Danny Miller is the author of the Detective Vince Treadwell novels, the first of which – *Kiss Me Quick* – was shortlisted for the CWA John Creasey New Blood Award. He started his writing career as a playwright and a scriptwriter, and has written for the BBC, ITV and Channel 4.

After a successful career writing for radio, **R. D. Wingfield** turned his attention to fiction, creating the character of Jack Frost. The series has been adapted for television as the perennially popular *A Touch of Frost*, starring David Jason. R. D. Wingfield died in 2007.

Titles featuring Detective Inspector Jack Frost

R. D. WINGFIELD
Frost at Christmas
A Touch of Frost
Night Frost
Hard Frost
Winter Frost
A Killing Frost

JAMES HENRY
First Frost
Fatal Frost
Morning Frost
Frost at Midnight

DANNY MILLER
A Lethal Frost
The Murder Map

Have you read all the books in the acclaimed Frost prequel series?

FIRST FROST

Denton, 1981. Britain is in recession, the IRA is becoming increasingly active and the country's on alert for an outbreak of rabies.

Detective Sergeant Jack Frost is working under his mentor and inspiration DI Bert Williams, and coping badly with his increasingly strained marriage. But DI Williams is nowhere to be seen. So when a twelve-year-old girl goes missing, DS Frost is put in charge of the investigation . . .

FATAL FROST

May, 1982. Britain celebrates the sinking of the *Belgrano*, Princess Diana prepares for the birth of her first child and Denton Police Division welcomes its first black policeman, DS Waters – recently relocated from East London.

While the force is busy dealing with a spate of local burglaries, the body of a fifteen-year-old girl is discovered next to the railway track. Then a fifteen-year-old boy is found dead on Denton's golf course, his organs removed. **Detective Sergeant Jack Frost** is sent to investigate, and when the murdered boy's sister goes missing, Frost and Waters must work together to find her . . . before it's too late.

MORNING FROST

November 1982. It's been one of the worst days of **DS Jack Frost**'s life. He has buried his wife Mary, and must now endure the wake, attended by all of Denton's finest.

As the week goes on, a local entrepreneur is shot, a valuable painting goes missing and a cyclist is found dead in suspicious circumstances. Frost is on the case, but another disaster – one he is entirely unprepared for – is about to strike . . .

FROST AT MIDNIGHT

August, 1983. Denton is preparing for a wedding, with less than a week to go until Detective Sergeant Waters marries Kim Myles. But the Sunday before the big day, the body of a young woman is found in the churchyard. Their idyllic wedding venue has become a crime scene.

As best man to Waters, **Detective Inspector Jack Frost** has a responsibility to solve the mystery before the wedding. But with nowhere to live since his wife's family sold his matrimonial home, Frost's got other things on his mind. Can he put his own troubles aside and step up to be the detective they need him to be?

A LETHAL FROST

Denton, 1984. After a morning's betting at the races, bookmaker George Price is found in his car, barely alive with a bullet in his head. As he's rushed to hospital, **Detective Inspector Jack Frost** and the Denton police force start their hunt for the would-be murderer.

But with a long list of enemies who might want the bookie dead, the team have got their work cut out for them. And with a slew of other crimes hitting the area, from counterfeit goods to a violent drugs gang swamping Denton with cheap heroin, the stakes have never been higher. Will Frost find the answers he's looking for before things go from bad to worse?

THE MURDER MAP

When art dealer Ivan Fielding is found dead of a heart attack in his home, it doesn't initially seem like a case for **Detective Inspector Jack Frost**. But then signs of a burglary are discovered, and Frost senses there's more to the story – even though the only thing taken was a worthless amateur painting.

Then a young girl is abducted outside the school, an infamous gangster fresh from prison arrives in the area, and dead bodies start turning up in the woods. As Frost and his team dig deeper, everything seems to lead back to Ivan Fielding's murky lifetime of misdeeds. Will they find the answers they need before the dead man's past puts them all at risk?

The Murder Map

A DI Jack Frost investigation

Danny Miller

CORGI BOOKS

TRANSWORLD PUBLISHERS
61–63 Uxbridge Road, London W5 5SA
www.penguin.co.uk

Transworld is part of the Penguin Random House group of companies
whose addresses can be found at global.penguinrandomhouse.com

Penguin
Random House
UK

First published in Great Britain in 2019 by Corgi Books
an imprint of Transworld Publishers

Written for the Estate of R. D. Wingfield by Danny Miller
Copyright © The Estate of R. D. Wingfield 2019

A CIP catalogue record for this book
is available from the British Library.

ISBN
9780552175067

Typeset in 10.24/12.46pt Caslon 540 by Jouve (UK), Milton Keynes.
Printed and bound in Great Britain by Clays Ltd, Elcograf S.p.A.

Penguin Random House is committed to a sustainable future
for our business, our readers and our planet. This book is made
from Forest Stewardship Council® certified paper.

MIX
Paper from
responsible sources
FSC
www.fsc.org   FSC® C018179

The Murder Map

Prologue

The old man had fought a long and hard battle, with fortitude and courage. As he lay in his hospital bed, tubes invading every part of him, the machine bleeped away, and the numbers flashed up, all telling him it was almost the end. That he was now on the losing side, as inevitably we all are eventually. The old man wasn't in fact that old. But it was clear he'd had a hard life, and time had really worked him over. And of course, the disease had eaten away at him.

The orderly working that shift on the palliative-care wing did something he should not have done. Something he had no right, remit, or indeed qualifications to do. He increased the level of morphine being intravenously fed to the dying man. He didn't do this on compassionate grounds, though he had struck up something of a relationship with the patient. He did it because the morphine loosened the man's tongue, got him talking.

The orderly knew who the dying man was even before he'd arrived at the Longthorn infirmary. In fact, he was the reason he'd applied for the post in the first place. And he treated him with a respect sadly not always afforded the old, the crippled, the dying. Especially in places like this. It was easy to see that in his pomp, his prime, he'd been a man of some status in his particular field of endeavour. One of the very best in his chosen profession. A thief.

So when the morphine worked its magic, and the man started talking, talking about a job he'd pulled off many, many moons ago, where he'd stolen something so precious, so unbelievably valuable, that it would mark him out for ever and make him as rich as Croesus, the hospital orderly listened. He listened good and hard and did whatever was necessary to keep the old thief talking.

He made sure he worked the night shift so he could be alone with the man. He befriended him, talked to him every night, sneaked him in cigarettes and miniature bottles of fine Scottish whisky. At this stage of his disease, stage four, it mattered very little. Together they treated every night like it was his last. And every night the dying man told him more and more of the story. And what a story it was.

This wasn't the last rambling speech of a mad man hallucinating on morphine. This was priceless. Once-in-a-lifetime stuff. It was the last will and testament of a true master. A deathbed confession. It doesn't get better than this, thought the orderly, as he switched on the night light and released the valve that sent the morphine into the old man's arm.

As the opiate worked its way through the patient's system, far from sending him into the land of nod, it livened him up. His rheumy eyes widened and glistened, and he looked twenty years younger as his mind scrolled back to the past.

'. . . It was a beautiful day . . . fantastic . . . I was there, you know?'

'Where?'

'Where? The hallowed turf . . . Wembley.'

'Yeah?'

'I wasn't . . . wasn't a big fan of football . . . but I couldn't turn down the opportunity . . . A friend of mine told me to meet him at Wembley . . . his name was Charlie . . . Charlie the Dip . . . he was a pickpocket, one of the best in London . . . and within minutes of mingling into the crowd . . . he'd got us a couple of tickets . . . I saw Bobby Moore lift the cup that day . . .'

'Ah. I've only seen it on TV. Geoff Hurst's goal. That famous commentary: "They think it's all over, it is now." That was 1966, wasn't it?'

The old man smiled, his grey teeth looking three sizes too big in his sallow and shrunken head. 'It was . . . It was a wonderful time . . .'

The orderly pulled his chair closer to the bed. 'But it was the year after, 1967, that you pulled off your greatest victory. Got your biggest score, wasn't it? Bigger than that bauble Bobby Moore lifted in '66, eh?'

The man attempted to laugh, but it just deteriorated into a hacking and wheezing cough that brought up a foul green viscous substance. The orderly mopped his chin. He then gave him his 'medicine' of two fingers of Glenfiddich in a plastic beaker and lit him up a Player's. With the morphine chaser, the orderly doubted that even the ubiquitous Larry had ever been happier. It was now that he struck:

'But the big question is . . . where you buried it all those years ago.'

'Buried . . . ?'

'The treasure . . . Where did you bury it?'

'Ahh . . . I buried it where no one would find it . . . *No one!*'

The orderly calmed him down. Sometimes when the dose was too high, the old thief would get excited, and he'd go off at a tangent. But he himself would remain calm; his bedside manner was impeccable, and he prided himself on being able to wheedle information out of people. So he waited a few minutes before asking again, softly, softly.

'Yes, my friend, very good. Now: where, *where* did you bury it?'

'The treasure?' The old man grinned, his eyes sparkled again, full of mischief. Then they narrowed suspiciously. He looked at the orderly, startled, as if he was a stranger. It was clear the fog had lifted, the drugs and booze had quickly worn off. 'Kevin? . . . You're not Kevin?'

'No. I'm not Kevin.'

'Where's Kevin . . . ? I want to talk to Kevin . . .'

'That's because Kevin knows, doesn't he? Kevin knows where you buried the treasure?'

'Kevin . . . Kevin knows . . .'

The orderly shook his head and let out a forlorn sigh, and repeated the old man's words, *Kevin knows*, because he'd heard them many times before.

But this was as far as the old thief would go. This was as far as he always went. It seemed that somewhere in that dying head of his was an insurmountable wall that just wouldn't crumble to reveal the vital information only he and Kevin knew: where it was buried. He was like a scratched record. Good up to a point, then useless. The orderly was satisfied that this was as much information as he would ever get from him. But it was enough. The rest he'd work out himself.

He turned up the level on the morphine release and watched the old man's eyes flutter and close. He then gently lifted his head, and went to plump up the pillow as he always did. But this time he picked up the pillow and placed it over his face. It didn't take long, the pillow barely moved.

They think it's all over, it is now. But in reality, it was just the beginning.

Sunday (1)

'Oh, please, call me Shirley. You wouldn't want me to call you Inspector Frost instead of Jack, would you?'

'Depends on the circumstances, Shirley.'

'Now you're talking. I've been guilty of a few crimes of passion in my time. It would have been interesting having you as the arresting officer. You'd have had to catch me, secure me, cuff me, bundle me into the back of your panda car and then give me a hard and thorough interrogation. Sweat me under the lights, as they say.'

Jack Frost laughed nervously, as had become his habit when talking to his recently installed neighbour. Shirley was of indeterminate age. Frost put her at around the forty-five to fifty-five mark, but doubted he would get a straight answer from her if he ever asked. She was originally from Rotherham, and her accent hadn't shifted a jot in the twenty-odd years she'd lived in Denton.

She had moved into Paradise Lodge a month ago, into number 142. Her abode was inconveniently situated between the lift and his front door. When leaving the elevator Frost had taken to padding across the carpeted hallway as stealthily as a cat burglar, as silently as his thick Doc Martens soles would allow, to get to the relative safety of his flat. And yet he still managed to stumble on the psychic tripwire she had rigged up in that overly made-up head of hers. Her door would burst open with a deafening *whoosh* as she sprang forth, all honey-blonde curls and plunging neckline, every time revealing more and more of her ample flesh. It was a twenty-minute conversation at least. She was a widow, she kept reminding him, and eventually she managed to drag his occupation and marital status out of him with the blunt determination of the Spanish Inquisition. On hearing he was a police inspector and a widower himself, anticipation seemed to palpably throb through her and she ran a muscular tongue around her glossy red lips. And that was it. Frost could feel the branding iron on his rump, and now it said: 'Property of Shirley'.

And here she was, actually in his flat, togged up in a turquoise towelling outfit, more suitable for the beach than landlocked Denton in January. She had just delivered a fish pie in a Pyrex dish, a dish that would need returning, so Frost knew there would be another round to go.

He said he'd have it tonight with his tin of peaches and condensed milk. She raised her blue-mascaraed eyes to the heavens and said she'd whisk up a trifle for him. He went into the kitchen and put the fish dish in the fridge.

'It's a nice view from here,' said Shirley with more than a note of sarcasm in her voice, as this side of Paradise Lodge looked out over the car park and the other blocks in the complex, Eden and Utopia. 'Me, I've got a pretty good view of the reservoir.'

When he returned from the kitchen, Shirley was shimmying away from the window and was soon sat, uninvited, on his sofa.

'Had a sense of humour, your mum and dad?'

'Sorry?'

'Jack, Jack Frost?'

'To be honest, they didn't – but everyone else did. My real name is William, but ever since the first day of school, *Jack* just sort of stuck.'

'Kids can be cruel.'

'Could have been worse – a kiddy in my year had the surname Anchor. You don't have to be much of a poet to get the punchline.'

She laughed, a little too keenly, so every part of her wobbled. 'Well, I must say, Jack, I like what you've done with the place – very swish, very tasteful.'

'Bit like the name, I can't take any credit for it. I moved in and got the furniture that came with it. I was supposed to have the ground-floor flat, the main show flat. But it was covered in parrot droppings so they had to repaint the place, even new carpets. I was in a bit of a hurry to leave my previous lodgings, so I took this one instead.'

Shirley wasn't really listening, and it was clear to Frost she had her own agenda. 'It must be fate, us landing on the same landing.'

'And the parrot droppings,' he muttered under his breath. 'Got a lot to answer for, that bleeding parrot.'

'What was that, Jack?'

'Just saying, the parrot.'

'Whose was it?'

'Belonged to Kenny Fong's mother, owner of the Jade Rabbit, and my old landlady.'

Shirley nodded over to the empty cartons of Kung Po on the dining table. 'Nice to see you're still in touch.'

'I miss Monty, the parrot. He was a very clever bird, helped us catch a felon.'

'How did he manage that?'

'A long story.'

'I've got plenty of time, Jack. And I'm quite a clever bird myself.'

She laughed hard and hearty, deep and dirty. Her ample flesh seemed to be rolling around in time inside the turquoise outfit, which had the effect of lowering the zip, each juddering laugh revealing more and more cleavage. Any more gags, Frost thought, and I'll have to throw a sheet over her.

When she did eventually stop, her hand patted the neighbouring cushion, inviting him to join her on the three-seater sofa. He noted that her long painted fingernails were the same colour as her outfit. The turquoise-talonned hand sported a chunky ring on every finger; every finger apart from the wedding finger, which stood out like a sore thumb, so to speak.

Frost stood resolutely by the mock mantelpiece, with his fists pressing down into his trouser pockets, rocking back and forth on the balls of his feet, but she continued to pat the cushion and fix him with a 'come hither' look. He'd run out of options and was forced to join her. But at a safe distance, his elbow weighing heavily on the armrest.

'Well, Jack, this *is* nice. I can't think of a better way to spend a Sunday. Who knows, I might even scrounge one of them cans of lager I saw you had in the fridge. Quite a few, I see.'

Frost tilted his wrist and read the digits on his Casio that told him it was 1.05 p.m. 'Bit early for me, Shirley. How about a nice cup of tea?'

'Oh, Jack, I must confess I'm in the mood for something a bit stronger.'

Frost felt a charge move through his lap. It was his pager going off. He read the message from John Waters: 'Fancy a pint?'

He sprang from the sofa, the grip of Shirley's hand on his thigh slipping away. 'Sorry, Shirley,' he said with serious intent. 'Police business. A dead body. *Murder.*'

Her red lips puckered then parted into a perfect O shape, then she seemed to melt all over the leather sofa.

'My old man was a chiropodist. You don't know how exciting that bloody sounds . . . *Detective Inspector* Jack Frost.'

Sunday (2)

'Cheers, Jack,' said DS John Waters, easing himself into the yellow Metro.

Frost had pushed the seat back for him as far as it would go. Still, as the tall, once athletic detective got into the car, Frost saw that beneath the mask of chirpiness lurked a grimace of pain.

The operations and skin grafts on Waters' back where he had received extensive third-degree burns had been a success, but the recovery process was slow. Inhaling all that toxic smoke as he rescued two women from a burning flat on the Southern Housing Estate had literally seared his lungs. It had happened over six months ago now, but his breathing was at times still laboured. To Frost, John Waters seemed to have aged ten years. It was understandable, and there was never any serious talk about the DS leaving the force. The union rep had of course spoken to Waters and Frost, and the idea of retirement on full pay had been mooted, and just as quickly rejected.

In fact, after the commendation for outstanding bravery in the line of duty had been approved, Frost immediately proposed to

Superintendent Stanley Mullett that Waters should be promoted to detective inspector.

But right now, DS John Waters was three days a week and desk-bound. His re-entry into the hubbub of the Eagle Lane incident room was to be slow and steady.

'Sunday, bloody Sunday. I *hate* Sundays. I needed to get out of the house,' said Waters as the car headed out of the close.

Frost caught sight of Waters' wife, Kim, at the window. She looked like a ghost, indistinct and sad behind the net curtains. Frost knew better than to ask, partly because he didn't know what to say. But when Waters was ready to talk, he was sure he'd be ready to listen.

'Your invitation for a pint was a lifesaver. I may have to move.'

'You've only just bought the place, Jack.'

'I'm afraid one day I might have one Skol too many and weaken. I lack the resolve of most men, John. I'm weak when it comes to the sins of the flesh.'

Waters laughed. 'Jesus Christ . . . I know it's Sunday, but what the hell are you on about?'

Frost filled John in on the Shirley situation: his very own Merry Widow on the landing, a landing that was now a minefield. Waters laughed harder. It was good to see him laugh, thought Frost, it had been a while.

The DI then pressed down firmly on the horn. A cheer went up from the nearby pavement. Frost had answered the request on the placard: 'Honk Your Horn To Show Support For Denton Woods'.

Though he agreed with the demonstration against the planned development of houses and shops that would encroach on Denton Woods, he'd hooted more to wind up PC Mills who was on duty. The protest had thus far been peaceful, but there had been anonymous threats sent to the *Denton Echo*, so Mills and two other uniforms were there to make sure nobody tried to break into the site and sabotage the equipment.

PC Mills responded to his superiors in the familiar yellow Metro with a two-fingered salute.

The car radio crackled into life just as Frost's pager bleeped. It was DC Susan Clarke. Frost reflected on his earlier excuse to extricate himself from Shirley's grasp. A dead body. Be careful what you wish for, he thought.

'No, *please* no! Ivan!'

'Could you take Mrs Fielding out of the room?' demanded DC Clarke, turning sharply to face the man who was holding back the near-hysterical estranged wife of the deceased.

'Yes, sorry, sorry about that.'

Stephen Parker, a tall willowy man in his forties, with an intelligent face under soft collar-length greying hair, held the sobbing Vanessa Fielding gently. She stood frozen just inside the doorway, eyes rounded in shock at what she saw, hands covering her mouth as if to stop a scream. He guided her out of the room, leaving Clarke alone with Dr Maltby.

'Yes, keep the family out, this next bit could be very messy,' said Maltby, returning his attention to the body. Maltby was always meticulous before signing the necessary documentation that consigned a corpse to the land of the not-living. Most of CID had heard Maltby's anecdotes about cadavers suddenly springing back to life just as the pathologist is about to crack open their chest for a closer look. Some of the younger lads even believed him.

DC Clarke had her head turned towards the door and was listening intently to what was going on in the hall outside. It was more of an effort at distraction, as Maltby had his latex-sheathed hand down the corpse's throat and was scooping out congealed vomit that was heavily marbled with blood. It sounded like sobbing Vanessa Fielding and soothing Stephen Parker had been joined by two others, Sally, the Fieldings' grown-up daughter, and PC David Simms, whose voice rose above the melee to try to take control of the obviously very emotional situation. She then heard footsteps exiting the house. Followed by a knock on the living-room door as Simms poked his head around.

'Sorry, DC Clarke, I didn't see them come in. I've got a statement from Sally Fielding, and I suggested they take Mrs Fielding home.'

Clarke watched as Simms pulled a grimace whilst the good doctor scooped a particularly vile-looking substance into a cone-shaped cardboard receptacle; it really did look like some grossly unpleasant raspberry ripple.

'Do you need me for anything?' asked Simms, swallowing hard.

Clarke gestured for him to wait outside and he closed the door behind him. She then marshalled all her attention back into the large living room and focused it on the body slumped on the Regency-style claw-footed couch, which looked like it belonged in an even grander house than the already rather grand one it stood in now.

Maltby surmised that Ivan Fielding had been dead for at least twenty-four hours, but not longer than forty-eight. Looking at the corpse, Clarke thought it must be longer. And Fielding certainly appeared a lot older than his purported sixty years.

She heard a car pull up outside with a screech. It was a familiar-sounding screech – like that of a yellow Metro narrowly avoiding the ambulance and other cars parked in the driveway.

More voices entered the house and the living-room door sprang open.

'Afternoon, Susan.'

'Guv.' Clarke smiled at John Waters, surprised to see him accompanying DI Frost. 'Hey, John, what brings you here on a Sunday?'

Waters tilted his head towards Frost. 'His nibs here. I just happened to be in the car when the call came through.' The DS raised his arms in a gesture of 'I'm hands off'. 'I'm strictly a passenger, forget I'm here.'

'You're my hero, mate, how can I ever forget you?'

'Ha, ha,' said Waters, dryly. He'd been getting a lot of that since the fire. It was something he almost wanted to forget – but with the commendation ceremony only a week away, his colleagues at Eagle Lane wouldn't let him. After taking a peek at the body and greeting Dr Maltby, Waters took himself out of the way and stood by the long mullioned window.

The house, large and old, was in Bolsyn, a sparse little village north of Denton, where the postbox was the only centre of activity.

'How are you, Jack?' asked Maltby, stripping his hands of the latex gloves and throwing them in a bag.

'Thirsty, looking at this lot. I take it this is what killed him,' said Frost, gesturing at the burr-walnut coffee table that held a drained full-size bottle of Beefeater gin, and two half-bottles – another of gin and one of Smirnoff vodka. There was also a crystal tumbler and an ashtray brimming with cigarette butts.

'I'd have thought it would put you off the wretched stuff.'

'Oh, yeah, keep forgetting you're teetotal now. Which is rare for a doctor.'

'Really?'

'My last medical, I told the doc I thought I had a drinking problem; he said if I drank more than him I had a problem. After he told me what he put away each night I went straight to the pub to celebrate my new clean bill of health.'

Maltby met Frost's grin with a cold hard fact: 'A myocardial infarction was the cause of death.'

'In layman's terms, his pump packed in?'

'Exactly. What brought it on will be determined by the PM. But without making any moral judgements, this little collection on the table certainly didn't help his situation. He was on all sorts of medication for his heart, according to his daughter.'

Frost studied the figure on the couch; he seemed vaguely familiar. He was wearing a worn-looking tweed suit that could once have been expensive, DAKS or some other quality outfitters, maybe even bespoke. A blue silk polka-dot cravat smartly did its job of covering a neck that was, from what he could see, scrawny with pouches of wrinkled loose skin. The suit jacket was undone, and the shirt neatly and tightly tucked in.

Fielding was cue-ball bald, and almost as white, apart from the brown spots clustered on the edges of his forehead, to match the liver spots on his hands. His half-moon spectacles were still perfectly positioned on his nose. He was clean-shaven, freshly so in fact, as just above the cravat there was a little patch of tissue with dried blood on it where he had nicked himself with the razor.

It seemed to the detective inspector that the heart attack hadn't done much attacking, and had instead ended this life quickly and without much fuss. He instructed that some photos be taken of Fielding on the couch before his body was lifted on to a gurney and conveyed to its next destination – the County morgue. Dr Maltby accompanied it.

Once the room was clear of all but his colleagues, Frost turned to Clarke.

'A heart attack brought on by too much of the mother's ruin, by the looks of it. Why am I here? Am I missing something, Susan?'

'That's what I thought, and initially I wouldn't have called you,' said Clarke. 'But PC Simms found something. With his magnifying glass, no less.'

Frost and Waters exchanged archly impressed looks at this. Rare was the copper who still carried one of these; that was now the preserve of Forensics.

The three detectives followed PC Simms, who was on probation for his 'step up' to DC, down some ancient-looking stone stairs and through to the kitchen and scullery area at the back of the house. Like the rest of the place, it seemed to have stopped acquiring new furnishings and equipment somewhere around the late 1940s. There was no washing machine, and even the green bulbous fridge was a survivor from the past. The kitchen table could have served as an Anderson shelter.

Simms led them over to a window that looked out on to the overgrown back garden, which was even more neglected than the front lawn and appeared to just meld in with the woods that lay beyond. The windowpane was broken but still in place, and the cracks in the glass formed an almost perfect square shape just above the latch.

Frost said, 'OK, Simms, so what does this tell you?'

'Well, guv, if you look carefully, you'll see that there's a gummy substance on the other side of the glass. I reckon it's from some gaffer tape, and it's been used to remove the glass.'

Simms handed Frost his magnifying glass. It was the classic round variety with an amber-coloured handle.

'What are you doing with one of these?'

'My auntie got it for me. Birthday present.'

'You must have been chuffed,' said Waters.

'I wanted a Scalextric set.'

Clarke said, 'Oh, she got it for you when you were a kid?'

'No, last month.'

Frost stopped peering through the magnifying glass. He was impressed, liked what he was hearing, but itched for more from the young PC. 'So the glass was broken, in an unusually neat shape, and there's some gunk on the other side. Though how you get to gaffer tape is beyond me.'

Simms bent down.

'What now, Sherlock?' said Frost, crouching down to join him. 'Some cigar ash that you can tell by the striations is a brand that can only be purchased from Dunhill of London?'

'Even better.' Simms pointed.

Frost caught the glint of glass slivers on the black and white tiled floor.

'These are fresh splinters from where the glass has been cut and pushed through earlier. Before I called DC Clarke, I put on my gloves, opened the window and tested the glass. It just popped out. It's been removed, then put back in place. I can show you if you like—'

'No, I believe you,' said Frost, getting to his feet. Simms followed suit. 'Let's get Forensics in here. But I've got a feeling they won't find any dabs. You can guarantee that whoever uses a diamond glass cutter, and not a brick, and bothers to put the glass back, will have been wearing gloves.'

The DI looked at the pane again. The cut-out square was big enough for a hand to be slipped through to release the latch. Once the window was open, the burglar climbed in and carefully replaced the square of glass. All of which might have been viewed as quite unnecessary, unless you were a stone-cold professional and it was second nature to you. Real professionals had a habit of tidying up after themselves, carefully and methodically going about their work so as not to leave any clues. It was cowboys who ransacked the place.

'Good work, Simms, good work.' Frost turned to Clarke. 'Remind me what Ivan Fielding did again?'

'He was a retired antiques dealer.'

Frost smiled. 'Well, this may be where they got in, but it wasn't their final destination.'

They all headed back upstairs to the living room, apart from Simms, who was sent back to Eagle Lane to find out what else he could about Ivan Fielding.

'I thought it looked wrong. The body. The way it was positioned, all wrong,' announced Frost after looking intently at the striped settee that Ivan Fielding had been discovered on. 'Sat bolt upright like that; you normally make yourself comfortable when settling in for a night like this.' He nodded towards the debris on the coffee table. 'And from the amount he drank, you're very unlikely to be sitting at all. Yet there he was, looking all prim and proper and perched on the couch. Not looking remotely pissed.'

'Agreed,' said Clarke.

'The jolt from the heart attack, that could make you sit up,' offered John Waters, playing devil's advocate.

'No, not like that – you can see the shock on their faces, their limbs are askew. Ivan Fielding looked like he was having tea with the Queen. Who found the body?'

'The daughter, Sally,' said Clarke.

'Did she touch it, move it, try and resuscitate him in any way?'

'I asked her the same thing when I got here. She said not. Said she knew he was dead the minute she clapped eyes on him; there were no signs of breathing, so she called 999.'

Frost began to pace around the room and gave some thoughtful clucking noises that were loud enough and long enough to make Clarke and Waters fix each other with looks to see who would laugh first.

'Nice place he's got here, or at least it was nice at one time. An antiques dealer, you say?'

'Mainly an art dealer, paintings, according to the family.'

'Yeah, you don't pick up classy gear like this at the local department store,' said Frost, tapping a knuckle on a rosewood side table adorned with silver candlesticks. Their quality forced Frost to take in the other items on display. Whilst the room was hardly cluttered, what there was on offer spoke of the man's previous profession. There were murky Dutch old masters up on one wall, and a huge gilt-framed mirror above a neoclassical fireplace that held a French ormolu mantle clock. In a display cabinet there was a collection of tortoiseshell and silver snuff boxes, and darkly patinated bronzes of reclining nudes and pouncing panthers graced the bookcase. He saw that every available flat surface seemed to hold something of beauty and no doubt value. But it was the paintings on the walls that really drew the eye, both classical and modern; there was obviously a refined and educated taste at work in this small collection. Frost, spellbound, looked up at a fleshy nude with some well-placed fruit barely covering her modesty.

'I know some of the dealers in the area, never heard of Ivan Fielding,' offered Waters.

'If you mean Del "The Knocker" Norris and that lot at the local boot fair, I think our Mr Fielding is in another class. He's Division One. Those other mugs are kicking about in the Alliance Premier.'

Clarke referred to her notes. 'Ivan used to have a shop in London, but he retired almost twenty years ago, in the late '60s, said his daughter.'

Frost tore his eyes away from the nude. 'Who was the attractive older lady?'

Waters shook his head and stifled a laugh. Frost and Clarke exchanged quick-fire looks before Sue asked, 'What's so funny?'

'Jack's developed a thing for older women. According to his neighbour.'

'And two-hundred-year-old nudes by the looks of it,' said Clarke, gesturing to the painting he'd been staring at.

'I was admiring the brushwork. So who is she?'

'Venus?'

'Not her, the tall woman in tears.'

'The tall woman in tears is Mrs Vanessa Fielding, Ivan's wife. But they've been separated for five years,' said Clarke. 'He lived here on his own.'

'Art dealer living out here on his own with all this, surprised the place hasn't been burgled sooner.'

All three of them considered this for a moment, before Frost added, 'So if Simms is right, what did they take?'

'And why would you leave all of this?' asked John Waters.

'Because you were disturbed?' suggested Clarke.

'Or you got what you were after, and it was worth more than all this put together?' Waters mused.

Frost fixed his two colleagues with a look that suggested he was happy to be in the room with them, at a potential crime scene, asking all the right questions, and not sat at home for a long, dull day, thumbing through the papers, watching *Ski Sunday*, or worse, waiting for that ominous knock on the door from that 'older woman' Waters had mentioned. It was a while since the three of them had been in the same room working a case together.

'Where to now? Ivan's wife and daughter?' asked Clarke.

'I'm going to the station, see if Simms has got anything on

Ivan Fielding, then I want to see what Dr Death has to say. I'll need you to wait for Forensics.'

DC Clarke nodded.

Waters checked his watch. 'I best be getting back.'

'I'll drop you at home on the way,' said Frost. 'Sorry about that drink. Another time.'

Sunday (3) ───────────────────────────

It was of course a solemn occasion. We come into the world alone, and leave it alone. But this funeral seemed even more lonely than most. Gathered on a patch of land in the corner of Longthorn Hospital known as the Peaceful Place Garden were the hospital chaplain, the chief medical officer, and the young art therapist who had worked with the deceased. No friends or family, just employees of the institution where his life had ended.

But Clive Banes, watching the scene at a distance through his high-powered binoculars, had expected to see one particular person there: Kevin Wheaton – a friend and confidant of the old man, probably his only one. Kevin was a young ex-con who used to visit him regularly. His absence was a surprise to Banes. And more importantly, it didn't fit in with his plans. In fact, he viewed Kevin's absence as a setback. If anyone knew the old thief's secret, it was Kevin. Where the hell was he? 'Where the bloody hell is he?' he mumbled to himself repeatedly like a mantra, hoping the answer would come. When it didn't, he took aim with his binoculars again and adjusted the focus on the zoom to get a clearer look.

A few words were being said by the chaplain, and the ashes were being scattered over a flower bed. A bed that was usually well tended and rich with colour. But in January, surely a contender for the real 'cruellest month', the flower bed was just soil. The only things growing there were the hardy and thorny stems of the red roses – their shrivelled heads the colour of congealed blood. As Banes watched the service come to an end, he wondered how many people would be at his own funeral.

He lowered his binoculars and again pondered where Kevin was. He knew he had to find him, before . . . before it was too late. He was sure Kevin wouldn't be that hard to locate. He knew the ex-con lived with his mother somewhere in south London. And he knew that Kevin was a repeat offender with a record as long as his arm, so there would be plenty of information on him.

'Clive? Clive, is that you?'

Banes turned sharply to see . . . Pete. He'd forgotten his surname. But he was pretty sure he'd never bothered to learn it in the first place. He knew that Pete was what they called a 'Longthorn Lifer', meaning he'd worked at the place longer than his probationary period, which was usually three months. Although, with the staff turnover at the hospital as it was, everyone joked they were lowering it to three weeks, three days, hours, minutes. Once he knew he'd been well and truly clocked, and there was no getting out of it, he smiled and said, 'Hello, Pete.'

Pete was as bubbly as his permed hair, which he wore gelled for that wet look. Or, he's as wet as his permed hair, thought Banes as he considered the man, who worked mainly down in the canteen. He'd obviously just come off shift, though what he was doing wandering along this road—

'I've started walking into town to get my bus now' – he patted his tummy – 'trying to get rid of some of the old Christmas excess.'

That explains it, and perfectly innocent, thought Banes, as he looked at Pete's expanding waistline.

'I thought I recognized you, Clive, from the van mainly. You've changed. Shaved off the beard, I see.'

'Yeah. People say I look younger without it.'

'And you're not wearing your glasses?'

'No. Contact lenses. People say I look less like a four-eyed git without them.'

They both laughed. Banes got off the wall he was sat on. Of course it wasn't the main perimeter wall of the hospital; that was much higher and festooned with razor wire. But you did get a good view of the hospital from here. Although only if you were armed with expensive high-powered binoculars. And only if you knew the right spot because you'd searched it out earlier.

'What you doing with yourself these days?'

'Oh, between appointments, as they say.'

'We all miss you, Clive.'

Banes gave an appreciative nod at this, but doubted its veracity. He was one of the many who failed to see out their three-month probationary period. Still, nice of him to say so, thought Banes, somewhat snidely.

'Well, I must be getting along. I'll see you around maybe.'

'What *are* you doing, Clive?'

'Like I said, in between appointments, but—'

'No, no. *Now*. What were you doing sitting on a wall looking through binoculars?'

Banes stopped looking chirpy. 'Nothing. Just taking a look at the old place.'

'You haven't been gone long, if you miss it that much I'm sure they'll have you back.'

'No thanks. Anyway, Pete, must be getting along—'

'Seems weird, though. You sat there' – he gestured to the binoculars in Banes' hand – 'looking through those.'

'Does it?'

'A bit.'

'How weird?'

Maybe Pete sensed the edge in Banes' voice, because he was

keen to explain: 'It's just that the top management have told us to keep an eye out. There's been some drugs going missing, you know the type.'

Banes did know the type. Opiates to relieve the pain. He'd heard some of the nurses had been sacked a couple of weeks ago for smuggling them out. He looked offended as he asked, 'What are you accusing me of?'

'Oh no, Clive, I didn't mean it like that . . . It's just we've been told to keep an eye out. Still, good to see you. I'll tell all the gang I saw you.'

'No need.'

'They all remember you. The ones who are left, anyway. I'll tell them I saw you.'

Banes considered his simple-minded friendliness, and viewed it like a threat. And one he knew that Pete would carry out, because he knew the idiot was chatty and friendly with everyone. Who knows, he might even tell the 'top management' about seeing him in relation to the missing medication. Totally untrue of course, Banes had no interest in that type of thing. He had a bigger prize than that to go after. But it could draw unnecessary attention to him. He reckoned Pete had so little happening in his life that bumping into him was tantamount to going to a Bruce Springsteen concert and being dragged up on stage for a dance and singalong with him. He knew what he had to do now. He matched Pete's gormless grin and said, 'Where you off to, Pete?'

'Like I said, going to walk into town to get my bus.'

'Tell you what, why don't we go for a pint in town, then I'll drop you home. You live local, don't you?'

'Yeah, I do.' Pete made a play of checking the time on his wristwatch and then pulled an impossibly big grin, like Bruce Springsteen had actually plucked him out of the crowd. 'Why not, Clive, why not indeed?'

They got into Banes' white Bedford panel van and drove off. Pete did most of the talking. Banes knew the type. Like most lonely people, he talked a lot when the opportunity presented itself. When Banes reached the spot he'd been heading for, he pulled the van over. It was a deserted stretch of road deep in the Suffolk countryside. Perfect.

'Sorry, mate, just got to take a leak.'

Banes got out of the van and disappeared behind the hedgerow.

Pete must have sat there for a good ten minutes, listening to Simon Bates on the radio, before he ventured out to check on Banes.

'Clive? Clive, you there?'

Pete heard a noise. A low groan of pain, perhaps. It came from behind a tree.

'Clive . . . You OK? Haven't got it caught in your zip, have you?' He laughed nervously, then stopped. 'Clive, you're worrying me, you OK? Clive . . . Clive, is that you? . . . What are you doing? What are you . . . ? No, please—'

The hammer smashed down on his forehead. It needed another three blows before Pete eventually fell. The first had stunned him, but barely dented his cranium. That part of the skull was very dense. His eyes were rounded in surprise and fear. He probably didn't feel much. Numbness brought on by the shock, a natural anaesthetic that no doubt nullified the pain. After the other whacks he stood swaying for a moment or two, blood oozing from his glistening wet-look perm, streaking down his face. Then he tumbled backwards, perfectly stiff, like a freshly felled tree.

Banes put the ball-peen hammer back in the pocket of his duffel coat, and went to get the shovel out of the van.

Sunday (4)

'Sign here, please, Mr McVale.'

'My pleasure. How are you today, officer?'

Jimmy McVale took the pen proffered by Desk Sergeant Johnny Johnson and signed the ledger. He knew the score – name, date of birth, time of signing in, and most importantly, his current address. So if anything dodgy happened locally he would be the first person they would visit. He'd been out of prison just over a month, and such was Jimmy McVale's case and reputation that he was to remain on licence for a full year. Forced to sign in at a police station twice a week – and not allowed to travel abroad, or more to the point, travel anywhere where he could not sign into a British police station twice a week.

Johnson spun the book around and checked the details – 'James McVale BA, MSc. DOB: 26/05/38. Residing at the Prince Albert Hotel, Denton.'

With his free hand, the desk sergeant clawed at his thick beard, as was his habit when confused, surprised, or indeed impressed, as was the case this time. This was due to the fact that McVale was staying at the Prince Albert, Denton's premier hotel, and that must have been costing him a pretty penny; and also because:

'Strewth, you've got some letters after your name, I see.'

'And hopefully there'll be more when I complete my doctoral thesis on the sociological study of crime and the urban environment. You have to spend your time wisely, you see, they offer all sorts of courses in the nick: ships in a bottle, needlework, origami. All a complete waste of time. I wanted a proper education, to help me understand the error of my ways.'

The ex-con winked, and Johnson laughed, uncomfortably. McVale handed back the pen and beamed a smile that lit up his broad handsome face. Beneath his pink shirt and lilac silk tie, worn under a well-cut double-breasted blazer, his six-foot-three frame looked bulked out with muscle. Not many men can wear a pink shirt and that colour of tie and get away with it, thought Johnson, much less manage to make it look as formidable as chainmail armour.

It was clear that Jimmy McVale's seventeen years in prison had been spent on self-improvement, not just of his mind through education, but of his physique, too. Prison hadn't dulled him; he looked in rude health, fizzing with energy and purpose. Ever alert to what was happening around him, his head turned fast to see who had just entered Eagle Lane police station when the swing doors opened. There were no soft edges to Jimmy McVale, he looked as lethal as his reputation, and yet he was a changed man – allegedly. But for all McVale's big smiles and bonhomie, Johnny Johnson was glad there was a desk between them.

'So if anyone calls out, is there a doctor in the house?'

'I'm not one yet, but even when I am I'd be about as useless as a pair of tits on a bull, I'm afraid.' Johnson laughed, and Jimmy McVale joined in. 'I'm afraid, Sergeant Johnson, my doctorate is not a medical one. And anyway, I hate the sight of blood.'

Johnson stopped laughing just as quickly as he'd started. There was something chilling in that statement, a statement so at odds with McVale's reputation, and the crimes he'd committed that had got him his life sentence.

'Is that it?'

'Yes . . . Doctor, you're free to go.'

'Not yet I'm not.' McVale smiled once more. 'A doctor, that is. But I am free. Or as any man can be.'

'Very philosophical. Oh, one last thing . . .'

Johnson looked surreptitiously around him, then reached under the desk and pulled out a hardback book. Its front cover had a sepia snapshot of a young boy wearing a cowboy hat and holding a pair of toy six-shooters like a quick-draw artist. On the back was a posed picture of the adult author, dressed as he was now in a smart suit. The book title read, *A Product of My Environment: The Early Years of the Notorious Jimmy McVale*.

'. . . You couldn't sign this for us, could you, Mr McVale?'

The ready smile lit up yet again. 'Of course I can, Sergeant. And seeing as I'll be in Denton for a couple of weeks, call me Jimmy.' Johnson nodded gratefully. 'Who to?'

'Oh, "Johnny Johnson" will do nicely. I've got to say, I think it's a great read. Very good. I especially liked hearing about what happened to Hacksaw Harry on the Heathrow job.'

'It's all behind me now, Johnny, I'm happy to say. But if people can learn from my experiences and mistakes then the book will have been worth it. And remember, I'm writing a follow-up to it, my prison years, attempted escapes, and, finally, my enlightenment.'

'Can't wait, Jimmy.'

Jimmy McVale signed the book with a practised flourish. Then turned sharply as the swing doors once more opened and the flash of a camera went off.

'Jimmy McVale, public enemy number one, as I live and breathe, in the flesh!'

Sandy Lane, crime reporter of the *Denton Echo*, swept into

reception accompanied by a photographer. Lane was physically the antithesis of the man he'd come to splash across his front page. His florid face had a tremble about it that suggested if he didn't get a drink down him in the next few minutes it might fall to pieces altogether; its strongest feature was his bulbous booze nose that positively glowed. His 24-carat Golden Virginia-tobacco-stained fingers gripped a reporter's pad and a well-chewed stub of a pencil. With his grubby mac, trilby, and shoes worn down at the heel, it hardly seemed necessary for him to introduce his profession, but he did:

'Sandy Lane, crime reporter for the *Denton Echo*,' announced the hack, flashing his credentials. 'We'd love to hear what you're up to, make a great front-page story. Ex-bank robber, reformed public enemy number one, suspect in the heist of the century, the world-famous Bond Street job?'

'I hope you put "allegedly" in front of all that. I'm very litigious these days.'

Undeterred, the hack pressed on. 'Is the *Denton Echo* going to get a world exclusive, Jimmy? Were you one of the infamous '67 Bond Street "Burrowers", and if so, what was in the vault, and where is it now?'

McVale offered a well-rehearsed mischievous smile to this question. 'You'll have to read my next book.'

'I know the story, Jimmy, everyone does, the stuff of legend.'

'I don't,' said the young photographer at Sandy Lane's side.

'You should read the bloody papers, son!' Sandy looked apologetically to McVale and explained. 'My sister's kid, he's on work experience.' Then he turned back to his nephew. 'In July '67, five robbers armed with high-powered drilling equipment burrowed their way under Bond Street to gain access to a private bank and raided the vault to get away with . . . Nobody knows. I heard everything from five million quid, enough diamonds to fill a bath tub, twenty-five Nazi-gold bars, to the *real* Crown Jewels. How about you, Jimmy, what did you hear?'

'I heard there were six robbers involved, not five. But don't quote me on that, I read that in the papers so it's probably wrong.'

Sandy Lane, knowing he wasn't going to get the exclusive he was after, licked the tip of his stubby pencil and prepared to scribble down some more banal titbits. 'So what are you doing in Denton?'

'I'm here to take in the beautiful countryside and work on my new book. I have an old friend who lives here, and I've taken them up on their offer to visit.'

'You like the town? You thinking of moving here?'

'Like I said, I love the surrounding countryside, and I'd also like to offer my support for the Denton Woods development protest. When you've been behind grey walls for as long as I have, you appreciate nature maybe more than most. Plus, the peace and quiet, away from the hubbub of London, will give me the chance to finish off the second volume of my memoirs. And I'd also like the opportunity to visit some local schools, young offenders' homes, and warn youngsters against a life of crime. Bring some positivity.'

'I hear they're planning on making a film of your life story – is it true that your part is being considered by a pop star? One of Duran Duran has been mooted for the role?'

'As long as it's not Boy George, I'll be happy.'

Five minutes later, and Jack Frost entered Eagle Lane to find Jimmy McVale posing with his new book in hand. The camera flash popped and Sandy Lane scribbled in his notebook as the smiling McVale smartly delivered some choice quotes from his book.

Frost beckoned Johnny Johnson to him. 'What the bloody hell is all this?'

'It's Jimmy McVale. He's just got into town, he's signing in.'

'I know who it is, I read the papers.'

'Funny though, he won't say anything about the Bond Street job of '67.'

'He's hardly going to deny it, and he's obviously not going to admit to it. It keeps the mystery going, so he can sell more of his tawdry little real-life-crime books.'

'You don't like a good crime book, Jack?'

'No, Johnny, I don't. I don't like true-life ones, and I don't like made-up ones either, because to me they're one and the same thing. You can tell who done it on page one. As for the ones he writes, pure self-aggrandizement, playing off some misguided romanticism around the great '60s capers. Making out like he's in *The Italian Job.* Try telling that to the bank manager's wife held hostage in her home by McVale to get the manager to open the safe. He poured petrol over her and held a match inches from her face. Or the security guard whose finger he cut off with bolt cutters to get the keys. Get him out of here.'

Johnson cringed. 'Yes, guv, I get the picture.'

Frost left the rebuked desk sergeant to it and went through to the incident room. But not before he caught Jimmy McVale's eye. It was cold and calculating as it quickly tried to work out who Frost was. Like the professional criminal he was, casing the joint. Once he realized that Frost might be someone to take seriously, his demeanour lifted and his trademark smile tore across his face. But Frost ignored the expensive dental work and concentrated on the eyes. They looked like they belonged to a creature scavenging the ocean bed.

Sunday was still Sunday, even in Eagle Lane, and if you didn't have to be there, you weren't. Just those on a scheduled shift, and those who had swapped with them because they were trying to pull in some overtime. So in the incident room it was just the skeleton crew of PC Simms, DC Clarke and Rita, a part-time civilian who answered the phones and input data on the computer. DC Arthur Hanlon was rumoured to be down in the canteen, but then again, the rotund DC was always rumoured to be down there.

Clarke glanced up from her paperwork. 'I left Forensics to it. I've checked and there's no record of Ivan Fielding reporting any burglaries or attempted burglaries from that address. And he's been there over fifteen years. But I'll be seeing Sally and Vanessa Fielding later, tell them what we've found out, see if they think anything is missing.'

'And he has no criminal record, not even traffic offences,' added PC Simms.

Frost looked impressed – even he had traffic offences. He kept his eye on Simms. Something was bothering him about the young PC. It was the same thing that had bothered him earlier at the Fielding house, but in the station, it seemed even more incongruous.

'Why are you in your Sunday best, Simms?'

The young PC turned towards his accuser, who was clearly running a disapproving eye over the copper's shimmering-silver boxy double-breasted suit with its big lapels and even bigger shoulder pads.

'I'm up for promotion, being reviewed for DC.'

'Yeah, I know, but why the civvies? Horse before the cart, son.'

Clarke looked up from her paperwork again. 'He asked me if he could wear plain clothes for the duration, and I said he could wear a tutu and some sling-backs if he got the job done. Which I think he has, plus he's got somewhere to stick his magnifying glass.'

Frost pulled out a pack of Player's from his bomber jacket, and looked at them like they had been planted there. He never smoked Player's, never even nicked other people's Player's, and he was always nicking other people's fags. Maybe they were Shirley's, maybe they were Ivan Fielding's? He frisked himself for a light and came up with a green Bic, sparked up and propped himself on Clarke's desk.

'That's the trouble with the new generation, you can't wait to get out of uniform, tarting around in your flash suits and Filo-faxes like you're some kind of City spiv. Me? I loved being in uniform. You know why, Simmo?'

Simms, who had been busy looking at the green names and numbers flashing up on the black screen of his computer as he checked the database, shook his head and asked, 'Why?'

'I'll tell you why, son. Not only because of the noble history and tradition that lie behind the blue and what it represented: a beacon of hope and security to the law-abiding decent citizens of Denton; people saw you and they knew they could come and ask you the time, directions, and approach you to get help. It wasn't all that. Which was bloody annoying enough.' Clarke and Simms laughed. 'No, it was also the fact that it saved me having to think about what to wear every bloody morning.'

At this, everyone in the incident room turned around slowly in unison, like in a well-rehearsed Busby Berkeley routine, to look at Frost. He was stood there in his battered leather bomber jacket, a pair of Lee Cooper beige cords that looked like they'd spent the night discarded on the floor, a burgundy Slazenger V-neck jumper whose creases had caught a fair bit of ash over the years, worn over a yellow Fred Perry tennis shirt, and a pair of cherry-red Doc Martens. His pillar-box-red scarf had fallen on the floor. It didn't look like a lot of thought had gone into the combo. And it was one that was very familiar to everyone at Eagle Lane – though the cherry-reds with the bright yellow stitching were new, and much frowned upon by Superintendent Mullett. Frost had pointed out that all coppers wore Docs, to which Mullett argued, 'Not that model, they don't.' Black and polished was the accepted norm – cherry-reds were the preserve of unsavoury elements. With everyone looking at him in dismay, Frost suddenly felt very naked. He mustered a defence.

'Einstein had five suits all the same so he didn't have to think about what he wore in the morning, thus giving him more time for his Theory of Relativity. You'd do well to remember that, Simmo.'

Frost turned on his bouncy Airwear heels and headed to his office.

'He's off to split the atom.'

'I heard that, Rita!'

Frost entered just in time to catch the tail end of a dull and buried ringing. Knowing he'd need both hands to burrow under the heaps of files and papers on his desk (it was a recurring problem and one proving harder to solve than the Theory of Relativity), he quickly stubbed out his Player's in a Mr Kipling's foil cake cup. This had been used incautiously as an ashtray, and was already filled to the brim with cigarette butts. He located the cord, and with some careful tugs he managed to yank the phone out from under the debris on his desk and into the flickering strip-light of day, with just the loss of an empty Lilt can (filled with more fag butts), a salt and vinegar crisp packet and a file marked *Urgent* in 1982, which all ended up on the floor. Before he could get his name out, Chief Pathologist Gerald Drysdale told him to 'get down here, sharpish'.

'I would suggest he put up a fight, or as much as a man in his condition could. But it was a brief struggle, as the markings indicate,' said Drysdale, aiming the business end of his stainless-steel Sheaffer ballpoint pen at purplish and grey markings around the corpse's collarbone, the base of his neck, and on his upper arms and shoulders.

Frost peered down for a closer look at Ivan Fielding laid out on the slab, and at the unmistakable bruising and red marks around his neck. He then considered Gerald Drysdale, whose pallor was about the same as Ivan Fielding's, who had been dead at least twenty-four hours. Tall and cadaverously thin, with his grey hair turning translucent and ghostly white, the Chief Pathologist really did suit his sobriquet, Dr Death, and not just because of his profession.

'Interesting, Gerald, very interesting.'

'Indeed. But let's not get too excited. Alcohol abuse causes cirrhosis of the liver, makes the skin bruise easily. But the marks are undeniably there. And whilst hardly the clear indent of a handprint, they could suggest that. What do you think?'

'They look pretty conclusive to me, like someone tried to hold him back or push him down. Or even pick him up, which is wholly possible, considering how drunk he was.'

'Yes, he was definitely inebriated. I've got the numbers there.' Drysdale gestured at a file on his desk. 'His blood-alcohol count is off the chart. The numbers give us some perspective on his condition: they're just a tad lower than yours, Frost.'

'Funny.'

'The problem with his condition is that he could have picked up the marks on his skin even whilst sleeping, just by rolling over on his hands.'

'Really?'

Drysdale shrugged. 'Devil's advocate. Putting up a spirited defence, if you manage to get someone in the dock. But they'll throw the cirrhosis back at you. Of course we'll conduct a full post-mortem tomorrow.'

Gerald Drysdale slipped off his blue scrubs to reveal he was dressed in as funereal a manner as ever, sheathed in his customary dark suit with a black tie knotted as neat and tight as a hangman's noose.

'Off anywhere nice, Gerald?'

'Cocktail party, wife's friend, something in the charity sector. So no, nowhere nice at all.'

'I know how you feel, you'd rather be cutting open a cadaver, up to your elbows, as it were?'

'No, I'd rather be in my favourite chair in my study listening to Elgar on my handcrafted and ridiculously expensive stereo whilst enjoying a balloon of Hennessy cognac with my feet up. Still, needs must. Although looking at our friend here . . . the pleasures of the grape and the grain are rather paling. God knows what his liver will be like, though we'll find out tomorrow. But as Maltby no doubt told you, it was his heart packing up on him, along with him choking on his own vomit, that killed him. The classic alcoholic's end. However, before the choking and the heart attack – as the marks suggest – I put it to you that he may have been involved in a struggle, and that's what may have triggered the event.'

'He choked on his own vomit, you say?'

'Very common alcoholic's death, the bile fumes alone can cause asphyxiation.'

Frost considered this, then laughed.

'What's so funny, apart from *la condition humaine*?'

'Sorry, funny film I saw last year, *This is Spinal Tap*?'

'Never heard of it.'

'It's about a rock band whose drummers keep dying. One died the same death as Ivan, but he choked on someone else's vomit. Another self-combusted.'

'Sounds ghastly, glad I missed it. But gallows humour, Frost, it's what gets us through, I suppose.'

'But it makes you think, they were both messy deaths, very messy.'

'I've seen self-immolation, not a pretty sight, but not spontaneous combustion. Sounds like the messiest of all deaths.'

'Do you have his clothes here?'

Gerald Drysdale gave a lavish sigh and shot up his shirt cuff to commune with his watch. He then led the way to the adjacent room where Ivan Fielding's clothing was boxed and bagged in plastic. Like their owner, they too had a tag identifying them. The clothes were themselves in some sort of purgatory; they would either be released to the next of kin, or taken to Forensics to be combed for clues, depending on Drysdale's autopsy and final conclusions on the cause of death.

'The shirt looks crisp and fresh and very clean. No vomit on it,' Frost commented.

'Like I said, he choked on it. If he'd vomited on his shirt, he'd probably still be alive.'

Frost threw Drysdale a quizzical look. Too fresh, too clean. Frost pulled some latex gloves from the dispenser on the table, opened up the sealed plastic bag and took out the shirt, cream-coloured with a fine blue thread darting through it. It had a white cutaway collar that was slightly fraying. Even through the gloves, the detective could feel the quality at his fingertips. Thick and soft Egyptian cotton. And the label spoke of quality too: 'Turnbull & Asser of Jermyn Street'.

'The world's finest shirtmaker,' announced Drysdale, impressed. 'I'll warrant this shirt is older than most of the PCs you've got running around Eagle Lane, and probably cost more than their combined monthly pay packets. A man of some sartorial discernment, our Mr Fielding.'

'I'm more Marks & Sparks myself,' said Frost.

Drysdale looked him up and down, then looked doubtful, as if even that was beyond Frost. Careful not to disturb the evidence too much, the DI peered inside the shirt and found a ticket for Wilson's the dry-cleaner's in Market Square pinned to the washing-instructions label.

'A man of discernment would take the safety pin out of his expensive shirt before wearing it, wouldn't he?'

Gerald Drysdale conceded the point by pursing his dry thin lips and emitting a low growl that took a sudden upward inflection.

Frost continued, 'Looks like after Ivan expired, someone changed his shirt for him.'

'Gussying him up to meet his maker?'

'Or hiding something. My money is on hiding something. It usually is with murder, if that's what we're calling it.'

'That's up to you. But I would suggest the bruising, as we've discussed, might indicate further investigation is needed. As for the business with this shirt, well, again, that's your whole field of play. Mine is in there,' said Drysdale with a nod to the adjacent room.

Frost watched as Dr Death stalked gleefully towards the corpse awaiting him next door. It sent a shiver down his spine, not just because it was always cold down here, but because he'd always hated the County morgue. Hardly an original aversion, he told himself, but enough to send him into a palpable panic when Drysdale turned the lights off without warning.

Monday (1)

'Foul play? Is that what they call it?'

'Yes, that's one of the terms,' said Frost. 'Of course, we won't fully know the causes of your father's death until the autopsy later today. But there are certainly some signs that warrant further investigation.'

Sally Fielding took this news with some solemn nods. She was a strikingly attractive woman of twenty-eight with lustrous raven hair worn in a Purdey style. Frost compared her with her briefly glimpsed mother, but more fully with the pictures of her mother scattered about the flat. They shared the same high cheekbones that gave them both an effortless unadorned beauty.

'She's still sleeping,' said Stephen Parker apologetically as he entered the living room. 'Do you need me to wake her up?'

Sally said, 'She took a tranquillizer, I think.'

'Sleeping pills, actually.'

'Same thing, no?'

Parker shrugged. 'I leave the medicine cabinet to Vanessa. It's a bit of a minefield, she has trouble sleeping, and with her nerves.' He smiled and injected some optimism. 'But she's getting better with more rest, calmer.'

Sally, pre-empting the two detectives, said, 'She's been exhausted by it all, wouldn't be much good to you, I'm afraid. There isn't anything that she knows about Dad that I don't.'

Frost doubted the veracity of that last statement when it came to husbands and wives. Clarke said, 'No, that's fine, we can talk to her another time.'

Parker came further into the room and sat down on the free armchair. 'It's been a terrible shock for her. I'm sure Sally will tell you the details.'

All eyes turned to Sally.

'As I said in my statement, I went round there yesterday at lunchtime to check he was OK, make sure he'd been eating. We have someone, Moira, who comes in three times a week, to clean, and prepare some meals.'

'When was the help last there?' asked Frost.

'Saturday morning, early.'

Clarke looked at her notes. 'Simms had a brief conversation with her yesterday evening. She's coming in to make a formal statement, but it seems she dropped in early on Saturday morning just to leave a meal in the fridge. On her way out, around nine, she took Mr Fielding a cup of tea. But he was fast asleep on the sofa, snoozing away, she said, so she left him to it. Didn't have the heart to wake him.'

'That sounds like Moira. She's a lovely woman; thank God she didn't find him. Mum used to do the shopping . . . But they hadn't been speaking these last few . . . well, probably four or five months now. As you know, my father had a drink problem. A severe one that just got worse and worse. We've almost been expecting something like this, a fall or just his body packing up on him. He was very frail. I try . . . tried to visit him as much as I could. But I have a young daughter, so it's difficult. And, well, *he* was difficult. His drinking made him almost impossible to talk to . . . like a child, a badly behaved one. It does that, the drink, infantilizes you.' She took a sharp breath, seemingly determined not to cry. 'My mother couldn't deal with him, and thankfully she didn't have to . . .' She looked over at Stephen Parker to take over the reins on the narrative.

He was in his early to mid-forties, with a soft boyish face, lineless and pale. If it hadn't been for his full head of almost uniformly grey hair that was on the cusp of turning white, he'd have looked at least ten years younger. It was a kind face, in a timid way, and matched his profession, thought Frost.

'Vanessa lives with me now.'

'How long have you been together?'

He looked surprised by this question, like it was none of Frost's business. Frost fixed him with an insistent look that told him everything was his business now.

'Three, almost four years. And without doubt, they've been the happiest years of my life.'

Frost glanced at Clarke to see if people really did say this sort of thing, outside of retirement communities. Clarke went out of her way not to look at Frost. He took it that they obviously did say this kind of thing, and his cynicism was misplaced. He watched as Sally Fielding smiled at this fact, like her mother deserved every minute of happiness.

'And you work at the university . . . Professor, is it?'

'That's right. I'm in the social sciences department. I'm a lecturer, not a professor. Not yet. I hope to—'

'So what do you think happened, Inspector Frost?' asked Sally, cutting Parker off.

'As I said, we won't know until the post-mortem, but we just need to be sure. We discovered there may have been a burglary at your father's house, probably very recently.'

'And you believe this has something to do with his death? He was . . . murdered, is that what you're saying?'

She had been stoic up to this point, but now Sally raised her hands to her face and began to cry. Stephen Parker sprang to his feet, went over to the packed bookshelves that lined the walls and brought back a box of Mansize Kleenex that Vanessa had obviously been grappling with earlier, as it was severely depleted. Sally followed suit; she plucked out a handful and buried her face in them. Stephen sat on the arm of the chair, his hands on her shoulders to comfort her.

The inspector was studying Stephen Parker, and his comforting gestures towards Sally. After all, in age difference, he was practically equidistant to the mother and daughter. But Frost couldn't spot anything untoward. In fact, he seemed ill at ease with the whole emotional element, patting Sally awkwardly on the shoulders like she was a child. She eventually gently shrugged him off and he took his seat again, a face full of stilted concern.

Frost thought he looked like the typical academic: analytical, theoretical and quantifiable, more at home with his books, research and references than the harsh and messy realities of life and death and grief.

'So how did he die, was he hit or anything? He was so fragile, it would just be too awful to think . . .'

Frost sparked up the last Player's in his pack and explained, 'No, nothing like that. We know he died of a heart attack, but we also believe there was someone else in the house. There was a window in the kitchen that had been forced open. The glass had been cut to gain access, a professional-looking job. And considering your father's profession, and the valuable items he had in the house, not that surprising. We'd like you to come to the house with us, to see if anything has been stolen.'

'If you're feeling up to it,' added Clarke.

Stephen Parker looked concerned at the cigarette Frost was puffing away on. A long striated rectangle of ash was already forming, and would soon be falling. There wasn't an ashtray on the table – never a problem or even a hint for Frost – so Parker got up to get one.

'Excuse me, Mr Parker,' said Frost, stopping him, 'but we'll need to know your movements for twenty-four hours before Mr Fielding was discovered.'

'Really?'

'Really. Actually, everyone's. Just routine, to eliminate as many people from the enquiry as possible. Just as we'll need to take everyone's fingerprints, again purely for elimination purposes, in case we find anything of interest.'

'Yes, yes, of course, of course.' Stephen Parker looked like he understood the logic, and sat back down to answer Frost's questions, and watch him drop ash on his oatmeal carpet.

Monday (2)

Grey Gables was the name of the house, built at a time when all houses of a certain size and stature had an official name rather than just a number. It was by far the biggest house in the village, which could have given its occupants a certain lord-of-the-manor status. But the building was in such a state of disrepair that it was probably a status the rest of the inhabitants of the village were happy not to have. It was Georgian and ran over three floors, if you included the attic rooms, which were closed off and home to squirrels and bats. The garden was overgrown, with a greenhouse that was boarded up due to nearly every one of its panes being broken. And as Frost had already spotted, if the brickwork wasn't attended to soon, the old pile would be reduced to a pile of rubble.

Still, the inside had not been subject to the elements too much. Some of the Regency-style striped wallpaper was peeling away and there were black speckles of damp in every corner, but it was clean and tidy and still very impressive.

Frost, Clarke and Sally Fielding were in the living room.

Sally stood by the fire, looking at the dead ashes, her long navy woollen coat wrapped around her to keep out the cold, which the house, now devoid of its owner, could no longer do on its own.

'I was never very happy in this house. We moved here when I was eleven, or twelve, from London. It belonged to my grandmother, Dad's mother. She was still here when we moved in. Always made us feel like lodgers. But she died shortly after we moved here. I'd hoped she would throw us out so we could go back to London. But even after she died, we didn't – that was never possible.'

'Why not?' asked Frost.

Sally shrugged. 'I never fully knew. A mixture of things. Dad's drinking had started to affect his business; there wasn't the money like there used to be. He had an antiques shop in Chelsea. It was very successful – until it wasn't. There may have been other reasons to leave, but I was too young to know. It all happened so fast. One minute we were happy in London, and then we were here.'

'Your father must have dealt in very high-class goods, to have a shop in Chelsea?'

'He did. He had great taste, and a wonderful knowledge of paintings. He started trading at a really young age, he had a stamp collection that he'd worked on since he was a child, and sold it at auction for a lot of money. Invested it all in a couple of paintings, sold those on for a huge profit and never looked back. My grandmother, who was a dreadful snob, thought he was turning into a spiv. So she sent him to a crammer boarding school in Brighton. His mother wanted him to be a doctor or a lawyer, like his father, but he refused. The only thing he'd wanted to do at university was art. Well, he wasn't any good at painting, so art school was out, so he went to the Courtauld to study art history. But once he was in London, he carried on his trading, gave up college after the first year and had a stall on the Portobello Road, and then in Antiquarius, an indoor market, and then opened a shop off the King's Road.'

Sally moved over to a nest of burr-walnut tables that held a cluster of photos in art deco silver frames. They looked like 1960s David Bailey portraits, and featured a young and blonde Vanessa Fielding with a Vidal Sassoon five-point haircut, in a miniskirt and knee-length white patent-leather boots. Against a white backdrop she looked like she was dancing on air. It was obviously a professional studio session.

Frost compared the pictures of the beautiful long-limbed Vanessa with pictures of the younger Ivan. He was portly, bespectacled, and what mousy hair he had he was losing fast. Frost reflexively ran a hand through his own hair. He breathed easy. It was still there. It was clear that Ivan was punching well above his weight with Vanessa. As Clarke and Frost looked at the photos, perhaps Sally could tell what they were thinking, because what she said next, she said with such a practised ease that she was obviously used to the comparisons.

'Back then Dad was witty, charming, confident, and had a deep knowledge of seemingly everything. My mum was from a working-class background, and Dad sort of did a *Pygmalion* on her. They made it work, they were happy, for a while.'

'What do you do, Sally, for a living?'

She pulled away from the photos to address Clarke. 'I went to art college, Dad's influence, but studied graphic design. I'm starting to get some work, now my daughter's a little older. She'll be nine next month.'

Frost had heard enough and wanted to get on. 'Well, this is as good a place to start as any.'

'I can tell you now, nothing has been taken from this room,' said Sally confidently.

Frost again looked at the photos, but at the silver frames this time. Even at this distance of a couple of feet he could see they were rather ostentatiously stamped *Tiffany & Co.* If this was a robbery, the value of what *hadn't* been stolen was adding up to a good few quid.

They went through all the rooms, and each time Sally came

up with a blank – nothing had been taken. She said she knew every item in the house intimately; it was the type of home where very little new was added, apart from the occasional broken cup.

And as they searched the house for that elusive missing item, Frost made a mental note in each room of the things that could have been taken, and how much they might have fetched. Whilst not cluttered, every room held something of interest and beauty and, more pertinent to the case, value. Maybe the burglar broke in and tidied up, and changed Ivan's shirt whilst he was at it, thought Frost with mounting frustration. The last room they inventoried was Sally's old bedroom.

'Embarrassing, pretty much as I left it ten years ago.'

'You left home early,' said Clarke.

'Yes. Met a guy at college early. Had a child early. He left us early.'

Clarke gave an understanding smile. 'You've got a head start on me – my son, Philip, just turned two.'

'They get a bad reputation at that age. They keep you busy, but there's nothing terrible about them.'

'My mum lives with me full-time now, makes things a lot easier. She's a rock, actually.'

Without saying any more, Sue and Sally seemed to be on the same page, as shared experience and understanding passed between them.

Frost wanted to add to the rock analogy about Susan's mother: cold, hard and craggy. But he refrained. In the brief exchanges they'd had recently, relations with the venerable Mrs Clarke hadn't improved. She'd even bought her daughter a new couch, feeling the old one that Frost had kipped on for a couple of months, when he was homeless, was somehow irretrievably ruined, maybe even possessed. He refocused on the bedroom. There was little of value in here outside of childhood memories. Some posters on the wall of David Essex, David Cassidy, Donny Osmond, and David Bowie in prime Ziggy Stardust mode, along with a stack of *Jackie* annuals, and another of LPs and 45s against the wall.

'Oh, that's weird.'

Frost and Clarke quickly turned to Sally, who was looking at an empty easel in the corner of the room. It was an antique-looking easel in a rich red wood, built for displaying paintings rather than the heavy work of producing them.

'There was a painting here, now it's gone. And it was still here three days ago, I know that.'

'Was it yours?' said Clarke.

'No, Dad was just storing it in here.'

'Was it particularly valuable?' asked Frost.

Sally pulled a face that looked like this was the most stupid question she'd ever heard. 'No, sorry – I would have actually paid someone to steal it. It was worthless and ugly. I'm pretty sure that's why Dad insisted on it being in my room, as no one really comes in here now – and he didn't have to look at it.'

'It wasn't of a clown with eyes that follow you around the room, was it?' Clarke explained: 'My nan had one of those in her hallway. It used to scare the life out of me.'

'We had the flamenco dancer and the green lady in our house,' Frost added to the bad-art debate. 'You normally had one or the other, but we managed to have both. Still, hid the rising damp. What was it a painting of?'

'From what I could make out, there was a hill, some trees, and a duck, or a chicken or something, didn't make much sense. Horrible garish things, they looked like they'd been done by a child, but without the charm.'

'*They?* There was more than one?'

'There were three of them, paintings, oil on canvas. Dad gave one to me and one to my mother, and there was also this one,' Sally said, gesturing to the now empty easel. 'I don't know where he got them, my mother thought he must have found them somewhere, literally on the street, or picked them out of a skip. He had a habit of doing that, bringing home stuff he found, like he was still collecting . . .' She stifled a sob. 'But it was always rubbish he brought home, stuff that people had thrown out. We just used to throw it out too. He'd never miss it, he was usually drunk when he brought it home.'

'Your father collected some modern art, could it have fallen into that category? You know, "matchstalk men and matchstalk cats and dogs".'

'No, Inspector, it wasn't anything like Lowry, or remotely conceptual. It honestly looked like it was scrawled by a five-year-old. It's completely worthless. To be honest, it just depressed me. It was just sad and pathetic. As you can see, my father was a collector and dealer in beautiful things, he loved and under-stood art. He was an aesthete. I thought the paintings were a sign of him losing his mind even more, trawling through skips. He'd let himself go so much, in all sorts of ways.'

'How so?' asked Clarke.

'Well, you know, not washing, shaving or getting dressed, constantly looking a mess, like a derelict . . . and just drinking himself to death.'

Sally sat down on the springy little single bed, cried, apolo-gized, and took a moment to compose herself. Sue Clarke sat with her.

Frost looked out of the window, at a view of Denton Woods, the north end, away from the impending destruction. He thought about the wreck of the alcoholic – he'd seen them before. As a PC he'd once kicked down the door of a neighbour when the bottles of milk lined up outside began to resemble the pins in a bowling lane. He'd found a man who had obviously given up. The bottles of booze scattered around the room, unlike the milk bottles, had been well attended to. He was wearing soiled pyjamas, a raincoat and shoes. Just enough to get him to the off-licence and back. There is a tipping point, a point when they give up, thought Frost. Had Ivan Fielding reached that point? And yet, at the time of his death, he'd been clean-shaven and smartly dressed. A blue silk cravat with white spots tied around his neck, hiding the marks that would soon show up as a bruise.

'The last time you saw your father, how did he look?'

'The same.'

'The same as you found him?'

'No, not at all. He was in his dressing gown.'

'Unshaven?'

'Yes, yes, he was always unshaven towards the end.'

'But not the day you found him. Do you know if he was expecting anyone the previous evening or that day?'

Frost stared intently at Sally as she thought about this. It obviously struck her as anomalous too. With her brow creased and lips pursed, she managed to look both confused and thoughtful as she ran through possible scenarios.

'No . . . no, there wasn't anyone to expect. Not any more.'

Monday (3) ————————————————

There was no sign of his neighbour, Shirley, as he twirled the key in his front door that night. But it was late, he'd made sure of that. He'd gone to the Spread Eagle pub on Eagle Lane to avoid her.

As he'd sat in the booth necking his second pint, refusing to look at yesterday's discarded *News of the World* that was rolled up on the seat next to him, he looked down at his developing paunch, and thought maybe he should make use of Paradise Lodge's basement gym, with its weights and resistance machines and its steam room and jacuzzi. The very second he thought that, he envisioned himself bubbling in the hot tub with a glass of bubbly, and the bubbly blonde Shirley dropping her towel and joining him. He squeezed his eyes shut to rinse the vision from his mind, and reprimanded himself for letting such a notion slip through. He'd decided to heed the much-touted advice about one's own doorstep, and what not to do on it.

Now safely in his flat, he poured himself three fingers of Teacher's whisky and slumped down on the sofa. He looked about the 'apartment' (as the brochure for Paradise Lodge had insisted on calling it) and was amazed at just how light his fingerprints on the fully furnished flat (as *he* insisted on calling it) were. Of course he'd jumped at the chance of the discounted weekly cleaning service on offer, so it seemed to always look the same; even his mess didn't last long. Apart from some books on the shelf (mainly military history, biographies of world leaders and war heroes, some Le Carré, and he was developing a liking for Trollope), some clothes in the walk-in wardrobe and a small pile of video cassettes by the TV, there were few clues that the place was inhabited at all. There were some stop-gap framed artworks on the walls, nothing like Ivan Fielding's, but also nothing like his mum and dad's green Chinese lady and flamenco dancer, either. There were some stacked boxes in the hallway closet that did contain important parts of his life: pictures of his wife, memorabilia from his marriage and his old home. The past, memories good and bad. But somehow Frost felt that he wouldn't ever be unpacking them here.

He reached for the remote and pressed the Trinitron into action. Denton Woods had made the tail of the local evening news, with a report on the growing opposition to the promised new housing development. It was certainly bleeding the force's resources, with Mullett having to ask the new Rimmington superintendent for some uniform back-up.

He flicked around the four channels. Four bloody channels, spoilt for choice, and yet never anything on. He took a swig of his drink. Then another, which finished it off. He got up and went into the kitchen and pulled a can of Skol out of the fridge. He paused for thought, then pulled three more out, knowing that, realistically, he'd neck them all. It made economic sense: saved him getting up again, and saved the little light in the fridge going on and off again. He glimpsed Shirley's fish pie in the fridge and knew he'd be laying waste to that around midnight.

The booze worked like a remote to change the channel in his mind back to earlier at Grey Gables, and Ivan's fate. He shuddered at the thought. Maybe a uniform would kick his front door down one day, and find him shipwrecked on his couch, surrounded by tins of Skol and bottles of Teacher's. And Shirley's Pyrex dish on the coffee table where he hadn't even been bothered to put her fish pie on a plate.

Maybe the fresh shirt Ivan was wearing at the time of his demise was his last attempt to claw back some dignity? The painting, the missing painting from Sally's old bedroom – maybe in a moment of sobriety Ivan had destroyed the childish daub he'd found in a skip somewhere to again try to get back some vestiges of his former self?

Frost slammed the freshly opened can on the frosted-glass coffee table, where it frothed up to leave a nice ring for the cleaner, and he got to his feet. He collected his keys from the breakfast counter and left the flat, determined not to let the rot set in. Barely ten seconds later he walked back in and picked up the can of Skol and took it with him – seemed a shame to waste it.

As Frost let himself into Grey Gables, he was aware that it still wasn't officially a crime scene. Even with today's autopsy, what would it show? Probably that Ivan died an alcoholic's death: heart and renal failure, and choking on his own vomit. The marks, perhaps signs of a struggle, were slight, and even Gerald Drysdale, who always veered towards the morbid and murder when he could, had said that the bruising could have happened by Fielding simply turning over in bed, such was the perilous state of his health.

But with seemingly nothing taken from the house, a house that was crying out to be robbed, Mullett would surely close the case down. No motive, no proof, no circumstantial. Death by alcoholic misadventure, another quick clear-up and better statistics for him. It was said that when it came to numbers of unsolved cases, Mullett always wanted his lower than the UK entrant's score at the Eurovision Song Contest.

With his gloved hand, Frost switched on the living-room light.

It flickered into life, soft and low. He began to pad about the large room, his carefully placed feet falling softly on the dark polished hardwood floor that was almost completely covered in Persian rugs, ranging from the plush to the threadbare, depending on the wear they got. Maybe they should have been rotated, maybe they had been at one time, but yet again, it was something that Ivan had let slip.

Frost eased himself down on the sofa and looked at the bottles on the table, the full ashtray. All the same brand of cigarettes, no lipstick traces on any of the butts to throw some interest into the mix; and all seemed to be uniformly smoked down to just above the print. All the work of one man. A creature of habit, and all of them bad by the looks of it.

There was a loud chime that made Frost jump and swear. In the corner lurked a grandfather clock standing on a rug. Frost checked the Casio on his wrist – either it was wrong or the clock was. He'd put money on it being the grandfather. The rug under it looked plush, no reason why it shouldn't; it was in the corner after all, not much foot traffic. There was also a slight tilt to the clock, a perceptible lean. Not much, you wouldn't really notice if you weren't looking. But Frost was looking. Hard.

He got up to make a closer inspection and noticed the varying imprints on the nap of the rug where it appeared the clock had been moved and not put back on its mark. As far as Frost could see, the back of the case was sealed and any necessary winding or maintenance could be done from the front. He eased the clock away from the wall, and manoeuvred it from side to side until he'd walked it off the rug. He then rolled up the rug and found what he'd been hoping for: a hidden trapdoor in the floorboards.

Frost quickly straightened up when he heard the noise. He wasn't being jumpy this time, but it didn't sound like the usual creaking, the moans and groans of old house beams and joists adjusting to the cold snap. No, this sounded louder, more pronounced. He quickly rolled the rug back over the trapdoor and made his way as softly as he could across to the hallway, picking up a heavy brass candlestick off a side table on the way. The light in the living room was weak, a low-wattage bulb that was about to blow, and it barely reached into the hallway. Still, he didn't turn the hallway light on.

He winced as he made his way up the staircase. Each step had its own distinct creaking sound, which you would probably notice only if you were walking carefully and trying not to be noticed. To Frost it was like moving along a big keyboard – if anyone was on the first floor they'd hear him note for note. It was pitch-black up there, like staring up into a tunnel. Like most people, Frost had a list of things that spooked him, but spooky old houses at midnight wasn't one of them. So he was surprised to feel his heart going about its work, and pumping away just a little faster than usual.

He was about to take the last step on to the landing when a door burst open and a figure rushed at him.

Frost grabbed at the banister, but his hand slipped and he was falling backwards, fast. He felt each edge of the steps on the base of his spine, then all the way down to his neck, one, two, three, four . . . Be stopped counting and concentrated on the pain. His back felt like cheese running down a blunt grater. His hand grabbed at a banister strut more successfully this time and that worked in slowing his descent, the top half of him anyway.

'Je . . . sus . . . bloo . . . dy . . . we . . . pt!'

His legs were up in the air, and he flipped over and barrelled down to the bottom of the stairs. As he hit the hall floor, face down, he just managed to raise his head to see the front door opening, a pair of feet darting out, and then the door slamming shut.

Tuesday (1)

The settled morning mist hung like a membrane around the base of the trees, and the ground was hard with frost underfoot. It didn't take long to find the protestors. There they were, crouched around a campfire, making themselves their morning coffee. In the clearing there was a Volkswagen Beetle and two camper vans, some single tents, and some family-sized ones. There were probably about fifteen people in all. Some looked like out-and-out hippies, others looked like the more thoughtful environmentalist types he'd read about.

As Clive Banes came into view they stopped talking. With his mousy and thinning hair, pilling grey polyester trousers, black moulded-sole BHS shoes and saggy navy duffel coat, he usually looked as inconspicuous and unthreatening as a mild-mannered geography teacher perusing the general-interest section of a bookshop. However, the protestors gathered around the campfire had good reason to be paranoid, and he probably looked like a copper to them.

But he put them at their ease – he was good at that. Banes prided himself on his disarming ability to slip into any guise, to talk to people at their level, befriend them, and gain their trust. It was all part of what he did, what he'd learned as a kid. When you grow up in institutions, you learn how to keep your head down, below the parapet. To keep quiet until danger passes, not speak until spoken to. Just in the same way you learn how to curry favour, to tell good jokes, pay compliments and sing for your supper. You make the best of what talents you've got, and when the opportunity strikes – you take it.

'Hello, hope you don't mind, I've parked down the way there. I heard people were protesting, thought I'd come and take a look. I hope you don't mind.' The big smile and wide-eyed innocent look he flashed them seemed to work. They all nodded in recognition. 'I used to live in Denton. Only spent a couple of years here, when I was a child, then we moved.' That was good, he thought. It gave him an emotional angle, but if they questioned him on details, he was just a kid at the time. 'When I heard they were planning on cutting down all the trees and building on the woods, I had to come back, take a look.'

'What they're doing is an abomination,' said an older man, probably in his fifties, in a cagoule and wellington boots. 'This place has never been officially designated an area of outstanding beauty, so the developers have jumped all over it. They'll be doing it all over the country if we don't stop them. Scarring the land with their carbuncles.'

'Yes. It's terrible.'

A tall hippy type rose from a crouch. He was wearing camouflage army fatigues, paratrooper boots, and his lank hair was matted together. 'We have to man the barricades, brother, or they'll take what's naturally ours! Are you with us?'

He wanted to say, 'No, I'm with the Woolwich.' But they probably wouldn't be amused, viewing him as capitalist scum. Instead he said, 'They won't be building this far in, will they?'

The older man pointed up the path, a path that was big enough to drive up. 'We've got people camped up there to stop them if they try. There are more of us than them, that's for sure, and our numbers are growing.'

Clive Banes looked impressed, and commended them for their principles and resolve to stand up to such dark forces. They seemed to like what he said, and told him they'd be happy to have him at their side if he wanted to join the protest. The tall hippy picked up a battered-looking acoustic guitar and began to strum it and sing Woody Guthrie's 'This Land Is Your Land'. They all joined in.

Mid-song, he waved his goodbyes and made his way up the track. He saw cars and camper vans parked up there too. He carried on until the track petered out to just a muddy path, bordered by denser foliage and trees, impossible to get a vehicle up. Away from the campfire the air smelt earthy, damp, and redolent of pine. A smell, ironically, he recognized from the little scented green tree hanging from the rear-view mirror in his van. On the road in one of those, things could get pretty gamey. Banes lifted his head up to the darkening sky, the trees greedily cramming out what light there was, and breathed in nature. He then spotted a glint of metal. He knew it was his man. Hiding in the woods. It was an Abi Monza 1200 CT touring caravan, *circa* 1972. The red Ford Cortina with the black vinyl roof was probably about the same age as the caravan. He'd seen the car before. In Longthorn Hospital's visitors' car park. He'd made a note of it. It was a good idea of the man he was after, Kevin Wheaton, to be here, to blend in with the protestors. It's certainly what he would have done, to hide in plain view; there was anonymity in a crowd, even if it was an angry and protesting one.

Banes turned around and walked back down the path, past the little encampment with the hippies, the middle-aged sandal-wearing liberal types and the Rambo done up in his army-surplus chic. He gave them a nod as he passed. They barely acknowledged him. Which was perfect, just what he wanted. There was only one track out of the woods for cars, so he'd wait at the bottom for him. Then he'd follow Kevin Wheaton, and take the necessary action.

It was the 9 a.m. 'morning scrum' at Eagle Lane, when a DS or DI stood in front of the incident board where the ongoing cases were chalked up and talked through their progress, or lack thereof.

Whilst the morning scrum was usually held in the CID incident room, with every officer sat at or on their desk, nominally paying attention as they drank their teas and coffees and rubbed the sleep out of their eyes, today was different. The team had been ushered by DC Clarke into the conference room, where Detective Inspector Jack Frost was waiting for them. Straight back, arms crossed.

Marked up on a flip chart in big red letters and underlined was a new case: <u>IVAN FIELDING</u>.

But as the troops trooped in, none of them were looking at what was written up on the flip chart, they were all ogling what was laid out along the conference table. There was a large and lavishly decorated Georgian silver-gilt punchbowl; eight tall silver candlesticks; a suite of jewellery by Cartier that contained platinum, ruby and diamond drop earrings, a necklace and bracelet; six oil paintings that had been cut out of their frames, all country scenes, *circa* 1800; eight Meissen figurines depicting a chamber orchestra; a coin collection featuring Krugerrands and sovereigns; and a large jewellery box out of which were spilling gold chains, brooches and rings like from a pirates' chest.

'What's all this, *The Generation Game*?' said DC Arthur Hanlon.

'More like *Going for a Song*,' said DS John Waters.

'No rotisserie or cuddly toy, bit crap this week,' joined in PC Simms.

'Why are you in civvies, Simmo?' asked the unnecessarily tall Pete 'Lofty' Pattison, a DC recently transferred from Rimmington.

'At least he can find a suit that fits him,' said Clarke, coming to Simms's defence.

'If you love him so much why don't you marry him?' quipped Lofty Pattison.

'Shut up, Lofty, or you'll be back on traffic duty in Rimmington.'

Once the banter had been quelled, and all the officers were gathered around the table, they got back to their ogling and making impressed whistling sounds, and guessing the value of the items presented.

'This little lot I found under the floorboards of Ivan Fielding's home,' said Frost. 'Who's Ivan Fielding? For those that don't know about the case, he's a retired art and antiques dealer, found dead at his home Sunday lunchtime. PC Simms first noticed that there'd been a break-in, with his trusty magnifying glass.'

Cheers went up for Simms.

'Bet that comes in handy when he needs a wazz,' said Arthur Hanlon.

More laughter. But it quickly petered out as all eyes turned to see Superintendent Stanley Mullett enter the conference room.

'As you were, as you were,' said Mullett, taking a leisurely stroll around the table as he inspected the goods. 'Carry on, Jack.' The super picked up the red leather Cartier jewellery case.

'I believe it's the good lady wife's birthday coming up, so we'll turn a blind eye if you like, sir,' said Frost.

Everyone laughed, dispelling some of the tension that always built when Mullett entered a room. The Denton superintendent was very hands off, seldom involving himself in the nitty-gritty of the incident room. He was presidential in his approach, preferring to work from his oak-panelled office, into which his secretary, the much-admired Ms' Smith, shapely in her tight-fitting trouser suits, would call officers when he wanted to be kept up to date and hand out his instructions. It was an arrangement that suited everyone.

Frost carried on. 'As Dr Maltby stated in his initial report, Mr Fielding died of a heart attack, and other complications brought on by his alcoholism. Then Dr Drysdale also found there were some marks on his body, his chest and around his neck, which may indicate that there was some kind of struggle before he died. This evidence is weak on its own. But it was our very own eagle-eyed PC Simms who discovered in the kitchen that a square of glass had been cut out of a window. It was a professional job, diamond-tipped cutter, glass removed, latch slipped, then the glass put back in place. And once the burglar was in the house . . . jackpot. A house that would pay dividends, full of quality goods worth nicking. And yet, nothing was taken.'

'He's disturbed by Ivan Fielding, there's an altercation, Ivan dies, burglar didn't plan on that and flees the scene empty-handed,' offered up Hanlon.

'I think that sounds about right, Arthur. Oh, there was one thing: a painting was discovered to be missing by Ivan's daughter. It was apparently completely worthless and Ivan might have got rid of it himself. But it's all in the report.'

Mullett cleared his throat, loud enough for all to look at him. Once he had everyone's attention, he said, 'Jack, I'd like a word. Alone, if I may.'

'Can it wait? I'm in the middle of a briefing.'

'From what I've heard, no, it can't wait.' Mullett's eyes swept those gathered around the conference table and he uttered ominously, '*Now*, please.'

Everyone looked at Frost. Their DI waited a moment, then gave a quick nod. A nod so quick you'd have had to be paying really close attention to catch it. It was the team's deference to Frost, and not to Mullett, that clearly rankled with the superintendent. It was only when Frost had given them the nod that they filed out of the room, studiously avoiding Mullett as they did so.

Frost could feel his cheeks prickle with anger.

Once the room was cleared, Mullett said, 'First off, what's this about DS Waters attending the scene of a crime? He is strictly desk-bound until further notice.'

'I was on call, he phoned up and asked me if I wanted to go for a . . .' He caught himself in time. '. . . a cup of tea. At the local café. We were in the car when I got the call.'

'I've made my position very clear on Waters. We see a bright future for him; his full and carefully managed recovery is of the utmost importance.'

'Yeah, yeah, I know, he's County's blue-eyed boy.'

Frost and Mullett fixed each other with uncertain looks at that last comment. But the super let it go.

'I spoke to Chief Pathologist Drysdale,' said Mullett. 'He told me about Ivan Fielding's state of health. And he also told me your ludicrous theory on his fresh shirt. According to you, this whole case hangs on a safety pin from Wilson's dry-cleaner's being left in it.'

Frost's mouth gaped, in both confusion and frustration. Eventually he got it together and said, 'It was an observation, one of many. I believe that's what we're paid for.'

'A common enough oversight, I've done it myself, I even use the same shirt service. What else do you have? A panel of glass was removed? That's not proof of a burglary; the glass may have been cracked and Mr Fielding might have replaced it himself.'

'Not according to Forensics. It had been cut, fresh slivers on the kitchen floor.'

Mullett dismissed this point like he was swatting away a fly. 'It's thin, Frost, *very* thin. And without any items being taken, can we really say that it was a burglary?'

Frost went to say something, but Mullett raised his palm imperiously. The super then pulled out a chair and sat down, inviting the DI to do the same. Frost pulled out the chair in front of him and lowered himself down into the seat, gingerly, trying to control the pained grimace that was creeping across his face as each bruised rib and vertebra adjusted to his new position. Once he was down, his spine pressing against the back of the chair, he breathed an involuntary sigh of relief.

Nothing escaped Mullett. 'What the hell's wrong with you, man?'

'That's what I was going to get on to next in the briefing, before you cleared the room. Last night, when I retrieved this little lot' – he nodded to the swag on the table – 'there was someone in the house. I obviously disturbed them. They pushed me down the stairs and made their escape.'

'Did you get a look at them?'

'It was dark. And I was too busy trying to stop myself from falling down the stairs – I failed on that score. But I did succeed in not breaking my neck. You'll be happy to hear.'

Mullett wasn't happy to hear, or certainly didn't look it. 'I see no case here. A robbery where nothing was stolen, and a murder where the so-called victim obviously drank himself to death and had a heart attack.'

'How about the man I disturbed?' asked Frost incredulously, his ire mounting. 'The man that may have caused Ivan Fielding's death and may have returned to get what he couldn't get before because he was interrupted by Fielding, and may well have struggled with him, causing his death!'

'Enough, Frost!'

Frost wanted to throw something against the wall, and there was enough ammunition on the table. But his pay packet wouldn't cover the damage.

Mullett continued, 'As you say, it was dark, who knows what you saw—'

'Are you doubting my word?'

'What time was this?'

'Midnight.'

'Where had you been?'

'How do you mean?'

'Before Ivan Fielding's house, where had you been?'

'I was at home.'

'Before you got home?'

'Am I being questioned, do I need my union rep?'

'Do you? It strikes me as a perfectly innocent question. Which I'll repeat: where were you?'

Frost could see where this was leading. 'The gym.'

Disbelief contorted Mullett's face. 'The *what*? The *where*?'

'There's a gym in my building.' Frost smiled to himself. There was no proof that he hadn't been there. And in the pub he'd been thinking about going to the gym, so put like that, maybe he had – maybe I just bloody well did go to the gym, he told himself.

'Before or after the gym, and before you got to Ivan Fielding's, had you been drinking?'

He was scuppered. 'I resent the implication.'

'I saw a can of Skol lager in your car.'

'What were you doing looking in my car?'

'I could hardly avoid it. As I parked next to you in the car park I saw the bright yellow can of Skol on the dashboard. Highly visible and highly inappropriate, wouldn't you say?'

Frost stayed shtum; he wouldn't put it past Mullett to launch an investigation.

'I take it these are stolen goods?' asked Mullett, gesturing to the antiques on the table.

'I have Rita checking the database now, but I suspect so.'

'Or they may be his property, his private stock, and he was merely hiding them?'

Frost conceded the point with barely a blink.

'In which case, again, if they are, they get handed to the next of kin, I imagine, or the tax man. Whichever comes first. If they are stolen goods, then you are to hand the case over to the Stolen Art and Antiques Squad. We have one blot on the landscape – the protest against the Denton Woods development. We know they have bused some protestors on to the site – outside agitators to stir up trouble. And we've been informed that there are more coming, and intel has told us that amongst them will be anarchists, communists and hooligans spoiling for a fight. Assistant Chief Constable Winslow wants us to up our policing of the area. We want the situation under control and we want to police them firmly.'

'Half our uniformed officers, and some of Rimmington's, are on the case already. I don't see what else we can do. Bring in the tanks? I don't think we've got another Greenham Common or a miners' strike on our hands, do you?'

'Have you heard of Operation Country Mile?'

Frost had. It was supposed to be secret, but everyone had heard about it. ACC Winslow, Mullett and the other County supers had hatched the plan. It involved taking pictures of and finding out as much as they could about the protestors, to investigate them, be on the front foot, seek out the agitators and those with 'subversive' political ideologies and 'police them firmly'. Proactive policing. Don't sit back passively and wait for things to happen, bring the fight to them.

'No, sir,' said Frost. 'Not heard a whisper. Sounds intriguing.'

This put a smile on Mullett's face, tins of Skol lager in the Metro seemingly forgotten as he launched into explaining Operation Country Mile. It held priority over everything, and he wanted most of CID concentrating on that. Frost nodded along to this, making all the right noises to Mullett, whilst all the time not giving a monkey's cuss about Operation Country Mile, and what the top brass considered politically or morally acceptable. He was going to crack on with solving a murder case.

Frost was flat on his back on his office floor, looking up at the post-mortem report that had just scrolled off the fax machine. It was pretty much as Mullett had predicted. Ivan Fielding had died of a heart attack and renal failure brought on by alcoholism; the red marks around his neck and bruising on his chest and collarbone were deemed inconclusive by Drysdale, and probably the result of advanced cirrhosis of the liver. The 'deemed inconclusive' gave Frost grounds to keep the case open, but not enough to assign to it officers and man-hours.

For some reason the pathologist's report seemed to sum up Frost's career trajectory of late. A lot of which was made up of going after cases that no one else was really that bothered about, or that were too much bother when the evidence didn't have a big red neon sign pointing at it. Frost could see why Mullett wanted the team on Operation Country Mile. It was big; it had the media involved, the national papers and TV coverage. And it had the kind of political edge that would put Mullett and the other County supers in the good graces of the powers that be.

Frost slapped the report on the floor. The sudden move sent

a wave of pain up his back, and gave him more facts to be considered. Just who the hell was in Fielding's house last night? What were they looking for, the stash under the floorboards? Frost felt another wave of pain move through him, not his back this time; it was the thought that maybe, just maybe, Mullett was right, there hadn't been anyone in the house last night, no one pushed him down the stairs. Maybe it was his imagination working overtime, fuelled by the Skol? Maybe he *had* had one too many . . .

'Bingo! Mr Frost?'

Frost rose up from the floor as slowly as evolution itself. He used every part of his desk as a handhold to get himself out of the primordial slime, to crouched primate, stooped Neanderthal, eventually to fully erect Homo sapiens.

'Ah, lovely Rita, what have you got for us?'

'What were you doing down there?'

'My back, Rita. I've done my back in.'

'Mmm. Best place for you, then. Did I tell you about the time I slipped a disc on the top deck of the number 34? Well, I was just . . .'

Rita was a woman with a fulsome and uncanny knack of lighting up a room – some unkindly said it was the garish velour clothes and the orange and electric-blue Crazy Colour hair dye that did it. But Frost was more charitable and thought it was achieved by the pure force of her sunny disposition and smiling countenance alone.

'. . . I said, I'm not buying an extra ticket, I can't bloody move!'

'Very good, Rita. Just out of interest – "Bingo", what did you find?'

'Well, Inspector, some interesting results. Eight of the thirteen items came up as stolen, including the Cartier suite of jewellery, and all eight give no details of the original robbery, or who they belonged to in the first place. They're marked under "special measures", and just give a number to call.'

As Frost considered this, a smirk crept across his face. Game on. 'Bingo indeed, Rita, bingo-in-bloody-deed! What's the number?'

'One hundred and *eeiigghhtttyyyyy*!' cried out Harry Baskin.

Keith 'Keefy' Keathson pulled his three arrows out of the red section, that precious sliver of real estate at the top of the darts board that was the El Dorado of the game. Grinning broadly, Keith was on fire, throwing the best arrows of his young career. In his flesh-pink silk bowling shirt, trimmed with purple, and with *The Coconut Grove* emblazoned on the back, Keith approached the oche once again.

Harry Baskin, Keith's manager, was sat at the bar, sipping his piping-hot morning tea and watching his young protégé practise whilst dispensing words of encouragement. 'That's magic, Keith, that's beautiful darts. Truly glorious arrows, son.' Harry had witnessed three 180s this morning alone, and even though it was just a practice session and not the adrenalin-fuelled bear-pit of competition, on today's showing, Harry was prepared to bet heavy on him.

The Coconut Grove was Denton's pre-eminent 'gentlemen's entertainment venue', as Harry called it. Whilst others referred to it in more prosaic terms – a strip joint. Just not in front of Harry. Harry believed that the success of movies like *Flashdance*, and all the female dance troupes cropping up on prime-time TV, like Pan's People, Legs & Co, Hot Gossip, had legitimized and elevated 'erotic dancing' to an art form. The girls at the Coconut Grove couldn't just stand there and peel off their kit, they now had to put in a shift and throw some moves: high kicks, splits, cartwheels and all manner of gymnastics were required if they wanted a gig at the Coconut Grove. And they did, because Harry Baskin paid good money. He looked after his girls, his 'Baskin Bunnies', as they had become known.

But Harry had greater ambitions for the club, and young Keith 'Keefy' Keathson was going to help him realize those. The dream was to watch the white-quiffed Dickie Davies, with his luxuriant moustache, announce on *World of Sport*, 'And now we go live to the Coconut Grove . . .'

Keith collected his darts and was about to go again when—

'Harry! He's here!'

The arrow shot out of Keith's hand and missed the board altogether. Baskin turned to see his biggest bouncer, Bad Manners Bob: baby's-bottom bald, six-foot-something-ridiculous and closing in on 300lbs. The trepidation on his face confused Harry. Being the size he was naturally imbued Bad Manners Bob with a certain bullish confidence; it was what he was paid for.

'Who's here? What's wrong?'

'He's in your office.'

Harry Baskin slammed the Charles and Diana commemorative mug of tea on the counter. His fleshy features crumpled in disbelief. 'Are you saying you let someone in my office?'

The big bald bouncer nodded, blankly.

'My office . . . my . . . my inner-fuckin'-sanctum?'

'I told him to wait at the bar, but he just sort of . . . breezed right past me.'

'*Breezed* past you? How did he manage that?'

'I stood aside.'

Bad Manners Bob seemed genuinely perplexed at his own actions. The huge unit of a man whose stock-in-trade was never to stand aside, never to let anyone past he wasn't supposed to let past, had ceded, taken a backwards step, and let someone *breeze* past him. He looked like a broken man. Who could have done this to Bad Manners Bob? Who would have the bottle? Who would dare . . . ?

Baskin then glanced down at the *Denton Echo*, and the front-page photo of a man holding up a book, with a uniformed and bearded copper beside him giving the thumbs-up. Bad Manners Bob was instantly forgiven. There were few men, and none in Denton, who would stand in the way of *this* man. He'd said that he'd be paying Harry a visit. He'd asked for a favour, and Harry had foolishly agreed to it. And now he was here to collect.

Harry Baskin made his way to his office. At the door, he composed himself, packed his face full of hail-fellow-well-met bonhomie, then whooshed it open with gusto. 'Here he is, a sight for sore eyes, handsome as ever, the man himself . . .'

Jimmy McVale was standing imposingly in the centre of the room, and he looked like he'd been stretching, or limbering up. He folded his muscular arms across the pronounced pecs of his chest. He had a light sheen of sweat over his dark handsome face, and was wearing a red Diadora tracksuit with white chevrons running down the arms and legs, and Reebok running shoes.

'What did you do, jog here?' asked Harry Baskin, ensuring the smile he'd forced on to his lips didn't slip.

'Six miles, I reckon, from the hotel.'

Harry Baskin pulled an 'impressed' face. 'You must be thirsty. The sun's almost over the yardarm, maybe not here but certainly somewhere in the world, can I get you a drink?'

'Club soda, ice and a slice if you've got it.'

Harry invited Jimmy McVale to sit down, and went over to the drinks cabinet and fixed them both a drink. When he turned around Jimmy McVale was, predictably enough, sat in Harry's seat behind his desk. Harry kept smiling, swallowed his pride, handed McVale his drink and sat down in the cheap seats opposite his guest.

'Been a long time, Jimmy. How are you adjusting to the world? Smooth re-entry?'

'As expected, Harry, as expected. You've done well for yourself. Put on a little weight in the intervening years.'

Harry Baskin contemplated his ample girth; he couldn't ignore it, and frankly he usually revelled in it. He hadn't been eating prison food for the last seventeen years. Harry kept smiling. He'd done some 'bird' himself, but didn't have the stomach for it like men such as Jimmy McVale. And Baskin knew that they were always chippy when they came out after a long stretch, like they resented everything you had.

'*Intervening?* I counted four syllables, I'll have to look that one up. So it's true, you have been at the old studies. I read it in the papers, you've got a university degree.'

'You have to fill your time, Harry. I had a lot of years to reflect on my actions, my life. I didn't want to fill them with bitterness or resentment for the past. I wanted to fill them with knowledge, to understand where I'd gone wrong. Hopefully be in a position to help others not make the same mistakes.'

'All right, mate, you're not talking to the parole board now.'

McVale laughed.

Harry nervously cleared his throat. 'Well, you're looking terrific, Jimmy. So, what are you doing in Denton? I thought you'd settle Kent way, what with you being from south-east London. Bermondsey, wasn't it?'

'I love the countryside around here, what can I say?'

How about the truth, you lying bastard, thought Harry. What he actually said was: 'It *is* lovely.'

'I've come to take you up on that offer.'

'Offer?'

'Short memory, Harry?'

'I've been very busy. A new venture. You know I used to do a bit of promoting, back in the Big Smoke.'

'I do, Harry. Unlicensed boxing above that pub you had in Hoxton. You staged some great fights there. I was there the night "Gypsy" Bradley bit Tommy "Sweet Face" Mullins's nose off.'

Harry smiled again. 'Ahh, wonderful days, I remember that night well. Still, can't get all misty-eyed and nostalgic. Onwards and upwards.'

'So you're back in the fight game?'

Harry stopped smiling and an air of solemnity came over him. 'Darts, Jimmy. Darts! I'm getting the place spruced up for Denton's first major darts tournament. We've just confirmed Jocky "At the Oche" Wilson; the Welsh Wizard, Leighton "Marathon Man" Rees; and from abroad, the Great Dane, Finn Jensen. As well as Cliff Inglis, Bill "Mr Consistency" Lennard, and Denton's very own Mr Talent himself, Keith "Keefy" Keathson.'

Jimmy McVale looked singularly unimpressed. 'They say golf is a good walk spoilt. I reckon darts is a good booze-up spoilt.'

Harry Baskin looked genuinely deflated. 'Jimmy, no, mate, it's a mixture of eye-to-hand coordination, strategy, mathematics – subtraction mainly – and showmanship. I'm getting measured for a gold-lamé suit. Every time there's a 180 we'll play "I've Got a Lovely Bunch of Coconuts". And then one of my girls wearing some kinky boots, a big smile and nothing else will hold up the score.'

'Classy. I wish you luck. Do you have the keys, Harry?'

'Keys?'

'When I saw you at my getting-out party last month, and said I'd be visiting Denton, you mentioned you had a place I could stay. A cottage you said, out of the way, nice and secluded.'

'Did I? I can't remember, Jimmy, I'd had a few drinks, I believe. Good party, though. Kind of you to invite me.'

'That's why I invited you. Because I knew you lived out here.'

Under McVale's unrelenting gaze Harry finally nodded along in recognition of this. It was nice and secluded, a little rustic bolt-hole, away from prying eyes, especially those of Mrs Baskin, where he could entertain the girls from the club who really took his fancy.

'Ah yes. I did mention that, didn't I? And here you are.'

Jimmy McVale placed his bottle of Canada Dry on the desk with a threatening thud, which brought home the very point that Harry had just made.

'It's undergoing a full restoration,' said Baskin. 'It's a building site at the moment. Hardly fit for habitation.'

'Running water, gas, electric?'

'I think so.'

'That'll do me.'

'What exactly are you going to do there?'

McVale deployed the smile again. 'One reason, and one reason only – to finish the new book I've started. Part two of my memoirs. To tackle the bit where I really started getting in trouble. The big jobs. And I need somewhere nice and quiet, secluded, no distractions, so I can get on with it. I can't do it in London, too much going on, too many temptations.'

Harry Baskin weighed this up. It sounded reasonable. 'So . . . so you've really given up the old life?'

'What more do I have to do to prove it to people? I've done my time and come out the other end a changed man. I've got letters after my name to prove my mind has now developed a richer moral and philosophical understanding of my place in the world. It's finished with the insanity, the greed, the covetousness, the need for power over others.'

Harry shifted uncomfortably in his seat, and focused on the Canada Dry bottle on the desk. That could so easily be a weapon in the wrong hands, Jimmy's hands, he thought. Jimmy then winked at Harry, and pulled the trigger on the smile yet again.

'Plus the fact my first book's on the bestsellers list, so there's more money to be made pushing a pen across paper than there is blowing safe doors off.'

Harry laughed along with him.

'Tell me, Jimmy, is this the book where you finally reveal the truth?'

'What truth's that, Harry?'

'The Bond Street job. I heard whatever was in those safe-deposit boxes was worth . . . millions. A king's ransom.'

'A king's ransom?'

Harry winked. 'Just a phrase. But there were rumours.'

'You should choose your words more carefully.'

'You can tell me, Jimmy – who am I going to tell?'

McVale picked up his glass, squeezed the lemon, and then downed his drink in a couple of thirsty gulps. 'You know, I was never actually convicted for the robbery. They tried to pin it on me, but they couldn't. Didn't have the evidence.'

'Just the head in the duffel bag . . .'

'To find out what happened, you'll have to buy the book.'

'You'll tell all? In a book?'

Jimmy squeezed out a nonchalant shrug. 'Double jeopardy rule. They can't touch me. But I've got to write it first. The keys, Harry.'

Baskin was looking forward to reading that, so he hauled himself out of his seat and went over to the portrait of Margaret Thatcher, and took it off the wall to reveal the safe. He spun the tumbler and opened it up. As he did so, he realized that he must really believe Jimmy had changed. He certainly wouldn't have opened up his safe in front of the old McVale. There were two metal objects in the safe: a Beretta 92 semi-automatic pistol and a jailer's ring of keys. He reached for the keys, slipped off the requisite one and handed it to Jimmy McVale.

'Do us a favour, Harry, don't tell anyone where I am.'

'You were never here.'

Tuesday (3) ———————————————————

'This is most interesting . . . most interesting indeed, Inspector Frost.'

'I was hoping it might be,' Frost replied with a satisfied grin as he watched DI Anthony Dorking of the Stolen Art and Antiques Unit. Dorking's eyes were gleaming and he was almost salivating at the Instamatic photos Frost had laid out on his desk.

It was quite a desk, rich mahogany with a green leather panel. And it was in quite an office, even by County HQ standards. An office that seemed to be stuffed with as many antiques and works of fine art as were listed on their computer database of stolen items. If this is where it all ends up, at least it's appreciated, thought the detective, giving Dorking the benefit of the doubt.

Anthony Dorking sat back in his chair and made a low purring sound, like he'd got the cream. He was tall and rake-thin in a pinstripe double-breasted suit that was cut perfectly to his gaunt frame. Everything about him struck Frost as public school, from his lank blond hair that came with a long foppish fringe, to his stripy tie, to the heavy gold signet ring that bore a family crest. A lot of his ilk, the ones who didn't get the tap on the shoulder at university to spy on the USSR, or for the USSR, ended up in forensic accounting, or Special Branch. Or some, like Dorking, used their natural affinity for the finer things in life by tracking stolen art and antiques.

'One of the paintings, an early Vogel, I can tell you now comes from a famous robbery, must be twenty-five years ago. The victim was the Earl of Penbury. We thought the painting had gone abroad. And there it was, under Ivan Fielding's floorboards. Tell me, Inspector, Ivan Fielding's death, do you suspect foul play?'

Frost had explained the case to Anthony Dorking over the phone, including the post-mortem report, but had hinted at other possibilities.

'Do you?' asked Frost.

'Well, let me put it this way, a sticky end for Ivan Fielding was never beyond the realms of possibility ... maybe even probability.'

'How so?'

'A fascinating character.'

'And a fence?'

'Oh yes. Of course. That's what you're here to find out, I take it. But much, much more than just that. And first and foremost, as I say, a fascinating character.'

Dorking offered him a Dunhill and Frost accepted. Dorking lit their cigarettes with an elegant gold rectangular lighter, which he kept in his left hand and smoothly rotated in his long fingers.

'You see, the painting was stolen from the upstairs sitting room of the earl's country house whilst there was a dinner party taking place downstairs. And Ivan was a guest. He was extremely well connected, and that's what made him perfect for this line of work. And the burglar who was robbing the earl during the dinner party was none other than Ivan's best friend and business partner, Conrad Wilde.'

Frost took out his notebook, and then frisked himself for the biro that was supposed to go with it. Anthony Dorking plucked a marbleized Montblanc fountain pen from his real marble desk set and handed it to Frost, who winced as he leaned over to take it.

'OK?'

'Back's playing up. Thank you, I must remember not to steal this by mistake.'

'I'll set the hounds on you if you do.' Frost believed him, for it was hard to believe they were in a government building and not in Dorking's country pile. 'I used to suffer with my back, to do with my height. I represented my school in the high jump; lots of Fosbury flops and awkward landings.'

'Sounds like my life.' Frost wrote down the name. 'Conrad Wild, you say?'

'With an "e" on the end.'

Frost added the 'e'. 'That's quite a name to conjure with.'

'He was quite a character to conjure with, too.'

'Like Ivan?'

'The polar opposite. Yet they complemented each other perfectly. The yin to his yang, if one goes in for Eastern philosophies. To understand Ivan, you need to understand Conrad Wilde. Where Ivan was small, plump, balding and somewhat professorial-looking, Conrad Wilde was tall, athletic and handsome. A leading man. In fact, rumour has it he was offered a film contract by Lew Grade on his good looks alone, and he did actually do some acting. But what really set him apart is that he was one of the best cat burglars in the business. He could climb anything and get in anywhere. The gossip was that he ran away to the circus as a child and did a high wire and trapeze act. He was fearless; the roofs of Belgravia were his sandpit. One of these real adventurer types, real *Boy's Own* material. I even heard a rumour he once—'

'I think I've heard enough rumours, Anthony, if you don't mind. Do you have any facts?'

Dorking stubbed out his barely smoked cigarette in the

crystal ashtray and pulled a face like it would be his last one. Frost took a long draw and carried on smoking.

'Fair enough, but with cases like this, it's hard to separate fact from fiction.' Dorking leaned back again and clasped his hands behind his head. 'But I'll give you their MO as far as I know it. Ivan used to set up the jobs and buyers for the goods, and Conrad used to steal the goods. Simple, really. And the jobs were always big. The grandest country houses. The finest collections. Home and abroad. France, Switzerland, Monaco, Italy. Ivan never used to send Conrad in to just grab whatever glittered before his eyes. Ivan would target the items, always knowing what he wanted. In fact . . . *rumour has it* . . . he told Conrad only to take what he'd earmarked to be stolen. Used to rebuke him if he filled his pockets with other trifles, said it wasted his time, distracted him from his real purpose, thus upping his chances of getting caught. Of course, Ivan had the items sold before Conrad had even scaled a drainpipe, slipped through a window or dropped down a skylight. They seemed to always get what they were after, professionals of the highest order.'

'You sound like you admire him – the pair of them, for that matter.'

'Well, it does all have a touch of the Raffles about it, and it all happened in the '60s, so I suppose it comes with rather a rosy glow of nostalgia about it. The way some see the Great Train Robbery through a mist of Robin Hood romanticism, but the truth was always a little more criminally prosaic. And so it was with Ivan and Conrad.'

'But all good things, depending which side of the law you're on, must come to an end?'

'Exactly. They'd ridden their luck, but as you know, in life sometimes you make your own luck. And Ivan Fielding certainly did that.'

'How do you mean?'

'Ivan was an informant. A select source. And a category A one.

Ivan was very well connected, as I said. He may not have been much to look at, but he was quick-witted, highly intelligent and immensely charming. He had that uncanny ability to mix with anyone, and knew everyone from society highlife to East End lowlife, and everyone of interest in between. Remember, this was during the Cold War, the Profumo affair was just unravelling. Paranoia was in the air and rumours of espionage were rife. And London was a hotbed of spies. So Ivan not only had his hooks into the criminal underworld, but he also had the ear of the aristos, the intelligentsia and the smart set, around whom diplomats, visiting dignitaries and people of note tend to cluster. And they were all spies, or certainly a lot of them were. It wasn't hard to be a spy in those days, everyone was at it.

'He proved invaluable not only to Scotland Yard but also to Special Branch, and even the Secret Service. And in reward, the Yard and everyone else would turn a blind eye to his activities. After all, Fielding and Wilde stole from the rich, and the goods were more often than not returned to the owners, eventually. After they had been rinsed through the market and everyone had earned a profit. Ivan often brokered the deals himself.'

'So he was getting it both ways?'

'Exactly – the art and antiques world is a murky one, it must be said.'

'I think I get the picture. So they rode the tiger's tail, but then how did it end for them?'

'Well, badly, as you've just told me about poor Ivan. I'd heard he'd left London and moved to the sticks, dropped off the radar and hadn't been active since. At least fifteen years ago, maybe close to twenty. But at least he had his liberty, even if he did squander it. But Conrad wasn't so lucky. He eventually got caught on a job and went to prison.'

Anthony Dorking gazed out of the fifth-floor window on to a view of very little, just another municipal block. He looked reflective, a little stumped.

'What happened to Conrad?'

The DI considered this, then turned his attention back to Frost. 'Rumour or fact?'

'I'll take either, seeing as they go together rather seamlessly in this case, like yin and yang?'

Dorking laughed and stubbed out his latest cigarette with a withering disgust. He dialled a couple of numbers and asked his secretary to find him the files on Ivan Fielding and Conrad Wilde. In the meantime, he told Frost what he knew about Conrad's arrest and imprisonment. Which was very little.

'To be honest, I'd moved out of London by then, so I'd lost touch. But it's always interesting to hear about a blast from the past, even if it is sad news about Ivan.' Dorking's eyes swept the photos of the stolen goods on his desk again. 'Still, every cloud has a silver lining, and these candlesticks really are a joy to behold. Can't wait to see them in the metal, any idea when that will be?'

Frost's mind was somewhere else. 'We've got another blast from the past on our patch. Jimmy McVale, released from prison last month after seventeen years. Another '60s face. Allegedly involved in the Bond Street job of '67.'

Dorking raised his eyes from the photos and squinted in concentration. 'Yes, yes, I read about his release. Nasty piece of work, from all accounts. Are you looking for a connection?'

'Always. Never one to leave it up to coincidence.'

'Then you'll have to cast your net wide. Every major crook in London and beyond was rumoured to have been in the frame for that caper at one time or another. I even heard that it was the work of a French outfit, seeing as they had initially gained their access to Bond Street via the unused basement of the Yves Saint Laurent boutique.'

'Was Conrad ever in the frame?'

'No. Not his style. It was a gang of five or more, using heavy drilling machinery, an oxyacetylene torch, and lots of hard graft. If I recall correctly, it took them the whole bank holiday weekend to get through the walls. Conrad worked alone. He was daring enough, but he had a lighter touch. More of a Raffles than a Reynolds.'

'Reynolds?'

'Bruce Reynolds. Masterminded—'

'The Great Train Robbery.'

Frost was about to ask something when there was a light knock on the door and the secretary entered, and promptly told Dorking that she couldn't find a hard copy of the files, and that the database stated they were 'under seal' and 'special measures' and had been given a D-Notice. Frost and Dorking looked at each other. They knew that meant the information was highly sensitive, and could involve national security. It had to be kept away from the media, and could be looked at only by those with special clearance. Dorking thanked the secretary and she exited as quickly and efficiently as she'd entered.

Frost watched him closely as he lit up another Dunhill; he seemed to be mentally retracing his steps, scrolling back into the past. He pointed his index finger up at the heavens as if an idea had struck him.

'Lionel, Captain Lionel Cavanagh, formerly of the Guards. He was Ivan's handler at the Yard. Long retired now, lives in the Cotswolds, I believe, though don't quote me on that. But I'm sure I can dig out his number somewhere. I'll tell him what you've uncovered. I'm sure he'll have the scoop on Conrad, and he'll certainly want to know about Ivan. I think he was rather fond of him.' Another thought struck him. 'If he's still alive, that is. It's been a while since I've seen Lionel, and he enjoyed a tipple or ten himself.' Dorking raked his fingers through his floppy fringe as his eyes flitted down to the five photos on the desk. 'Meanwhile, you'll certainly make a lot of people happy uncovering this little lot. When can we pick them up?'

'We might need to keep hold of those for a while longer.'

'Really?'

'Yes. The more this unfolds, the more I believe we have a murder enquiry on our hands.'

'I trust they're under lock and key?'

'The usual security measures. They won't go missing from the lost-and-found at Eagle Lane, it's on the top floor. *Where Eagles Dare*, as we call it. Not even Conrad Wilde could get hold of them.'

Anthony Dorking looked doubtful about that.

Tuesday (4) ————————————————

Jimmy McVale pulled up sharply. Took time to regain his breath. His stamina was still low, well off the mark for what he wanted it to be. Pumping weights in prison was one kind of fitness, but a long run in Denton Woods, out in the open, was another. As well as taking the opportunity to finish his second book, McVale was going to get in lots of long runs in the beautiful countryside he'd spoken so glowingly of, to anyone who would listen. It was a solid alibi.

He was on the edge of the woods now. He heard them long before he saw them. They were chanting, 'WE'LL BRING JARRETT'S TO THEIR KNEES BEFORE THEY TOUCH OUR PRECIOUS TREES!'

As he looked about him, the cold January day didn't seem bleak and grey in Denton Woods, it was multi-hued and verdantly alive and glorious. Before, it had been just a notion; now, in an instant, it was a deeply felt belief. He liked a good fight, maybe more than the next man, and this seemed like as good a one to join as any, for all sorts of reasons.

McVale ran over to the demonstration, and soon found

himself in the thick of it. There were about two or three hundred protestors. The thin blue line of combined County police forces kept the crowd away from Jarrett & Sons Ltd's onsite HQ, with its stacked Portakabin offices. Hard-hatted men in high-vis jackets walked about with rolled plans under their arms, trying to ignore the melee that they were fenced off from. There were rolls of razor wire festooning the high perimeter fence to ward off anyone who fancied scaling it. There were three yellow bull-dozers lined up like tanks primed for destruction, and men stood ready with the lighter artillery of chainsaws. The battle lines were clearly drawn.

And there were TV vans and cameras rolling to capture the action.

McVale looked at those around him, young men in combat fatigues and black CRASS T-shirts and Mohican haircuts ready to get stuck in, given half a chance; but there were also older people, the kind who had gathered in Trafalgar Square to Ban the Bomb in the '60s, and were probably more attuned to Gandhi than Guevara when it came to changing the world.

The 'reformed' villain hadn't shouted so loudly since he was a nipper standing on the Millwall terraces at Cold Blow Lane, or when he led a handful of Cat A prisoners on to the roof at Parkhurst to protest the conditions and the brutality of the screws. They pelted the bastards with slates for six solid days until they ran out of roof to stand on.

'Jimmy McVale!'

He turned to see Sandy Lane of the *Denton Echo*. He was with his pimply work-experience nephew, who as a photo-grapher looked like he didn't know one end of a camera from the other.

'You said you'd be here, and here you are!'

'It's a disgrace,' said Jimmy with a surge of indignant rage. 'To destroy an inch of Denton Woods is truly a criminal act, a decimation of natural beauty, and we're here to ensure that crime does not happen!'

Sandy Lane scribbled down the words of the eminently quotable ex-con in his notebook.

'Go on, Degsy!' came the cry from some of the more hardcore protestors, as a bottle got thrown over the fence of Jarrett & Sons.

Sandy Lane instructed his photographer to 'get in there, son!', pushing the fearful young man further into the crowd.

McVale surged forward and soon put himself at the front of the now baying mob, who were forcing the uniformed coppers to link arms and push back. Things were getting nasty, truncheons were being drawn.

'KILL, KILL, KILL THE BILL! KILL, KILL, KILL THE BILL!' was now the chant from the younger more militant members of the protest. Some more bottles, stones and other missiles were launched from the crowd into the blue line of coppers, a line that was looking frayed and weak as it became clear they'd misjudged the force of the opposition.

'KILL, KILL, KILL THE BILL! KILL, KILL, KILL THE BILL!'

A black flag went up showing the interlocking emblem of CRASS. Then another, showing the scratchy encircled 'A' of Anarchy. What had been promised in the UK in '76 seemed to be getting delivered in '85. The Queen was never much of an enemy, benignly smiling up at you from your one-pound note when you collected your dole money. It was Maggie. *She* was the enemy. And Denton Woods was just a convenient battleground.

In amongst all the surging forward and pushing back, a copper, a young WPC, got pulled into the crowd, and blows rained down on her.

'KILL, KILL, KILL THE BILL! KILL, KILL, KILL THE BILL!'

Jimmy McVale coursed forward, his red-tracksuited figure slicing its way through the muted colours of the protestors like a knife. He was soon in the eye of the storm – a storm that swirled around the young WPC. She was terrified, humiliated, and was getting hit and kicked as she fell to the ground, a ground of churned mud, her truncheon as useless in her hand as a dry twig.

McVale grabbed her, pulled her up from the mud, wrapped his arms around her and carried her through the hostile crowd, which was now overrun with black-T-shirted anarchists. One spiky-haired punk went to throw a punch at him, but McVale pulled his head back, like cocking the hammer of a gun, then he pressed the trigger and shot his forehead on to the bridge of his would-be attacker's pierced nose. Blood exploded into the air. Other black-clad eco-warriors reeled back. They got the message. They were dealing with a different force here, someone used to the dreadful intimacies of violence, not just shouting and throwing things from the collective anonymity of the horde.

Just as McVale delivered the distressed young WPC into the hands of her colleagues and commanding officer, who were about to wade into the squall of the mob to save their fallen comrade, the camera flash popped. And Sandy Lane had his front page yet again. For the hack, the ex-public enemy number one was proving a godsend.

When Frost arrived back at Eagle Lane the first thing he saw was Desk Sergeant Bill Wells.

'What you doing here, Bill, I thought you were on nights this week?' said Frost in surprise.

'You've not read the papers this morning, then?' Bill Wells reached under the desk and pulled out the *Denton Echo*. 'Mullett didn't want it in the station, but saves me explaining what happened to Johnny.' He handed it to the DI.

And there it was, splashed across the front page, Johnny Johnson stood next to convicted murderer, armed robber, all-round arch criminal, and now apparently reformed character, Jimmy McVale. The image was obviously staged; Frost was there, saw what happened. Johnson got caught up in the moment with Sandy Lane barking instructions and setting the whole thing up, resulting in that ridiculous photo.

'I take it the superintendent's seen this?'

'Sent Johnny home, suspended until further notice. But it looks bleak – ACC Winslow's on Mullett's case, apparently. Throwing Eagle Lane into disrepute is the accusation.'

Frost knew that Mullett was right. After all, even a broken clock is right twice a day. 'I'll have a word with the super when I can.' Frost dropped the paper on the desk and went through to the incident room.

There was only one case that seemed to be taking up everyone's attention: Operation Country Mile. On the long incident board, photos and names were pinned up; some had been taken at the site in Denton Woods, others, of known agitators who were expected to turn up, had been sent over from the police intelligence unit.

Frost looked at Rita at the computer, inputting new names into the database; her colourful fingers, each nail painted a different shade, were darting across the keyboard faster than Bobby Crush on amphetamines. Frost reached into his jacket pocket and pulled out his packet of cigarettes, Dunhills. He remembered that for once he hadn't nicked them, Anthony Dorking had given them to him as part of his long-running effort to give up. The DI looked at his team all beavering away, and wondered if this was the new face of policing. Everyone would be sat at their own computer, checking everyone who would be on the database. They'd be able to know what everyone was up to and their whereabouts 24/7 at a keystroke. Unless they had a D-Notice, like Ivan and Conrad.

Frost went over to Clarke's desk. 'Get your coat, you've pulled.'

'That may be the best offer I've had all day. The get-my-coat bit, not the last bit.'

'Got some interesting news about Ivan.'

'Go on.'

'I'll tell you in the car on the way.'

'Where we going?' She slipped on her jacket.

Frost took out the packet of ibuprofen that Rita had got for him and downed a couple with a mouthful of Susan's coffee, which turned out to be cold.

'How's your back?'

'Still making its presence felt.'

Clarke called out to PC Simms, who was just about to go out of the door. 'Do you want to come with, Simmo?'

Simms turned to Clarke, his face lit up with excitement. 'The super wants me at Denton Woods, collecting info on the protestors.'

Before Clarke could say anything, Simms shot out of the door. 'Good for him. I thought he was supposed to be shadowing me this week.'

Frost smiled. 'We'll be working for him one day. Young Simms is ambitious, knows the high-profile cases to jump on and the back-burner ones to avoid. He knows which side his sliced white has marge on.'

Tuesday (5)

Banes didn't have to wait long for Kevin Wheaton to show up. It was only a couple of hours before the Ford Cortina drove slowly down the now boggy track, out of the woods and towards what passed for civilization in this part of the world, Denton town centre. It was dark now. All he saw were the headlights emerging from the thick blackness. But as the Cortina passed him, he recognized the burly ex-con immediately. Kevin had his inside light on, probably had a map on his lap, so there was no mistaking him. Just as he had recognized him at Longthorn, when he came to the infirmary. Always with a smile on his face, trying to look as jolly as possible, to lift the mood of the dying man he was visiting.

Banes started the van up, turned it around and followed Kevin down the track. He knew all about Kevin Wheaton, he was like him in some ways, an impostor of sorts. And they both had the same information, and they were both after the same prize. Wheaton had no interest in saving the woods, he was there to hide. The protest made for good cover, provided him with an excuse to be camping out in January. But Banes knew that Kevin wouldn't be gathering around the campfire with the protestors and singing songs, because they would soon suss him out as the impostor he was. Kevin wasn't quick on his feet, couldn't adapt to his environment, improvise and blend in.

Kevin Wheaton was a thief. He may not have been much good at anything else but, to his credit, he was a good thief. He'd learned from the best, he'd learned from Conrad Wilde.

Banes followed the Cortina at a safe distance into the town, into Market Square, where the shoppers were finishing up for the day, and the market traders were taking down their stalls, bantering loudly about how slow business was after Christmas, even with the sales, and hoping for better luck tomorrow.

The Cortina parked up just off the square in East Street. Kevin got out of the car, locking up and looking around him with all the natural suspicion of an ex-con. They treated the whole world as though it was just like them. Satisfied that no one was on his tail, Wheaton slipped into the Lamb and Flag pub.

'Mind if I join you?'

He did mind, of course he did. But he wasn't going to say anything, wasn't going to cause a fuss and draw attention to himself. The pub was reasonably full, and as Kevin Wheaton looked around the saloon bar, he could see it wasn't an unreasonable request to ask to share the table.

The burly ex-con was reading the local paper, the evening edition of the *Denton Echo*. The front page was all about the protests, which were hotting up and becoming newsworthy. There'd been some real violence, the front-page photo showed some big bloke in a red tracksuit stepping in and helping a copper . . . and then Kevin lowered the paper and the story was lost to him.

Kevin nodded bleakly to the man before him. It was permission for him to sit, but was also a warning to him not to try to engage him in conversation, no matter how vacuous.

'How are you, Kevin?' asked Banes as he put his pint on the table, and before Kevin could respond, quickly added, 'We've met. In Longthorn.' He sat down opposite the ex-con. 'Bet you don't remember me, do you?'

Kevin's aggressive expression turned to one of blankness.

'My name's Clive. Clive Banes.'

The blankness continued. Which was exactly what Clive Banes had expected. Even after shaving off his beard and getting rid of the fake glasses, he was seldom remembered, rarely recalled, and always quickly forgotten.

'I worked in the Longthorn infirmary. I was an orderly. I used to see you visiting your friend Conrad, Conrad Wilde. I used to talk to Conrad. He was a lovely man. An interesting man.'

Kevin was of medium height, but bulky in build. Maybe made to look bulkier than he was by his blue quilted ski jacket. His hair was short on top with a neat side parting, but the impression of neatness was undone by a flange of rat's tails hanging down his back. He wore a gold ring in each ear. His knuckles were inked with prison tattoos that were little more than blue blobs. Banes assumed they were supposed to read as LOVE and HATE. But his stubby fat fingers had worked like blotting paper and soaked the ink up to render their message indecipherable.

Kevin took a sip of his pint. 'I've never done a day's prison in me life. And my name's not Kevin.'

'We both know that's not true. And strictly speaking, Longthorn isn't a prison. It's a secure hospital for the criminally insane.'

'I'm not a nutter!'

'No, technically. But you were visiting someone who was certified as being one.'

'You're getting on me fuckin' nerves, mate. Maybe you should take your pint and piss off.'

'Listen, Kevin, there's no need for the aggression. We're on the same side. We want the same thing.'

'Do we?' Kevin Wheaton lifted his pint off the soggy beer mat.

'That's why we're here. That's why you're camped up in the woods.'

'You following me?'

Banes lowered his voice and leaned in. Kevin Wheaton lowered his pint and listened.

'When I used to speak to Conrad, towards the end, I sometimes think he looked on me as a priest. Someone to unburden himself to of all his sins. I know he looked on you as a son, he told me as much. I was surprised not to see you at his funeral.'

Kevin looked sheepish and guilty as his eyes flicked down towards the thick head of froth on his lager; it seemed to hold his attention like a child staring up at clouds in the sky, trying to discern shapes of animals. Banes suspected the guilt came not from failing to attend his mentor and father-figure's funeral, but from his reason for being in Denton. Once Banes had arrived in town, he'd scoured the local paper, and had found out about the death of Ivan Fielding, the former Chelsea art dealer, and the suspected break-in at his property that might have precipitated his untimely demise. Just a few paragraphs in the *Denton Echo*, but the article had immediately caught Banes' eye. It was the only crime in the local paper that looked in any way relatable to his and Kevin's common cause.

'Where did you first meet Conrad?'

'The Scrubs,' muttered Kevin, looking almost tearful at the memory. 'My first real stretch. I was just a kid. Conrad had been there for a few years. People were wary of him, he'd got into some fights. But he was good to me.'

'He looked after you. Taught you the ropes, how to rob a place, what to steal . . .'

Kevin Wheaton nodded slowly, his mind obviously scrolling back to the past. Happy days. 'He did. He taught me everything I know. I've only done five years in prison since I met Conrad – and that was only because of grasses. Conrad showed me how to case a place, how to bypass alarms. He always told me to stay focused once you're in, and to just go after the prize you were after. Get what you come for, then get out.'

'Good advice. And you got it, right, Kevin? You got what you were after?'

Kevin Wheaton broke out of his nostalgic reverie and pondered his more recent crimes. Banes knew that Conrad might have taught Kevin a thing or two, but not enough. Conrad was cunning, smart, sharp. Kevin was the opposite of all that, as his next utterance proved.

'I didn't kill him.'

Banes gave an internal smile of satisfaction but remained outwardly unmoved, businesslike. 'I didn't say you did.'

'I swear on my mother's life, he was alive when I left him . . . I swear on my—'

Banes quickly raised a halting hand for Wheaton to stop. 'Kevin, please . . . please, I don't want you to swear on your mother's life, it's meaningless. I read the papers. They said he was dead. What I want to know is, do you have it?'

'Have what?'

'You know.'

'I don't.'

'*You do.*'

'I swear on my—'

'Kevin, please, no more swearing on that poor woman's life. You know what I'm talking about. Conrad told me *all* about it. Now, again: do you have it?'

'The painting?'

Banes smiled. 'Yes. That's it. The painting.'

Stephen Parker answered the door. He stood there, seemingly reluctant to let Frost and DC Clarke cross the threshold.

'She's still very upset, and tired, very tired.'

Sue Clarke issued her standard understanding smile. Which always impressed Frost; he could never quite muster it.

'Yes, Mr Parker, we can appreciate that, of course—'

'But we still need to talk to her,' said Frost bluntly.

'Who is it?' came a voice from inside, presumably Vanessa Fielding's. It was loud and strong.

'She sounds good to me,' said Frost.

Parker turned his attention from the two detectives and called out into the hall behind him, 'It's the police, about . . .'

There was a pause. Then came the voice again, weaker this time, emotional, like she'd just been reminded of her loss. 'It's OK, Stephen, let them in.'

Frost and Clarke made it clear to Stephen Parker that they would like to talk to Vanessa on her own. She didn't protest. And Parker slipped away, said he had some papers to mark.

They were soon sitting in the living room, drinking coffee from an exotic-looking service, which was out of keeping with the rest of the house, all neat and tidy and modern and very beige. The only other real splash of colour came from the spines of the books on the pine shelves that took up two walls of the room.

As Vanessa poured, she explained, 'It's Clarice Cliff. Very of the period. Her designs were all the rage in the early '30s. It was something that Ivan instilled in me – not the coffee set, I bought this myself, but a love of extraordinary things. A gift or a curse, because once you understood Ivan's philosophy and aesthetic, you just simply couldn't bear to have the ordinary around you. It makes you very judgemental. Ivan loved being surrounded by beautiful things.'

Her eyes swept around the room, almost apologizing for the blandness of it. Her assertions would sound immodest, bordering on the boastful, if it wasn't so damn true, thought Frost. Vanessa, in her late fifties, appeared to have changed little from her 1960s photo shoot. She was in black slacks and a black roll-neck sweater that just seemed to accentuate her swanlike poise, and her blonde hair now had shimmers of silver running through it. She wore no make-up, but you would have needed PC Simms's now legendary magnifying glass to see the fine lines on her taut alabaster skin.

'It's those beautiful things that we need to talk about,' said Frost. 'After a search of the property, we found some items that were hidden. And according to our database, they were stolen.'

He reached into his jacket pocket, pulled out the photos he'd shown DI Anthony Dorking and handed them to Vanessa. She carefully worked her way through them, satisfying Frost that she was getting a good look at each one. When she'd finished, she placed the photos in a neat stack on the coffee table.

'Do you recognize any of the items?'

'Never seen them before in my life. There's quite a lot – where on earth did you find them?'

'I found them under the floorboards of Grey Gables. There was a trapdoor under the grandfather clock in the living room.'

'I swear to you, Inspector, I had no idea they were there. I haven't lived at Grey Gables for well over four years.'

'The items were stolen over twenty years ago,' said Frost, 'in various robberies. How long they've been under the floorboards, I couldn't say.'

'And neither can I, Detective.'

'Would you like to take another look at the pictures?' offered Clarke.

She shook her head. 'I will swear on a stack of Bibles now that I have never ever seen any of those things in my life.'

Frost wanted to move things on, so he changed tack. He laid out all that Anthony Dorking had told him, from Ivan's criminal partnership with Conrad Wilde, to Fielding being a secret police informer, to Conrad's eventual arrest and the dissolution of their felonious enterprise. When he'd finished, she seemed to be digesting the information with a slight pursing of her lips and an agreeable murmur of accord. She seemed neither shocked by what she had just heard nor indeed familiar with it. She just sat there, perfectly poised and amiably unfazed.

It was only after a prompt as to whether she knew Wilde that she said, 'Conrad Wilde? I don't suppose that's the kind of name you easily forget.'

'So you never met anyone by that name, were never introduced to him, however fleetingly?'

She laughed, and shook her head like it was the most ridiculous thing she'd ever heard. 'Ivan was very successful and knew lots of people. And when we lived in Chelsea there were lots of parties, and naturally I was introduced to lots of people. So I don't know, maybe, maybe not. What do they say about the '60s? If you remember them, you weren't there.'

'How convenient. But pithy little aphorisms don't pass for facts in police work. And even through the haze of all the funny cigarettes, you just said you wouldn't forget a name like that.'

'Then that answers your question: I never met him or heard of him. Ivan always kept his business dealings away from me, and from Sally.' She gave an apologetic shrug. 'Would anyone like any more coffee?'

As Frost and Clarke finished their drinks, he considered Vanessa's story. Plausible? Up to a point. Whilst it may have been the swinging '60s, and bras were being burnt, Ivan could have been old-fashioned enough not to divulge his business affairs to her. Especially the more dangerous elements. And she was incurious enough not to ask, to just enjoy the glamorous life that he was providing for her. As Frost had first noted, and Anthony Dorking had pointed out, the art and antiques trade was always murky, and if Ivan had erred into out-and-out criminality, then Vanessa wasn't too shocked. But she remained innocent to it. That was her story, and she was sticking to it. And for now, Frost couldn't see a way of disproving it.

Frost and Clarke thanked her for her time and got up to leave, intoning the customary formula that they would be in touch. But before they'd made it to the living-room door, Frost spun around.

'One last thing: your daughter noted that the only item missing from the house was a painting.'

'Oh God, which one? I know we can't touch anything in the house until you've concluded your investigation, but really, Inspector, I do worry that with the house being empty someone might—'

Clarke calmed her. 'It's OK, Mrs Fielding, nothing of any value was taken. Just the opposite, in fact. It was in Sally's old room, and it was rather on the ugly side, she said. Not any of the ones on the sitting-room wall.'

Just then, Stephen Parker gave a little knock on the glass panel of the door and entered the room. 'I'm sorry, I thought you were finished.'

Frost reckoned he'd probably been stood by the stairs ear-wigging, as he'd left the door ajar earlier. Which was perfectly natural and hardly against the law, but Frost still fixed the lecturer with a hard stare.

'I'm sorry, I don't know of any such painting,' Vanessa said.

Clarke expanded, 'Sally said there were three of them. Ivan gave one to Sally and one to you? Your daughter thought he found them on the street, or in a skip? The one in her old room was of some hills, or something similar.'

'Here.'

They all turned around to see Stephen Parker holding up a painting. It was about eighteen inches by twenty. He'd managed to slip out of and back into the room without being noticed, which struck Frost as very achievable in someone so bland.

Parker said, 'It's kept under the stairs. Pretty horrible . . . I'm sure you'll all agree.'

Vanessa's expression changed from innocent bemusement to sour contempt. 'Oh, yes. *Those* pictures. I'd completely forgotten about them.' She turned to her boyfriend. 'I thought you were going to throw it out,' she said, looking annoyed at Parker for not doing so. 'If you'd like it, Mr Frost, or you, Miss Clarke, you're more than welcome to it.'

Frost and Clarke had their faces scrunched up in embarrassment, caught in the unforgiving glare of the picture's artistic ineptitude. It was eye-achingly awful. It featured what could have been a hill, rendered in thick globs of glossy green oil paint; some long brown vertical strokes suggested trees; there was a streaky blue sky and some white splodges for clouds. If the missing painting was similar, Sally Fielding was right in her description: it looked like the daub of a child. The two detectives didn't take up Vanessa's offer.

Parker rested the painting against the wall. 'Part of a triptych, I believe.'

'Well, there were three of them,' said Vanessa dismissively. 'I think that's a slightly grandiose term. I believe a triptych is three paintings that can be hung separately and still look good. This looks like one painting has been cut into three parts. It's just . . . ugly and meaningless.'

'Why would anyone steal the one from Sally's old room?' asked Parker.

'Sorry, sir?'

'You said, Sally reported it stolen.'

Frost smiled – *nicked* – Parker had obviously been eavesdropping. 'No. Not quite. She just noticed that it was missing from the house. Sally assumed that Ivan must have thrown it out. We just thought we'd let you know.'

'And following Ivan's lead, that's exactly what I shall do to this one, throw it out,' announced Vanessa.

Tuesday (6) _____

'It's very . . . awful. I mean, no offence, but you can tell it's the work of a madman. Or a two-year-old child. Or a mad two-year-old child. Mmm?'

'He wasn't always that way,' said Kevin Wheaton with an earnest tone in his voice. 'The system did it to him.'

Clive Banes nodded his approval at that. 'So true, Kevin, so true. No truer statement ever made than that one. The system did it.' Banes turned away from the painting that was propped on the small blue Formica table in Kevin Wheaton's caravan. Either side of the table were padded benches that could be converted into beds. Banes and Kevin Wheaton were drinking beers.

'What happened there?' asked Kevin as Banes lifted the can of Hofmeister to his lips.

Banes looked at the still livid stripes on the back of his hand. 'A cat scratched me. Big . . . ginger Tom sat on a wall. I think I might need a tetanus jab. Teach me to be so good-hearted.' Kevin looked like he was about to share a tedious cat anecdote, so Colin cut to the chase. 'So, you've found no clues on the painting, nothing that means anything to you?'

'Like I said, nothing. You saw yourself, nothing on the back, nothing hidden on it. I've looked all over.'

'Tell me again, what he told you.'

'Conrad?'

With an edge of impatience to his voice, Banes said, 'Yes, Conrad, of course.'

'When he got ill, knew he was dying, he just told me he pulled off a big job and buried the loot in Denton. Didn't tell where he'd got it from and I didn't ask. I did ask him where, but he couldn't tell me. He just said he'd done some paintings, paintings that showed where it was buried. And he gave them to his old friend Ivan Fielding.'

'Painting*s*?'

'Yeah, painting. He liked painting. Wasn't any good at it, but he liked it.'

Banes leaned forward, to spell it out for the thief. 'No, you said painting*s*. Paint*ings*. Plural, as in more than one.'

Kevin took a swig of his beer and pondered this. 'Yeah . . . so I did. Paintings. I think that's what he said – in fact I'm sure he did. But this was the only one I found at Ivan's. I mean, unmistakable. I'd seen Conrad's paintings over the years, they used to let him out into the grounds to paint. And they were all rubbish. Like this, but different. But all rubbish.'

Banes stood up and considered the picture again. Not that he really needed to, the tight little two-berth caravan offered more or less the same perspective wherever you stood. The composition was mainly blue for the sky, green for the land, some brown lines for trees, maybe some stumps and logs. He got close to the painting, and with his finger he traced what could have been a hill that went up sharply and off the canvas.

'That makes sense. Cunning old Conrad: he sent them one at a time so you couldn't get the whole picture. So it wouldn't mean anything until you had them all, like a jigsaw puzzle.'

'Why would he do that?'

Banes shrugged. 'Maybe he thought it was safer, in case it got into the wrong hands. Maybe it was his way of toying with us. Who knows how his mind was working towards the end.'

'What did he tell you?'

'Me?'

'Yeah, what did he tell you about the painting?' said Kevin.

'Nothing.'

'Nothing?'

'Yes. Nothing.'

'Well, he must have told you something, or you wouldn't be here.'

'You're not going to like this, Kevin.'

'I'm not too sure I like you anyway, *Clive*.'

Banes smiled; it was sly and knowing. 'Conrad told me that he'd told you where he'd buried his fortune. He said, "Kevin knows." And that after he died, you were going to find it.'

Banes was right, Kevin didn't like this. 'That's all?'

'That's all.'

'You didn't know about the painting?'

'No. Not until you told me.'

Kevin Wheaton drained his can of Hofmeister and crushed the tin in one effortless clench. Banes saw the power in the stocky thief's frame, and slipped his hands into his coat pocket. Ready for whatever Kevin might want to throw at him – a punch perhaps, a barrage of indignant rage and swearing. Whatever it was, he was ready.

But all he got from Kevin was another question: 'Did you know about Ivan?'

'No. Not until I got to Denton, then I read about it in the local paper. The death of an art dealer. Seemingly natural causes. Signs of a break-in at his home. Police still investigating whether they're connected. It was the kind of thing I was looking for. I put two and two together. Doesn't take a genius to work it out.'

'So all you had to do was follow me?'

Banes considered this carefully before answering. 'You could say that. But don't feel bad about it. Conrad gave you some information, and you got the painting. Conrad gave *me* some information . . . and now I've got you.'

Kevin shot to his feet, his inky fists clenched, blue blotches against white, bloodless, furious. 'I loved Conrad! I loved him like a father . . . You were just a fucking screw!'

'No, Kevin, I was never that, I was an orderly in the infirmary. I was there to look after him, to make sure he was comfortable . . .'

'I should kill you now! Who would know?'

Banes closed his eyes and breathed steadily, almost Zen-like in his concentrated calm, his eyes closed to the danger in front of him. His hands in the pocket of his heavy duffel coat, his right shaping itself around the haft of the ball-peen hammer. He counted to eighteen in his head. Then the next thing he heard was the familiar sound of gas escaping from a can of beer as the ring was pulled. Banes opened his eyes to find Kevin sat back down and glugging on a new can of Hofmeister.

'Kevin, you're not a killer. You're a good man who's lucked into a fortune.'

'And what are you?'

'The man who's going to make sure you realize that dream of the good life and help you get your hands on that fortune. The reason Conrad told me about you was because he loved you, he loved you like a father would. He died without issue, you were the closest he ever came to a son and heir. He thought the world of you, Kevin, wanted you to have his fortune. And the way I looked after him, he trusted me. He trusted me to look after you, he wanted me to look after you. That's why I'm here, Kevin, to look after you.'

'I can look after myself.'

'Well, that's not strictly true, is it? I mean, you're already being sought on a potential murder charge.'

Kevin balled his fist and hammered it down on the fold-out Formica table, almost snapping it off its aluminium hinges. 'I never killed anyone!'

Banes made some placating gestures, then in a hushed voice

said, 'I know that, but the law don't. So we have to make sure they never find out, right?'

Kevin Wheaton wasn't the sharpest knife in the caravan cutlery drawer, Banes knew that. But he wasn't entirely stupid and without qualities. And he wasn't a killer; Banes knew that was one quality he didn't possess. So there Kevin sat, looking daggers at him, but not prepared to actually take one out and plunge it into Clive Banes' chest. With this little fact firmly established between them, Banes pressed on.

'We can work together, Kevin.'

'Why should I trust you? You're just some geezer who happened to be at Longthorn.' His anger returned. 'You weren't a friend of Conrad's, you're just a bloody screw!'

'No, Kevin, that's not true. You see, I may not have known Conrad as long as you, but it was my preordained fate and good fortune that I should meet him. You see, I was sitting in a pub one day, just minding my own business, reading the classifieds. I was between appointments and was looking for a "new challenge", as they say. I got talking to a couple of blokes who saw me circling jobs in the paper. They were temps who worked at Longthorn. They said they were always looking for people. I had some experience working in a retirement home, said I'd give it a try. They told me some of the funny stories about some of the nutters they had locked up there. One of them, who worked in the infirmary, said there was an old bloke in there, dying of cancer, kept calling out in the night that he had stolen a fortune and buried it.

'These blokes in the pub didn't take him seriously. Why would they? The place was full of nutcases. They told me his name. *Conrad Wilde.* For some reason, it stuck in my head. I liked the name, it was impressive. So I did my research. Looked through library press cuttings, archives, made it my purpose to find out about Conrad Wilde. You could say, Kevin, that I got a bit obsessed with it, like a detective. I found out that Conrad was a top-class burglar, a master of his trade. I also found out something else. What do you know about the Bond Street Burrowers?'

Kevin Wheaton, with his mouth ajar, shrugged. 'Not a lot.'

'In 1967 an undisclosed fortune was stolen from a vault in a private bank. Shortly after the robbery, Conrad Wilde was sent away to prison for an old job he'd committed much earlier. As we know, he never resurfaced. And neither did the proceeds from the Bond Street job. Coincidence? I don't think so.'

Kevin Wheaton's dull eyes sparked into life. 'You think Conrad did the job and buried it here?'

'Very good, Kevin. And once I put two and two together . . . I applied for the job at Longthorn. And one week later I was working in the infirmary and making myself known to the great man. Gaining his trust. Sneaking him in fine ten-year-old malts and those big cigars he liked. We became friends. He trusted me. And I knew it wasn't the morphine-addled rant of some madman. I asked him about the '67 job. He winked at me, but he would never say for definite if he'd pulled it off. Did he tell you?'

Kevin shook his head blankly. His answer seemed genuine enough, but still Banes was doubtful. In these situations, he'd learned, there was always something to hide.

'Are you sure, Kevin?' he pressed.

Again Wheaton balled his fist, but stopped short of hitting the table, as it looked like it couldn't take another pounding. 'I bleedin' said he didn't, and he didn't. That's the way it is with thieves. You don't ask too many questions or you come across like a grass. Conrad told me what he wanted to, and that was good enough for me.'

'I believe you. And I hope you believe me when I say there's a fortune buried out there, and it's my destiny to find it. And it's yours too, Kevin. You believe that, don't you?'

Kevin finished his German lager. He was calm now. In fact, Banes could see that Wheaton seemed almost hypnotized by his words; his clear and measured explanation was obviously comforting to him. The none-too-bright thief was finding succour in someone else knowing what they were doing, taking charge and showing him the way. Wheaton said he believed him.

Banes stood up, stretched, and stamped some life back into his feet that had been tucked under the little table. The flow of blood gave him a renewed sense of urgency. 'We have to act fast, in case anyone else knows.'

'How do you mean?'

'Well, I know for a fact that the morphine loosened his tongue, that's how I found out. The blokes I met in the pub who used to work there and told me about him, they obviously knew. But I'm wondering, who else did he tell?'

'Who else would believe him?'

'I did. All it took was some research. A little effort.' Banes turned his attention back to the painting. 'Which brings us back to this little puzzle here.' He sat back down on the vinyl padded bench opposite Kevin to ponder the picture.

'Another beer?'

'Very kind of you, Kevin, very kind.'

As Kevin pulled two beers out of the fridge, Banes picked up the evening edition of the local paper that was folded on the bench beside him. It was the one Kevin had been reading in the pub. The front-page story about the Denton Woods protest had piqued Banes' interest earlier and he read on avidly.

Wednesday (1)

'Why exactly are we meeting here?'

'I'm having my office refurbished.'

'Really?'

'You sound surprised, Stanley?'

'I confess I am. I always thought it was . . . rather perfect as it was.'

Stanley Mullett had been called to this 7.30 a.m. walk around the duck pond in Rimmington Green Park by Assistant Chief Constable Winslow. Both men were sheathed in their police-issue overcoats to keep out the biting cold; the winter sun wasn't due to make an appearance for at least another hour. The pond was large enough that three times around it was more than adequate exercise for this time of day. Winslow swore by it as his daily constitutional. He enjoyed throwing some stale bread to the flotillas of ducks and the stately hissing swans, prodding the occasional rough sleeper to move on, and he'd even boasted of stopping a mugging once. But for Mullett, being asked by Winslow to join him seemed most irregular, most irregular.

'I'm a firm believer that one's office space should reflect the occupant.'

Mullett agreed. Then he gave an involuntary shiver as the thought of Jack Frost's abomination of an office flashed through his mind. 'So what are you having done to the office?'

'Bigger. Just made bigger.'

Mullett had always known it was wise to attach himself to Winslow's star, he was nothing if not ambitious, and certainly on the up.

'How's Operation Country Mile going?' the ACC asked.

'Very good. Keeping order, gathering intel. We've already identified some subversive forces. Though they're rather easy to spot, mainly because they have *Anarchy* written across their T-shirts and leather jackets, and most have anti-social haircuts.'

'Anti-social haircuts?'

'Oh, you know, dyed lurid colours, spiked, or just unkempt.'

'Yes, yes. Although, to be honest, they're not the ones to worry about. As you say, easy to spot, the foot soldiers. The prince of darkness is a gentleman.'

'Sorry?'

'An expression. He won't come snarling, swearing and spitting into the world like Sid Vicious, he'll be sedately dressed, blending into the populace so as to quietly plan and spread sedition and goad the crowd into action with misinformation – then he'll slip away quietly into the night.'

Mullett mulled this over. Winslow was well read, privately educated, and knew how to turn a phrase to *stiffen the sinews* and *summon up the blood* of his troops.

'Don't be fooled, Stanley, they're as likely to be the sock-and-sandal followers of Mr David Steel's Liberal Party as they are the beret-wearing brigade of the Socialist Revolutionary Party.'

Mullett was about to congratulate him on this observation, when Winslow stopped in his tracks, reached into the brown paper bag he held in his black-leather-gloved hand and turned his attention to the pond.

'The red-breasted merganser, and my favourite, the tufted duck. See his fulsome plumage, rather like your colourful agitators at Denton Woods.'

Winslow threw them all the bread in the bag. With this act, the volume at the pond got turned up significantly. Lots of squawking, clattering of bills and flapping of wings. Then the natural pecking order was restored when a grand swan sailed into the fray like an ocean liner surrounded by the smaller grey tugboats of her cygnets.

'Beautiful creatures. But I hear they can break your arm with a flap of their wings. Anyway. We need to talk about *Inspector Frost.*'

Mullett hated the way the ACC had rolled that name over his tongue. It sounded like he was contemplating two extremes: either he was going to promote Frost above Mullett, or sack him for harbouring the recalcitrant detective in his police station.

'What about him?'

'Whilst most of your CID has been seconded to Operation Country Mile, he seems to be pursuing a burglary.'

'Well, in all fairness, there are extenuating circumstances—'

'Yes, I know all about the Ivan Fielding case. I'm not at liberty to tell you everything, because everything has not been made clear even to me. But I have been advised that Eagle Lane CID should drop the case, certainly, for now, anyway.'

Winslow turned his attention away from the ducks, who were also turning away from him once they saw him scrunch up the brown paper bag and put it in the bin. The ACC carried on walking. To Mullett, he seemed agitated, on edge, put into a position he didn't much care for.

'Frost has a habit of digging into cases that appear dormant. But to his credit' – and it pained Mullett to admit it – 'his instincts, if not always his actions, have proved fruitful in the past.'

'I don't doubt it. But in this case, they won't.'

'Sir, his investigation is only three days old, I think it's too early to "drop it", and I don't know how we could. Fielding's family and friends will be expecting answers.'

'I didn't say it isn't to be investigated, just not by Frost, or the Denton force. The case will be looked at, eventually. But I believe Dr Maltby's report and Dr Drysdale's post-mortem results give a more than adequate account of Ivan Fielding's demise.'

Mullett looked surprised at this. This was low-grade detail for someone as lofty as Winslow. 'Yes, sir. But there is the matter of the suspected break-in, and the stolen antiques concealed under the floorboards and—'

Winslow coming to an abrupt halt was enough to stop Mullett talking. He was shorter than Mullett, but still managed to stare him down.

'There are ducks that need to be lined up. There are higher forces at play here, Stanley. Forces that go right to the top. Do I make myself clear?'

Higher forces . . . ducks. At times like this, Mullett really did wish he was in the Masons, as he knew Winslow to be – he even knew which lodge and his position in it. Then he was sure whatever it was could be made clear with a handshake, and he of course would follow unquestioningly. As it was, he was left flailing in the wind. Every exchange with Winslow or other superiors, no matter how casual, felt like an audition for the favoured fraternity. Mullett always suspected that to gain entry to that hallowed lodge he would be set a series of undisclosed moral tests. And this, with its whiff of secrecy and 'higher forces', made him feel especially tested. He had to tread carefully; if he followed Winslow's orders too slavishly, he'd be viewed as weak-willed and disloyal to his own team at Eagle Lane. If he proved too intractable, he'd be considered an unreliable rebel, like one of those sock-and-sandal prince-of-darkness liberal types that Winslow so despised. Mullett erred on the side of caution.

'Yes, you make yourself perfectly clear. Don't worry, sir, you can rely on me.'

Longthorn was a large red-brick Victorian building with an even larger modern concrete annexe. There had been no attempt to assimilate the two; they were just stuck next to each other and somehow managed to cancel each other out. The schizophrenic design suited the institution, though. It was hidden away from view and as far from the general public as possible, deep in the Suffolk countryside. A solid and dependable storage facility, that's what you got with Longthorn, the secure hospital for the criminally insane.

Frost was in the office of Dr Graham Edmunds, Longthorn's chief medical officer. It was tantamount to being a prison governor, if you peeled away the thin veneer of its hospital status.

'I'm sorry you've wasted your time, Inspector Frost.'

'How long ago was this?'

'Conrad Wilde passed away three weeks ago. Oesophageal cancer. He'd battled for almost five months, but in the end . . .' Dr Graham Edmunds let out a philosophical sigh.

'He died here?'

'Yes. Due to our high security status we of course have our own infirmary; as you know, we are in fact a registered hospital. We also have a palliative-care wing equipped like a hospice. Less austere surroundings. A window, with bars of course. A great number of our "patients" smoke, obsessively, and suffer physical health problems as much as mental ones. Unfortunately, life expectancy is short at Longthorn.'

'I'm surprised he ended up in here,' Frost ventured.

'You do know Conrad Wilde's record, his prison record?'

'From Pentonville, Parkhurst, Durham, then transfers all over the place. It took quite a bit of hunting down to find him here. Most of his records have been redacted, such as the reasons for his transfers, and what brought him here. He seems to have been almost lost in the system.'

The doctor had a full beard the same colour as his shoulder-length light-brown hair. He wore a pair of round wire-framed John Lennon glasses, and was probably in his early forties. His voice was soft and empathetic as he said, 'I've only been in this post a year and a half. But I have to say, I think there's been a miscarriage of justice somewhere. You say lost in the system, I would say buried. Conrad only came into the prison system for a five-year sentence for burglary. A non-violent crime, with no other previous for violence at all. It was his first prison sentence, and if he'd kept his nose clean he would have been out in three years. According to his records, he never settled into prison life. Eight months in and he got into a fight with a fellow prisoner. He pleaded self-defence, but ended up being sentenced to ten more years because he was considered so dangerous. Then he kept trying to escape, showing more and more erratic behaviour. Apparently.'

'You sound uncertain?' Frost prodded.

'Well, all before my time. I've only seen the records, which as you say, are heavily redacted or skimpy at best. I don't think they would be acceptable by today's standards.'

'So I take it he was repeatedly picking up more years and getting transferred?'

'Yes. It was a terrible spiral for him that eventually brought him here.'

'What was he like?'

'Interesting question.'

'How so?'

'There is an assumption that once a person reaches here, that question becomes irrelevant. They are beyond redemption, beyond the pale, their personality and very being are fixed in one state, that of insanity. It took a while to get to know him, as when I first arrived here, he was heavily sedated.'

'Whacked out on the chemical cosh?'

'Exactly. When I took over, I found that the chemical cosh, as you put it, was wielded rather too heavily under the previous regime. Whilst there's very little hope of rehabilitation, I felt that the management had lost touch with the fact that we are dealing with mental health issues, albeit of the most extreme and dangerous kind. I wasn't sure Conrad Wilde even belonged here. The system had failed him somewhere along the line, and this is where he ended up.

'The first thing I did was lower his meds. And it yielded results, his true personality began to emerge. I believe he thrived. He'd come to terms with his lot, seemed to find some kind of acceptance and peace. The times we spoke, he was civilized, amusing even, interested in the outside world and events.'

Frost considered Edmunds – he seemed young enough and intelligent enough to be the reforming modernizing type. 'That would go along with my impression of him, from what I've heard. Tell me, did he do any painting whilst he was here?'

'We have an art therapy workshop three times a week. I believe he attended that.'

'Do you have any of his paintings?'

'There's a session going on today. Would you like to join the inmates?'

'I've always had the feeling it was only a matter of time.'

Edmunds smiled politely at his gag. 'I'll take you down myself, Inspector. We're short-staffed. To be honest, we're always short-staffed. One of our orderlies quit a couple of weeks ago, another's not bothered to turn up at all. It's a tough job. Frankly, it can be depressing, so the people who work here need to have good mental health themselves to do the job. I'm trying to improve the conditions for patients and staff, but needless to say, we have a very high turnover.'

Wednesday (2) _____

When Jimmy McVale arrived at the Little Chef restaurant they were already enjoying breakfast. The choice of venue was his. They offered to meet him at his hotel. But Jimmy McVale couldn't afford to be seen with them; they were, after all, his former associates. And if he was caught fraternizing with them it would break the rules of his licence agreement, and he could end up back in prison. Plus the fact that, with what they had to discuss, McVale thought the anonymity of the Little Chef, next to a service station on the Denton bypass, offered the best setting; no one remembers anybody in these places.

So there the three big men sat, cramped in the little red booth. There had been some small talk, some catching up. His two former associates, Eddie Tobin and Tony Minton, had done very well for themselves, gone legit, well, semi-legit anyway. There were some scrapyards and some shrewd property investments in Docklands. Very nice. They were living on the Algarve half the year, swinging golf clubs and swigging the local beer. And watching their wives broil in the midday sun as their complexions began to match their crocodile handbags.

Foreign climes hadn't staunched their appetite for English cuisine, and the two men squeezed the life out of the ketchup and HP Sauce containers, smothering their extra-large full Englishes.

Jimmy McVale contented himself with some orange juice and looked at a copy of the *Denton Echo*, which the two men had laid out on the table when he arrived. Its front page held the picture of him protecting the young WPC from the baying mob. Jimmy smiled, it was a great shot. He would definitely be putting it in the book.

'Titian.'

'Sorry?'

'It looks like a Titian,' said Eddie, wiping a napkin around his mouth. 'Sort of epic, you the mighty warrior, saving the damsel in distress.'

McVale laughed. 'Getting a bit grandiose there, Eddie.'

'You're not the only one who's done a bit of self-improvement over the years, mate,' said Tony, coming to Eddie's defence. 'That's your trouble, Jimmy, you always took us for a pair of mugs.'

'And we ain't,' said Eddie.

Before McVale could defend himself against the charge, Tony cut in. 'So much for keeping low-key. I thought you wanted out of the newspapers. Start a new life with your new education . . . Doctor Doolittle, Professor Plum or whatever the fuck you are.'

'And now we've found you,' said Eddie.

'I wasn't hiding. Obviously.'

'What are you doing here, Jimmy?' asked Tony.

'Didn't you read the article in the paper? Or did you just look at the picture?'

'There he goes again, Tone, taking us for mugs.'

'Cut to the chase, boys. What's on your minds?'

Tony Minton gave him the headlines: 'We've not forgotten, Jimmy. We can't forget, never will. It's stuck in our claw.'

'*Craw.*'

'What?'

'It's stuck in your *craw*, not *claw*.'

Eddie and Tony looked at each other and laughed. Then Tony said, 'All this education has turned you into a real prick, Jimmy, you know that?'

Now McVale laughed.

Tony Minton continued: 'As I was saying, we've never been able to let it go. And over the years we've kept our ear to the ground. We've paid good money for information when it's been available. Truth be told, we've spent a small fortune over the years. We've had contacts in prison, both cons and screws, so we've heard the rumours, the rumblings, the gossip, the prison jungle drums. Conrad Wilde.'

'I've heard the name. What about him?' asked Jimmy McVale, after a sip of his orange juice.

'He was in the country-house game. One of the best.'

Jimmy McVale knew what that meant. He wasn't just your average burglar, he pulled big jobs, could bypass sophisticated alarms and specialized in country houses, stately homes, fine art. 'What about him?'

'He died of cancer not long ago. We heard through the grapevine that towards the end he was blabbing away to anyone that would listen that he buried a fortune in the countryside. Whatever it was he buried, it was worth millions upon millions, he said. It was almost a deathbed confession, to be taken very seriously. But he was banged up in the nuthouse, so no one did take him seriously. Including us. Just another rumour. We'd heard hundreds of them over the years. Then we did take it seriously. Because this Conrad said he buried this fortune in Denton. *Denton*. Where you're staying right now. Coincidence?'

Eddie Tobin took over: 'We hired a private dick to find out about this Conrad Wilde. He found out that Conrad used to work with a character called Ivan Fielding. Big-time art and antiques dealer in his day. And an even bigger fence. Ivan Fielding was found dead—'

'Yeah, I read about it in the local paper.'

'That's right, the local paper you're on the front cover of. Which begs the question—'

'Did I kill him?'

'That's jumping the gun a bit, Jimmy,' said Tony Minton. 'But since you mention it, did you?'

Jimmy McVale laughed good and hard. 'Course I didn't. I don't know what you're talking about.' He stopped laughing. 'I'm here because an old mate has a cottage here. You know him, Fat Harry Baskin. I asked if I could stay here for a few weeks so I can finish my new book. Somewhere quiet, out of London and away from distractions. Away from idiots dragging up my past and asking stupid questions.'

Tony Minton and Eddie Tobin gazed with narrowed eyes at the man opposite them finishing off his orange juice.

Tobin spoke first. 'I don't believe in coincidences.'

'You calling me a liar, Eddie?'

'Heaven forbid. But I do believe in . . . *serendipity*.'

Tony Minton nodded, proud. 'Big word that, Jimmy, told you we weren't mugs.'

'Five syllables, you're on a roll,' quipped McVale, echoing Harry Baskin's earlier jibe.

'Tell him, Eddie.'

'We don't know what happened, but we think that somehow, over the years, it ended up here. In Denton. And we're gonna find it.'

'Let it go, boys. I have,' McVale said.

'No, mate. We had it. We had the prize. We got it! And it escaped us. It was stolen off us!'

Tony Minton said, 'I won't lie, Jimmy. If you'd escaped from prison and got away, never to be seen again, like Lord Lucan or Shergar, I'd have thought you'd double-crossed us.'

Eddie Tobin nodded his agreement. 'After all, you were the last one to see it.'

McVale glowered at the two men opposite him. '*I* was the one who did the time for killing the barrister' – he spat out the words like poison – 'the not-so-honourable Mr Charles D'Arcy. *I* was the one who did the work to try and find out what happened to it. *I* was the one who did the time,' he repeated. 'Seventeen years on circumstantial evidence. I could have grassed you slags up at any time—'

'We know, Jimmy, and we're grateful—'

'—*and* I would have got a reduced sentence! But I stood staunch, kept my mouth shut.'

'Jimmy—'

'Shut up!'

Eddie and Tony did as they were told. It was like old times again. They were doing as they were told. As a 'firm' they were always equal in everything. All had a say in what jobs they'd pick, each got an equal share of the haul. But leaders always emerge. Those who go just that little bit further to get the job done. And Jimmy McVale was always the first amongst equals. A natural leader. At the table were three of the original five of the gang; the other two had met violent ends.

'You've both done well for yourselves whilst I was rotting in prison.'

'We've put some aside for you,' said Eddie, 'we told you that.'

'That's not the point. If I can swallow it, why can't you? You've grown rich and fat, so why do you want to risk everything going after it now?'

The two men turned towards each other, and Tony gave Eddie the nod to speak. As if they'd thought long and hard and rehearsed this moment, and now it was here.

'Because we're cut from the same cloth, Jimmy. We're thieves, always will be. No matter how much you put on our plate, we always want more. And because it was ours. Because we had it, we had the prize. It was our biggest job, it was our Everest, and we had it snatched away. And this is the only concrete news we've heard about it in over seventeen years. It all makes sense.'

Like in a well-drilled double act, Tony Minton took over. 'Come on, Jimmy, you know it makes sense. And you're just like us. Reformed character? It's in your bones. If someone offered you a million quid not to steal ever again, you'd tell them to go fuck themselves, then work out a way to steal it off them.'

'We're not calling you a liar,' said Eddie, 'but the minute we heard you was in Denton, we knew you'd heard what we heard.'

'Right, Jimmy?'

Eddie and Tony stared him down with expectant eyes.

Jimmy McVale picked up the *Denton Echo*, looked at his picture, then rolled the paper up like a cosh and gave both men a playful whack over the head. They smiled; just like old times.

'Like I said, I was the one who did the time. Of course I heard the rumours. Heard the same as you. A mate of mine inside, he said a mate of his had got nutted off, certified insane and sent to the funny farm. Said this Conrad Wilde has been singing like a bird. Of course, he's dead now. Maybe he took the secret of where exactly he buried it to the grave with him – but maybe he didn't.'

'And his partner, Ivan Fielding, he's dead too,' added Tony.

'But the trail's not.'

Eddie and Tony smiled again. They were back in business. Eddie, more out of habit than necessity, scoped the Little Chef to see if anyone was earwigging – the place was empty. The three men leaned into a huddle; just like old times.

'It was always the same, country idylls, green hills, blue skies. Or sometimes it was the ocean, with old ships. Conrad used to say they were pirate ships, because they were free to sail the seven seas, they could go wherever they wanted. But it was always the great outdoors. Freedom beyond the walls of prison, I suppose.'

'And was he always this bad at painting?'

'Afraid so,' said the young art therapist, with some sadness. She was in her twenties, wore a pair of paint-splattered Lee dungarees and a white shirt. 'But painting kept him calm, and of course he was let out into the grounds, which are quite extensive.'

Frost and the therapist were looking at a selection of Conrad Wilde's paintings. They were unmistakably by the same hand as the painting belonging to Vanessa Fielding that Stephen Parker had shown him.

'Did he ever say what they meant?'

She looked confused, then glanced at the paintings, then back at Frost, still confused. 'In art terms, they meant exactly what was on the canvas. I'm afraid, Inspector, you may be looking for meaning where there is none. You'll find no melting clocks like in *The Persistence of Memory* here.'

'Sorry?'

'Salvador Dalí, his most famous work, with the melting clocks.'

'Yes, I know the painting, but not the title. Did Conrad have titles for his paintings?'

'If he did, he never mentioned them.'

'I take it patients are allowed to give their work away, to family, friends?'

'Yes. Depending on the content, of course. Some images can be . . . rather disturbing.'

'Did Conrad?'

'Yes, I believe he did once. They usually give them to visitors, but with Conrad, I think he posted his out. I remember because he had to pay for postage and packing himself.'

'Do you remember who he sent them to? Or have any records of this?'

She shook her head, doubtful. 'There may be some records at the post office in town, but we wouldn't keep them. We don't have the resources, I'm afraid.'

'Would you mind if I borrowed one of the paintings?'

'No, not at all. Take your pick.'

'Inspector?'

Frost turned to see Dr Edmunds approaching with a folded sheet of lined paper.

'You asked about visitors?'

'Yes, thank you.'

'Conrad had just the one visitor in the time he was with us. He's an ex-offender, I believe, served time with Conrad, not here though. He was on file as the next of kin. Conrad didn't have any family. I tried to contact him to tell him about the small funeral service we had for Conrad here, but I couldn't reach him. His mother said he'd gone away. Make of that what you will.'

Frost unfolded the sheet of paper and saw a name and address for one Kevin Wheaton.

This part of south London had a weary uniformity about it, long litter-strewn streets that you could get lost in. Well off his patch, Frost wasn't even sure he was in London any more. He wasn't really, he was in Norwood. It was city sprawl, where London just didn't know where to stop. These weren't so much proper destinations as names on a map where the tube didn't reach, and they were dotted with forlorn little train stations that led to better places.

He scoured the streets looking for a blue police box, but failing that, a red public one would do. His bleeper was going like the clappers. It was obviously something DC Clarke didn't want put over the radio. Across the street he glimpsed a red box. He pulled the Metro up sharp and parked on a double-yellow and put his police-on-business sign on the dash, next to the Skol can he'd forgotten all about, and made the call.

'Where are you?' said Clarke.

'You sound concerned, Susan?'

'The super wants to know. He started coming out of his office, patrolling the incident room, arms behind his back like he's inspecting the troops. Everyone's working the bloody Denton Woods demonstration. I'm not even sure what we're doing is legal. Taking pictures of people, checking for criminal records, and then putting them on a database, when they haven't even done anything yet. I feel like we're living under Stalin.'

Frost agreed. 'And I thought *1984* was supposed to happen last year.'

'Waters says if he's not working a real crime soon he's going to tell Mullett to stuff his bravery award!'

'Tell him to hold on, this is the January slump. After Christmas and the sales, everything goes quiet, even crime. It's like no one can be bothered to kill each other and no one wants to rob anything any more, so we make work for ourselves. But the good news is, I've got something for us.'

'I'm all ears.'

'I've just come from Longthorn Secure Hospital . . .'

Frost loaded nearly all his change into the payphone and filled Clarke in on the plight of Conrad Wilde, including his artistic endeavours at Longthorn.

'. . . The style is unmistakable, awful, but unmistakable. Conrad painted the pictures and sent them to Ivan . . .' The pips went and Frost slotted in the last of his coppers. '. . . Now we have to work out why Conrad sent them to him, and why one of them was stolen.'

'You think it was stolen?'

'Check the records on one Kevin Wheaton, he's a convicted burglar, and a prison friend of Conrad Wilde.'

'Will do.'

'One last thing: can you call DI Anthony Dorking of the Stolen Art and Antiques Squad, and ask him if he's been able to contact Captain Lionel Cavanagh?'

'Who's Captain Cavanagh when he's at home?'

'He knew Ivan and Conrad. Ivan was his snout in the '60s.'

'Ivan was an informer?'

'That's not the half of it.'

Then the pips went again and Frost was out of change.

'They must have gone on holiday.'

Frost took his thumb off the doorbell and turned around to see a woman in a turquoise raincoat, headscarf and cat's-eye specs at the gate. It was cold, and the coat she wore didn't look like it could keep it out. But he reckoned she probably wore the same coat in the summer too, so things evened out.

'On holiday?' echoed Frost.

'The caravan's not there. Must have gone away. Who are you?'

He came down the steps and showed her his warrant card. 'Inspector Frost, Denton CID. You know Mr Wheaton?'

'Kev? I know the little bugger. In trouble again, is he? Doesn't surprise me. He's been the bane of his poor mother's life. Flossy. Lovely woman. She thinks the world of him. Personally, I'd have kicked him out years ago. Still, he's her only child. I've got four of them, I can afford to be a bit more choosy.'

'So Kevin lives here with his mother?'

'Course he does, couldn't look after himself, could he? Probably why he likes prison. You know what they say: two hot and a cot. They get used to it.'

Frost couldn't help but laugh at the streetwise old bird. He then turned his attention back to the house. It was a pebble-dashed council house on the edges of West Norwood, with a small patch of grass out front marked with what he now assumed were caravan tracks.

'Where do Kevin and his mum go in the caravan?'

'What's he done now? Don't tell me, been on the rob again. He's got the good sense not to do it round here, we'd shop him straight away. He took ten bob out me purse once, he was six years old! I said, "Flossy, he's a wrong 'un." But he's her—'

'Yes, love, her only child, you said. He's not done anything, we just need to ask him some questions about a friend of his.'

'Isle of Sheppey, Folkestone, Deal, Romney Marshes, Whit-stable, Broadstairs, Margate—'

'Right, thanks. So Kent. All over Kent.'

'Kent, yes, always Kent. Flossy likes Kent.'

With some effort he managed to get rid of the neighbour. She was nosy, but not nosy enough. She hadn't noticed the four pints of milk and the tub of cream on the doorstep. Frost had one more go on the doorbell, then peered through the letterbox to be met with a small dim hallway leading to a kitchen, and a dead cat on the linoleum floor.

He went around the side of the house and found the back door. With his gloved hand, careful not to wipe off any existing prints, he turned the handle and the door opened. He took a big breath, then stepped over the threshold into the kitchen, expecting the worst. First up was the cat. It was a tortoiseshell moggy. There was half-eaten food and curdled milk set out for it. And there was blood where its head had been bludgeoned, matted in the fur, but very little on the floor.

After checking downstairs in the well-kept but cluttered and chintzy house, the detective found her in the bedroom. She was laid out on the bed, looking like she'd fallen asleep on a red pillow. Frost left the curtains closed, but switched on the pink ruffle-shaded bedside light to reveal what he'd suspected; she'd suffered the same fate as her cat, and the blood-soaked pillow had originally been white.

'Poor Flossy, she'd had a hard life, and for it to end like this doesn't bear thinking about,' pondered DI Dave Garside of the West Norwood police.

'Kevin was known to you, was he?'

'Ever since he was a kid he was in trouble. Flossy tried, but his dad was a bad example. He died when Kevin was a kid. Fell off the roof.'

Frost noted the complete lack of empathy at the patriarch's demise. He nodded towards the house. 'That one?'

'No, the church roof. He was robbing the lead.'

'Tell you what I don't get, Dave. The cat. Why kill it?'

'You're in the Big Smoke now, more nut-jobs and sickos per capita than your neck of the woods, I'd imagine.'

'Sod off, I'm in West Norwood, and in Denton we've got more than our fair share.'

Garside laughed, but agreed that the killing of the cat added another sadistic dimension to the already horrific murder of Florence Wheaton.

Garside was a squat bullish man with no discernible neck

and a tight crop of grey hair, a few years older than Frost's. He seemed like a copper after Frost's own heart: called a shovel a shovel, asked awkward questions, and carried a hip flask to 'keep out the cold'. It hadn't taken the two detectives long to break down the formalities of their different jurisdictions and chew the fat like they'd shared an office for the last ten years.

They were standing in the small back garden in the failing light, next to a rusted old swing that they both suspected a young Kevin Wheaton had once played on in more innocent times. The road in front of the house was swarming with rubberneckers from the estate, and more women in raincoats and headscarves. And the inside of the house was now swarming with crime-scene officers taking pictures, and Forensics taking a fine-tooth comb to the place for clues and prints. They were into their second JPS, their fourth nip from the hip flask, and Frost had filled in DI Dave Garside on the case thus far.

'Did you see the state of the back of her skull?' asked Garside, shaking his head in revulsion.

'I'm going to have to work hard to forget it.'

The London DI offered him the hip flask. Frost considered it for a second. It seemed like the slippery slope, but the fumes of the Scotch helped cover the stench of blood that still clung to his olfactory senses. People think that blood is odourless, but enough of it like that, soaking into the pillow, into the bedlinen and mattress, has a metallic smell about it. In the cold light of day, Florence Wheaton looked as white as her sheets must have been before the attack.

From what they could ascertain, the sixty-two-year-old woman had been knocked unconscious downstairs, probably in the kitchen where the cat was, then taken upstairs where the job was finished off. It made sense: the bedroom was more secluded, fewer windows to contend with, easier to muffle the victim's screams. He took another swig from Garside's flask.

'You're way off your patch, Jack, your super's gonna love you going out scouting for murder cases. Nothing going on in that teeming metropolis of Denton? Didn't I see some kind of big protest in your neck of the woods on TV? New motorway.'

'More than just the neck, the actual woods themselves. New houses, shops and a leisure centre.'

The two detectives glanced over to the house; the crime-scene officers were taking Florence Wheaton's body out through the back door. The morgue van had pulled up the drive to avoid the gathering crowd out front. It refocused the two coppers' minds.

'So, no sign of forced entry, came in the back by the looks of it,' said Frost, prompting them into action.

'Kevin's not here, and neither is the caravan.'

'Florence has been dead for at least forty-eight hours.'

'And why kill the cat?' Garside repeated Frost's earlier question.

'It suggests another psychological twist to me. Another way of hurting Florence? Maybe the cat got it first. Then . . . then Mum. I think you've got your prime suspect, Inspector Garside.'

'Matricide. Makes sense to me. Christ knows, Kevin had given her enough to complain about. And maybe it was just one thing too many.'

Frost nodded in agreement, then glanced down at his Casio. He wondered how long it would take him to drive back to Denton.

Thursday (1) _____

The hammering was unbearable. Smashing down on his head,
squeezing his skull, pulping his brain. Frost hadn't heard or felt
anything like it since . . . since the last one. But this one was
made worse by the unrelenting ringing that came with it. It was
a mighty carillon of deafening unpleasantness. He grabbed the
pillows and sandwiched his head between them. Still the hammering and the ringing continued. That bloody doorbell will have
to go, he thought. And now came the voices, a chorus of urgency
that just wasn't going to go away and demanded an answer.

'Frost! Get up, we know you're in there, Jack! Frost!'

By the time he'd got back to Denton from Norwood, it was
too late to report back to Eagle Lane and check in with Mullett, who was, according to Clarke, fuming at his going MIA.
Frost reckoned he was allowed two, maybe three solid radio-
silence MIAs a year. He was sure that by the time he returned
to Eagle Lane in the morning, armed with the murder of Florence Wheaton and the connection of her son to Conrad Wilde,
he could make the case for a fuller investigation and his absence
would be forgiven, if not quite forgotten.

So he'd taken the opportunity to pop into the Prince Albert Hotel, Denton's pre-eminent, if not only, four-star hotel. He knew that's where Jimmy McVale was staying, and was hoping to catch him in the bar. Given his new information about Conrad Wilde, maybe he'd find out what McVale knew of him, if anything. But when he arrived, he found that McVale had checked out the previous day. The author had let it be known to the chatty barman that he was heading back to London for some book signings and lectures. Frost finished his brandy and thanked the young barman for the info. Then disaster struck.

They were a team of very attractive double-glazing saleswomen from Southend who were celebrating their success at convincing most of South Denton and all of East Rimmington about the wonders of UPVC. They were insistent that Frost join them for *one* glass of champagne. Who was he to say no?

'No . . . No! . . . He's not here!'

'Get up, Jack!'

He threw the top pillow across the room, flung the duvet off and sat up. He staggered to the door and opened it. There he was met by DC Susan Clarke and PC David Simms: one was laughing, the other was wincing. Frost felt the cold gust from the hallway. He felt it everywhere; it's particularly strong this morning, he thought. He looked down and realized he was naked.

'Take that smirk off your face.'

'Smirk, sir?'

'You think this is funny?'

'No. I don't.'

Frost didn't think it was funny at all. But in his attempt to stem his anger and block out what Superintendent Stanley Mullett was saying, he found himself thinking about last night. It was on uncorking the fifth bottle of Moët that the girls pulled him down to the floor for an impromptu version of 'Oops Up

Side Your Head', and on emptying the decanter for his fourth glass of port that, he was pretty sure, he'd signed on the dotted line for a full set of new windows to replace the new windows in his brand-new flat.

'I have the report from the super at Norwood. You were a long way from home, Frost. It makes interesting reading.'

Frost was in Mullett's office, and he hadn't been invited to sit down. The superintendent sat at his desk, imperiously peering through his tortoiseshell glasses at the statement that Frost had made for DI Garside.

'Time, money and resources investigating a crime—'

'A murder.'

'Ivan Fielding died of a heart attack. That's clearly stated in the reports from both Dr Maltby and Chief Pathologist Gerald Drysdale.' Frost went to say something, but Hornrim Harry raised his hand. 'I know you have theories as to what brought it on, but you have no proof. As for his ill health, his liver apparently looked like and had the consistency of a tinned tomato.'

'A what?'

'Gerald Drysdale's words, not mine. I've never knowingly eaten a tinned tomato in my life. Whilst his morbid sense of humour is questionable, his expertise is not.'

'Florence Wheaton was bludgeoned to death with a ball-peen hammer. That's murder in my book.'

Mullett's voice rose to a barely controlled bellow. 'Yes, and the prime suspect is now her son, Kevin Wheaton. Apparently they had a volatile relationship, and he's a repeat offender. The Met are on the case and it has nothing to do with you or Denton CID—'

'Wheaton was a prison buddy of Conrad Wilde. And I've found a connection between the Ivan Fielding case and Conrad Wilde, who I believe—'

Mullett again raised a hand in front of Frost's face, like a big fat 'Stop' sign being wielded by a ferocious-looking lollypop lady.

'This case is closed, Inspector. Ivan Fielding died of a heart attack in his home after drinking half a distillery. And from what I hear, this Conrad Wilde died of cancer. All very sad, but no crimes committed. As for this Wheaton murder, let the Met handle it. It's not your job to go out scouting for crimes, prospecting for cases, we have quite enough on our hands in Denton.'

'I spoke to a very reliable source, one Inspector Anthony Dorking of the Stolen Art and Antiques Squad, and he said that—'

'There are no files or records connecting Ivan Fielding to Conrad Wilde. It is all hearsay. I have it on good authority that Dorking regrets talking to you about it. And I have arranged for the items that you found at Ivan Fielding's to be collected by Dorking's team. And as far as I and Denton CID are concerned, that's the end of the case.'

'The painting Conrad Wilde sent to Ivan, and which subsequently went missing from the house, is proof that they knew each other. And I can prove Ivan Fielding was an informant. His contact was a Captain Cavanagh, retired now. I'll call Dorking to—'

Mullett slapped his hand down on the edge of his desk. It was loud and looked like it hurt. His face reddened. 'No, no, you won't. If you contact anyone about this again, you will answer directly to the ACC, not me. And you will be suspended from duty immediately. It's not just your career that's on the line, it's your very job. Your pension. Starting from today. I repeat, any further involvement in this case and you will be immediately suspended from duty. *Do I make myself clear?*'

He did. For now Frost was sure there were forces working behind the scenes to bury the case. Just as they had buried Conrad Wilde. Just as they had put a D-Notice on Wilde's and Fielding's case files.

Nonetheless, thought Frost, looking at the still-fuming Mullett who was now sat at his desk going through some paperwork in an effort to restore some of his authority and equanimity, in for a penny, in for a pound.

'Talking of suspensions, sir, would this be a bad time to bring up Desk Sergeant Johnny Johnson? I think his suspension, although not official yet, is a bit harsh and—'

'Get out!'

'I can't believe it. I mean, it's just unbelievable,' said John Waters, backing up what he'd just said with a slow shake of the head.

'It's true,' said Frost, 'the whole thing. It was all laid out in front of Mullett. The connections with Kevin Wheaton, Conrad, the paintings, and Ivan, certainly enough to warrant further investigation. And all he could do was threaten me with suspension if I carried on.'

'No,' said Waters, still shaking his head, 'I can't believe that grown women still do the "Oops Up Side Your Head" rowing dance!'

'You're not taking this seriously, are you?'

They were at the Jarrett & Sons site in Denton Woods, in an unmarked maroon Datsun Cherry, the worst car in the Eagle Lane carpool, but good enough for this type of work. They were on 'obs' duty at a safe distance from the demonstration. They were to take notes, use the telephoto lens, observe, collect info, and generally liaise with the uniforms who were on the front line. Although, from what they could see, it all seemed pretty peaceful. The Jarrett workmen charged with clearing the forest weren't due to go in for another four days, when it was thought the final appeal against the planning decision would be rejected in a hearing on Monday, and the diggers and chainsaws could swing into action.

Waters shrugged. 'The path report was pretty conclusive, and Dr Death hasn't let us down in the past. As for this Conrad and his paintings? I don't know that it amounts to much, if I'm honest, Jack. So they had a past, who doesn't? And it's not as if they were criminally active recently.'

There was a tap on the window – it was WPC Hayley Jefferies.

Frost opened the door and she handed in two Styrofoam cups of piping-hot tea.

'Thanks, Hayley, where d'you get these?'

'The protestors, they've got a tea urn in one of the tents. I know we're probably not supposed to fraternize with the enemy, but they seem nice enough. I think some of them are a bit embarrassed about what happened, the older ones, anyway.'

'I used to play in these woods as a kid,' said Frost. 'Who knows, if I wasn't doing this I might join them, manning the barricades, power to the people, and all that.'

Waters and Jefferies were united in throwing him sceptical looks.

'That for us too?' asked Frost. Jefferies handed him the *Denton Echo* that was tucked under her arm, and he opened it up.

'How you feeling?' Waters asked the young WPC. 'Happy to be off the front page, I bet.'

'Not exactly one for the scrapbook. My mum said I should sue them for dragging my reputation through the mud. I had to point out to her, I was literally dragged through the mud. The only person to come out of that looking good was Mr McVale.'

Frost didn't glance up from the paper, but gave a gravelly murmur of disapproval at the mention of the name. 'An opportunist with an eye for publicity,' he said sourly.

Jefferies smiled at Waters. 'Nothing like what you went through, Sarge. You saved two women, I had to *be* saved. Bit embarrassing, really.'

The DS never liked being reminded of his bravery in the line of duty. It came wrapped up in too much personal grief and pain, which he'd not really shared with anyone else. Waters knew that Kim had told some of her colleagues in Rimmington CID, so maybe it wasn't such a secret.

Jefferies said, 'Still, looking forward to Sunday when they give you the award, sir, no one deserves it more than you.'

Frost saved Waters any further discomfort by giving the paper a thoroughly good rustle, like he couldn't believe what was printed on it. 'I stand corrected, Hayley, even chip paper comes up trumps every now and then!'

'Guv?'

Waters and Jefferies both looked at Frost, whose mouth was distinctly ajar, his gob looking well and truly smacked. She said she'd leave them to it, and ambled back to join the thin blue line.

Frost showed Waters a half-page ad featuring a photo of the Conrad Wilde painting still in the possession of Vanessa Fielding. Frost read out the accompanying text:

' "A substantial and negotiable reward is offered for the return of a painting, very similar to the one shown. The painting is of no value other than sentimental to the family. All information will be treated in the strictest confidence. Contact Dr Stephen Parker at the University of—" '

'So what's the problem?'

'Well, for a start, "all information will be treated in the strictest confidence" is a load of old bollocks! 'Scuse my bloody French, but despite Mullett and Winslow's protestations, this is still an open case, there's still questions need answering.'

John Waters gave a guarded nod of agreement.

'A substantial reward? For what? Why does he want an ugly worthless painting?'

'Like he said, sentimental value, maybe the estranged wife wants it, the daughter. People think differently once things are gone.'

'No, they wanted shot of the one they've already got, never mind paying for a new one. So what's changed their minds? *That's* what I want to know.'

Frost twirled the key in the ignition.

Waters grabbed the steering wheel. 'Whoa, whoa, where do you think you're going?'

'To the university, talk to Stephen Parker.'

'You're under orders to stay off the case, under pain of death. That's why we're here.'

'Acting like the Stasi, taking pictures, names and addresses? It's 1985, John, 1984 has been and gone and Big Brother didn't show up. This is England: if people want to protest, then good luck to them, there's a long tradition of it. We're wasting our time sitting here; I'd rather be directing traffic than doing this. Do you want a proper case, to get back to work, or do you just want to let them pin that medal on you on Sunday and sit you in front of a computer screen for life?'

Waters thought about it for approximately three seconds before releasing his grip on the steering wheel. 'Lead the way.'

Thursday (2) ─────────────────────────

The university was a plate-glass affair, brutalist in its architecture, with grey concrete blocks clustered together, and space-age walkways connecting various buildings and floors. The grassy quad was busy with students on their way to classes; others sat around the focal point of the campus, the fountain, smoking, eating crisps and making plans for a big night out, or the overthrow of the capitalist system.

Frost found Stephen Parker's office on the fourth floor of the social sciences department. He was between lectures and was marking a stack of papers. When Frost knocked on his door, he greeted the detective with a surprised diffidence. As if he couldn't possibly be the one the inspector wanted to see, looking around his office to check that his girlfriend, Vanessa, wasn't there.

Parker offered him a seat, one of six that had been set out for an imminent seminar. Without explaining why he was there, Frost placed the *Denton Echo* on the desk, and fixed the academic with a questioning look. The lecturer didn't open the paper.

'Ah, yes, I have a copy, obviously. No calls as of yet, I'm afraid.'

'It's not against the law to offer a reward for stolen items, in fact it's sometimes encouraged. But in this case we still haven't completely ruled out that Ivan suffered a heart attack because of an intruder, which makes it a potential aggravated robbery leading to manslaughter.'

'Yes, I did think of that. But who knows, it might shake things up, smoke them out.'

Frost pulled a puzzled expression. It was confirmation of what he'd heard about academics: a string of letters after their name, like someone had thrown a Scrabble board at them, but none to spell out *common sense*. So he attacked the issue from another angle.

'It does seem strange that you would offer a reward after everything we discussed. Mrs Fielding seemed to have no interest in the painting at all. In fact, she found it abhorrent. And her daughter thought it a blight on her father's memory, what with him having such impeccable taste.'

'Let me give you a clue, Inspector.' With a sweep of his hand Parker directed Frost towards his bookcase.

Frost got up and read some of the spines on offer. It began to make sense.

'Your specialist interest is in . . . criminology?'

'Indeed.'

Frost picked out one book that caught his eye like a rusty hook: Jimmy McVale's memoir. 'I take it you know he's in Denton? Or at least, he was staying at the Prince Albert.'

'Yes, I was going to seek him out, get him to sign a copy, maybe even do a talk for the students. I hear he's on the lecture circuit now. But I read the book, and I'm afraid it added little to the field of research; it's all rather self-absorbed, lacking the objectivity of truly good biographical studies.'

'I could have spared you the three hundred pages, Doctor.'

'Oh, please, Inspector, call me anything but doctor. I leave that title to the medical profession. I'm just a humble PhD.'

'Maybe you should leave the catching of criminals to us. If

the painting was indeed stolen from Ivan's house, should whoever took it come to collect the reward, you might get a nasty surprise. Trust me, *Mister* Parker, some criminals are best viewed through the pages of a book, rather than up close and personal.'

'I fully understand, Inspector. My interest is purely academic, and I appreciate your concerns, and I certainly don't mistake the work I do for the real investigative work of real policemen. Work I can only applaud you for, but never hope to emulate.'

Frost couldn't help but smile at the fawning explanation. 'Criminology is a pretty broad subject, so what exactly is your field of interest?'

'The post-war period, with a focus on the increase in organized crime in the '50s and the '60s, the economic and cultural implications, and the growing cultural iconography of criminality at that time, and how it has fed into the present day.'

Frost's smile slipped, as he couldn't stop himself looking perplexed at the convoluted statement.

'It was a period, Inspector, when Conrad Wilde would have been very active.'

'So Mrs Fielding told you about Conrad?'

Parker looked momentarily offended. 'Of course, Inspector, Vanessa and I share everything.'

'Of course.'

'With my research into the underworld of the period, I'd heard of Conrad Wilde, but only as a fringe figure, certainly not as part of any larger criminal conspiracy. But I had more or less forgotten about him, until Vanessa mentioned your belief that Ivan did business with him.'

'You sound doubtful.'

'Vanessa says she'd never heard of him, and I believe her. But as we know, Inspector, that isn't proof that their paths didn't cross, just proof that Ivan didn't want her to know about his criminal activity. However, once Vanessa told me what you had said about him, it got the cogs turning, mobilized the grey matter. And I discovered that due to his dashing looks, he was a bit-part actor in some British films and television shows of the time. Which again piqued my interest, as far as cultural iconography goes – in many ways, there couldn't have been a more swinging '60s figure.'

'I heard he was in *The Saint*.'

Parker pulled an excited grin. 'Yes. I'm trying to source a copy, maybe we can . . .'

'We can what?'

'I was going to suggest, watch it together?'

'It's a date. I'll bring the popcorn.' Frost's delivery was so dry that it mopped up the smile on Parker's face. 'You're obviously a man who enjoys his research, so did you know anything about Ivan and Conrad before the former's death and our investigation?'

Parker gave a vigorous shake of his head. 'I didn't have a clue about Ivan's criminality or the extent of it, no. I was as surprised as Vanessa when she told me.'

Frost considered this. He really wasn't sure if he believed him. He let the moment hang in the air, like he wanted Parker to register his disbelief, then asked, 'And why does she want the painting now?'

'Sorry, I thought I made myself clear, *she* doesn't. *I* do. If what you say is correct, Inspector, who better to write a book about the topic than me? This Conrad Wilde sounds like a fascinating subject, don't you think? I've already made some phone calls.' Parker grabbed a pen and opened an A4 notebook, as if ready to scribble more. 'He died in Longthorn, the high-security psychiatric hospital, I believe. I'm only at the early stages of my research but I'd love to ask you some things, pick your brains.'

Frost didn't expect this, to find himself being questioned. 'Like I said, there's nothing illegal about what you're doing, Mr Parker, but maybe you should be careful. The idea that Ivan was killed for the painting is still a possibility, for reasons we haven't fully discovered yet. But I have ideas, theories of my own—'

The door swung open with a clatter.

'Jack, we have to go!'

Waters had 'emergency' written all over his face, his voice a veritable siren of urgency. Frost shot to his feet, didn't quibble – he'd heard enough from Parker anyway.

'Maybe I could set up an interview, Inspector, I'd love to hear more of your thoughts on the case, your theories. I could buy you lunch . . .'

He thanked Parker as he darted out of the office after Waters.

The lecturer watched the two detectives bolt down the corridor and turn the corner. He closed his office door and sat back down at his desk with a satisfied sigh. He then took his pipe out of a drawer and unhooked the little leather tobacco pouch he kept hanging from the wooden frame of his cork noticeboard. He filled the bowl, tamped it down with a little tamping tool he'd picked up in Paris, and fired it up with his copper petrol lighter purchased in Lisbon. He was five billowy clouds of smoke into his pipe when he heard the timid knock on the door. Invigorated by the rich aroma of the shag, and emboldened by his exchange with the policeman, he barked out, '*Entrez à vos risques et périls.*'

The door eased open and a man in a dark-blue duffel coat and grey beanie hat entered. Parker prided himself on knowing his students and the entire faculty – but not this one. In fact, he didn't really look like anyone from around there, not really. Once the hat had been removed, Stephen saw the man was far too old to be a student, and a little too diffident in these surroundings to be a member of the faculty. He had thinning mousy hair and a narrow face with indistinct features. To Parker, he sort of looked like someone you might know but couldn't quite place . . . or he sort of looked like no one at all.

'How can I help you?'

'Professor Parker?'

'Doctor.'

'Ah. I used to be a school prefect. I wanted to shout out to those two fellas coming out of your office, *no running in the hallway!*'

Parker didn't join the man in his chuckling. He just repeated his question: 'How can I help you?'

'I've come about the painting,' said Clive Banes.

Stephen Parker had cancelled his next lecture and seminar. He was now sitting opposite Clive Banes in a greasy spoon not far from the campus, but far enough away that it never seemed to be populated with students, or anyone really. It was one of those businesses that seemed to have gone out of business, and was now just a pastime for the elderly couple who barely ran it. This was reflected in half the menu being off the menu. Just the greasy-spoon basics. They sat drinking tea from chipped mugs and eating slices of white toast that had simultaneously the texture of coarse sandpaper and the viscosity of chewing gum.

'Of course, if you do have the painting, I suppose I need to ask you where you got it.'

'Yes. I can see why you would need to ask that question.'

Parker and Banes had been playing cat and mouse around each other, neither wanting to commit. Banes had said he hadn't taken the painting, but knew who had; Parker had said he wasn't interested in calling the police, he just wanted it back. But in the brief game that played out between the two men, it had become clear to both that it wasn't just a case of returning a painting and getting a reward. There was more to it. A *lot* more.

'But I don't have the painting, not really. As I say, I just know who has it, but I don't really know how they got it. I'm sorry to say, Mr Parker—'

'Doctor.'

'Yes, sorry. Doctor. My mistake. But I can get hold of it, easily. How about you, Dr Parker?'

'How about me . . . ?'

'Do you have . . . the other painting?'

'What other painting?'

Banes, who was about to bite into another triangle of toast, let out a weary sigh, then placed his slice of Nimble back on the plate. 'I'm sorry, I thought I was dealing with a man of intelligence. The other painting in the advert in the paper.'

'Yes, of course I do. It belongs to Mrs Fielding, it was a gift from—'

'Her husband, Ivan. Who was given it by . . . ?'

'By . . . ?'

'Yes, by . . . ?'

Now it was Parker's turn to drop his toast on the plate. 'You have the advantage over me, as I know next to nothing about you, just your name, Mr Banes. But I confess, me putting the advert in the paper was something of a fishing expedition.'

'And you've reeled me in.'

'Indeed. So, we're both sort of at an advantage and a disadvantage. But I'm sure we can both agree that the man who gave Ivan Fielding the painting is key to this situation?'

'We can agree.'

'Good. So how about if I say his Christian name. Then if you can say his surname, I will know we are on the same page, as it were.'

'Agreed,' said Banes.

There was a pause. Then realizing he had to go first, Parker apologized and said, 'Conrad.'

'Wilde. With an "e" on the end. He was very insistent on that, was Conrad. Didn't want it to be mistaken for the adjective, wild. Because it's the last thing he was. He was caged. He saw his name as a cruel irony.'

'You met him?'

'That's what brought me here, to Denton.'

'What was he like?'

'By the time I met him he was a changed man, years of prison will of course do that. I found him to be a thoughtful, softly spoken man.'

'How did you meet him?'

Banes remained silent. More than that, he completely ignored the question and got on with eating his toast and drinking his tea.

'I'm . . . I'm considering a book on him,' said Parker, feeling he must fill the awkward silence. 'So . . . so anything you could tell me would be of the—'

'First things first,' said Banes. 'What do you actually know?'

Parker pushed his plate to one side, the toast abandoned. 'I know that in 1967 something of great value was taken from a private bank vault—'

'In Bond Street.'

'I see you've done your research, Mr Banes.'

'I'm not an educated man, but I like to read up on things that interest me.'

'Tell me, do you really believe the paintings hold the secret to where it's buried?'

'Yes. I have it on good authority. From a trusted source.'

'The man who stole the other painting?'

'Let's not hold that against him, Dr Parker. I don't think any of us involved in this . . . *undertaking* want the police involved.'

'Quite.'

'That policeman leaving your office in a hurry, what does he know?'

'Inspector Frost. Yes, he looks like a bit of a scruffy yobbo, but he's sharp, clever. In a household full of valuable things, the only thing taken was Conrad's contribution. For a detective of his stripe, it's just the kind of anomaly you look for. It would have been better if your . . . "trusted source" had also stolen some other things, to cover his tracks.'

'Unlike your detective, he's not sharp or clever. But in all fairness, he was only taking his mentor's advice. Get what you came for, then get out.'

'Still, with my *Echo* advertisement, well, I rather fear I may have alerted him to the possibilities of the painting having greater meaning. But we're not the only ones after it, you know that?'

Banes nodded. 'I read about him in the local paper. Jimmy McVale. And, of course, he's a dangerous man. Him being in Denton would be a bit of a coincidence, wouldn't it?'

'Yes, it would. But don't you see, Mr Banes, it adds validity to our shared beliefs.' Parker's eyes shone, he was excited now. 'It's just another piece of the puzzle all coming together. Maybe that's why Conrad painted three pictures, because it was safer that way. You don't see the bigger picture until you get all three of them in front of you, and then the mystery—'

Parker broke off. He cursed himself inwardly. Like a true academic, he was prone to getting carried away and expounding his theories through thesis and antithesis. You could do that with students, but not with men like Banes.

'. . . You didn't know about the third painting . . . did you?'

Banes smiled. 'It doesn't matter, Stephen. Now we really are on the same page.'

'I heard a car pulling up behind us. There was a skidding sound. Not an emergency stop, but just like they'd spotted a parking space. I was going to turn around, take a look, like you do. Then Ruby started telling me about ... about her Cabbage Patch dolls ... how she enjoys looking after them ... but how she feels that she loves Miss Lucy most of all ... and how sad that makes the others ...'

The sheer torturous strain of recalling her child's abduction was finally proving too much, and Gail Hanson's valiant efforts in giving as detailed an account as possible faltered. She buried her face in the wad of Kleenex that was already in her hand.

Frost was with DC Clarke in the Hansons' home. It was a modern home, aggressively so, with a split-level bunker-style design, made of glass and concrete in equal measure. It reminded Frost of the campus he'd just left. Inside was all very minimal, too, with blond wooden floors, two Italian steel-framed black leather sofas either side of a vast smoked-glass coffee table, and some impenetrable modern art on the walls. But for all its sophisticated design, given the Care Bears on the floor, and three Cabbage Patch dolls propped up on one of the sofas, it couldn't quite disguise the fact that there was an eight-year-old living here.

An eight-year-old who had just been snatched from the arms of her mother.

Gail Hanson had some grazes on her forehead and some bruising on her arms and back where the assailant, or assailants, had rushed her from behind and forced her face down on to the pavement. They'd grabbed little Ruby Hanson, still clutching her mother's hand, and pulled her into a car. When uniforms tried to put Gail into an ambulance to take her to A&E to get her checked over, the distraught mother had become insistent that she needed to be at home for when Ruby came back.

She was a slim attractive woman in her early thirties, with dark straight shiny hair worn in a pageboy style. She matches the house, thought Frost: expensive-looking, modern, sophisticated. But she can't hide the fact that right now her heart is breaking.

Frost gave DC Clarke the nod to resume the questioning when she thought it appropriate.

'The car, Gail, I know you said that you didn't see it approaching, it was behind you, but when you got up, what did you see?'

'Nothing . . . It was too late by then. By the time I got up the road was empty, I didn't see any cars . . . not even the sound of an engine.'

'How long were you on the ground?'

'I don't know . . . I just froze . . . I didn't know Ruby was gone. I thought they'd taken my bag . . . you know, just mugged me. So I just lay there, waiting for them to go . . . I didn't think for a minute they'd take Ruby. I squeezed her hand . . . muttered, it'll be OK . . . It will be OK . . .'

Little Ruby looked just like her mother. A mop of dark hair, hazel eyes, small doll-like features. DC Arthur Hanlon was organizing the door-to-door. Uniforms were showing copies of the Hansons' photos of Ruby. Hanlon, knowing that time was of the essence, hadn't bothered going back to Eagle Lane – he knew a photocopying place that was much closer. For a big man, Arthur Hanlon could move quickly when necessary (three kids of his own, he said, was all the incentive he needed).

'OK, Gail, you're doing great. We just need to be clear on what you saw, no matter how seemingly small.'

Gail Hanson gave an energetic nod of her head, and pulled herself together for the umpteenth time. Frost threw her encouraging looks.

'Of course . . . It was when I tried to squeeze Ruby's hand that I realized she was gone. I got up, there was the van . . . A green van with some writing on the side. A furniture van? I don't know, it was parked there, it blocked my view . . .'

Frost had made a note of the van earlier. The abduction had taken place on Penfield Road in West Denton. Tree-lined, well lit, nice detached houses. He knew it was a removal van. When he'd first arrived at the scene it struck him as being very conveniently parked for the abductors, almost as if they'd timed it to perfection. The van obscured the view from the other side of the street, and the high walls and well-kept hedges obscured the view from the houses on this side. It was the perfect place to strike.

'. . . By the time I got past the green van, the car was gone. I assumed it had turned into the next road . . . I can't remember the name—'

'Chesterfield Avenue.'

She looked up at Frost, surprised. He'd introduced himself but it was the first time he'd spoken since. She saw that he had a cigarette in his hand. Unlit. Rotating it in his nicotine-stained fingers, like a prop or some worry beads.

'Yes. Thank you. I think I might have seen the car otherwise. It's a long straight road, I'd have seen it.'

Frost smiled. 'You say a car. Are you sure of that? Not a van or . . . sounds silly, but a minibus?'

Gail Hanson tilted her head to the side as though the suggestion offered a new perspective. 'I know what you mean. I assumed it was a car because it just sounded like a car. But I can't be sure.'

'That's OK,' said Frost. 'We have officers covering the whole area, going door to door. They always find something out, someone has always seen something.'

She drew a deep breath that indicated she derived some comfort from that. She then turned her attention back to DC Clarke, but Frost wasn't finished yet.

'Can I ask you something else, Gail?'

'Of course.'

'Did you smell anything?'

'Sorry?'

Frost said, 'You said this person pushed you down, so they were on top of you, or certainly close to you, right?' She nodded. 'Did you smell anything . . . a scent, aftershave, perfume, something distinctive or everyday, cigarette smoke, BO, anything?'

Mrs Hanson closed her eyes, as if shutting off her senses, all apart from one, as she relived the moment. If Gail had seen her assailant she would have obviously known the gender. If pressed now, she would have probably said it was a man. Because even without the statistics in front of them, Frost and the team knew it was a crime that was committed more often by men than women. And that lazy assumption could be the difference between finding a victim in twenty-four hours rather than forty-eight, between life and death. But sensory recall could sometimes be just as potent. The smell, the weight, the feel, that too could lead to something beyond probabilities and statistics, to something more like the truth.

Her eyes opened suddenly, big and round, as a fresh memory spiked. 'I could smell smoke like cigarette smoke – no, no, stronger than that. More like cigars. My father smoked cigars. My mother hated them but I always liked the smell.'

'Would you say it was a man?'

'Didn't I already?'

'No.'

'It was a man, I'm sure of that.'

Frost pressed her. 'A big man, heavy man, small man? Take your time . . .'

She sat forward, head in hands. As she thought, Frost glanced over at the tape recorder on the coffee table to make sure it was still rolling. When possible, he always insisted they tape these interviews. The victims of a crime were usually a bundle of jangling nerves, talking nineteen to the dozen, and it was easy to miss clues buried within clues, whilst every little detail mattered at this stage. Frost liked to have the tapes transcribed, then play them again with a red pen in his hand – listening for the inflections, the trembles, the assertions and the false notes.

Gail lowered her hands and looked at the detective. 'My legs went first, like in a rugby tackle, I guess. My husband plays rugby, I go to watch him sometimes. Don't know why I said that. Maybe because I always cringe when he gets tackled. It felt like that. Then he pushed my head down. He had big hands, I could feel them all around the back of my head. He didn't lie on top of me, but from his hands . . . and just the way he felt, his presence . . . does that makes sense?' Frost gestured that it did. 'So yes, I would say he was a big man.'

'How tall are you, Mrs Hanson?'

'Me? Quite tall, five foot eight.'

There was the sound of a key scraping in the lock of the front door, some fast footfalls in the hallway and Richard Hanson entered the room. He looked in pain. Gail rushed over to her husband and folded herself into his arms. Frost recognized him from the framed photos on the side table. He was a big fella, around six two. You would know if you'd been rugby tackled by him, thought Frost. A handsome-looking man with thick dark brown hair swept back, a lantern jaw sprinkled with designer stubble, and a slender nose with a crook in it. He was fashionably dressed all in black, with a long raglan-sleeved coat that almost reached the floor. Like a cloak, it gave him a dramatic sweep.

Frost couldn't imagine what the perfect couple looked like,

doubted there even was one, but against the backdrop of the designer house – he an architect, she a homemaker – they wouldn't have seemed out of place in one of those glossy magazines that Sue Clarke was always flicking through. It just showed: no matter how perfect someone's life appeared, they couldn't insulate themselves from the world's imperfections, the failures and sickness of others.

The drive here must have been hellish, and fast. Richard Hanson's face looked like he had had the blood drained from it. He peppered his wife's face with kisses, a face that was now damp with tears.

Through thick breaths he asked, 'What's happening? Are you going to find her?'

Frost confidently said yes, then added, 'You're an architect, Mr Hanson, is that in Denton?'

'Yes, yes, that's right.'

'Is that where you've come from now?'

He shook his head, looking like he was trying to work out the reason for the question.

'We need to know where everyone was at the time of the abduction, and that means everyone. Eliminating everyone we can from our enquiries. You understand?'

'Yes, of course. I was in Wilsmere today, seeing a client.'

Frost carried on staring at him with an unrelenting and questioning gaze – he wanted more.

'I was there from about midday . . . until I got the call from Tony, one of my partners, then I drove straight here.'

'*Wilsmere*. Where have I seen that?' Frost stuck the unlit cigarette in his mouth.

'It's a small town near—'

'I know where it is, Mr Hanson, but I want to know why it's ringing bells.'

'Jarrett & Sons have their head office there. Wilsmere is mentioned on all their billboards. They're still a local family firm, very proud of it, employ most of the town in one capacity or another . . .' Richard Hanson must have read Frost's face. '. . . You don't think this has got anything to do with . . . ?'

Frost ignored the unwritten but obvious house rule and did what he'd been threatening to do since he'd got there: he lit his cigarette. No one protested. Sated, he thought to himself, *Let's hope so, let's bloody well hope so.*

Thursday (4) _____

As Banes approached the caravan, he could see the light was on.
He wondered whether Kevin Wheaton was reading the paper.
One of the nationals, the red tops, not that little rag that Denton put out, which was only concerned with what was happening
in its immediate environs. Although Banes had to admit, there
did seem to be a lot happening in Denton since he'd arrived.

He'd discovered a path to get to the caravan without passing
that awful hippie encampment, with its smelly protestors, how
he loathed people like that. And he certainly didn't want to be
bumping into them tonight. He had a copy of the *Daily Express*
tucked under his arm, just in case Kevin hadn't read the papers.
He suspected Kev was more interested in the stash of porno
mags he'd glimpsed under his yellowing quilt.

But there was one story that would certainly interest him: a
woman bludgeoned to death, with a ball-peen hammer most
probably, in West Norwood. It had made the nationals. And, of
course, they mentioned the demise of the cat. If it had been a
dog, no doubt it would have made the front page.

Banes thought about the cat, that bloody cat. That untypical bloody cat. When he struck the first blow at the back of her head, the thing jumped up at him and clawed and chewed at his hand, as if it was trying to get the hammer out of it. He didn't expect that kind of bravery and loyalty from a cat. That was usually the preserve of dogs. Cats, shallow, callous things, they just move on to the next person laying out the Kitekat for them, purring away and rubbing themselves flirtatiously against your ankles till the bowl is full. First sign of danger, they dart out of the way. But not this one. It certainly left its marks, sinking its sharp claws and little needle-like teeth into him. He'd always been allergic to cats, the fur-balled little fuckers, making his eyes run and his skin bubble up and itch. This one deserved everything it got.

Kevin would be a trickier proposition altogether.

He was a big lad, a right lump, a capable-looking unit, as they'd say on the prison landings when weighing up the competition. And he had, like himself, spent time in institutions. You learned not to turn your back on people. You were always aware of your space; it was precious, it was limited. It was yours. And if you wanted it to remain that way, you were wary of who was around you, eyes in the back of your head. That's how Banes had survived the institutions, ever since he could remember, ever since he was a child.

He knocked on the caravan door.

'Yeah?'

'It's me, Clive.'

The door opened. And there stood Kevin. King of his domain. A pair of Wrangler jeans undone at the waist, relying on a failing zip to keep them up. His beer gut flopping over the straining fabric like some malignant old tumour about to burst. Thankfully, he was wearing his vest, a patchwork of unpleasant yellows and worrying browns covering his whiter-than-white skin. On his left forearm, a luminous blue prison tattoo advertised 'Cristal Palas FC'. How could he get it so wrong? The tattoo on his right arm he'd managed to get right, the spelling at least. But with only three letters, and two the same, how could he go wrong? It was a dagger going through a heart, and in the heart bore the legend 'MUM'.

Which brought Clive Banes to his point.

'Can I come in, Kev?'

Wheaton shrugged. 'I guess.'

Banes stepped in and closed the tinny little door behind him. He'd obviously disturbed Kevin catching up on some light reading. A copy of *Razzle: Readers' Wives Special Edition* was prominently laid out on the blue Formica table. Kevin pulled out a couple of cans of Hofmeister from the fridge and sat down on a camping chair, which looked like its spindly aluminium frame would collapse at any minute.

The painting was propped against the wall under the window. It had a floral Brentford Nylons sheet over it, a polycotton blend, according to the label that was visible. Funny the things you notice, thought Banes: 20 per cent cotton, 80 per cent polyester. That would be all he would really remember about what he would do tonight. The rest would be blanked out; as with the painting, a sheet would be thrown over it, 20 per cent cotton, 80 per cent polyester . . .

'How are you, Kevin?'

'Worked it out yet?' asked Wheaton, gesturing to the painting.

'Getting warmer, Kev, getting warmer. I've discovered that the painting is part of a triptych.'

'Trip what?'

'One of three.'

'Yeah, that's right. You said you thought there were others. You know what I think?'

'What?'

'I reckon I made a big mistake.'

Banes sat on the corner of one of the fold-down beds. 'How so?'

'I took Conrad's advice. Maybe I shouldn't have listened this time.'

'What advice was that?'

'He always said, go for the prize only. Grab what you came in for and get out quick. Most burglars get distracted, stay too long, leave too many clues and get caught. Ivan's house was stuffed full of quality gear . . . And I came away with that piece of shit.' Kevin stabbed a fat finger towards the painting. 'I can't even bear to look at it.'

'You'd always listened to Conrad before, and he always steered you right.'

'But not this time. He was off his head on morphine, he was dying.'

'You're not losing faith, are you?'

Kevin shook his sad-looking head, pulled the ring off his Hofmeister and tossed it over his shoulder with weary disdain. He then took some big glugs and followed these by a big burp. 'I don't know if I'm cut out for all this. Send me in to rob something, and I'll rob it. I'll get the job done. But all this bleeding treasure-hunt nonsense? It's not my game. Don't have the patience for it, to be honest. Wasting my time going after something that might not even exist? I'm thinking of going home, get on with some real robberies and earn some real fuckin' money.'

'Back to Mum?'

Kevin Wheaton glanced around at him. He obviously didn't like the tone, sort of snide. 'You taking the piss?'

'No, mate, no. Not at all. You're lucky to have a mum, a mum that loves and looks after you. I never had that. Don't know who my mum and dad were. I never had a home. I still don't, not really. So I've got nowhere to go. This is it for me, Kevin.'

Wheaton greeted this admission with blank indifference. Or maybe it was just all the booze he'd drunk that was keeping his eyelids at half-mast. Dulling his senses, blunting his responses. There were a dozen or so empties stacked up in the corner. Banes certainly hoped this was the case.

Still, Wheaton tried, and eventually managed to squeeze out a barely audible 'Sorry to hear that.'

Banes was undeterred by his less than enthusiastic audience. He liked talking about his past, his truth. Especially when he knew his secret wouldn't be revealed.

'I was what they call a "foundling". I grew up in lots of homes. But like I say, never a "home". Care homes, orphanages, mainly. I was fostered out a couple of times ... But it never worked out. I never really fitted in. I realized that fitting in was something you had to work at. A skill you had to learn.'

Kevin gave some slow, bored nods to this, then concentrated on chewing his damp and blunt thumbnails down to the quick.

'I worked on a building site in Stratford once,' said Banes, smiling at the memory. 'Got talking to this fella, fellow labourer. Found out all about him. He was about my age. Single. No family to speak of. Seemed a bit lonely. So I became his friend, his fast friend. And I found out everything about him. Detail by detail, bit by bit. Every day I learned something new. It wasn't hard, no one had taken much interest in him, so he liked me asking questions about him, taking an interest in his life ... Until I had it all. His whole life mapped out: all the important dates and what-not. He was a good lad, no criminal record, no record at all. His name was Clive. Clive Banes.'

Kevin stopped admiring the raw mess of his now over-chewed thumbnail and grimaced in confusion. 'That's *your* name?'

'It is now. But in the words of the immortal bard, "What's in a name?" You've not read the papers today?'

'Nah, not been out.'

Banes glanced over at the open copy of *Razzle*. He knew there was a stack of similar publications under the very bed he was sitting on: *Asian Babes*, *Jouncers International*, *Fiesta* ... He handed Kevin the *Daily Express* he'd brought.

'Ta. So ... what's your real name?' he asked, turning his attention to the paper and flicking through it.

'It's all bad news, though, these days, Kev. You're from Norwood, right?'

Kevin didn't remember telling him that, but nodded along to it anyway.

'Page ten. Terrible thing. Terrible, terrible . . .'

Kevin turned the pages, in no great hurry, nothing much fazed him once he'd had a few lagers. Then, once he'd happened upon page ten, the paper in Wheaton's tattooed fingers began to rustle, then visibly shake. He buried his face in the newsprint, eyes bulging, his cheeks reddening at the pictures. A posed photo of Mum in her Sunday best with her boy . . . then Mum with the cat . . . then . . . partially blacked out due to the graphic nature . . . Mum . . . on her bed . . . lying in blood, the headline . . .

He turned to face Clive Banes . . . or whatever the hell his name was. But he wasn't sat on the bed now. Kevin had not kept his eye on him. That was a mistake. In prison you always had to stay alert. You needed eyes in the back of your head. And if that had been true, he'd have seen that Banes, or whoever he was, was now poised behind him. Like an executioner.

Friday (1) ————————————————————

Superintendent Stanley Mullett stood with his back to CID, in front of the main board in the incident room. He had the dusty old blackboard eraser in his hand. With assured sweeping movements he rubbed out all the information pertaining to the Ivan Fielding investigation, and wrote 'RUBY HANSON' in large capitals. He then performed a sharp Prussian-officer turn and addressed his troops.

'Inspector Frost will be leading the investigation to secure the safe return of little Ruby Hanson. It's our top priority, nothing else matters until I personally say it does. Right, Jack?'

All eyes were on Frost. It was the '9 a.m. briefing', a three-line whip, everyone was expected to attend. And everyone was there. Sipping coffee, indulging in the first cigarette of the day, but all silently studying the photocopies of the facts of the case thus far. It was standing room only. And it was only 7.30 a.m. Whenever there was a missing, or in this case, even worse, an abducted child, the incident room at Eagle Lane was an adrenalin-fuelled engine room of efficiency and determination. Coppers pulling double shifts, treble shifts. Only knocking off when they got too knackered to have a quick kip in the locker rooms, where there were foldaway cots.

The first forty-eight hours of any investigation were always the most important, but in a missing-child case even more so. Every passing minute was precious. In most murder investigations the worst that could possibly happen already had. With missing kids, the very worst that could happen was still feasible, still ahead of you, waiting in the dark recesses of the imagination.

Everyone knew that Mullett had had his size-eleven boot on the DI's throat of late. All eyes were on Frost.

'That's right, Superintendent Mullett.' It was loud and clear. 'Our *full* attention. Give it everything. What Eagle Lane always gives in these cases, right?'

They matched Frost, loud and clear, and responded with a thunderous 'Right!'

Mullett smiled, and left the team to it, assured that he would be kept informed of the progress every step of the way. All existing office politics and animosities were out of the window. Mullett's job was to focus the media on the case, get maximum exposure and publicity – TV, newspapers, radio, Saturday-morning pictures if need be – to jog memories, prick consciences, alert the world to the plight of Ruby Hanson.

'Arthur was in charge of the door-to-door after the incident, so . . .'

Frost gave Hanlon the nod and the DC got to his feet, and with his notes in hand went over to the area map pinned up on the incident board. All roads around the crime scene were marked in red.

'Initial house-to-house enquiries brought up three vehicles seen at the time of the abduction that warrant investigation. On Preston Road, Ardale Road, and Chesterfield Avenue, which as we all know leads to Penfield Road. These cars were all reported as speeding. Only two vehicle models identified: a light-blue VW Beetle, and a dark-green Triumph Dolomite. No number plates identified. So, three cars going in different directions, take your pick. No other verified sightings of young Ruby with either a man or a woman. Ruby's school, Mountview Juniors, is on Mountview Road.' Hanlon pointed unnecessarily to the school on the map, everyone knew it. 'It means parents walking kids home is such a common occurrence, no one takes much notice. Kids shout and scream and no one comes out to complain or is even curious. It's just what happens between 3.30 and 4.30 on weekdays. That this happened a little later in the day may have some significance . . .'

DC Clarke followed this up. 'Gail Hanson picked Ruby up a bit later that day, 5 p.m., because Ruby attends after-school dance classes.'

'The green van parked on Penfield Road?' called out DS Waters. 'That bothers me, who does that belong to?'

Hanlon checked his notes. 'Yes, a removal van, arrived yesterday for a Mr James Golding, lives at 38 Penfield Road, he's moving today; the movers started packing up yesterday early afternoon. They'd gone home by five. It checks out and so do they.'

Frost took Hanlon's place at the board. 'As stated in your notes, Ruby's father, Richard Hanson, is an architect. He's a senior partner in a practice, very successful, or certainly on the way up. What makes his profession of interest is that he is currently under commission from Jarrett & Sons, the developers about to dig up Denton Woods.' Murmurs of discord went up from the gathered officers. 'Richard's firm has had a part in designing some of the new homes. So, we could have a motive for Ruby's abduction. It's extreme, very extreme. But as we know with the protest thus far, passions are riding high. So it's an area we need to investigate.'

Universal nods and mutterings again. There was almost a palpable sense of relief that that might be the case. Because every officer knew that the alternative was a lot worse. DI Jack Frost designated everyone their duties. His biggest job was to stress at all times the logic and solvability of the crime; to treat it like a robbery or a fraud case. To look for clues, motives, links and chains that would lead you to the answer. A child being taken off the street in a random crime wasn't worth contemplating at this point, it served no purpose other than to drain the energy and confidence of the team. You didn't want it to be bad luck, the wrong place at the wrong time, some lone wolf sticking a pin in a map to decide where to snatch a kid off the street.

Ruby's young life would be gone through like she was a criminal. It sounded harsh, but it often worked. Who she was friends with, who she was enemies with, what was her routine, and had anyone been taking a special interest in her. No one was above scrutiny. Trusted public servants like teachers, doctors, lollypop ladies, anyone in her orbit. Her family. Her parents. Sometimes, especially the parents.

'Sally?'

Sally Fielding halted her full shopping trolley with some effort, and turned to see Stephen Parker ambling up the aisle with a basket. There was a single item in it, a tin of Heinz spaghetti hoops. She greeted him with a half-smile, still obviously grieving for her father. And he gave her an understanding look, and then smiled broadly at Ella, her almost-nine-year-old daughter, who was gripping the bar of the trolley.

'Hi, Ella, and how are you?'

'I'm fine, thank you very much.'

'No school today?'

The smile fell from Ella Fielding's face, and she shook her head. The strands of her black hair fell on to her face as she began to examine her shoes. Her mother ran her fingers through her daughter's hair, and gave her a gentle smile, then spoke in a hushed tone.

'School's closed today, Stephen. You must know why, it's been on the news?'

'Ah, yes. Does Ella know the . . . ?'

'Yes, she does, they do ballet and modern jazz together. They were rehearsing yesterday after school.' Sally Fielding took a deep breath, and mouthed to Parker, '*It could have been Ella.*'

'Terrible. Do you know the parents?'

'Yes, we've met. Lovely couple. I can't imagine how they must be feeling. Just awful, awful.' She turned to Ella. 'Darling, why don't you go and get yourself a *Bunty*?'

Ella ran over to the magazine rack, knelt down on the floor and picked out some comics, *Bunty* being one of them.

Keeping one eye on her daughter, she carried on talking to Parker. 'And of course, it has upset Ella, and she'd already taken the loss of Dad quite badly.'

'I see. Were they very close? I don't recall . . .'

'Well, before he got really bad with the drink, they spent a lot of time together. Dad was good with her.' Sally pulled a Kleenex from out of her sleeve. 'I was looking through some old photos of them together – when Ella was younger, they used to play pirates. He actually had outfits for them, God knows where he got them from. You know what he was like . . . everything had to be just so with him . . . He was so lovely with her then, Dad . . . then the drink just wiped all that away . . .'

'And how are you holding up?'

'Like I said, it was sudden yet not unexpected, but you know . . .'

Ella returned with *Bunty*, *The Beano* and *Smash Hits*. 'Can I, Mummy?'

'As long as there are no rude lyrics in *Smash Hits*. You're too young for Run DMC.'

'Mummy? Are you OK?'

Sally tilted her head back and took in a big breath, in an effort to pull back all her emotions and stem the tears that were building up behind her eyes. Then she forced a big smile on her face and squeezed Ella's hand.

'Yes, darling, I'm fine. I hope you're not surprising Mum with dinner tonight, Stephen?'

He followed her withering gaze down to the lone occupant of his shopping basket, the tin of spaghetti hoops.

'Oh no, heaven forbid I should offer this up to your mother. They're for me. Delicious on top of cheese on toast.'

'I like them,' said Ella.

'Then I shall invite *you* to lunch, Ella.' He smiled, but didn't indulge the little girl any further. Instead he got to the point, and the real reason he was there. Because it certainly wasn't the spaghetti hoops, they were merely a ruse; he'd picked them up when he'd followed them into the supermarket. 'Sally, I was wondering, those paintings of Ivan's – Ivan gave one to you, and one to your mother?'

'Yes, those ugly things, what about them?'

'Well, I'd be happy to take it off your hands.'

'Really, why?' But before Parker could say anything, Sally Fielding added, 'Funnily enough, I sold it.'

'Sold it?'

'Yes. A couple of weeks ago. They had a jumble sale at Ella's school to raise money to pay for the goats' vet bills.'

Stephen Parker was staring down at the tin of spaghetti hoops in his basket. 'Who to?'

She shrugged and ignored this. 'Ella's school keeps five goats, don't they, Ella?'

Ella smiled and nodded effusively. 'Mopsy, Rocky, Bowie, Lola and Cliff.'

Sally laughed. 'Cliff's my favourite, as in cliff edge. The kids love them. They *are* sweet, cheap to feed, but the vet's bills do add up. One had an impacted tooth and almost bankrupted the school—'

'Please! Sally, if you can remember . . .'

She looked startled, then offended. 'Stephen, please don't shout. We've got a lot on our plate at the moment. I don't care about that painting. I'm much more worried about the real ones that belonged to Dad. They're worth a lot of money, but the police are saying they may be stolen so we can't take them, and without anyone in the house they could be—'

'Was it a man, a woman?'

'Was what a man or a woman?'

'Who you sold the painting to.'

'Why do you need to know?'

'Why do . . . Why do I . . . ?'

'Yes, why?'

Now he thought about it, knowing if it was a man or a woman who had bought the painting at the jumble sale would hardly make a jot of difference. Under Sally's unrelenting and questioning gaze, he bit down on his bottom lip. A nervous tic in his reddening cheek was like Morse code spelling out his deception. Why, oh why, he wondered to himself, can't it be easier than this?

Friday (2)

RUBY HANSON WILL DIE! HER YOUNG LIFE
CUT DOWN NEEDLESSLY LIKE A YOUNG TREE,
UNLESS JARRETT & SONS AND THOSE WHO
WOULD SEEK TO DESTROY OUR PRECIOUS
LAND STOP AND WITHDRAW FROM DENTON
WOODS <u>IMMEDIATELY</u>!

The message was written in green felt-tip pen, in shaky
block capitals. At the bottom, it was signed 'RUBY', in red. The
red looked like dried blood.

The letter was addressed to Superintendent Stanley Mullett.
It was the only piece of paperwork on his polished mahogany
desk. Gathered around the desk were Frost, Clarke and the new
fella from Forensics whose name Frost could never remember.

'So what do you think . . . ? Sorry, it's . . . ?'

'Thales, Martin Thales.'

Frost nodded, knowing he would always forget his name; it
just seemed so instantly forgettable.

'Matching envelope and paper, bought as a set. Cheap paper,

won't give us a watermark. We'll get it under the ultraviolet, might be able to get a trace on the paper and felt-tip used. As for the blood, we'll be able to match it against Ruby Hanson's blood type, to hopefully eliminate that possibility.'

'Could it be animal blood?' asked Clarke.

Thales shrugged. 'At this point, I wouldn't like to speculate – blood is blood, dried like this it's hard to tell. We'll know more once we're in the lab.' Thales turned to Mullett. 'Are you the only one who touched the letter, sir?'

'Ms Smith handed it to me, but I'm the only one who's handled the letter properly, yes.'

'Good, we might be able to get fingerprints, even if they're just trace ones.'

'Well, Frost, you suspected it was coming. Either this is for real, or it's an opportunist who's heard about the case on the news and is appropriating it for their cause. Though what they hope to achieve – apart from the antipathy of even those people who support their cause – is beyond me.'

Frost agreed. 'We'll visit every protestor in town; we can start using the information on the database that we've been collecting the last few days.'

Frost gave Hale, *Twail*, whatever his name was, permission to remove the letter, and the new Forensics man bagged it up and took it away for examination.

'One other thing, sir,' said Frost, 'can we get Desk Sergeant Johnson back where he belongs, on the desk? He plays a blinder getting the right info out of people on the phone, and we need all hands on deck.'

Mullett assented with barely a second thought, and Frost and Clarke left the super's office and made their way through to the incident room.

It was busy, very busy. Phones were ringing off the hook, the map of Denton and the surrounding area was dotted with red pins indicating where there had been various unverified sightings. Photocopies of a police artist's drawing were plastered around the room, showing Ruby in the outfit she was wearing when she got snatched, along with photos of the same clothing: a red woollen coat with big black buttons manufactured by Ladybird with matching red shoes, also made by Ladybird. She had carried a blue rucksack featuring the characters from the TV show *Cockleshell Bay*. There were also photos of items identical to those in her rucksack: her pink dance leotard and pumps; a paperback copy of *Black Beauty*; a Mountview Juniors exercise book; a Kermit the Frog pencil case; and her beloved Little Miss Lucy Cabbage Patch Kid doll.

'Shall we tell the Hansons we got a letter?' asked Clarke.

'No, not yet. They'll want to see it, or know what was written in it, and I don't want to do it over the phone. We'll visit them later when we get the results back from Forensics. Meanwhile, gather up some troops and we'll go knock on some tent doors.'

'Do tents have doors?'

'Flaps?'

Clarke peeled away to check the rota. Frost went to make a phone call, but quickly stopped when he clocked PC Simms's latest outfit.

Like an overgrown Boy Scout, he was obviously prepared to enter the wilds of Denton Woods, in camouflage army trousers tucked into wellington boots, a green cagoule and a waxed flat cap.

'What the hell are you wearing now, you little tart?'

Waters laughed, more at Frost's reaction than Simms's outfit, though that must have accounted for some of it.

Simms, baffled by their reaction, looked down and inspected himself. 'I'm in plain clothes.'

'Every time I see you, you're wearing something different.'

Waters agreed. 'You should be like Jack, the same clobber day in, day out.'

'Exactly,' said Frost proudly.

'I'm just trying to be professional. It helps me blend in, not stick out like a sore thumb, or a copper.'

'Got news for you, son, plain clothes isn't an opportunity for you to raid the fancy-dress shop, you're not Mr Benn.'

Frost scoped the room, looking for Clarke. He saw she was on the phone, raking a hand through her hair like she wanted to pull it out in frustration. Her voice kept rising above the urgent whisper she was trying to maintain.

'. . . Look, Mum, just do as I say, I don't want you taking Philip out today, just wait till I get home . . . No, I'm not being silly, just . . .'

Clarke turned and saw Frost behind her. She quickly wrapped up the conversation, pacified by the promises from her mother to do as she said.

'We ready?' said Clarke, forcing a smile on her face.

'I don't know, are you?'

She bit her lip. 'Sorry, I was just on the phone—'

'To your mum, telling her not to take Philip to the park today. I understand.'

'It's every parent's nightmare. Sounds trite, sounds obvious, but it's not until you have to deal with it . . . and that letter and the lack of confirmed sightings. And now we have civilian volunteers about to search the parks and wastelands . . .'

'I've never been a parent, but I've been through this before. It's important we don't get emotionally involved. As harsh as that sounds, it's not what Gail and Richard Hanson want from us. They want to see stone-cold professionalism. Especially from you, as you'll mostly be dealing with Gail. She can't see your fear. She doesn't want to. She wants to see you efficient, determined and capable of getting her daughter back. OK?'

Clarke took a deep calming breath, and nodded in agreement.

'Right, let's go and do that, then.' Frost headed out of the incident room with Clarke at his heels, and they picked up Simms along the way. 'And anyway, Sue, I wouldn't worry about little Philip. No one would dare go near him with your mother about, Attila the Hun's got nothing on—'

'Jack! You were doing so well until then.'

*

'Where's the painting?'

Parker slammed the car door shut, hard enough for it to feel like the little Citroën 2CV would collapse around them. But in all fairness, the 'Tin Snail', as it was known, always did that; even rolling the window down made it feel like bits were falling off. Once the car had settled and stopped shaking, he turned towards Banes, sat expectantly in the passenger seat, a seat which was little more than a deck chair.

'She's sold it.'

'*Sold it?* Who has she sold it to? It's worthless to anyone not in the know!'

'At a jumble sale.'

Banes buried his hands deep into the pockets of his duffel coat, one of them gripping the hammer. He looked around him, there was no one in sight. They were in Parker's pale-blue 2CV. They had agreed not to look at each other's painting until they had all three together. That was Banes' idea; he didn't trust Stephen Parker, but only because he didn't trust anyone. And he suspected that Parker didn't trust him. And with all those letters after his name, he can't be a complete idiot, thought Banes. So he believed that the suggestion would lull the lecturer into a nice false sense of security, give him the impression that they were equal partners in this exciting little venture, as he was sure Parker viewed it. Nothing could be further from the truth as far as Banes was concerned.

But now all that had changed. Now there was no third painting. Just the two. Maybe Kevin Wheaton was right, thought Banes, maybe it's all pointless? As simple-minded as Kevin seemed at times, his criminal acumen was gleaned from the best of them. And going after something that may or may not exist might not be the best use of his time . . .

He turned to Parker, who had just finished lighting up that pipe of his. Like some stinking old compost heap in a barrel. As Parker gripped the briar shank of his pipe for a long draw, Banes gripped the hickory haft of his hammer and was about to draw it out of his coat pocket—

'Lucky for us I know who she sold it to.'

'*What?*'

Parker stopped inspecting the burning embers of his pipe, and turned towards his passenger, who was now breathing heavily.

'Oh yes, I managed to get that out of her. Charles Wilkes. He's an artist, or certainly professes to be. He has a gallery and craft shop in Gisborough, the next village up from Ivan's. He sells his paintings there, mainly local scenery.'

'If he's an artist, what would he want it for . . . You don't think he knows about it?'

'No, why would he?'

'You said he lives near Ivan. Maybe they were friends, maybe they used to meet up for a drink? Maybe Ivan got drunk one night and told him about the paintings?'

'That's an awful lot of maybes. In academic terms, one needs more solid empirical evidence to consider it a thesis.'

Banes ran his tongue around his gums on hearing this. 'This isn't an academic exercise. And what I've discovered in life, *real* life, not books, is that it's the "maybes" that can get you what you want, and the "maybes" that can get you hanged.'

Parker considered this. It didn't seem to make a lot of sense to him, but he wasn't about to debate the point. 'Sally sold the painting to him for ten pence.'

'Then if we offer him twenty, he's made a profit, hasn't he?'

'Yes. Although he might put it in his shop. Though I can't imagine he'll sell it to anyone else.'

'That could be another *maybe* he will, *maybe* he won't. But we need to stop that happening.'

The urgency in Banes' voice alerted Parker to the danger, so he turned the key in the ignition and the 2CV rattled into action.

Friday (3)

Denton CID had a list of hardcore activists who were to be brought to Eagle Lane station and questioned immediately. Some had a criminal record, others had affiliations to groups known to advocate the violent overthrow of the system. These ranged from the Red Hammer socialist group to Anarchy in the UK Today!

Frost was without political prejudice, apart from the politics that traded on people's prejudice, but he still wasn't happy about Operation Country Mile. It seemed to be persecuting people for their beliefs, not their actions. This lot were protesting because of something they believed in – and the powers that be were collecting their personal information for what? Frost didn't quite know. Subversive? Hardly, he thought. There were some bad apples who would get agitated at the opening of an envelope if they thought they could get in a fight with the police. But most were just ordinary decent middle-class citizens imbued with the very English spirit of protest, from the Levellers of the 1640s, through the Kinder Scout Mass Trespass of 1932, to Ban the Bomb more recently. Not a lot had changed. But right now, even he had to admit, he was more than happy to have a list of names in front of him. It gave them a good starting point.

At the camp around the Jarrett & Sons site they managed to find five of the ten they were after. They were summarily pulled from their tents and brought in for questioning. It was still early enough for most of them to be caught with their pants down and tucked up in their sleeping bags. None of them had time to 'flush their stash', and most of them were caught in possession of lumps of hash, about the same size and consistency as Oxo cubes, and sealed in clingfilm. There were also Dexies and amphetamines to be found in the pockets of punked-out and studded black leather motorcycle jackets, stencil-sprayed with CRASS, GBH, Dead Kennedys, Anti-Nowhere League, Thatcher on Acid, to name but a few.

The drugs stash proved good leverage. Those questioned all denied having anything to do with the abduction of Ruby Hanson. Most agreed it wasn't a bad idea, the type of action that needed to happen, but they wouldn't actually do such a thing themselves. Frost believed them, they looked like they'd have messed it up if they'd tried. But as the team expected, when threatened with some real prison time for drug possession, they all turned on each other. They may have looked like the cast of *Mad Max 2*, but all lacked that real apocalyptic edge, and all wanted to be back in their nice little middle-class homes when their camping trip was over.

One name kept coming up, though. One who was just a little bit more extreme than the others. He took things a little further than most. But no one knew where he was. Word was, he'd gone deep into the woods. Gone upriver, as it were. Gone native. He knew how to survive out in the open. Word was, he didn't even need a tent, or a sleeping bag, or takeaways delivered from any of Denton's pizza parlours, chicken joints, burger bars, or Frost's beloved Jade Rabbit Chinese restaurant. The town's thriving takeaway industry was doing good business with the protestors, delivery boys were run off their wheels. There was always a queue at the phone box in the woods car park, from which people hungrily placed their orders. But not this fellow; word was, he had the knowledge to survive out in nature on a diet of berries, selected mushrooms, skinned rabbit, baked hedgehog and water from the streams.

His name was Degsy.

She could hear them arguing, voices raised. They were using words that Mummy and Daddy would never use. She heard them make a phone call to someone. When she pressed her ear against the door she could hear the static crackly voice of the person at the other end of the line; he too was angry, and very loud, yelling at the men in the next room. That's what really frightened her. It was the not knowing what she had done to make them all so angry at her.

Ruby moved away from the door and covered her ears and sat on the bed until she could hear the shouting no more. The room was small, a lot smaller than her one at home. And it was old, and a bit smelly. There were mottled black patches in the corners, and the crispy old wallpaper was coming away from the wall, and she could see the wood coming through where the plaster had crumbled away. There was a small electric fire, two blazing orange bars, but the heat didn't travel very far. She kept her red coat on, and her mittens that Mummy had stitched into the sleeves so she wouldn't lose them.

The single bed she sat on was hard and lumpy. Like the one in hospital when she had her appendix out. Her feet didn't touch the ground. They'd given her a glass of milk and some biscuits. She told them she only drank milk with banana Nesquik. They didn't say anything, they just looked at each other. Ruby couldn't tell if they were angry because they were wearing masks, rubber masks of the same man. The face was of a man on the telly, not the good telly, but the telly that Mummy and Daddy watched in the evenings. They liked the programme, it made them laugh. It was like a *Muppet Show* for grown-ups with politicians instead of Kermit and Miss Piggy. She couldn't remember his name right now . . . but he was the president of America, she thought. He had a nice smiling face, and the mask captured his likeness perfectly.

The two men had been in the room twice today: the first time when they left the milk and a plate of biscuits on the side table; then about an hour later, when they came back with the banana Nesquik and stirred it into the milk. Then they left, and locked the door behind them.

Mummy and Daddy never lock her bedroom door. When she was smaller she couldn't sleep when the door was closed. They used to leave a small light on in the hallway. But now, at home, she closes the door, she closes it so she can't hear Mummy and Daddy. It upsets her, it makes her cry.

Mummy and Daddy are like the people in the American president's masks now. They argue. They argue a lot, and they shout, at night, when they think she's asleep. She sneaks out of her room at night and crawls along the landing to the top of the stairs to listen to them. She gulps down her breath, trying not to cry, trying not to shout out to them to stop. Because little Ruby knows, she now knows that Daddy doesn't love Mummy any more. And that they would soon not be living together in their house any more, the house that Daddy built for them. Mummy has been shouting at him, telling him that he'll never see Ruby again, she'd make sure of that.

Ruby wondered if they would come to collect her, or if she would never see them again.

Banes snapped away on his Olympus Trip 35. He thought he'd be needing it to take some photos of the paintings. Now he was in the academic's Citroën 2CV taking snaps of Parker, who was on the other side of the road, talking to Charles Wilkes. Banes could see it wasn't going well. Wilkes' little gift shop-cum-art gallery was closed, and Parker was talking to him on the doorstep of his flint-walled cottage, attached to the shop. The road, little more than a lane, was lined with similar old cottages and a tea room, a second-hand bookstore and a bric-a-brac shop.

The village of Gisborough was picturesque and old. And so was Charles Wilkes, with his generous unnaturally auburn curls hanging down in clusters like bunches of grapes, and a paisley cravat tied around his long neck; he cut a tall, eccentric, bohemian figure, straight out of the Bloomsbury set. But for all the flamboyancy and dabbling with hair dye, he must have been in his seventies.

Old and intractable. Whatever Parker was saying to him, it was going down like a chipped cup of cold tea. Banes tutted and clicked away, as a flustered Parker gesticulated wildly, until the old man gave him a two-fingered salute and slammed the door in his face.

Well done, cracking job, you idiot, thought Banes, as he watched Parker ringing the man's doorbell again. Banes had suspected that Parker wouldn't handle it well, but he'd let him have a go anyway. Trouble with Parker was, at his core, he was a teacher. He was used to a bunch of snot-nosed students hanging on his every word whilst he pontificated. He seemed mild-mannered and ineffectual enough, at first glance, but take him out of his comfort zone, out into the real world away from his ivory tower, and he just sort of fell apart. Got all niggly and flustered and couldn't con a toddler out of a jelly baby.

Banes laughed as Parker now banged on Wilkes' door with his fist. The door flew open and Charles Wilkes came out, with his dog, a yappy Jack Russell, straining at the leash to bite Parker. The good doctor of philosophy jumped back into the road. And the door closed on him again. Old Wilkes may have looked a bit of an intellectual old fop, but he obviously had steel running through him and wasn't to be messed with. Banes put the camera back in his pocket.

'Bloody hell, *bloody*, bloody . . .'

'That went well, then,' said Banes, his voice brimming with contempt and sarcasm as Parker got into the car and petulantly slammed the door shut, further profanities falling from his twisted mouth.

'I went from a pound for his trouble to offering him two hundred pounds! Two hundred sodding pounds – and he said no. I begged him, said it was Vanessa's painting, sentimental value, gift from her dead husband, you know, really laid it on thick. And he still said no. How unbelievably heartless. Do you know what he said to me?'

'My lip-reading isn't what it used to be, but from here I got a pretty good idea.'

'He said it's too late.'

'What do you mean?'

'He agreed the painting was an abomination, but the only reason he bought it was because it was a ready-made stretched canvas and it was the perfect size. The old fool said that he's had an artistic breakthrough. He's entered a golden age and is producing some of his best work, and he's already started painting over the canvas.'

'He's painting over . . . over the painting?'

'Yes. Happens all the time with artists, he says, artists are always on the lookout for cheap paintings, they're cheaper than buying blank canvases sometimes.'

'So even if we get the painting, he's painted over it? We're fucked!'

Parker flinched, as if he'd never ecountered such fury before. Parker stopped looking at Banes, and stared ahead of him, like he didn't want any distractions as a thought struck him: 'No. No, we're not. At the university we run an MA in art restoration, we could get the new paint removed. They do it all the time. They unearthed a lost series of Dutch old masters under some 1940s paintings of cats in baskets; they'd been found in a shed, covered in filth. Sometimes the back of a painting can tell you as much about it as the front: the wooden frame, the type of materials used in the canvas, the age. One of the lab guys was telling me about it the other week . . .' Parker rapped his knuckles on the steering wheel in frustration and muttered some curses. '. . . But it's all a moot point, as we can't get it anyway.'

Banes ignored Parker's defeatist hissy fit and gave some thoughtful little nods at the idea of restoring the painting. It made sense. He knew they could perform wonders these days, find out all sorts of things.

'We need to get in there and get that painting back.'

'How are we going to do that? I offered him a small fortune, he could buy a hundred blank canvases to paint his master-pieces on.'

'Don't worry. Where there's a will, there's a way.'

'He's a deluded artist, there isn't a painting in his shop he'd sell at that price. He's . . . he's crazy.'

So am I, so am I, said Banes to himself.

'We're a peaceful protest protecting our mother. Mother Nature. When she cannot speak for herself, we shall stand up and speak for her. Because when she is gone, there will be no one left to speak. We don't want any trouble.'

'Then put down the weapon,' called out PC Simms.

Frost and Clarke exchanged quizzical looks at this.

The protestor looked at the branch he was fanning the camp-fire with. 'It's not a weapon.'

'It's a stick and you're pointing it at me, which makes it an offensive weapon.'

Frost and Clarke, who were just behind Simms, waited to see how far the keen PC would take this.

'I'm not pointing it at anyone,' said the man with a long grey ponytail worn under a broad-brimmed bushman's hat. 'I'm just holding it, and it's got leaves on it, hardly an offensive weapon. It's not even a stick. It's a branch.'

The other three men and two women gathered around the fire for warmth all hummed and muttered in agreement.

Frost put his hand on Simms's shoulder and whispered, 'Stand down, son, I think they've got a point. You couldn't beat a carpet with that, never mind an overzealous PC who's about to blow his shot at promotion.'

The DI stepped forward into the small clearing where the tents were pitched. There were four small tents, army-style ones, and one big enough to stand up in, with clear plastic windows. Frost couldn't help but think it looked like the set of *M*A*S*H*. These people were in it for the long haul.

'We're not here to break up the Swamp, no matter what Radar over there says.' Whilst Frost chuckled, they looked at each other blankly. 'You don't watch much TV . . . ?'

'We don't have a television set. Not even at home,' said a woman, also with a long grey ponytail worn under a bushman's hat.

Clarke distributed some missing-person pictures of Ruby Hanson and filled them in on the case. It seemed they hadn't been listening to the radio either. They looked genuinely disturbed by the fate of the little girl, and that the protestors had fallen under suspicion.

'I don't for a second believe that any of you had anything to do with it,' said Frost, 'and I can see you're as appalled as us. But I'm sure you understand just how vital it is we get Ruby back with her family, so anything you can help us with, we'd be grateful.' They all readily agreed: anything they could help with they would. 'One person keeps coming up in our enquiries, a man in his twenties who goes by the name of Degsy?'

This got a reaction. The man with the *stick* and the bushman's hat spoke for the group. 'He was here, we asked him to leave. To be honest, our ethos is that through persistent peaceful protest, we will prevail. He thought force and violence were the way forward. He wanted a revolution and the violence that came with it, and he was using the woods as an excuse for that, we believed. We told him, we are all one with nature, every living thing. We asked him to leave our camp and he did.'

'Can you give us a description?' asked Clarke.

The tall 'bushman' gave a description that pretty well matched what they'd already been told by others. But still no one seemed to know his real name, assuming 'Degsy' wasn't it.

'Do you have any idea where he is now?' asked Frost.

A tall skinny man leaning on a hand-tooled wooden crook, or as Simms would probably have it, a Kalashnikov, pointed northwards.

Frost, Clarke and Simms followed the directions and headed deeper into the woods. The peaceful protestors had told them that there were a few people setting up camps further into the terrain, so that if the main body of them couldn't hold the line, they would be a reserve force to keep up the good fight.

It had been a while since Frost had been into Denton Woods, certainly this far in. But at this stage it wasn't just the woods that were being searched for Ruby; already civilian volunteers were sweeping the parks, fields, the wilder environs of Denton and even the Southern Housing Estate. There was always a sense of desperation when these scenes were shown on the TV, it looked like the last resort when the police had run out of ideas or options. But in reality, the desperation was always there from the start. It was just a horrible fact in these cases, that from the outset every wheelie bin and tip and skip were searched.

'Look at this,' said Simms, pointing into the distance at another clearing.

Frost and Clarke caught up with Simms, who was leading the way. The great outdoors seemed to suit him, and his sheer enthusiasm and ambition were becoming as exhausting as they were exasperating.

'What am I looking at?' queried Sue Clarke.

'Exactly!' said Simms, as he started to pull away some branches and hold them up.

'Oh, more deadly weapons. Nice one, Simmo. Best take them with us in case we come across a bear or a pack of wolves . . .'

'I heard there was still an escaped panther from Denton zoo on the loose,' said Frost.

Clarke said, 'I heard there's definitely wild boar still out here.'

Frost laughed. 'Big Foot.'

'King Kong, or the—'

Sue Clarke stopped talking and Frost stopped laughing as Simms pulled away more branches to reveal a car. A red Ford Cortina with a black vinyl roof, and behind that, again almost totally obscured by branches, fern fronds, bracken and anything else that could be thrown at it to camouflage it from view, was the cream 1972 model Abi Monza 1200 CT touring caravan. The car and caravan had travelled as far up the muddy track as they possibly could before the woods had closed in and made it impassable.

Simms held up a branch, and pointed to the white flesh of the wood where it had been torn from a tree. 'Freshly cut, about twenty-four hours ago, I'd say. It's still sappy.'

'Just like you, Simms.'

Clarke laughed, but couldn't help but look impressed. 'Your Boy Scout training is really paying off, Simmo.'

Frost made his way around to the door of the little cream-coloured caravan. 'Hold on to your woggle, I'm going in.' With his gloved hand, the DI tried the door handle. It opened. Frost gave a dispiriting groan.

'What's wrong?' asked Clarke.

'Last time I got this lucky with a door being unlocked was in Norwood. You wait here.'

Frost pushed the wobbly aluminium door and stepped carefully into the caravan alone, and found Florence Wheaton's son in much the same condition as he had found her – dead.

Kevin Wheaton was face down on the linoleum floor, a floor that was almost completely red where he had bled out from deep and penetrating wounds. By the look of the head trauma, Frost straight away suspected the same weapon had been used on both Kevin and his mother. A cluster of blows had reduced the back of his head to a pulpy mess. There was blood, splinters of bone and fragments of brain matter splattered on the walls.

By the position of the wounds on the head, and the body on the floor, it looked like Kevin had been sitting down when he met his fate, his head bowed.

There was a *Daily Express*, soaked in blood, lying on the lino. It was open at a report of the murder of his mother. Frost took a sharp intake of breath and blew out a tremulous stream of air, as a genuine cold charge travelled up and down his spine. He felt nauseous. Not just because of the carnage in the caravan, but because of the heartless distraction he believed the killer had used. Did the killer hand Kevin the paper because he knew his victim would dip his head in grief? A distraction. But it had its own macabre logic. If the killer was of average height, because of the limited size of the caravan, he'd be unable to fully raise his arm, so he would need his victim to be seated, bowed, to inflict the fatal blows. A skilful, calculating and practised killer, thought Frost.

Also capable of abducting and killing a child? Without a doubt. They had come out to the woods to find Ruby Hanson's abductor, and had discovered the Norwood killer. Were they one and the same?

'What is it, guv?'

'Jack?'

The voices of his colleagues outside the caravan broke his gruesome but necessary train of thought. He stepped back out of the doorway, and closed the tinny little door behind him. If you didn't have to see it, you were better off not seeing it.

'Kevin Wheaton?' asked Clarke.

Frost nodded. 'Same as his mum. I think we've got a psychopath on our patch.'

The crack of a twig sounded like a gun discharging, such was the silence and solemnity of that brief moment as they reflected on the danger they faced. The three of them turned sharply in the direction of the sound, and saw a crouched black-clad figure dart into the undergrowth away from them. For a moment they thought it could have been an animal, even the escaped panther that had forced the zoo to close down in '79, or one of the fictional beasts they'd teased Simms with. It was getting dark now, and the tree canopy made everything darker. They took a collective sharp breath and went after whatever it was.

Frost stopped Clarke. 'You stay here, but don't go in the caravan.'

'Sod that, Jack, I'm not staying here.'

Frost got her point. 'Fair dos.'

Simms was already disappearing into the gloom of the dense woods, torch in hand, again leading the way. Frost soon lost sight of him. He called out to the young PC, but nothing came back.

'Over there!' Clarke pointed to a flash of light.

'And there!' Frost pointed to where, about thirty feet away, a torch beam raked the trees. The two shards of light circled each other, then one shot off, with the other giving chase.

Then there was a sharp cry – *Jesus!* – and one light disappeared. Frost and Clarke heard a pained whinnying sound. They raced towards it, the bushes slowing them down, tearing at their clothes.

'Simmo?'

'Over here . . . Jesus wept!'

'Hold on, Simms, we're coming!'

When they reached the young PC, he was rolling around on the ground, as much as he could. His left foot was ensnared in some kind of animal trap. The trap was old and rusted, but very heavy. There was no blood.

'You're all right, Dave,' soothed Clarke. 'Can you move your toes?'

Simms nodded.

Frost bent down to look at the damage. 'If you can move your toes, it's nothing serious. That'll teach you to go charging off. You should always keep close to your colleagues, no matter where you are. Got it?'

Simms nodded again.

Frost tried to open the trap's jaws, but to no avail. The mechanism had stopped short of sinking its blunted brown teeth into Simms's foot, and had probably tripped him as much as trapped him. But it was proving equally intractable in freeing him.

'We'll need some WD40 to get that off.' Frost said to Clarke, 'You wait here.'

'Where are you going to get WD40 from around here?'

'Don't be a wally, I'm not, I'm just saying. I'm going after him, or whatever it is!'

There was no argument this time from Clarke, as Frost grabbed the torch that was still in Simms's hand, and took off after whoever it was disappearing down the narrow path.

Clarke made sympathetic faces at Simms, who was now looking more embarrassed than pained. 'How do you feel, mate?'

'To be honest, I think I can wiggle my foot out of it.'

'Then get wiggling.'

Simms sat up and started to pull his foot out of his wellington boot. It slipped out easily enough, just serving to deepen his blushes.

'Ahh! . . . *Gordon bleedin' Bennett!*' came a cry in the distance. Frost was the only person Clarke knew who still used that arcane expression.

She stood up and headed in the direction the cry had come from. Simms, leaving his welly in the trap, hobbled after her. About seventy yards away, Clarke saw the flicker of torchlight; it was climbing a tree. What the hell is he doing up there? thought Clarke.

'Jack?'

'*Down here!*'

Simms had caught up and was at her side. They looked around at each other, trying to work out where the voice was coming from. 'Where are you?'

'*Don't come any closer! . . . I've fallen in.*'

Clarke and Simms dipped their heads down to where the

voice sprang from. Not the tree in the distance, but a hole in the ground. Frost had fallen into another trap, a covered pit.

'You all right?' asked Clarke.

'Silly bloody question,' Frost said, slowly getting to his feet and straightening up in staggered stages of grimacing pain. 'My back . . . my bloody back . . . just as it was getting better.'

Clarke looked around at Simms, who wore the same expression as Frost, and was rubbing his ankle. Useless, she thought, the pair of them, bloody useless.

'Get me out of here!'

The pit was about twelve foot deep, and about that again wide, and sheer and slippery on all sides.

'How?'

'Is there a ladder?'

'A *ladder*?'

'I don't know . . . a rope ladder or something . . . how about some rope?'

'Oh yeah, the rope ladder, it's in the same place I found the WD40 to get Simms out of the trap.'

'Yeah?'

'No, you *wally*. You'll have to wait here. I'll go back to the car and call it in.'

'You can't leave me here . . . Can you?'

'Teach *you* to go charging off,' muttered Simms.

Friday (4) _____

'I didn't do it, I swear I didn't do it!'

'Didn't do what?'

'Didn't take the girl! I'll admit to everything else, but not the girl.'

'We're not interested in anything else,' said Frost, 'we're only interested in the girl.'

Frost and Clarke were in Interview Room 1, with a pale and frightened-looking Gordon Alistair Dellinpile, otherwise known as Degsy. Frost suspected it was a self-appointed nickname, much in the same way he always suspected that Sting had called himself Sting. His only interest in Sting being the name of his band, but it irked Frost; you shouldn't get to pick your own nickname. Frost hadn't picked 'Jack', that was the work of some genius primary-school wit pointing out the bleedin' obvious. Both Sting and Degsy obviously wanted to get away from Gordon. Posh-boy Degsy was straining for working-class street cred; Sting, obviously, and without any irony, was straining for cool.

Frost refused to call him Degsy. Gordon Alistair Dellinpile, who was twenty-three, had turned down a solicitor or any kind of legal assistance whatsoever. He said he wanted to come clean, said he wanted to help with the enquiry, as he'd realized the error of his ways. But what became most clear was that Gordon Alistair 'Degsy' Dellinpile didn't want his parents to know where he was, or what he'd been up to, as it might interfere with his annual allowance from his trust fund.

There he sat, eyes brimming, his pinched little public-school face twitching with trepidation, looking faintly ridiculous in his anarchist's gear – black jeans, shirt, biker jacket, twelve-eyelet Doc Martens, and eyeliner that was now smudged.

Laid out on the table in plastic evidence bags was the same stationery as had been used for the blackmail note. It had been found in Dellinpile's rucksack, which he'd stashed up a tree. A tree he'd been hiding and sleeping in, with a platform he'd fashioned from some branches he'd rather expertly woven together. It even came with its own pull-up rope ladder. The very ladder Jack Frost could have made use of to get out of the hole he'd fallen in. Luckily, he wasn't down there too long. Clarke had made her way back to the car and alerted Eagle Lane to their location, and predicament. Soon uniform were swarming in the woods, and Dellinpile was discovered up his tree, the tree Frost had seen him climbing by torchlight, just before he fell in. If Dellinpile had switched his torch off, Frost would never have seen him or been able to find his hideout.

At first Dellinpile refused to come down. Then Frost said he'd cut the tree down himself, with an axe he kept in the car, and he couldn't rule out what he'd then do with the axe. Dellinpile scuttled down the tree as fast as a squirrel.

'I heard about the little girl on my transistor radio last night. Who she was . . . that she was the architect's daughter. I thought I could use it to our advantage.'

'Whose advantage?'

'The cause.'

'This cause, is it organized?'

He shrugged. 'Not really. No one else knew I did it. There's only a few of us who really know how to protest against this kind of stuff, the rest are just amateurs.'

'Or just law-abiding citizens,' countered Clarke, 'who probably have a lot more influence on changing things than you do.'

'What about the bear trap, and the pit?' asked Frost.

'I thought if anyone came after me, I could slow them down.'

Clarke said, 'Oh, Mr Dellinpile, you certainly did that.'

Frost ignored Clarke's jibe.

Dellinpile bowed his head in shame. 'Sorry.'

'Sorry are you, sunshine, is that right? You could have taken PC Simms's leg off with that thing.'

'I don't think it's a bear trap.'

'It was old enough to be one, when bears roamed Denton Woods. How long have you been up the tree?'

Dellinpile raised his eyes from his bootlaces, still unable to look the DI in the face, and examined his ragged nails that had chipped black nail varnish on them. 'A few days. Three or four.'

Frost leaned across the table and got in his face. 'Bear traps, digging pits, sleeping up in tree houses. Anyone would think you're feral, raised by wolves, a sort of Home Counties Mowgli. But you're not, are you? You're a well-educated and well-to-do lad from fine upstanding stock. Your father is Sir Malcolm Dellinpile, the renowned surgeon at King's Hospital. Your mother was the lady mayoress of—'

'I know who they are.'

'So where did you learn all this, then?'

'All what?'

'All this Trapper John stuff. Without being too judgemental, most kids in Cure T-shirts and black eyeliner can barely get the cap off the Evo-Stik to sniff it, never mind construct reasonably sophisticated tree houses. I mean, we're not talking the des res of the Swiss Family Robinson, but it wasn't bad.'

Dellinpile managed to look both proud and ashamed. 'I learned it at boarding school. They made us spend half the week camping in the grounds, which were considerable. Joining the army cadets was obligatory. Almost everyone who went there ended up at Sandhurst, then a commission and off to foreign lands to kill people and spread their despicable imperialism.'

'Have you ever killed anyone?'

'*What?*' He blew out a blast of air that flapped his lips. 'No, of course not.' Dellinpile raised his black spiky head and looked up at Frost, saw he wasn't joking. He glanced around to Clarke, and saw she wasn't smiling, either.

Frost said, 'Tell us about the caravan.'

'What caravan?'

'The caravan that you covered, camouflaged, just like you did the pit I fell into.'

Degsy shrugged. 'I don't know what you're talking about.'

'You've been in the woods for three, four days. You've set up traps, were building a little tree house for yourself, had made the woods your home – and about a hundred yards from your tree, there was a cream caravan. Not big, two berths. But big enough to notice.'

Dellinpile shook his head.

Next to the plastic evidence bag was an A4 Manila envelope. Frost opened it up and laid out the four Instamatic photos that had been taken of the inside of the caravan.

Gordon Alistair Dellinpile's purposefully pale and intro-spective face now looked bleached and bloodless, as he inspected the carnage in the photos.

'What are these? Who is this?' Dellinpile's voice was now threaded with genuine fear.

'This – this is who we found in that caravan.'

'So . . . What's this got to do with me? I just wrote a letter to the police . . . That's what this is about, right? The letter? I've said I'm sorry . . . I really—'

'That's enough, Gordon. We're not interested in apologies, you can save those for the judge at sentencing.'

Dellinpile stifled some tears, snorted back up some snot from his runny nose, and really did look distressed.

Frost didn't let up. 'We found a bow and arrow in your ruck-sack, up in your tree. Sounds like a kid's toy, but it isn't, this one looks like a proper one. And a large hunting knife.'

'I'd never use it . . . It's just a tool for cutting wood and things.'

'Things?'

'The plan was to forage, maybe snag a squirrel or rabbit if I couldn't get to the shops, skin it and cook it.'

Clarke joined in. 'Learned that at school, did you, snagging squirrels and skinning them? How about the bear trap and the pit? Bit big for squirrels and rabbits?'

'It was . . . it was . . .'

'What, Gordon?' pressed Clarke. 'A *prank*? A bit of a public-school lark?'

'I wouldn't do that . . .' He pointed at the photos. '. . . I *couldn't* do that.'

Gordon Alistair Dellinpile's head swivelled from side to side, trying to find an understanding face between Frost and Clarke. All he got was hard stares. His shoulders went first, juddering up and down as the tears began to fall.

'I'm going to terminate this interview,' said Frost. 'And I would suggest that you make use of that phone call and contact your father. Tell him to get the most expensive lawyer he can find.'

Dellinpile was then taken to his cell, crying and protesting his innocence of everything, apart from everything that he'd already confessed to being guilty of. Which was more than enough to bang him up in the cells for the night. They wanted to make him as uncomfortable as possible, what with PC Simms now limping around Eagle Lane with a bruised ankle. And Frost lurching around with the now familiar stiff upright gait, due to having freshly aggravated his back injury.

Frost came through into the incident room, his Doc Martens leaving a trail of muddy prints on the grey carpet tiles. Most were far too busy to notice him. But those that did tittered with laughter at the sight of him, until the DI fixed them with a don't-even-think-about-it death stare. He headed straight over to John Waters' desk.

'Got a job for you.'

Waters turned, suppressed laughter, then asked, 'What the hell happened to you?'

'Didn't you hear? I fell down a hole.'

'You look like you've been digging one.'

'Never mind that. I want you to ring Longthorn pronto. Get as much information as you can about the comings and goings of all their staff in the last . . . say, six months. Pay special attention to those who left recently. But mum's the word, this is just between me and you.'

'Gotcha.'

'You need to talk to a Dr Graham Edmunds, the head honcho there. Tell him we've just discovered Conrad Wilde's frequent visitor at Longthorn, Kevin Wheaton, murdered in Denton Woods.'

'Are you sure you're not looking for one of the patients?'

'Maybe. Or maybe the lunatics have taken over the asylum.'

Waters jotted down the info. Frost glanced up and saw Superintendent Mullett approaching.

'Just like they have in this place,' muttered the DI as he made his way over to the superintendent. It was 5.30 – Mullett was usually seen easing himself into his maroon Audi 4000 S about this time for the leisurely drive home back to leafy North Denton.

'Still here, sir?'

Mullett looked Frost up and down, and took a deep measured breath, as if trying to calm himself – count to ten, man. He gave his habitual withering stare of disgust at Frost's familiar less-than-orthodox attire of battered bomber jacket and equally battered cords. To Mullett, the DI looked like his only business in a police station was to be lined up in an ID parade, not leading an investigation. But what really got Mullett's goat were the obnoxious pillar-box-red scarf and cherry-red Doc

Martens. All of which Frost was wearing now, and covered in mud.

Getting Frost out of the pit, for his rescuers, had proved tricky, and messy, and funny. Watching the DI trying to scramble up the walls had elicited laughs from most of the Eagle Lane uniforms present at the scene. Frost swore revenge on them all. Eventually, they had to use a rope tied around his chest to pull him up, which at times made him look like the losing side in a tug of war. Still, all in the line of duty.

'I need a word, please, Jack.'

'Sir.'

'If you even so much as look at one of the chairs in my office, much less try and sit on one, I'll have your badge and your pension.'

'Fair enough, sir.'

Clive Banes sat in his white panel van, a full-size Bedford CF. It had been good to him over the years. Even acted as a home at one time or another, when he'd travelled up and down the country looking for 'interesting projects' to busy himself with. Sleeping in it was no problem. He'd learned you could stretch out in it quite happily, no problem at all. And having never really had a real home, the mobility of the van had the obvious advantages of one without any of the drawbacks. Home and creature comforts, he didn't miss any of those, had never really known them. And for some reason, the van offered an anonymity that cars lacked – any car – with its particular colour, make and model. People just didn't take any notice of white vans. You could follow someone for hours in one. And in worker's overalls, a yellow high-vis vest, a hard hat, and with a tool belt around your waist, you quite literally didn't exist.

So as he watched Charles Wilkes lock up his premises, he was sure that the painter hadn't noticed him. Wilkes pulled a ring of keys out of his coat pocket and doubled-locked what looked like a heavy mortice lock. Banes saw the red box on the wall above the door, a burglar alarm. Banes was many things, but a skilled burglar he was not. He was missing the services of Kevin Wheaton already, he thought, with a not completely ironic smile on his mouth.

Wilkes had his dog with him, the lively and yappy Jack Russell. Banes liked dogs, definitely more than cats. The scratches and bite marks on the inside of his wrist from his last encounter with a cat, in West Norwood, were still unusually red and livid. But this dog, the Jack Russell, alarmed Banes as much as the red box above the door. It looked noisy.

Banes got out of the van, made his way over the road and waited at the bus stop with Wilkes. There were five others forming a loose queue, but there was no tiresome conversation about waiting hours for a bus, then two turning up at once. They didn't even make eye contact. The number 12 to Denton town centre arrived and everyone got on.

Wilkes alighted from the bus at Market Square, and Banes followed him along a series of well-lit streets, full of people who'd knocked off from work, and young couples meeting up for dates.

The Coach and Horses was on Mantle Street, two doors down from the Denton Repertory Theatre. And into the pub he followed Wilkes and the dog. Inside was a shock of red: red flock wallpaper, red carpet and red velvet-covered bench seating. The occasional respite from the red came in the form of the theatre posters on the wall, and framed signed photos of the 'stars' from the theatre who had popped in for a tipple of port and lemon. Everyone from Roy Hudd and Emu to a young Peter O'Toole had graced its stage and trodden its boards. It seemed to be the preserve of regulars. Charles Wilkes ordered his drink, a bottle of stout, chatted with the barman, who he was on first-name terms with, then settled at a table with a cluster of friends.

Far from the curmudgeonly old git that Banes had witnessed on the doorstep with Parker, Wilkes was full of garrulous bonhomie. His voice was plummy and he seemed well educated.

The more that Banes considered him, the more he suspected that he could well have been friends with Ivan Fielding. In fact, this might very well have been a pub that Ivan frequented. The crowd Wilkes was seated with looked like a cast of interesting characters: late '50s Soho artists, wasted old writers, worn-out chorus girls, stage hands, resting actors gone to rack and ruin. All perfect company for an alky antiques dealer with a dark past. It was just the kind of demi-monde that Ivan Fielding would have sought out once he'd washed up near Denton.

'. . . I said to him, dear boy, the only difference between the saint and the sinner is that every saint has a past, and every sinner has a future!'

They all laughed as Wilkes took the credit for this lesser-quoted bon mot. But there was someone at the table who wasn't laughing, not even smiling. It was in fact glaring at Banes with a positive snarling menace across its muzzle.

The bloody dog. Whatever that sixth sense is, dogs have it, thought Banes.

'What can I get you, my friend?' asked the publican.

The dog barked, pulled at his leash and snapped at Banes.

'Plato!' called out Wilkes, pulling the dog back and petting him till his barks subsided into a sustained low growl, like an engine left turning over. 'What's wrong with you, boy, what's got into you?'

The publican said to Banes, 'He's got the hump with you all right – what did you say you wanted?'

Banes left the pub without saying a word.

'Tucked under the bench in the caravan we found a black plastic Gola sports bag with tools in it, burglar's tools, including a diamond-tipped glass cutter,' said Frost.

'Put all this together with the fact that he was best friends with Conrad Wilde, or like a son to him, and it looks like your theory is right, Jack.'

The Denton DI gave an appreciative gesture to his Norwood

counterpart, DI Garside, who, with Frost, was sitting in Superintendent Stanley Mullett's office. (The super had insisted Ms Smith put newspaper down on Frost's chair first.) Mullett considered the information before him, including from the scene-of-crime officers and Forensics reports, as well as other supporting evidence dredged up by Garside and his team investigating Florence Wheaton's murder.

Mullett put down the thickening case file and turned to the officers. 'Do we think that the killer of Florence Wheaton and her son Kevin has Ruby Hanson?'

Frost and Garside exchanged anxious looks. Frost said, 'Until we get the post-mortem report on Kevin to confirm that the same weapon was used on mother and son, we don't know for sure that it was the same killer. But from the initial inspection of the body, it looks like it.'

Mullett met this with a murmur of accord. Frost knew it was the kind of due diligence he enjoyed.

'As for Ruby,' continued Frost, 'Kevin Wheaton's caravan was parked up in the woods, not far from the protestors who have embedded themselves there. Ruby's father is the architect for the new housing development, so yes, there's an undeniable connection.'

'The one you have in custody?'

'Gordon Alistair Dellinpile, who we're holding as a suspect for the Kevin Wheaton killing, denies both the killing and the abduction – but admits to writing the letter that was addressed to you.'

'Who signed "Ruby" in blood?'

'Yes. But not Ruby's blood, not even animal blood. It's a vegetable dye. He lacks a credible alibi, but he seems to me an unlikely candidate for the abduction. He's a loner. My gut feeling is that more than one person, at least two, are involved in the kidnapping. But I don't want to turn him loose yet. I've been wrong before.'

Mullett nodded. 'Agreed.'

'Thought you would, sir,' muttered Frost under his breath.

'So how are we playing it?' asked Garside.

'A joint operation,' said Mullett. 'The killer of the Wheatons is obviously at large in the Denton area. We must find him before he kills again.'

Garside assented. 'We've been liaising with Suffolk police, and they've had a missing person just been reported by an ex-girlfriend of one Peter Allerton. He works at Longthorn Secure Hospital, in the canteen.'

Frost and Garside focused on Mullett. Eventually he spoke. 'What we don't want is the spectre of Ivan Fielding and Conrad Wilde, and this business from 1967, to colour this case. At this stage I'm only interested in getting Ruby Hanson back home, and the Wheatons' killer behind bars. Anything else is a distraction. Is that clear?'

Both inspectors gave solid nods in deference to Superintendent Stanley Mullett's clarity.

Frost was up before the wailing siren of his new digital alarm clock had time to pierce his subconscious. He'd replaced the old wind-up one – it was too easy to throw it across the room, which happened on a regular basis. This new one was plugged into the mains and could make tea for him, though he'd never put that function to use. The main thing was, it was too big to throw across the room.

The gods were smiling on him this morning – the Metro started up first time, and he hadn't bumped into Shirley, his neighbour from across the landing. He'd seen her collecting her two pints of full-cream, bending down in a revealing dressing gown, offering him a cuppa before he left. He'd always declined, it was easy to do so in the mornings, always in a hurry, things to do, people to see, crimes to solve. Shirley would give a deep heaving sigh when he hinted at his heroics on the streets of Denton.

The traffic was good, he beat every red light, and his parking space at Eagle Lane wasn't taken. And everyone was present and correct for the morning briefing in the incident room.

Frost stood at the board, where there was a new name written up in block capitals to accompany Ruby Hanson's: KEVIN WHEATON.

Frost briefed the team on the murder and told them they'd be working in tandem with DI David Garside from West Norwood CID. They were soon all up to speed on the case. And with the pictures of the horrific injuries that Kevin Wheaton and his mother, Florence, had sustained pinned up on the board too, everyone knew the killer had to be caught before he, literally, struck again.

Frost was just about to answer questions about the possibility of the Wheaton murders being connected to Ruby's disappearance, when Sue Clarke told him that Gail Hanson was on the phone, very distressed.

'It came yesterday, the second post.'

'Who else has touched it, read the letter?'

'Just Richard.'

'Where is he?'

Gail Hanson turned away from Frost, couldn't meet his eye. She went over to the window, perhaps hoping to see her daughter coming up the path. He repeated the question.

'He's gone into work,' she said, still averting her eyes. 'That's where he keeps all his paperwork, so he can organize getting a loan from the bank, paying the money . . . doing what they want.'

She collapsed rather than sat on the sofa and stared at what was on the smoked-glass coffee table before them.

It was an unwrapped brown paper parcel that contained the head of Little Miss Lucy, the Cabbage Patch Kid doll that Ruby had with her when she was snatched off the street. It had been a present for her birthday, some five months earlier. And in the short life of faddish toys and children's whims it had remained a favourite and a constant companion.

It was a special-edition doll, quite rare and sought after. With its head had come a note typed on a sheet of white A4 copy paper. The text's uniformity and lack of impression suggested to Frost that an electric typewriter or a word processor had been used to produce it.

The demand is for £70,000 in cash. To be delivered to a location you will be informed of soon. Somewhere you will know, somewhere you have been. There will be no need for hysterics, this is a business transaction. Do not call the police, or you know what will happen: her real head will be cut off. WE MEAN WHAT WE SAY.

On looking at the severed doll's head, its macabre aspect, all Frost could think about was the carnage in the caravan and in the bedroom in Norwood. The use of 'we' in the note went along with what he suspected, that there were at least two abductors. One driving the car, ready to pull away at speed, and one doing the actual snatch. Gail in her statement thought she had heard the car engine running whilst Ruby was being taken, and the tyres screeching almost as soon as the door slammed shut.

'Does your husband know that you've called us?' asked Susan Clarke.

Gail Hanson shook her head. 'I thought we should. He thought we should just do as they say. Pay them and get Ruby back.'

'That's a lot of money,' said Frost.

'Richard assured me he could get it, borrow against the house, the business, whatever it took. Nothing else matters, nothing.'

'You made the right decision calling us,' said Clarke.

Gail Hanson squeezed her eyes shut and gave a quick shake of her head. 'He'll go mad, Richard, when he finds out. We argued about it all night, but he was insistent. Kept saying we couldn't rely on you, we just had to pay.' She looked up at them. 'Sorry, I shouldn't be saying this.'

'We understand. We understand how you're both feeling,' assured Clarke.

'Now you need to call Richard,' said Frost. 'We need to make sure we're working together to get Ruby back. There's no need for who's responsible for taking Ruby to know that we know about this. Nothing else matters to us either, just getting your daughter back safely, that's the priority. Then we'll worry about the culprits. We've been in this situation before, we know how to handle it. OK?'

Mrs Hanson managed a small smile, like all her questions had been answered. 'That's what I said, we can't afford any mistakes . . . you have to know.'

Frost returned her smile with some encouragement on top. Then with his gloved hand Frost picked up the doll's head. Funny-looking thing, he thought, nothing like Tiny Tears, that's what all the girls had when he was at school. He never did work out how you filled them up. Did the head come off, like the top of a bottle? He glanced around to see Gail padding into the hallway to make the call.

'Gail, can you tell us where you got this doll from?'

'Richard got it for her.'

'Actually, don't call him. I'll go and see him. I have his work address.'

Clarke turned away from Gail Hanson and gave Frost a quizzical look.

DC Arthur Hanlon held the Hornby model of the Flying Scotsman with the reverence of an archaeologist who has just dug up a perfect and priceless Etruscan pot.

'Breaks my heart, it does, John, breaks my bloody heart.'

'What does?'

'The day I sold my train set. Had it set up in the spare room. Made un-spare by the arrival of Arthur Jnr.'

'You make him sound like an unwanted guest.'

'No, love him to bits, most of the time. Should have seen it, John, full steam ahead, it was magic. I had the OO gauge, all the scenery, the sidings, crossings, trees, bushes, the backs of houses – not just a train set, the whole world . . .'

'I had Subbuteo as a kid, I get it. Twelve teams, including Ajax for European nights. Had the Jules Rimet trophy. Had the stands, the floodlights, even had the little St John Ambulance men on the sidelines.'

Waters saw that Hanlon wasn't listening, as his gaze drifted into the middle distance, and the memories rolled back, like the wagons on his OO gauge.

Waters and Hanlon were in Chamleys & Co., Denton's premier toyshop on the high street. It had been there almost as long as the high street itself, and for a toyshop it had a sombre feel about it. With its dark wood and glass cabinets, it was very much from the Victorian era, and still sold wind-up Schuco tinplate toys and spooky-looking bisque dolls, as well as the more modern fare of My Little Pony, Atari, Fisher Price Ghetto Blasters, Light Sabers, Scalextric and the ubiquitous Cabbage Patch dolls.

'Here we are, gentlemen.'

Mr Chamley, fourth generation, emerged from the back room to rest a large red ledger on the counter. With his white hair and a white Laughing Cavalier beard, he had, appropriately enough, more than a touch of the Kris Kringle about him, though he was lacking the girth.

'Special edition, Cabbage Patch Kid, Little Miss Lucy. We were the only store in Denton that stocked them, not even Woolworths or Aster's could get their hands on them. We had five of them, we sold five of them. It does annoy me, they're no more special than any of the others, but they advertise them as such to drive up interest. Instils the collecting bug. That's what all the best toys do, make you want to collect them. Not even play with them, just collect.'

'Tell me about it,' murmured Hanlon, still lovingly holding the model train.

'That's quite some record you have there,' said Waters,

looking down at the neat entries. The hypnotically slanting writing looked like it was done with a calligraphy pen.

'We do all our own accounting, so it's best to keep it neat.' Mr Chamley ran a finger down a column and stopped abruptly about halfway down. 'We sold three for cash, and two on credit cards.'

'Do you have the names of the card holders?'

'Yes, I do. And I also have the names and addresses of the cash purchasers.'

Waters looked impressed, and took out his notebook to write down the details.

Mr Chamley became distracted by Hanlon fiddling with the locomotive he was holding, opening its doors, running it along his arm to test the wheels.

'Excuse me, officer, are you buying that locomotive?'

Arthur Hanlon looked at the model train in his hand like he would never put it down. 'The missus will kill me.'

Waters winked. 'Go on, Casey Jones, treat yourself.'

'Yes, yes, I bloody well will. I'm gonna start over again.'

'Were you ever going to tell us?'

Richard Hanson was angered to see Frost, and angered that his wife had gone against his strict instructions and called the police. The DI was on his own; he'd left Clarke with Gail Hanson, partly to monitor any phone calls and see if the 'alleged' abductor made any further contact. But also to make sure she didn't call her husband. Foretold is forewarned.

'Yes. Once Ruby was home. Then you could do as you pleased.'

'As I explained to your wife, we've done this before, Mr Hanson, and we will get her back. But for that to happen we need to work together, we need your complete cooperation.'

'I know what your job is, Mr Frost, and no offence, but you're not bloody Scotland Yard.'

'No, we're not, I think our clear-up rate per capita is far better. And it's *Inspector* Frost.'

Sometimes they need reminding, and this is one of those times, thought Frost, as he stood with Richard Hanson in the open-plan office of Hanson & Partners Architects. It was located on the ground floor of a building in Denton's plush new business park. The empty office was similar to Hanson's home, all polished minimalist chic, and steel-tubed black leather seating. On one of the walls something rather non-architectural caught Frost's eye. It was a huge black-framed poster of a striking Japanese girl in a weird-looking white dress, like some sort of parachute, and black shoes with corrugated platform soles that were so high that if she fell off them, she'd need the parachute to land safely. All made the more precarious because she already stood on a concrete block, like a plinth. Inscribed on the plinth was: 'Comme des Garçons Spring 1985'.

Frost didn't like trendy shit, and this stank of trendy shit. In the reception area, as well as all the usual architectural magazines there were copies of *The Face*, *Creative Review* and *i-D*. It made him wonder what the hell Hanson was planning for the new development in Denton Woods. Turning the beautiful ancient woodland into some concrete wasteland with smoked glass, steel and black everywhere to house designer-stubbled, Paul Smith-suited, Audi-driving, Bang & Olufsen-playing, Sade-listening, Filofax-carrying, Rolex-wearing yuppies. Still, back to the business in hand.

Hanson had stopped pacing up and down on the polished concrete floor, and was now slumped on a black leather sofa that had expelled a *whoosh* of air as he sat down. Frost placed himself opposite, careful not to expel a similar *whoosh*.

'What have you done so far, in terms of getting the money?'

'Called the bank manager. Luckily, he was in this Saturday. I have some money in my accounts, I can secure a loan. I can get it and I will get it, I must.'

Frost took the letter in its plastic evidence bag out of his jacket pocket and looked at it. 'The letter says that you're to deliver the money to "Somewhere you will know, somewhere you have been." Now, that could be interpreted as you knowing the abductors. How else would *they* know you've been there?'

Hanson bristled at this, looked pantomime confused. 'Or it could just mean that it will be in Denton. Which is obviously a place I know. What are you suggesting?'

Frost carried on reading: ' "There will be no need for hysterics, this is a business transaction." What do you think they mean by that?'

'That . . . that if I stay calm . . . I'll get my daughter back. What do you think it means?'

'Of course. It's an emotionally charged situation. Is there something we need to know, something you may think is none of our business, and may not have anything to do with your daughter?'

'I don't know what you mean.'

Frost let out his own *whoosh* of exasperated air, from his mouth, not the cushion. 'I think you do know, I'm talking about your private life, personal life, love life, to be frank. Any indiscretions we need to know about that may—'

'What the hell is this?'

'My colleague is asking your wife the same questions. We have to, it's procedure. And the tone of the letter leads me to believe it's a good idea. Because aspects of it, around the edges, sound personal. As we widen the search we also dig deeper – every aspect of your life will be inspected. We will be looking at your phone records, both at home and at work. It's a hoary old cliché, but the truth will out. In cases like this, it always does. And for your daughter's sake, sooner rather than later is the way to go.'

Richard Hanson didn't flinch at this. Not even a blink. It looked to Frost like he'd been expecting it. 'Yes. Yes, of course. If your colleagues are talking to Gail, I'm sure they'll find out she had an affair three years ago. His name was Jamie Bucknell, he was a teacher at Ruby's old school. We almost came to blows . . . Or, rather, I almost beat the crap out of him. The police were going to be called, but Bucknell certainly didn't want to take it any further. So the whole thing was dropped.'

'Nothing was reported to us. It's not on our database. We checked if you had a record, of course. What happened?'

'It was a bit of a scandal. I confronted him at the school. There were no kids around. I just . . . I pushed him over some desks. Like I said, someone saw me do it and reported it to the headmaster.' He expelled a short sour laugh. 'Just like school kids really, and someone told on me. Bucknell lost his job, they sacked him. Good job too. But it didn't end there.'

'How do you mean?'

'You know how mothers like to gossip at the school gates. It became impossible to keep it secret, so we took Ruby out of that school in Rimmington, and moved her to Mountview.' Richard Hanson, tearful now, sat forward on the sofa, elbows on knees, hands clenched, trying to hold it together, his voice laced with bitterness. 'But hey, it wasn't all Bucknell's fault, was it? Takes two to tango, as they say. She didn't love him or anything like that, said she didn't, anyway. Christ, I felt like killing him, but I didn't, obviously, just pushed him over a desk. He was . . . he was just a little guy, didn't look like much at all. I know how this will sound, arrogant, egotistical, but I just couldn't see what Gail saw in him. She said most of it was a cry for attention that just got out of hand, to punish me for neglecting her. The affair began about the same time I was starting out on my own, starting the business. I was working twenty-four seven, I was neglecting her, neglecting Ruby. She felt alone.'

'You forgave her, but things have never quite been the same since?'

'That's about right. Have you been there, Inspector?'

Frost couldn't quite remember, but he suspected that his late wife had, at one point, been seeing someone. He had no proof, just maybe some vague hope that she was. She probably deserved more than he'd been able to offer her at the time, wrapped up as he was in his job, like Hanson, twenty-four seven. He shook his head to answer him, not that Hanson was paying too much attention. He was too caught up in his own personal trauma.

Saturday (2)

Ruby took her ear away from the door and stepped back, careful not to tread on the creakiest of the floorboards. She was getting to know them by now. Some sounded like an alarm going off, and when she triggered it, the men in the next room would fall silent, like they knew she was listening. Sometimes the handle would turn and a head would pop around the door. A Ronald Reagan head. Ruby now remembered the name of the American President, and the TV show he was on, *Spitting Image*. He was funny on the TV, always forgetting things. Sometimes this Ronald Reagan here would ask if she needed anything. The voice was rough, but not unkind, there was no edge or threat of violence to it; in fact, it tried its best to sound nice and friendly.

The two Ronald Reagans had been on the phone again, but there was no shouting this time, either from the Ronald Reagans or from the man on the other end of the line, who, even though he was on the other end of the line and not in the room, managed to sound louder than the two Ronald Reagans.

Ruby thought the men sounded like Darren Blake's dad,

who was fat and had tattoos and ran a garage, and always tried to talk to Mummy at the school gates. And she always tried to avoid talking to him, because he was fat and had tattoos and ran a garage. Mummy described him as 'not really our kind'.

The men in the Reagan masks were funny. Sometimes they told each other jokes. Ruby didn't always understand them. She thought they played cards a lot, and probably for money, not chocolate buttons or counters like she did. There seemed to be a lot of disputes and swearing during these games, and often one of the men would reprimand the other, saying, 'Shut up, the kid will hear you!'

They smoked, a lot – cigars, she thought. She'd smelt cigars before. Granddad smoked them sometimes at Christmas and on his birthday only, otherwise Nanna would tell him off. The two Ronald Reagans were smoking them now. They seemed happy, like whatever problem they had, they'd sorted it out and come to some kind of agreement. Which made Ruby happy, or at least happier. She assumed that the dispute was about her. And she didn't like it when grown-ups shouted. She always knew that's when bad things happened.

She went over to the telly and turned it on. It was *Button Moon*, one of her favourite programmes. Even if she did feel she was too old for it now, it still made her laugh. She turned up the volume, as loud as it would go. Ruby then went over to the chest of drawers. It was empty and not very heavy, and she carefully pulled it away from the wall. She then removed the piece of carpet that was rotting and smelly and coming away from the floor. The floorboards were in similar condition to the carpet. The nails had rusted away, and the wood was rotten with damp.

Ruby had discovered all this yesterday, a day after they'd put her in the room. There was nothing else for her to do other than sit on the bed and cry, and by Friday she was sick of that, she'd done enough crying at home. So she searched every inch of the room for a possible escape route. The bed was too heavy and noisy to shift; it was set on these squeaky old castors that barely moved anyway. But the chest of drawers was made of flimsy grey plywood.

She peered down into the hole in the floor and saw there were shafts of light. This told her that there were gaps in the outside wall, or maybe some kind of window in a cellar. She also saw that there was a big enough space for her to crawl along. She quickly put the floorboards back in place, and also the damp, smelly patch of carpet, and the cheap little chest of drawers. She knew that one of the Ronald Reagans would soon be bringing in her elevenses of banana Nesquik and cookies.

She sat on the bed, trying to control her breathing. The butterflies in her tummy fluttered away because it was exciting, it was scary – but it was also, strangely, fun. She'd never really been on an adventure before, not like this, and now she was on one. It was like some of her favourite films: the end bit of *ET*, most of *Peter Pan*, or *101 Dalmatians* with Jasper and Horace now played by Ronald Reagans. And all of the Famous Five books she'd read. But this was real, and it was hers. Of course she was scared, but she also knew that if she wanted to get out of here, she would have to rely on her wits. The grown-ups weren't going to save her, they never did, they were always a bit useless in these situations and never around, or when they were they just panicked and cried and made all the wrong decisions. It was the kids who worked it out, it was the kids who saved the day.

'Ruby. It was all about Ruby. That's why . . . that's why I stopped the affair. It was nothing to do with Richard, no matter what he thinks.'

Gail Hanson took a sip of her coffee, and Sue Clarke did the same. They were both on the black leather sofas. The big shiny cafetière that sat on the smoked-glass coffee table was almost depleted.

'Tell me about Jamie Bucknell.'

'He was the opposite of Richard, in all ways. Maybe that was the attraction. He was modest, sensitive, attentive, and he listened. Of course, we met at Ruby's school, but I used to see him in the park, and we got talking. We'd meet up for a coffee and a chat.'

'When did it end?'

'Three years ago.'

'I'll ask again: when did it end?'

Gail Hanson's head drooped and she squeezed her eyes shut, as if to block out the reality of her situation. It didn't work. She raised her head again and her eyes sprang open.

'It hasn't. Not really. I tried to end it . . . But he wouldn't listen, and I couldn't . . .'

'When was the last time you saw him?'

'We arranged to meet up . . . Thursday morning. The day Ruby was taken. I'd arranged to meet Jamie at a hotel, in London. That's where he lives now. I told him it was over, that I couldn't do it any more. We'd been meeting up once, twice a month. We'd book a room. It sounds seedy, I know that. But sometimes, sometimes we'd just lie on the bed and cuddle, and talk. And when we talked I never wanted to leave him. But when I got home, with Ruby and Richard, I always knew I would never leave them, especially Ruby. Richard has always said he'd fight me tooth and nail for custody.'

'Did you tell Jamie Bucknell this?'

'Yes. That morning. He went mad, I've never seen him like that before. It was the most angry I've ever seen him. He said he'd lost everything for me, his wife, his job . . . everything. Then he stormed out. Of course, we haven't spoken since.'

'How angry, Gail, angry enough to abduct Ruby? After all, she's the reason you can't be with him. Did he know this?'

She squeezed her eyes closed again, and raised her hands to her face, for good measure. Clarke didn't have the patience, and Ruby didn't have the time. She grabbed Gail's wrists and firmly yanked her hands away from her face.

'You said he stormed out, what time did he storm out?'

'You don't think he could have—?'

'Are you telling me you haven't thought about this possibility?'

The answer, like a child's guileless guilt, was etched all over her face. 'About eleven . . . twelve at the latest. We always met in the morning, it gave me plenty of time to get back to Denton to pick Ruby up.'

'Midday?'

'Yes.'

'Can I use your phone?'

'Does Richard have to know?'

Clarke heard a car skid to a messy halt outside. It was Frost in his yellow Metro – he didn't believe in using the brakes sensibly, preferred a sort of emergency stop that inflicted whiplash on any unlucky and unsuspecting passenger. Sue had got used to grabbing the dash whenever they arrived at their destination – there were the crescent-moon indents of her nails in the moulded plastic to prove it.

Richard Hanson let himself and Frost in. His wife didn't close her eyes now. What good would it do? There was nowhere to escape to.

Saturday (3) _____

Frost was sitting on a chair in his office the wrong way round, with his arms perched on the backrest and his aching back pressed against the radiator. Heat. That was the thing, that and lying on the floor, and popping ibuprofen like Smarties, to give him relief and help stave off the pain.

John Waters was pacing Frost's office, energized by facts and possible leads on Ruby's abductors.

'Chamley's was the only shop in Denton that stocked these limited-edition Cabbage Patch dolls—'

'Not even Aster's department store?'

'Nope. Three bought for cash, one bought on an Access card, the last one bought on a Bennington Bank credit card.'

'That's not that great, means you can't trace three of them.'

'Yes, we can, and we have. You see, these Cabbage Patch dolls come with a "Birth Certificate", with the kid who owns it being the mum.'

'Or dad?'

'Fair point, or dad.'

Frost shook his head, 'Jesus wept, I don't remember toys being this elaborate in my day. Bloomin' ridiculous.'

Waters handed him a list of names and addresses. 'As you can see, Ruby's name is there.'

Frost's phone rang. He winced as he made some geriatric attempts to dismount from his chair, but Waters saved him further humiliation by picking up the receiver and handing it to him. It was a DI from the Met, telling Frost they'd made a call to an address they had for Jamie Bucknell, a bedsit in Tooting Bec. Bucknell wasn't there and his landlord hadn't seen him in a couple of days. Frost explained that Bucknell was now a priority suspect in the Ruby Hanson abduction.

The DI from the Met assured Frost they'd treat Bucknell as such, and would put an unmarked car on surveillance at his address. Frost thanked him, put the phone down and told Waters the score.

'What do you want to do about the other names on the list?'

Frost, still thinking about Jamie Bucknell, and with other little thought worms burrowing around his grey matter, looked blank. 'The list? What list? Help me, John, I'm confused, un-confuse me.'

'The idea was to find out who else had the same doll as Ruby, and might have a connection to her, to eliminate potential hoaxers.'

'Of course. Yes, we're on it.'

'You want me and Clarke to go, so you can rest your back?'

He looked affronted at the very suggestion. 'No, I bloody well don't.' Frost this time levered himself off the chair with a determined look on his face, pulled out his box of ibuprofen, popped a pill from the blister pack, and necked it with the dregs of his now cold and bitter Mellow Bird's coffee. A thought struck him: 'How about Longthorn, any joy?'

'Didn't you get my message? I left a note on your . . .'

Frost and Waters glanced down at the mess; needles and

haystacks came to mind as they both realized the futility of trying to find anything on the DI's desk.

'Spoke to Dr Edmunds,' said Waters. 'Nice guy, very helpful. He's going to fax over a list of ex-employees from the last six months. Said he'd try and make it as comprehensive as possible, but they've had a huge turnover of staff the last few years. Something he's trying to put a stop to.'

'That's what he told me,' said Frost, biting down on the butt of the Rothmans he'd just put in his mouth to help disguise the pain as he straightened up.

Waters looked concerned. 'You sure about coming along?'

'It's barely a twinge. And anyway, Susan's at the Hansons' waiting for a call from the potential kidnapper. And probably stopping the two of them killing each other. I knew it was too good to be true.'

'What was?'

'People being happily married.'

'Tell me about it.' Waters shook his head ruefully.

'It's just awful, our prayers are with Ruby and her family. Sorry I couldn't have been of more help.'

'You have, Mr Bridges,' said Waters, 'you've taken your name off the list.'

'I'll tell you one thing,' said Tony Bridges, holding up the doll with its accompanying certificate and, most importantly, its head still intact. 'This doll cost an arm and a leg and my daughter doesn't even play with it any more – now it's all about My Little Pony.'

Tony Bridges closed the door of 13 Arcadia Avenue, home of Little Miss Lucy Number 67, the 'daughter' of Debbie Bridges, aged seven and three quarters. In the three homes Frost and Waters had visited thus far, all of the Cabbage Patch dolls still had their heads attached, and lived in middle-class comfort with families who would no more abduct a child than rip the head off their kid's dolly. Still, the detectives lived in hope – three down, two to go.

*

Frost and Waters were on the doorstep of 52 Montpelier Road, not far from the university. The buzzer had sounded, and there were some yelps of excitement and screams of pure joy from inside. They came, the detectives saw through the frosted-glass door, from the figure of a young woman in a lilac dressing gown. When the door was opened, she didn't disappoint – she was in her early twenties, with a scramble of long, just-got-out-of-bed blonde hair, bright blue eyes with just a hint of a heavy night fraying their edges, and lips that looked set in a permanent pout.

'Oh, you don't look like the pizza delivery.'

'Bit early for pizza, I would have thought?' said Frost.

'Not if you'd had the night we've had, sweetie.'

The two detectives showed their warrant cards.

'Oh, Lordy Lord, what did we do last night? Nothing that bad, I'm sure.'

John Waters gave her his best, relax-it's-nothing-to-worry-about smile, and backed it up with, 'Probably broke a few hearts, I imagine, but it's not last night we've come to talk about.'

'Will you be needing to come in?'

'I think so,' said Frost.

She then turned her head and called out, 'Ladies, make yourselves decent, we have company – it's the police. And I'm not bloody joking!'

Frost and Waters were led into the living room to be greeted by two other girls, also in jim-jams and dressing gowns. Both at various stages of glowering hangovers, and drinking some rough-and-ready Bloody Marys, as indicated by the bottle of super-market vodka and the cans of V8 juice on the coffee table. It was very much a student house, with worn mismatched decor, made cosy and feminine by fairy lights around the fireplace; and colourful cushions and fluffy throws over the dull rental three-piece suite.

They were Katy, Abbie and Harriet, and they were all

twenty-one. But no Louisa Hamilton, who was the 'mother' of Little Miss Lucy Number 654.

'She's moved out,' said Abbie, cross-legged on the floor.

'She didn't move out, we threw her out,' clarified Katy, the one who had answered the door and was now propped on the arm of the sofa, playing with Harriet's long red corkscrew curls.

'That sounds worse than it is,' said Harriet, who was laid out on the sofa, obviously suffering the most, swatting Katy's hand away from her hair. 'Louisa was a nice girl, just not our kind of nice girl. She was . . . a bit too prim and proper.'

'And *weird*,' added Abbie, studying the split ends of her black crimped hair.

'What was weird about her?' asked Frost.

On hearing this, they all sort of perked up and paid attention, as if realizing for the first time they were in the company of police officers, and not overgrown nosy pizza-delivery boys.

'Sorry, I shouldn't have said that.'

'It's OK, Abbie, we're just trying to find out where she is. Has she left town?'

They all looked at Katy, as if she had become the designated adult in the room. Katy said, 'We three were all at uni together, she wasn't, so it must have been hard for her coming in to the house. But she just wasn't our type. Very . . . *intense*?' The others nodded. 'She left two weeks ago, she may have gone back to her parents', I think they live locally, maybe Bamford or Rimmington. She wanted to be in Denton for work, you know, because Denton's where it's at.'

'So they tell me,' said Frost, unable to tell if she was being ironic or not. That was the usual assumption when it came to the town he loved and served.

'I know she lost her job, she was pretty upset about that.'

'Yeah, really upset, *intensely* upset,' opined Harriet, sitting up, as if forced from her prostrate position on the couch by the sheer strength of the thought. The other girls agreed and echoed the word *intense*, obviously Louisa's defining feature.

Harriet added, 'It was only a temp job anyway, but she said she got plenty of overtime, and the money was turning out to be very good with lots of perks.'

'Where was this job?'

The girls all looked at each other. There was some umming and ahhing and scratching of heads, then they all started giggling. Frost and Waters glanced at each other. The girls just carried on giggling as if they weren't there. Then the giggling completely took them over, and soon all three of them were on the floor, practically beating the carpet, doubled up in hysterics.

The two detectives pulled stern-looking faces, cleared their throats, muttered warnings about this being a serious matter, and then tried their damnedest not to start giggling themselves, such was the infectiousness of it. Waters was almost crying with laughter when he caught sight of something and nudged Frost to get his attention. Tucked under an armchair was Culture Club's *Colour by Numbers* LP. On the record cover were various items: a packet of ten Bensons, with the top of the gold box shredded where it had been used to make a roach; three torn-open fags; a pack of green Rizla papers; a small lump of rocky Lebanese and an even smaller one of Moroccan black; and a recently extinguished, expertly rolled, six-paper conical joint of epic proportions.

That explained why Katy had shouted over her shoulder to warn the girls to make sure they were decent before she let the detectives in; why the window was flung open to the January cold, yet the electric fire's faux-coal fascia was glowing hellishly and all three bars were throwing out a fierce heat; and why the air in the room was eye-wateringly thick with pungent hastily sprayed Honeysuckle Glade.

Busted.

Waters crouched down and retrieved the Culture Club waccy-baccy platter and rested it on the coffee table, alongside the arbitrarily more legal high of supermarket vodka.

On seeing this, the girls stopped giggling, sat back up in their respective positions, and looked completely crestfallen.

Again Katy, the designated adult, spoke: 'Oh God, I'm so sorry, we had guests last night, some guys, and they must have . . . have . . . have left it here?'

Waters raised some unbelieving eyebrows at this. 'Lying to a policeman, Katy, that's . . . that's really bad karma.'

The girls flicked looks at each other, as if to ask, is he being serious, he looks like he's joking?

'What do you think, Jack, shall we ask again – where did Louisa Hamilton work? – or come back when the giggles have worn off?'

But Jack Frost wasn't paying attention, he was looking at the discarded footwear on the floor by the armchair.

There were three pairs altogether: some cowboy boots, some knee-high grey suede boots and a pair of black shoes with a thick corrugated platform sole. Frost bent down and picked one of them up.

'Whose are these?'

Harriet raised her hand, like a schoolgirl in class.

'Comme des Garçons,' said Jack Frost without needing to peer inside at the label. 'Spring '85 collection.'

Yet again, the girls flicked questioning looks at each other – was this fuzz for real? And Waters joined them in incredulity. How the hell would Frost know that? In their brief amount of time together, it was already clear to the girls that the DI was obviously the most unfashionable, untrendy man in all of Denton, if not the whole county. The black detective obviously had some style, in so much as what he was wearing didn't look slept in.

Frost held up the shoe again. 'Tell me about them, Harriet.'

'Well, they're very uncomfortable, I tripped and almost broke my ankle going into the club. But still kind of worth the discomfort cos they look so bloody amazing and—'

'Tell me something I don't know. Like: where did you get them?'

'Oh . . . oh . . . shit. Sorry, they belonged to Louisa. She left them here, said she didn't want them any more.'

Abbie spoke. 'Oh, yeah, I remember, they were a gift from her boss.'

Katy said, 'That's right, now I think of it, she fell out with him, big time, think that's why she left the job, or got sacked.'

A memory struck Harriet. 'I asked if she was shagging him, and that's when she got all prim and proper. She said he was married, and huffed off to her room to play with her cuddly toys.'

'Cuddly toys?' asked Frost.

'Yes, I mean, *ridiculous*. I've got a Paddington, but that's cool.'

'I've got my Snoopy,' said Katy.

Harriet and Katy looked at Abbie, but she shrugged. She had nothing similar, and couldn't care less.

Katy winked at Abbie and mouthed cattily, *So mature*, then addressed them all. 'But Louisa, she had Peter Rabbit, Winnie the Pooh, Babar the Elephant, and—'

'A Cabbage Patch doll?'

Katy shrugged and sneered at the thought. 'Yeah, probably, they were all on her bed, like tucked in. I mean, you bring a guy back and he sees all that . . . weird. Plus it takes about twenty minutes to get them off the bed!'

They all laughed, but stopped when they saw that the two detectives were engaging in some serious looks.

'Louisa didn't work at an architect's, did she?'

'Yes!' they all called out in unison, beaming big smiles. Then Harriet stopped smiling and looked deadly serious too.

'The shoes . . . I swear, she did give them to me, I didn't steal them.'

'God no, she left them here and Harry got first dibs.'

'Yes, absolutely, it's not like we killed her or anything, and stole her clothes!'

'Shut up, Abbie, that's not even funny!'

'I'm not being funny! Am I? I don't know . . . Oh God . . .'

'I swear, we didn't kill her or anything, you can search the house!'

'And the garden . . . we didn't bury her, or anything really bad and bitchy like that, I swear—'

Waters raised his hand to calm them. 'Girls, you've had the munchies stage, but no pizza. You've had the giggles stage. Now, unfortunately for you with two coppers in the room, you're having the paranoia stage. Relax, we don't think you've killed her.'

'Where's the phone?' asked Frost.

Katy pointed to the kitchen and Frost went out and made a call to Clarke at the Hansons'.

'How are they both doing?' he asked.

Sue's voice was hushed; she was obviously taking the call in the hall, but was not fully out of earshot of the Hansons. 'Once Richard found out the truth that she was still seeing Bucknell, he looked like he was about to cry his eyes out, or go ballistic. Thankfully he did neither, and held it together, stayed calm. She explained what had happened, how she tried to end it that day with Bucknell, but Bucknell stormed out. Then she started crying and Richard hugged her. They've been sat on the sofa in silence, holding hands, waiting for the kidnapper's call. Tell you what, Jack, after what he's been through, I'm impressed. Hope I meet someone like him, sensitive, understanding, forgiv—'

'Well, bollocks to all that! The marriage-guidance counselling service is over. I'm on my way.'

Frost put the receiver down. There was a tug at his elbow. It was a doe-eyed, near-tears and very contrite-looking Katy.

'We're ever so sorry, Inspector, for everything, absolutely everything. Would you like a cup of tea?'

The doorbell rang; through the glass it was easy to see who it was. Frost smiled. They were good kids, young, having fun, and not about to be nicked for possession. 'No thank you, Katy, we'll leave you to your pizza.'

Saturday (4) _____

Clarke answered the front door. Frost said nothing as he stepped into the clean sweep of the hallway, with its blond wood floor, the reeds in tall glass vases, some Miró prints on the walls. A world away from the shared cosy clutter of the three girls he'd left munching on pizza. The house's clean minimal design and order no longer spoke of an architect's tasteful aesthetics, but of coldness, lies, deceit and a concealment of emotional chaos that went straight to the very heart of the home.

Clarke led the way into the living room, and there they were, on the chrome-framed black leather sofa, holding hands and looking up at him expectantly, like a couple of contestants on the daytime quiz show *Mr & Mrs*, but utterly clueless about each other, and definitely not about to win the jackpot prize.

'Any news, Inspector Frost?' asked Richard Hanson.

Frost considered them. 'I'd like a word with you, in private.'

The Hansons turned to each other in round-eyed bemusement, then back at Frost, like it was the strangest request in the world. Frost glared as if to convey his impatience. Richard read the look perfectly, disentangled his hand from his wife's and got to his feet.

Hanson led the detective through to the kitchen, which was sufficiently far away to allow for some frank discourse. There was a breakfast island with six stools gathered around it, and what wasn't a sparkly grey granite surface was a brushed-steel one. Hanson headed to the shiny-looking Italian coffee machine – no Mellow Bird's for this couple.

'Would you like some coffee, Inspector?'

'Louisa Hamilton.'

He stopped fiddling with the Gaggia, and looked around at the detective. 'How do you know . . . ?' He leaned heavily against the granite work surface. 'I guess it doesn't matter . . . Just doing your job.'

'And you're not helping.'

'No. Louisa worked for me, it was only ever a temporary position, but I think she thought it was more . . .'

As Hanson tailed off, Frost assumed the architect realized just how bad that sounded. 'So you fired her?'

'After three months. Of course, I shouldn't have got involved with her.'

'She was young, vulnerable – her first job out of poly, I believe.'

'Yes . . . but she was twenty-one, not a complete child. And I didn't realize how immature she was. But thanks.'

'For what?'

'For not saying anything in front of Gail.'

'Expediency, not empathy. I don't care about saving your marriage, just getting your kid back as quickly as possible, and I haven't got time to sit through you and your wife tearing strips off each other. Though I have to say, it goes a fair way to explain your magnanimity at *her* indiscretions. I think Louisa Hamilton is just the tip of the iceberg with you, right, *Dick*?'

Hanson looked like he wanted to address this slight, but stayed quiet.

Frost continued. 'And I'll be taking the names and addresses of all of them, just in case there's any wronged woman with a score to settle.'

'Please, I'm not that bad, it's just—'

'Let's start with Louisa Hamilton first, shall we? You think she's capable of something like this?'

'Taking Ruby?'

Frost glared.

'God, no.'

'You're lying.'

'I'm not . . . I swear. I wouldn't, not now.'

'But you're not certain, though, are you – how could you be?'

Hanson shook his head.

'Let me tell you what I think, and certainly the way it would look in a court of law. You didn't want us involved when you got the doll's head. You were annoyed with your wife when she contacted us, because you wanted to handle it yourself. Because you probably suspected that it was from Louisa, and even if she doesn't have Ruby, she's playing on it. She wants to hurt you, she wants money off you, a pay-off for the way you treated her, and now's the time to get it because you're vulnerable – right?'

The architect staggered over to the breakfast island and propped himself on one of the stools. 'I panicked. I don't know. To be honest, she's crazy enough to do something like this. She knew Ruby had that doll because she was the one who bought it. It was Ruby's birthday, I wasn't going to leave it all to Gail, thought I'd get her a surprise.'

'Make yourself look good in front of the wife, I get it.'

Hanson gulped hard, the irony of it wasn't lost on him. 'I didn't know what to get her, Louisa said she knew exactly. She bought the Cabbage Patch Kid. Ruby loved it. Of course, I reimbursed her.'

'Like the efficient secretary remembering the wife's birthday and the perfume she likes?'

'Yes, I guess so. It's all turning into pretty cliché, grubby stuff, isn't it, Inspector?'

It was. But Frost didn't comment. 'Louisa also bought herself a Little Miss Lucy doll, right?'

'That's right, she did. Seemed a bit strange. I was going to offer to pay for it, but somehow that seemed stranger.'

Frost couldn't argue with that. 'Were you in love with her?'

'No.'

'Did you give her the impression that you were?'

'She was young, it was a mistake. I've admitted that. It wasn't tit-for-tat, but this did happen after Gail's affair.'

'You bought her presents, though. Those shoes. Comme des Garçons?'

Hanson shrugged, looked confused. 'Yes, yes I did. How do you know?'

'She left them at the house she was renting a room in.'

'I was in Japan, on business, doing some freelance work for my old firm, I picked up some samples. I thought she might like them, obviously not.'

'Have you tried to contact her since Ruby was taken?'

He nodded. 'She's not at her old place, as you know. I don't know where she is. The more I think about it, the less I know about her. The job was paid cash in hand. I put a note in the *Denton Echo*, junior secretary wanted. She turned up . . .'

Frost raised his hand for Hanson to stop talking. His eye was taken by something on the American-style fridge. Farmyard-animal fridge magnets held in place some photos. He went over to take a closer look.

'You know Sally Fielding?'

Hanson shook his head, then joined Frost over at the fridge. It was a photo of six mothers with their respective daughters, all dressed in netball kit.

'The school has a parents and pupils netball event once a month. Gail enjoys it.'

Frost pointed to Sally Fielding and her daughter.

Richard Hanson shrugged. 'Yes, I may have seen her about, but I don't know her.'

'Are you sure?'

'What are you suggesting? I'm not that bad, I promise. After what happened last time at Ruby's old school in Rimmington between Gail and that little wimp Bucknell, I wouldn't do anything to jeopardize Ruby's happiness ...' Richard let out a strained sigh, turned his back on the fridge and slumped down on one of the stools, like the full weight of his actions had just hit him. He asked tearfully, 'So tell me, Inspector, what the hell happens next?'

Frost exited the kitchen without answering.

Sunday (1)

Dogs. Man's best friend. He liked them well enough, in theory. The idea of them. Their loyalty, their reliability, their guilelessness. If you had a dog you had a routine. And Charles Wilkes had a dog. And if Banes couldn't get him today, he'd get him tomorrow.

But Clive knew that time was becoming of the essence, he knew he'd have to move on soon. As invisible as he was, as anonymous as he was, the police would close in eventually. He'd budgeted for a couple of weeks. From the first blow to the last. So he still had time. There was no forensic trace to nab him, no prints, he'd made sure of that. He always cleaned up after himself, every teacup, every beer can, every surface was memorized, accounted for. Shoe prints on the sticky blood-drenched caravan floor? No chance, not him.

And there was no description of him, either. A name might come up soon, but it would be just that, a name, and not the right one. But then again, he'd had so many, it was hard to remember what the right one was. As a foundling, he was given a name. Then, as a foster child, another name. And when that one didn't work out, he was given another, and so it went on until no one would take him any more. No one would give him their name.

But he didn't care, names meant nothing to him now. You could go to a cemetery in any city or town and find a name on a gravestone of someone who was roughly around your age, and starting from something small – a membership of a club, say the Airfix modellers' club, or a subscription to an innocuous magazine paid for with a postal order – you could start a whole new identity. People didn't care, no one checked, as long as they got their money. Before you knew it, you had enough paper proof to get a utility bill, a bank account, a chequebook, a driving licence, a passport. You just had to be patient, watch the detail and be consistent. He had a knack for detail because that's where the devil was. And he also knew that when it came—

Ah, there he was. Banes stopped thinking about how good he was at not existing, and concentrated on the victim at hand. Charles Wilkes stepped out of his cottage, his springy little Jack Russell energetically trotting off in front of him, straining at the leash to cock its leg somewhere. Once that was done, they headed off in the direction of the fields, and beyond that, the river. It would be a nice long early-morning walk. Man and his best friend. It would be their last.

'How's the back, Jack?'

'You being funny, Johnny?'

Desk Sergeant Johnny Johnson thought about it, then laughed. It was more a laugh of relief. 'After you getting me back at work, perish the thought. In all seriousness, though, was it a deep hole, the one you fell into?'

'Not as deep as the one you're digging for yourself.'

Frost had just entered Eagle Lane, and he was patting himself down for a cigarette and coming up blank. Johnson was a complete waste of space, didn't smoke. Still, the copy of *Viz* he'd just swiped off his counter held the DI's attention for a bit.

'You twist my words, guv, but I do have to admit I've missed our banter. That'll teach me to fraternize with the likes of Jimmy McVale. Don't know what I was thinking, it all happened so fast. One minute I'm standing there, next minute McVale's put the book in my hand and Sandy Lane's taking pictures.'

'I saw what happened.'

'He's an arch manipulator, that McVale.'

Frost dropped the *Viz* back on the counter and headed for the swing doors to the incident room . . . then stopped as a thought struck him. 'Tell me, did you actually read McVale's book?'

'I did. And I have to say . . .' Desk Sergeant Johnson did an archly comical glance from side to side, keeping an eye out for Mullett, Frost supposed. '. . . It was absolutely riveting.'

'What was his MO? I remember hearing McVale and his mob developed a technique for kidnapping.'

'That's right. They did it first in '63. They'd kidnap the bank manager when he left his house on his way to work. They'd drive him to a secure location and tell him that they had his wife and kids too. Then two of the men, armed with walkie-talkies, waited until they got the word, then strolled into the bank just as the bank manager was telephoning through to his assistant to say he was being kept hostage, and to do as they said or they'd harm him and his family. That way they'd get into the high-value vault, not just the cash tills.'

Frost made a low growly sound in his throat as he considered the audacity of the technique. 'It's a cunning stunt, Johnny. Adds another emotional angle to the fear. More than just having a sawn-off pointed at your head.'

'Worked every time, according to McVale. There were variations on the theme. They'd find out where the bank manager lived, force their way in, then hold the family hostage, and in the morning make the bank manager go to work as usual. Then two of the gang would walk in, and the bank manager would—'

'Would lead them down to the prize. Thanks, Johnny!'

Invigorated, Frost burst through the door into the incident room like one of Jimmy McVale's robbers bursting into a bank. He was met by Sue Clarke, notebook in hand, looking equally invigorated as she said, 'Just got off the phone from a DS Raines at the Met. They found Jamie Bucknell, in a drying-out cell in Streatham. At the time of the abduction, Bucknell was downing his sorrows in pubs all over south-west London and telling anyone who would listen that he was going to join the French Foreign Legion. Eventually, he got thrown out of a boozer at 5 p.m., then arrested at 5.45 p.m. for kicking over traffic cones and assaulting an officer with a kebab, then attempting to take his own life by throwing himself from a police car.'

'Typical night out in Streatham, I'd imagine. Any news on Louisa Hamilton?'

'I visited her mum who lives in Bamford first thing this morning. Last she heard, Louisa was staying with mates in Bristol, where she went to poly. Mum doesn't have an address or number, but she's worried about her, said she sounded upset last time she rang.'

'Right. We need to find her. Let's get a picture of her out there in the world, get on to Bristol CID, get back to her mum, get names of all her friends, call her old poly, the usual.'

Clarke nodded and went off to do 'the usual'. Frost looked around him, at the faces of his team, ears to phones, flipping through lists, ogling the green text coming up on their IBMs. Hard at it, yet looking despondent as the hours slipped away. He also knew that he'd have to release Gordon 'Degsy' Dellinpile soon. Releasing suspects never looked good in the press. It suggested wrong turns, mistakes, that somehow the case was getting away from you.

Frost saw the pack of 555 cigarettes on Arthur Hanlon's desk and plucked one out of the box without the burly DC seeing him, wrapped up as he was in trying to work out some simple equation. In for a penny, he then took another fag for 'Ron' and slipped it behind his ear.

'You're nicked!'

Frost spun around to see John Waters approaching. The DS mouthed the word *Longthorn* and handed Frost a Manila file. Frost took it and headed off to his office, before Hanlon, who was now counting the cigarettes in his packet, could say anything. Waters followed him.

Frost closed the door behind them and sat down, back again pressed against the radiator for pain relief. He opened the file; inside was a list of about forty names.

Waters explained, 'That's all the recent employees of Longthorn Secure Hospital, the last six months. Here's the funny thing: because it's not actually deemed a prison, they don't keep as tight a record of employees coming and going. And photo ID is pretty sketchy, too – when they leave they're supposed to turn in their passes, but half of them don't. They have lots of agency temp workers, cleaners, orderlies, and none of them stay too long. Even the psychiatric nurses tend not to stay the full term of their contract. Apparently, the place has a bad rep.'

'Yeah, when I spoke to Edmunds, he said that when he took over it was a dangerous place, for both patients and staff.'

The phone rang. Waters and Frost both looked around, trying to locate where the ringing was coming from, and where the actual phone was. Waters looked flummoxed, and left the office muttering something about not knowing how he could live like that.

Frost followed the cord from the socket in the wall, gripping it like a mountain climber easing up the rope, careful not to pull too hard as the whole edifice of heaped paperwork on his desk would fall to the floor. Once he answered the phone, he recognized the voice on the other end straight away: it was DI Garside, his opposite number from West Norwood.

'Got some more bad news for you, Jack.'

Frost let out a dispirited sigh, then nestled the receiver into his neck and sparked up the 555. 'That's our stock in trade around here.'

'Suffolk police have been on the blower. They think they've got something that links in further with the Wheatons' murders. A rambler found a bus pass yesterday in woodland near Longthorn. It belonged to Peter Allerton, the missing canteen worker. It was found beside a pile of leaves that were soaked in blood. There were also bone fragments. Their path bloke identified them as skull fragments.'

'Jeez. Sounds like the same as the Wheatons. Ball-peen hammer to the head. His weapon of choice. Perfectly legal to carry one, and perfectly lethal in the wrong hands. Looks like all roads lead to Longthorn. I've just had a list of ex-employees sent over.'

'Employees? How about patients!'

'Yeah, we discussed that. Maybe someone's not locking the door at night.' There was a pause down the line that turned into a deep silence, as Frost's throwaway statement seemed to take on a terrifying possibility. 'You know what, maybe that's not such a mad idea. Maybe they do need to look into their security.'

Garside agreed. 'You want me to go up there and check on it?'

Frost glanced at the map pinned up on the wall. Longthorn was quite a drive for either of them. 'I'd appreciate it, Dave. As you can imagine, we've got our hands full here.'

Frost hung up. But didn't move, just sat there mulling the conversation over. The phone rang again. 'DI Frost.'

'Jack, me old mucker, long time no see!'

Frost groaned. It was Sandy Lane of the *Denton Echo*. 'What can I do for you, me old muckraker?'

'What's this I hear about murder and mayhem in Denton Woods? I'm hearing rumours, Jack, everything from a mad axeman running around killing people, to a wild animal on the loose, eating people! Big Foot? An escaped big cat, a gorilla?'

'You've had the press release: a thirty-three-year-old man was found dead in his caravan. We're still investigating, a full statement will be available when we—'

'Spare me the press releases, Jack! Give me something I can splash on the front page. Either that, or I'll have to run with you falling down a hole. That's what I heard, Jack. A stumbling detective got chased by a madman with an axe then fell down a hole.'

'For the record, that's all true, but I was being chased by Godzilla.'

Frost slammed the phone down. But he knew they'd have to give the press more information soon. They'd held off because they didn't want to link the murders of the Wheatons with the abduction of Ruby Hanson. The public was still a major factor in the case, any sightings from them could be invaluable and their vigilance was still needed. Any speculation about a serial killer on the loose would change the emphasis and focus.

He stuck his hand in the pocket of his leather bomber jacket and pulled out the photo that had been on the Hansons' fridge. He didn't ask to take it, he just did. That was to be his next call, but he was beaten to the punch by the phone ringing once more.

'DI Frost.'

'We need to talk. Not at the station. Somewhere private.'

'Who is this?'

'Somewhere you don't usually go. Do you understand, eh?'

The voice was deep and throaty, and indicative of the upper classes with its clipped authoritative tone.

'Again, who is this?'

'Who is this, you ask?'

'Yes.'

'As well you might, as well you might.'

The man laughed huskily; it sounded like it could easily segue into a hacking cough. Frost cut through the phlegm-fuelled guffawing with a loud and impatient sigh, and was about to hang up.

'Don't hang up! I'm sorry. Should have said. This is the only person alive who knows what really happened in 1967.'

Sunday (2)

He went to smash the hammer down on to the dog's skull.
There was a yelp of pain. But not from the dog – from him.
Banes cursed. The little bastard saw it coming just in time, let
go of his leg, then shot off into the undergrowth to make its
escape. Banes had cracked himself right on the shin bone, and
was now rolling around on the grass grabbing the pummelled
limb; it throbbed, it bled.

Banes wanted to scream out in pain but knew he couldn't.
They were deep in some copse, but still, he probably wasn't
alone, there were likely to be other dog walkers with equally
vicious little bastards off their leashes not too far away.

He rolled up his left trouser leg to inspect the damage. There
were four puncture wounds where the terrier's fangs had sunk
in. The damned thing had put its heart and soul into the bite,
and it wouldn't have been satisfied until the top set of teeth had
connected with the bottom and it had made off with a lump of
his leg. Luckily, me hammering down on me own leg stopped
that happening, thought Banes, with enough irony to elicit a
brief and bitter chuckle. The bruised skin around the bite

marks would soon be a lavish mix of blues and purples. He was sure he'd chipped the bone. There was a serious numbness at the epicentre of the pain.

Banes straightened up, and cursed as he saw the tough little terrier disappear further into the thicket. It had been watching him.

He hadn't planned on such a ferocious attack from the dog. It wasn't an Alsatian, a Dobermann or a Rottweiler, it was a small terrier. But it knew how to jump and it knew how to bite. And it had done all of that in a sustained, if brief, spell of terror inflicted on Banes. He felt waves of indignant rage pass through him, like the hot throbbing pain in his leg. He felt like *he* was the victim.

At least Wilkes, the dog's master, lay on the grass thoroughly dead. He had been easy: Banes just snuck up from behind, the long damp grass cushioning his footfalls. Before the dog could bark into action, the hammer had gone down on the back of Wilkes' head. Then some follow-up blows until Banes saw what he knew was irretrievable damage. There was no coming back from that kind of injury, it was direct trauma to the cerebral hemisphere, you were gone. All in a matter of seconds.

Banes steeled himself: he would blank out the pain. He had too much work to do.

He was sitting, appropriately enough, in one of the green leather chesterfield armchairs by the fireplace. He already had a tumbler of whiskey going. There were others in the lounge of the Prince Albert Hotel, but with his officer-class carriage and impressive moustache, Frost could tell right away that this was his man. He was also wearing the brass-buttoned blue blazer with the crest of his regiment and the old school tie that he said would mark him out.

'Captain Cavanagh?'

'Ah, Inspector Frost,' he said, rising to his feet with the spring and agility of a pole vaulter, and not a man in his seventies.

Firm handshakes were exchanged, with Frost putting in some extra effort to keep up. 'I've heard great things, great things, from our mutual friend, the delightful Tony.'

'Inspector Anthony Dorking?'

'Ha! Bless him, that old fraud, he's no more a detective than I am!' Cavanagh said, lowering himself back into the armchair. Frost sat opposite him, and some more whiskeys were ordered.

'Before we start, Captain, I am intrigued – you said Anthony Dorking is no more a detective than you are?'

'Ah, yes, that was wrong of me, I'm being cruel. Anthony may well have taken some exams to become a policeman, but initially, he was like me, a civilian, brought in by the Yard because of his expertise in fine art and antiques. In fact, I recommended him. He was writing the catalogue at Sotheby's at the time, which naturally enough I think he found incredibly dull, and rather fancied himself as a Bulldog Drummond type. But me? No, I was never a detective. I was a captain in the Guards, but never took any police exams, or even had much in the way of formal training. An old chum of mine in the robbery squad gave me a badge and some paperwork. After all, can't go knocking on a crook's door without the right credentials. You see, Inspector, you can train a policeman to detect the crooks, but it takes a special knowledge to identify the goods they trade in. Tony and I have that knowledge.'

'So, 1967.'

'Yes. The end of an era, and now, for me, it's finally come to pass. When Anthony told me about Ivan, I knew it was finally over. And of course, Conrad dying before him, by only a matter of weeks, I hear. Both driven to the grave by their demons. But certainly, that was just the end result, the inevitable result.'

'Of what?'

'The past, of course. A past they couldn't outrun, and the one action that ultimately set them on their path to destruction.' Captain Cavanagh gave a sorrowful shake of his head, picked up his freshly replenished glass of Bushmills whiskey, took a sizeable sip and then turned his attention back to Frost. 'How much do you know, Inspector?'

'To be honest, I feel I know nothing. Just rumour, conjecture, hearsay, and a fair bit of mythologizing.'

'Yes. People tend to look back at the '60s through rose-tinted spectacles. What do they say: if you can remember it, you weren't there.' Frost nodded. Vanessa Fielding had said the very same thing to him. 'Well, I was there, Inspector, and I remember it like it was yesterday.' Cavanagh put his glass on the table. Frost leaned in.

Cavanagh began: 'On May 25th 1967, Conrad Wilde was at work. A job in Belgravia, Eaton Square. The job was lined up for him in the usual fashion by his partner in crime, Ivan Fielding. Conrad was confident that the house would be empty. He knew that the owner would be at a shooting party in a pile out in Berkshire that weekend, because it would be the same party that Ivan, along with his wife, Vanessa, would also be attending.

'Conrad was after a particular painting that night, a Vermeer that had been stolen from the Rijksmuseum in Amsterdam just over a month before. It was hot, and it was being lined up to be sold. Conrad, through his usual athletic daring, had managed to beat the alarm system which was, in consequence of the owner's reputation and what he was guarding, rather sophisticated for the time. He'd also located the secret room in which the painting was stored. It was a largish room that was rather stuffed with stolen antiques and artworks. The entrance to the hidden room was behind a wall lined with bookshelves. Pull out a first edition of *Oliver Twist*, and Open Sesame.

'So there Conrad stood, swathed in black – black evening suit, black calfskin gloves, a black silk scarf and black Oxfords with a rubber sole so as not to be heard on the marble staircase. And there, the prize, the Vermeer on the wall in front of him. Of course, there were other items he could have filled his pockets with that night. Wasn't there a diamond and sapphire suite of jewels resting in a velvet case from Van Cleef & Arpels? You bet there was, Inspector Frost, you bet there was. However, Conrad Wilde was a professional, and heeded his friend Ivan's advice, always go for the prize, and just the prize. Don't get distracted by other items, time is of the essence. Ivan never sent Conrad in blind, everything was meticulously worked out, and the goods he was after were already sold. "The only people who get caught, are people who want to get caught," he'd say.'

Frost didn't know if he totally agreed, but he was hungry for more information and didn't argue the point. 'Go on, Captain,' encouraged the DI with a smile; it wasn't every day you got to use that title.

The captain dispatched his Bushmills, and like some masterfully prearranged operation, or in a West End play, a fresh Bushmills was brought to the table with barely a nod to the waiter. Frost had only had a sip or two of his and refused another. Pointless going up against a captain, he thought.

Once refreshed, Cavanagh continued: 'Conrad was just about to take the picture off the wall when he heard someone take the first edition of *Oliver Twist* off the bookshelf. As luck would have it, there was a black lacquer six-panel screen in the corner, just waiting for someone to hide behind it. Wilde, quick as lightning, did exactly that, and in stepped the owner of the house and another man. The owner of the house was one Charles D'Arcy QC.'

Of course, Frost knew the name.

'D'Arcy, a barrister from one of the smartest of the smart Lincoln's Inn chambers. A legal genius, one of the best in the business, soon to be appointed a judge. But with a fatal flaw. He liked to own beautiful things, no matter how briefly, and had a self-destructive urge that had led him into trading in the beautiful – but stolen – things he so coveted.'

'And the other man with the barrister?'

'Jimmy McVale.'

Frost acknowledged this with barely a blink. Of course he'd

read all about the slain barrister, the murder that got McVale a sentence of twenty-five years. He'd served seventeen. Even though, as McVale would have it, there was no hard evidence proving that he'd committed the crime and it was a fit-up.

The captain carried on, hardly missing a beat. 'Of course, Conrad was shocked to see D'Arcy, he was supposed to be absent, and of course, Ivan had had no means of warning Conrad. The bent barrister had slipped away from the house party to take care of this piece of business, and once taken care of, he probably planned on slipping back to Berkshire.

'Charles D'Arcy then took a painting off the wall to reveal a safe. Now that the job had gone so off-piste, this obviously piqued Conrad's attention: a safe within a safe?

'Conrad knew of McVale by reputation. As well as being extremely vicious and violent, he was known for pulling off very big robberies. As far as high-value crimes were concerned, he was a serious man.

'Conrad, eagle-eyed at the best of times, thanks to a gap in the screen was able to use a pocket-sized telescope to watch the barrister spin the tumbler and work out the combination. McVale was also dressed in black, but he looked drained, absolutely exhausted, his forehead covered in sweat. Conrad recognized the look: McVale had just come from pulling a job. And a big job at that, Conrad assumed . . .'

Captain Cavanagh was smiling now, his old grey eyes lit up and animated. Maybe it was the Bushmills loosening his tongue, making him loquacious, or maybe he was a natural-born story-teller. Or maybe, just maybe, thought Frost, this is the story he's been dying to tell for almost two decades, and he isn't going to let the opportunity go to waste.

'. . . Anyway, with the safe open, McVale then handed D'Arcy what he was clutching in his hands. It was a small leather holdall. D'Arcy put it in the safe, closed the door and spun the lock. D'Arcy replaced the painting on the wall and he and McVale left the "secure room" without exchanging a word.

Conrad waited for their footsteps to fade to nothing on the marble staircase, and the solid glossy black front door to close behind them with a reassuring thud, before he stepped out from his hiding place . . . his vantage point, as it were. He took down the painting, and turned the tumbler . . . Hey presto! Conrad took out the bag, unzipped it and saw what was inside. A box.'

'A *box*?'

The old soldier flashed a teasing grin at the detective, who was now on the edge of his seat. 'He never told me what it was made of. Just said it was a box. Maybe that's something we'll find out. But needless to say, when he opened up the box and saw what was inside . . . Well, he knew straight away, Vermeer or no Vermeer, this was the *real* prize. So he made off with the box without a second thought for the Vermeer he'd been sent in to steal.'

Cavanagh arched his unruly and wiry white eyebrows to emphasize that fact, and left a hefty pause for Frost to absorb the information. In that pause he soaked up the last of his Bushmills.

'I know it's obvious,' said Frost, eventually, 'but just for clarification, and my own sanity, I need to hear someone actually say it.'

The captain let out an explosion of laughter followed by a salvo of small coughs. 'I understand, Inspector, I understand. I'll lay it out for you, as much as I know, which is as much as anyone. Jimmy McVale and his gang definitely pulled off the Bond Street robbery of '67. On Friday at 5 p.m. the gang took up their position and got to work. They gained entry to the private bank, and the high-value vault, at precisely 6.30 p.m. on Saturday evening, and McVale was at the Eaton Square home of Charles D'Arcy at 9.15 p.m. Conrad Wilde was out of there by 9.25 p.m.'

'The robbers were robbed?'

'Indeed. A bitter pill for any criminal to swallow, never mind a man like Jimmy McVale. The first victim was Charles D'Arcy. His head was found wrapped in a shopping bag and washed up on the banks of the Thames, by the Royal Festival Hall. His torso befell the same fate, further downriver in Wapping. His limbs were never recovered. It was clear he'd been horribly tortured before being dismembered. One can almost feel sorry for D'Arcy, he'd got in over his head – no pun intended – and paid the price.'

'And what happened to Conrad?'

'Here's where things get really interesting, and tragic. Scotland Yard were hot on Conrad's heels, not for what had just happened, but for a previous burglary. And the man who'd informed on Conrad was none other than his best friend. Ivan gave him up because they were after *him*, the brains behind the operation. And Ivan knew that he couldn't do the prison time. Like I say, Ivan and Conrad both knew the jig was up, and stealing the Vermeer was to be their last job. So when Conrad turned up empty-handed, Ivan thought he'd double-crossed him, pocketed it for himself. Of course he hadn't. He was, in fact, protecting Ivan.

'McVale wasn't taking his losses lying down. He was keeping a close eye on proceedings, carrying out his own violent investigation, kidnapping and torturing those who he thought might have information about who had stolen the prize from him, listening intently to the underworld rumour mill. And if it became known that D'Arcy's stolen Vermeer had turned up, the trail would easily lead to Conrad and Ivan. Conrad had a choice: steal the painting or open the box. And of course, like with Pandora, once the box had been opened, there was no going back. He had to have them. If this was to be his last job, believe me, Inspector, there could be no bigger haul. In fact, that was to prove the problem, it was *too* big. It didn't take long for Conrad to realize that he had bitten off more than he could chew.'

Frost gave the captain a reassuring nod. 'So, then Conrad got arrested, right?'

'Eventually. But not before burying the treasure, because that's what it was, you know. *Treasure*. The Crown Jewels, but better. The Crown Jewels would need to be broken up, the stones re-cut, the gold melted down. But these beauties could not be tampered with. Conrad's plan was simple, don't pass Go, don't collect two hundred pounds, go straight to jail.'

Captain Cavanagh laughed good and hard, like he'd been sitting on the joke for about seventeen years – which he probably had.

'But of course, Frost, the good thing was, he'd never been caught before. So as a first-time offender, as it were, he was assured he'd only get about five years, seven at the most. Then, by the time he was released, hopefully the heat would have died down and he'd be able to sell the haul and disappear abroad. Australia, South America, Canada – with that kind of money he'd be able to live like a king wherever he was.

'Conrad was a lion of a man, never happier than scaling up a wall and leaping across the roofs of Knightsbridge to commit a burglary. Very much an outdoors man, a man of action, a commanding presence who wouldn't let anyone push him around. Seemed cruel to box him in, cage him. And he couldn't take it. The minute he was pushed around, he lashed out.'

'You sound like you were very fond of him, Captain.'

'I profess I didn't know him very well, not like I knew Ivan, obviously. More by reputation. But I'm not a bad judge of character and, let me put it this way, if I was going into battle I couldn't think of anyone finer I'd want at my side. And I served with some very brave, tough men.'

'Fair enough.'

'When I heard what was happening to him in prison, I reached out, tried to stop it. But as I discovered, there were darker forces at play. There were people that wanted Conrad, if not dead, then certainly buried. And that's what happened to him. His various escape attempts led to him being shunted from prison to prison, held in solitary, then goaded by the prison wardens.

They soon got what they wanted, he was certified insane. He got into some scrapes, but he didn't kill anyone. They said he attacked people, maybe so, but I know that at Durham the warders bloody well paid people to attack him.'

'Why? Why single him out for this treatment?'

Cavanagh considered this, then tilted his head to the side and gave his companion a curious glance. 'Funny thing is, Frost, you haven't once asked me what was in the box. That's usually the first question anyone asks about a box: what's in it?'

'Not in this case, it isn't.'

Cavanagh's expressive eyebrows again shot up at this, and his moustache rippled on his top lip like a caterpillar crawling across a leaf.

'Only because I don't think you've ever told anyone this,' Frost clarified.

Everything about the captain got raised further, including the glass in his hand, in a gesture of acknowledgement. 'How could you tell?'

'Because of the way you tell the story. You've relished every minute of it. You're a trustworthy man, a man who's good at keeping secrets, and you've kept this one for a long time.'

The captain took a deep unsteady breath that was full of emotion. 'And the only reason I'm telling you now is because both the players are dead. It can't harm anyone. Apart from me.'

'And now me.'

'Only if you find out what was in the box.'

'Ruin my illustrious career?'

'This information has been kept secret for a good reason.'

'Could it topple governments?'

'Worse. Nothing so transient as mere governments. They come and go. This, Inspector Frost, goes right to the top and is always with us.'

The captain leaned forward to give Frost the information he'd waited so avidly to hear. Frost did the same, but when he glanced around, there was a waiter at his side.

'Anything else, gentlemen?'

Cavanagh's and Frost's eyes met in agreement. 'Why not? Be rude not to.'

Before the waiter crept away, Frost reached into his trouser pocket and pulled out his wallet. 'Please, allow me.' He took a tenner and put it on the waiter's tray.

'Ah, one thing I miss about the job, that expense account. And I have to say the Yard was rather generous and forgiving when it came to the bar bills—' Cavanagh broke off as he spotted something on the table. It was a photo that had fallen out of Frost's wallet. He picked it up and went to hand it back to the DI, then he stopped. His eyes narrowed and the dense nail of his forefinger tapped a figure in the picture. 'Is that the missing girl?'

'What makes you ask?' queried Frost.

'Seems familiar, thought I recognized her face from the newspapers, terrible business.'

Frost corrected him. 'No, Ruby Hanson is the girl on the end with her mother. The girl you pointed out is Ivan Fielding's granddaughter, with her mother.'

'Her . . . mother?' The captain's eyes narrowed further, as if trying to bring something, or someone, into focus. Like with one of those spooky old photos where the faint outline of a spectre haunts the frame.

John Waters was stood in front of the full-length mirror. He was wearing a midnight-blue Armani suit, crisp white shirt and skinny black tie. It was the suit he'd bought for his wedding to Kim less than two years ago. And the nearest he'd got to a tuxedo, seeing as he didn't own one, and certainly had no intention of hiring one at Moss Bros. Whilst hardly dead man's shoes, he didn't really savour the idea of wearing other people's clothes and paying for the privilege. The Armani didn't come out to play often, and now seemed like as good a time as any.

It was supposed to be his big night, the regional copper-of-the-year ceremony, and he got to pick up his commendation for bravery. A medal would be pinned to his chest for saving two women from a blazing fire started by some drug dealers who were trying to run them off the Southern Housing Estate, all because they had the temerity to stand up to the scumbags. Ella and Cathy didn't want anyone else's children dying on the cheap smack the dealers were putting out in the area. They had both already lost their only sons.

He was proud of the work he'd done on that case. But it had come at a price. It had marked him for life. Physically, he still wasn't at full capacity, wondered if he ever would be again. He still felt taut, fragile, vulnerable, a dry autumn leaf ready to crumble underfoot at any moment. He just couldn't shake the feeling that if he came up against anyone, challenged anyone, he'd come off second best. It wasn't a good feeling. You needed confidence: it was your armour. You couldn't just rely on your badge and cries of 'Police! Stop!' Sometimes they didn't. And that's when you really proved your worth.

But then again, he'd listened to Frost. His DI, who had famously stopped a bullet in a bank robbery – with his face. He always said the bullet just grazed his cheek, but in reality, it took a fair amount of skin with it and left a nasty little scar. Frost never talked about it. He didn't even bother to pick up his medal of commendation. Threw a sickie on the night, said he was struck down with a migraine. Of course no one questioned it. But Albert Briggs from Rimmington CID said he saw Frost in the Feathers pub that night, knocking back the Teacher's and Hofmeister like a man on a mission.

The only time Frost had talked about it was when Waters was in the hospital. Jack said he wouldn't be without his scar. It served as a reminder of what the job was really about at times, and how fragile existence is, all the time. It was his badge.

Still, it niggled and surprised Waters that Frost was complaining about simple back pain since taking a header down the stairs, and then falling into a pit, whilst he'd had to endure three months of skin-graft surgery on his back where the flames had flayed off his skin. The scars were still too unsightly to be worn with pride, though they were healing, turning from a livid red to a more palatable pink. Kim said she didn't notice them. Which, for a man of his colour, was an out-and-out lie. But where he couldn't bear to look at them, she certainly didn't have a problem rubbing aloe vera over them. It was a recommendation from his mother, an old Island remedy that seemed to be working.

But he couldn't stay too mad at his colleague and friend. Jack Frost could be an insensitive prick at times, but nine times out of ten, he got the big things spot on. And maybe he had every right to whinge about his back – after all, as some streetwise philosopher once pointed out: it ain't the earthquakes that kill you, it's the stubbed toes.

'You look great.'

'I don't feel it,' said Waters, looking at Kim reflected in the mirror. She was wearing a one-shoulder turquoise taffeta dress, studded with the occasional rhinestone. With her frosted hair, the glitter accentuating her cheekbones and her glossy pink lips, she looked gloriously inappropriately attired for a sombre civic do at the dusty and musty town hall. It was the most colourful he'd seen her in a while. It was a first-date, let's-go-dancing outfit. Since her miscarriage, she'd been in mourning; and this outfit looked like it marked an end to that.

'You look beautiful. You always do.'

'That's not true. I'm sorry.'

'For what? You don't have to—'

'Yes, I do.'

She came up to him and took his hand.

'I haven't been a wife to you, I know that.'

'That's not been on my mind.'

There they stood, their reflections looking perfectly suited, almost like a picture in a glossy magazine. Waters turned away from the image to face the reality of his wife. She was even more beautiful to him in the flesh. He kissed her. He drew her into him, began to gently peck at her neck, a neck fragrant with Rive Gauche. Then he stopped. Just as he could feel himself tense up, he could feel her do the same. He released her waist; his hold on it had been tentative at best.

Her head dipped, she wouldn't look at him. 'Not now. I've just got dressed, made up.'

It was a practical but poor excuse, and one he'd heard, with variations on the theme, too many times over the last six months. *Six months.* She stepped out of the room. And he glanced towards the mirror again. Never believe what they try and sell you in the glossy magazines, he thought.

Sunday (3)

The function room at Denton town hall was swathed in blue, there were blue cloths on the tables, blue crêpe paper was tacked to much of the walls, and there was a strip of blue carpet to replace the red one at the entrance. They'd gone all out for the boys in blue. The decor was rather stating the obvious and, as some concerned coppers had pointed out, it had cut into the budget, the drinks budget that is.

But by the time Frost arrived, everyone was on their third or fourth drink, and decor and fiscal concerns had pretty much left the function room; it was just full of coppers from the county turning the air blue with blue jokes now.

Frost had shoe-horned himself into his best suit that seemed to be inexplicably getting tighter and tighter each year. He'd had to buy it for his wife's funeral, more than two years ago. Frost blamed the copious Kung Po at the Jade Rabbit, not the Harp, the Hofmeister, the Holstein, or even the Heineken when the other three weren't available. He emptied his can of Top Deck shandy into the glass and took his inaugural swig of the brew. He winced, almost in pain, as it fizzed its sickly-sweet way down his gullet. He thought he'd take his foot off the gas after his meeting with Captain Cavanagh, who, boy oh boy, even though he was a captain in the Guards, drank like the captain of a pirate galleon on shore leave after six months at sea.

He was still wincing when Stanley Mullett sidled up to him. 'Cheers, son, I'll have a pint of . . . Oh, sorry, sir, my mistake, I didn't recognize you in that outfit, thought you were a waiter. *Very* smart.'

Mullett, in full evening dress – a satin stripe running down his trouser leg, satin cuffs and shawl collar to his DJ, and a bow-tie that was probably a real one, that he actually knew how to tie – sat down next to Frost. His hair was heavily brilliantined, matching the effulgence of his patent-leather shoes. Authority loves to dress up, loves to press its case, thought Frost.

'That tie, Frost . . .'

'Clever, isn't it? Very good use of the space, I thought.'

'It's unbecoming in a senior officer.'

'We're not the fashion police, sir. Which will be my standard reply this evening.'

Mullett raised his withering, hornrimmed gaze from his DI's neck, and fixed him firmly in its glare. 'Where were you this afternoon?'

'Most of my time was spent with the Hansons. We've had a breakthrough, I believe.'

'Yes, I heard. They've both been engaging in extra-marital affairs. Where else?'

'Where else, how?'

Frost could see he was frustrating Mullett with his picture of innocence, and Mullett cut to the chase: 'I hope Ruby Hanson is getting your full undivided attention.'

The DI took another swig of his Top Deck, to rid himself of the bad taste that was developing in his mouth and replace it with the bitterness of lemons and limes instead. 'With all due respect, I don't think you're aware of just how bloody awful that sounds. A young kid is missing, and you're suggesting that I—'

Mullett raised a placating hand. 'I know you've been obsessed with the Ivan Fielding case, and all the rumour and intrigue swirling around it. It's tempting for a detective to get drawn into that kind of thing. Solve an historic case, get your name in the papers, on TV.'

'Not me. Not when a kid's life is in danger. I leave all the heroics and glory to others.'

Mullett must have noticed the indignation emanating from Frost, because he sat back in his chair, took an engine-turned silver cigarette case from his inside pocket and relieved it of a dainty-looking cocktail cigarette that he lit up with an impossibly slim rolled-gold lighter. Notoriously tight, he didn't offer Frost one. And maybe that's why Frost had taken to stealing Mullett's cigarettes off his desk at every opportunity he got. And he got a lot, the amount of times he was summoned to his office for a bollocking.

'So I have your word that you have not been actively pursuing the Ivan Fielding case?'

Frost followed suit and relaxed back into his chair. He pinched out a cigarette from the crumpled box of B&H on the table and sparked it up. He took a long slow draw on the coffin nail and cogitated on what his super was asking. He didn't want to get caught out in a career-ending lie. He eventually released the smoke and plumed it out in the direction of Sandy Lane, who was by the bar with his snapper, recording the event.

'I have not.'

'Are you sure?'

Just what the hell did Mullett know? 'Yes, I'm sure.'

Of course he wasn't sure. But he was pretty sure he hadn't been *actively* pursuing it, rather the case just kept on presenting itself to him. After all, it was Captain Cavanagh who had contacted him for the meeting earlier today, not the other way around.

'My full attention is on getting that little girl back. And with the leads we have, I'm sure we'll be achieving that within the next forty-eight hours.'

Mullett expelled a breath of relieved air. 'That is excellent news, excellent. She's alive. After the death of the two boys last year, I don't think the area could take another tragic loss of a child.'

'No, sir, I know what you mean.'

With that, the superintendent stubbed out his barely depleted cigarette in the ashtray, shot his cuffs and stalked off.

Frost watched as Mullett weaved his way through the mass of blue tables and over to ACC Winslow, the real power in the room that night. In Winslow's party were the four supers from the other four regions in the county. Once Mullett had taken his seat next to Winslow, the two top brass drew their heads together in a secretive huddle. Frost knew what the subject was, though. And he also knew that buried somewhere in the Fielding case was a cover-up, a cover-up that went right to the top. Captain Cavanagh had alluded to it, but held back from telling him the full story. Maybe he didn't know? Or maybe all the booze at the hotel had got the better of him and he realized he'd said too much. Or maybe, just maybe, under all the bluster and confidence the old warrior was . . . scared.

It wasn't just the fabulous wealth of the object that was taken that night in 1967 . . . it was more. It was history. It was information that could rewrite history. And who knew, maybe change the course of it.

So when ACC Winslow's shadowy glance eventually made it over to him, Frost met it with a raised can of Top Deck. Surely the ultimate insult, he thought.

'Guv?'

He turned sharply around, too sharply, and felt a ripping pain in his back. He muttered some curses, and saw PC Simms hovering at his side holding a couple of expensive-looking drinks. They certainly hadn't been budgeted for, none of the complimentary cheap stuff they were doling out.

'Back still playing up, guv?'

'Only when I laugh. Who are you now, James bloody Bond?'

Simms looked down at himself, as if he'd forgotten what he was wearing – again. He too was togged up in a tuxedo. 'Nice, eh? It's rented.'

'I'd find it deeply disturbing if you owned it, especially on your wages.'

Simms straightened his bow-tie and flicked a speck of lint off his satin collar. 'That said, I could get a taste for this.'

Frost dropped his spent cigarette in the empty can of Top Deck and heard it fizz away. 'Sorry to be the bearer of bad news, son, but I can guarantee you that nothing that great in your life will happen on a regular enough basis to justify the expenditure on a penguin suit. Unless something really bad happens, you get the sack, and are forced to get a job as a waiter. Anyway, how did you get a ticket for this, Plain Clothes Only, you're not a DC yet.'

'The super got me one. A thank-you for my work on the Denton Woods demonstration.'

'Oh yeah, you still working for the Stasi, taking names and addresses?'

Simms shrugged. Probably more familiar with Spectre than the realities of the Stasi, thought Frost. He pulled out a chair for Simms to join him. 'Put the drinks down, *garçon*, don't want them curdling in your hot little hand.'

Simms looked down at the fancy whisky cocktails. 'Ah, yeah, these are for the super and ACC Winslow.'

'Bloody nerve of those two, you might look like a waiter, but you're not one yet. Sod them' – he jabbed a finger into the table – 'we'll have those, they can get their own.'

'They didn't ask me to get them, I found out what they were drinking and decided to take the initiative. Nice tie, by the way, guv. Can you play *Goldfinger* on it?'

'Very smart, Dave. You look like a bad magician,' said Sue Clarke coming over with two pints of Hofmeister.

'Or an emaciated bouncer,' laughed Frost.

Clarke put the drinks on the table. 'You looked like you could do with a pint.'

Simms looked sheepish, and went off to deliver his drinks to the top brass.

'What do you think?'

Frost picked up his pint and downed a substantial amount, then wiped the froth from his lips with the back of his hand before answering. 'Very good, just what the doctor ordered.'

She groaned. 'I meant my frock.'

Frost sat back and took it in. It was a black and magenta off-the-shoulder number with ruffles and puff sleeves, adorned with flamingos in sequins.

'Give us a twirl, Anthea.' Clarke obliged. 'Oh, yes, very nice. The business, the bee's knees.' He took another swig of his lager and Clarke sat down next to him. 'We're going to have to do something about Simms.'

'What's wrong?'

'He needs to have his nose surgically removed from Super-intendent Mullett's arseh—'

'He's young, he's keen, he's—'

'A brown-nosing little prick who's at risk of making enemies amongst the rank and file,' persisted Frost.

Sue Clarke shook her head.

'You don't think he's overly ambitious? I'm telling you, he needs reining in.'

'I fully agree. I'll have a word. That's not the reason I'm shaking my head, Jack. You're wearing it, then? You're actually, actually, *actually* wearing it.'

Frost followed her withering gaze and glanced down at his tie. 'I thought you'd be pleased. You always say what a scruff I look. Thought I'd save it for a special occasion. What better than John's big night.'

'And you do look very smart . . . apart from the tie.'

'It was a gift, Susan, from *you*, if I remember correctly.'

'Yeah, I got it for you this Christmas, as a secret Santa. It was . . . a joke? I got Arthur some Incredible Hulk underpants.'

'And I'm sure he's very grateful and probably wears them every day.' Frost flipped the skinny PVC tie to examine its keyboard design. 'My only other black tie had a couple of big fag burns on it. Last wore it to Mary's funeral.'

She winced. 'That's the problem. It's not a black tie. It's a black and white tie, like a keyboard.'

He shrugged. 'It was the nearest I could get.' He then craned his neck as he spotted Kim and Waters entering the function room.

Clarke waved at the couple and Waters came over, leaving Kim to chat with her colleagues from Rimmington CID.

'Here he is, the man of the moment!'

'Copper of the year!'

'Nice tie, Jack.'

'Sue bought it for me. Secret Santa.'

'She got me a "I Shot JR" T-shirt,' said Waters, winking at Clarke. 'Four years after the event, but I treasure it.'

After some more banter about the pros and cons of Frost's tie – pros: it angered Mullett; cons: everything else – they sat down and more drinks were ordered. Kim came over, Frost and Clarke stood up, greetings were exchanged, cheeks were kissed, and again, all praised the man of the moment, John Waters. Kim and Sue complimented each other on their frocks, agreed they both looked far too glamorous with their sequins and taffeta, rhinestones and ruffles, gelled and glittery hairdos, and would be more suited to a South Beach disco in *Miami Vice* than a municipal building in downtown Denton.

Meanwhile, Crockett grabbed Tubbs' arm for a private conflab, and ten minutes later they were on the marble stairs of the town hall, and out of sight or hearing of Mullett and Winslow. And yet, as Frost filled Waters in on his meeting with Captain

Cavanagh, there was still enough conspiratorial intrigue swirling around the subject for both men to speak in hushed tones.

'. . . So what was in the box?'

Frost gave a slow and sly smile as he saw that Waters was sporting the same look that he himself must have been wearing when Captain Cavanagh told him the story. John was practically drooling.

'A clue. It's Russian, it's beautiful, very precious, and it's made out of metal. And it's not a Lada.'

'Come on, Jack, what was in the bloody box?'

Frost shushed him. 'An egg. A Fabergé egg. But a very special Fabergé egg. About twelve inches in height, about six inches at the fattest part.'

Waters' face stretched in all directions as his eyes widened, his jaw dropped, and he still managed a grin from ear to ear. 'My God, I've only ever seen photos of them. And that one in *Octopussy*.'

Frost raised his eyes to the ceiling and shrugged. 'I stopped going after *Diamonds Are Forever*.'

'This one sounds huge. They're not normally that big, are they?'

'No, never. It's a complete one-off. But as big as it is, and believed to be the largest and most jewel-encrusted one ever produced . . . that's not what made it so special. It was made for the Romanovs.'

'The executed Russian royal family?'

'Unless you know of another.'

'Get on with it!'

'It's not just one egg we're talking here. The egg was designed like a Russian doll, each one contained another. Eight eggs in all. The largest outer egg representing Mother Russia herself. The other seven representing members of the family, the second largest being Tsar Nicholas II, then the tsarina, gradually going down through the children to the very smallest, little Alexei. The smallest egg is carved from Alexandrite, a precious stone found in the Ural Mountains in Russia, and named after

Alexander II, an earlier tsar. Each egg is engraved in Cyrillic with the name of the family member.'

'And this Captain Cavanagh told you all this?'

'In great detail. He even showed me a facsimile of the original design as drawn by Carl Fabergé himself, specifying the jewels to be used.'

'And it's never come on the market?'

The DI gave a solemn shake of his head. 'It was commissioned by Tsar Nicholas himself and went straight to the royal family. A Christmas present in 1916, a gift from a grateful nation, as the Tsar described the expense. Or as the Bolsheviks would have it, more precious baubles paid for by the blood and toil of peasants. Either way, the egg disappeared just before October 1917. Never to be seen again.'

'So what's its value? I forget how much the one in *Octopussy* went for . . .'

'Forget bloody fiction, John, this is real! Those eggs can go for five, ten million? Twenty . . . ? But this one, who can say?'

'Priceless. Making it . . . worthless?'

'There's always someone willing to buy something like that for whatever the seller is asking for it. But the thing that makes it so valuable, and dangerous, is the secret that brought this Russian artefact to London in the first place. And that alone could, according to Captain Cavanagh, not only have brought down the government of the time, but the Royal Family.'

'*Our* royal family? The House of Windsor?'

'Unless you know of another.'

John Waters shook his head in disbelief. He then started to laugh.

'What's so funny?'

'I can't believe I'm being told this by a man in a piano keyboard tie.'

'I'm wearing Frosty the Snowman socks, too.'

'Secret Santa? I got you those. So this big secret that could topple the House of Windsor, what was it?'

'Captain Cavanagh wouldn't tell me that bit. And who knows, maybe he doesn't know. And by the sounds of it, knowing what the secret was could be worth more than your life is worth.'

'How about Conrad Wilde and Jimmy McVale – they must have known?'

Frost considered this. 'Only after opening the box. My theory is: McVale and his team knew there was a big pay-off in that vault, but didn't really know what it was. And if they'd known all the aggro it would cause them, maybe they wouldn't have stolen it in the first place.'

'Like the Great Train Robbers?'

'Exactly. But that was bundles of cash. This was a box full of secrets. A right Pandora's box.'

'If McVale and Conrad knew the secret . . . they've done a good job of keeping it quiet.'

'They had to. If they admitted knowing the secret, they would have to admit to stealing the box in the first place. And two criminals like that? The powers that be would have them snuffed out in a minute. That's the real curse of the Bond Street caper, the information. Once you set eyes on it . . .'

John Waters mouthed *bloody hell* then said, 'Maybe that's why they buried Conrad in the prison system? He started talking, so they had him certified and stuck away for life?'

The inspector blew out his lips and raised his hands palms up in a gesture of complete cluelessness. 'I'm the only one not togged up as James Bond tonight, but I reckon spooks are definitely on the case. Who knows, maybe in Denton right now.'

Sunday (4)

'. . . I'm very grateful for this, it means a lot. But I was just doing my job. And it could have been any one of us stood up here getting this award. Because I know my colleagues at Eagle Lane, and I know that every copper in this room would have done the same . . .'

Applause went up for this, and there were a good few cheers of approval from the audience. John Waters was up on stage to receive his award, something modern-looking in stainless steel and Perspex to collect dust on the sideboard, as well as a very official-looking medal in a velvet case, which would probably live in the sideboard drawer. His speech was short and sweet and very heartfelt.

It was when Waters got around to thanking his wife, Kim, who was sitting with Frost and Clarke, that the first tear fell from her eye. Frost and Clarke exchanged nervous glances surreptitiously, but not surreptitiously enough. Everyone knew that Kim had lost the baby, it was a badly kept secret. Naturally enough, she had taken time off work after the miscarriage, and to help John through the early stages of his recovery. But now the rumoured cracks in Waters' marriage were becoming visible, and public. Frost and Clarke had noticed that Kim was necking the white wine at an alarming rate, and by the time John had stepped up on stage to collect his award from the ACC and the mayor, the tabloid term 'tired and emotional' could have been coined for her.

'You know . . .' said Kim, seemingly addressing neither Frost nor Clarke, '. . . we're all sitting here, having a drink, a laugh, and slapping each other on the back for all the great work we do . . . and yet there's still a little kid out there . . . Ruby . . . missing . . . not home with her mum and dad . . .' Now she focused in on the two detectives, as if demanding an answer.

Clarke said, 'That's what we do, though, isn't it? We do the work, we do it as well and as hard as we can. We're all on call now, all night. We do our job, but we can't take it home with us every night. We need a night like this, Kim. To let off a little steam, and to celebrate the victories, and celebrate what your husband's done.'

'But sometimes we *do* take it home . . . every night, for ever . . . we do . . . we bloody well do!'

Kim shot to her feet, almost fast enough to knock the table over, and certainly fast enough to knock over some glasses. All the attention in the room was now centred on her. Up onstage, her husband stopped talking and turned towards her.

There she stood, frozen in the moment, tears coursing down her glittery cheeks, a trail of mascara advertising her emotions. Clarke grabbed her hand. Frost didn't know if she was pulling at it, trying to get Kim to sit back down, but the move failed. Kim ran out of the function room, bouncing off the backs of her colleagues' chairs like a pinball until she reached the exit. Clarke wasn't far behind, ready to catch her if she fell, but realizing that her leaving the room was the best thing.

John Waters cut his speech short, got a round of uncomfortable applause, and left the stage to tend to his wife. He had to pass Frost's table to get to the exit and his DI was ready for him.

Frost blocked his way, his hand resting on Waters' chest, where he could feel his heart thumping away.

'Susan's got it, John . . . she'll talk to her . . . trust me, mate,' he whispered in Waters' ear.

'You've got a kid, right?'

'I have. A boy.'

'Philip?'

'That's right.'

'John's mentioned him. Said he's got a wicked little smile.'

Clarke pulled a wicked little grin herself at the thought of him. 'He has. But to tell you the truth, he's got a wicked little everything at this age.'

Kim and Sue were on the same steps that Frost and Waters had been sitting on earlier. The ladies' toilet had proved unsuitable for a good chinwag, heart to heart, or whatever this conversation was turning out to be. But they were in the loo long enough to freshen up, powder their noses, reapply some lippy, and for Kim to wipe away her panda eyes.

'This is my first missing-child case since I've had Philip,' said Clarke. 'We've had them wander off the Southern Housing Estate for a few hours, run away and come back, stay at friends' and forget to tell their mums. Then there was . . . well, the two boys last year from the SHE. Dean and Gavin. But this is the first time there's been anything like this, an abduction.'

'How does it make you feel, as a mum?'

'Not as a policewoman?'

'I'm a policewoman, Sue, I know how that feels.'

'It scares me. I know he's safe, tucked up in bed by my mum, who's probably read him more bedtime stories than I ever could. But I can't separate the two. I was a copper long before I had Philip. And as Ruby's case goes on, the deeper we dig, there are clues that tell us it's not just a random snatch. And that's what I wanted to hear. It sounds horrible, but to me that was the most important thing . . . still is. That there is a reason behind it, something in the past to do with an adult. Somehow it makes me think that if I can keep my side of the road clean, I can keep my boy safe.'

'I bet you're a great mother.'

'I'm not. *I've* got a great mother, who sometimes annoys the hell out of me, but takes up a lot of the slack. Like tonight, as I say, she'll read him as many stories as he wants.'

'Must be hard, working and . . .'

'Life is. Sometimes. And, yes, I'm a single mum, so people automatically assume it is.'

'I didn't mean—'

'That's OK. But I wouldn't have it any other way. Or maybe I would, you know – being married to Richard Gere would be quite nice. But seeing as I'm lucky enough to live in Denton, which is nice and flat, and Richard lives in Beverly Hills, and I don't like hills, I'm sort of contented with my lot.'

This achieved what Sue had set out to do and got a laugh out of Kim. Clarke knew the Rimmington DC wasn't by nature the morose woman she had been in the last six months, and it was nice to see her smiling.

'And anyway,' continued Clarke after the laughter subsided, 'I wanted a child more than a man. You're lucky. You can't see it, but you are. You can have both.'

'I don't know if I can . . . If I'll be able to conceive again.'

'You've been told that?'

'It's a feeling.'

'Don't mistake those for facts. If there's one thing this job has taught me, it's that.'

'Then here are some more facts. I don't know if I want to try again. I don't know that John wants to try. He wasn't that keen in the first place. Maybe . . . maybe he got what he wanted, and maybe this is a good place to end it. The marriage.'

Clarke wasn't expecting this. In an effort to modulate her surprise, and as her mind scrambled for something appropriate to say, she focused on a green mark four steps ahead of her. She soon realized it wasn't something totally disgusting, just a crumpled and waxy lime-green Opal Fruit wrapper.

'Listen, Kim, I won't even pretend to understand what you've been through, and maybe I'm completely out of order and have got it completely wrong, but that just seems—'

'I don't know if I love him any more . . . or if he loves me. The house has become like a bad flat-share. Sometimes I dread it when he comes in, I pretend to be asleep.'

'Have you spoken to him about this?'

Kim shrugged, and now seemed to be focusing on the same Opal Fruit wrapper.

'Can I take that as a no?'

'Probably.'

'I think that might be a conversation you'd really, really remember, Kim?' Again, Kim laughed. 'And for what it's worth, I think that might be a conversation you need to have. With him, not me.'

'That's the conversation I'm dreading. I know we can't go on like this. Maybe I'll find out stuff I don't want to.'

'I don't know, Kim. At one point, I thought I wanted to make a go of it with Derek, Philip's dad, but he went and got himself killed, didn't he. Doubt it would have worked. Without wanting to sound like a really crap song, I don't know what love is, not really. Which sounds sadder than it is, and I have to admit every now and again I feel a little bit lonely, but not much. And I'm sure I've never felt that strongly about any bloke, not really, not until they're gone, walked out the door.'

Kim sat up straight as a thought hit her. 'That sounded like two crap songs . . . and one really quite good one.'

'Sing it.'

'Which one?'

'Whichever one you fancy.'

'Don't tempt me, I'm drunk enough.'

'And the acoustics in this place are perfect . . . Go on, sing it.'

'I can't.'

'Yeah, you can, why not?'

'I'd like to say, because I don't want to make a complete arse of myself, but I think it's too late for that.'

'Probably. But I'll be more than happy to join you, if you feel like making even more of an arse of yourself.'

'Where is our man of the moment?' asked Sandy Lane.

'Last I saw him, he was with Frost,' replied Mullett.

Lane shook his head. 'Scuppered, then. Looks like you've lost him if he's with Jack. Jack hates these things, far too stiff for him.'

'*Stiff?*' repeated ACC Winslow, obviously incredulous at the idea that the event was in any way deficient.

Lane was with his young nephew snapper, angling to take a group picture of John Waters together with Stanley Mullett, John Barksdale (the new Rimmington super), ACC Winslow, the mayor, and a local Tory councillor, who soon drifted off once he realized the photo op with the hero cop wasn't forthcoming.

The mayor was the next to make his excuses: 'If Shaft turns up, I'll be in the gents, then I'll be at the bar.'

'Don't forget to pull your chain, your lordship.'

'Very good, Sandy, never get sick of hearing that one.'

The hack turned his caustic attention to the three senior coppers. 'Tell me, Mr Mullett, what was all that about with his missus? She ran out in floods, got some nice pics, real top-tier pap stuff. But we need some background.'

Winslow and Mullett, obviously embarrassed at Kim's antics, pretended nothing had happened. Sandy Lane told them it *did* happen, and his spotty nephew had the pictures to prove it. But Lane stressed again he needed some background.

'I need you to dish the dirt on the couple, to add the big emotional angle and turn the night from a dull public service event into something more newsworthy and sexy. Like the Oscars, Miss World, Rear of the Year. Imagine the headline, fellas.'

Lane winked, stretching out his hands before them as if to frame the front page. 'Wife runs out in floods of tears due to high price of heroism . . . Personal cost of copper bravery breaks up happy home . . . Heartbreak and loss of copper couple . . . Rumours of three-in-the-bed romp finally tear apart hero copper's marriage—'

'How dare you!' said Winslow.

'Disgraceful!' said Mullett.

'Ever drop litter in Rimmington and we'll bang you up for life!' said Barksdale.

The reporter raised his hands in surrender to fend off the two supers and the ACC.

'There is no such story to be had, Lane,' said Winslow, with an authoritative edge hardening his voice.

'DC Kim Waters is a professional of the highest order,' added Barksdale, the Rimmington super.

'All our officers are professionals to their very core,' stated Mullett. 'They're not given over to tawdry, rash displays of emotion and—'

All in the function room stopped talking and every head turned towards the doors. If they could have, they would have all carried on towards the huge marble staircase that swept up from the entrance hall of the grand old Victorian building. Because it was here that Kim Waters and Sue Clarke, arms around each other's shoulders, were belting out the big power rock hit of last year:

'. . . I want to know what love is!'

They were, if not pitch-perfect, then certainly word-perfect. Like they were singing the lyrics straight from a copy of *Smash Hits*.

Then they segued effortlessly into another big hit from a couple of years ago.

'. . . A total eclipse of the heart!'

Arthur Hanlon was the first to raise his Bic lighter above his head and fire it up. Taking the big fella's cue, the rest of the

Denton and Rimmington coppers followed suit with their Bics, Zippos, Ronsons and Swan Vestas, and joined their two vocal, but unseen, colleagues, and before long the whole room raised the roof and belted out the finale . . .

'. . . Purple rain! Purple rain!'

Sunday (5) _____

At this time of night, Harry Baskin's Coconut Grove was the only joint in town where you could get a drink. It was also the only joint in town where you could watch cavorting strippers and strobe-lit pole dancers, and be served drinks by the seriously underdressed Baskin Bunnies. You could press a fiver on them for a tip; but try pressing anything else and Bad Manners Bob, the 300lb bouncer, would launch you out through the back door.

But not tonight, because tonight it was all about the rigours of elite sport. It was all about darts. The strobe lighting had been replaced with bright halogen spots to illuminate the oche, the board and the 7 feet and 9¼ inches of hotly contested air that separated them.

The only real allusion to the club's other enterprise was that every time a 180 was scored, one of Baskin's topless Bunnies would parade in front of the crowd, a score card held aloft. The celebrity MC came out with some gamey quips whenever it happened, and it had already happened twice since Frost and Waters had entered the club. Local player Keith 'Keefy'

Keathson was on fire; and every time his arrows hit the top-twenty spots, or the grandstanding bull's-eye, the crowd erupted.

Frost and Waters soon found themselves ensconced in a booth, furthest away from the action. They'd had their heart to heart on the way over, in the cab, and it had lasted about six and a half minutes. It mainly consisted of Frost saying, 'Don't know what to tell you, mate,' and 'I'm sure you'll make the right decision,' and eventually, 'I don't know, mate, when it comes to this stuff, I haven't got a naffin' clue.' All of which was true. He had no advice for Waters because, as Frost told him, everything he said would just have sounded trite, like lines off the telly, the usual second-rate, hand-me-down received wisdom that people like to spew out at times like these; more for their own benefit than that of the poor sod who had to listen to it. And anyway, who the hell was he to impart his insights on other people's marriages when his, by the end of it, was little more than a sham. Waters would have to work this one out for himself.

However, he wasn't all callous indifference to Waters' domestic plight. Frost had seen the glint in the DS's eye when he told him the news from Captain Cavanagh, and he knew that work would take Waters' mind off his floundering marriage, even if only for a momentary respite. And work was the reason they were here.

On entering the Coconut Grove, Frost had put into action the plan they'd hatched in the remaining ten minutes of the cab ride over to the club. It wasn't long before one of Baskin's Bunnies, with two bull's-eyes about the size of bottle tops replacing the customary tassels, had sashayed over and told them Harry would see them now. Of course he will, thought Frost, my message written on the back of a napkin wasn't that cryptic. It alluded to what Baskin had always suspected, but was dying to know for sure.

'Unbelievable . . . unbelievable . . . I really can't—'

'Believe it?'

'It's unbelievable.'

Frost and Waters glanced at each other, both with bemused smiles. They'd never seen Harry Baskin so undone by a piece of information. The club-owner was at his desk, dressed in the same formal evening attire as the famous comic MC out front.

There was a depleted bottle of Johnnie Walker Blue on the desk, and Frost's and Waters' crystal tumblers accounted for some of its sorry state.

'But Harry, you've always suspected that Jimmy McVale had something to do with it,' said Frost. 'You've always had him in the frame.'

'Yes. But to hear it laid out like that . . . well, it beggars belief. And Conrad Wilde . . . he nicked it off him and buried it in Denton?'

'That's what we've heard.'

'Reliable source?'

'The best. Wouldn't be wasting your time otherwise, would I?'

Baskin nodded in agreement. 'So why *are* you wasting my time with it?'

Frost shrugged. 'No reason – like I said, Harry, nothing you didn't know already. Just thought I'd satisfy your curiosity. And if you hear anything on the grapevine, you know, you scratch my back, quid pro quo?'

Harry Baskin raised a glass to this. 'You haven't told me what was in the box.'

Frost shrugged. 'Don't know. That bit my reliable source couldn't tell me.'

Waters piped up, 'But whatever it was that Conrad Wilde buried, McVale's obviously found it.'

Harry took some meditative sips of his whisky, then asked, 'How do you know he's found it?'

'Because of the land he's buying in Denton. We've just come from the town hall, a contact in land registry told us. Still all very hush-hush, but the word is, he's bought some sizeable acreage, including a parcel in Denton Woods. Plans on building a place from scratch, like Southfork, I'd imagine, knowing the ego on him. Invest in some other properties around town. Makes sense, there's a boom on.'

'He'll be your new neighbour,' said Waters. 'There goes the neighbourhood!'

Frost laughed along. 'Yeah, just a heads-up, so now you know where your new neighbour got all his money from, and it's not from selling his rubbish book, it's from finally getting his hands on the Bond Street haul.'

Harry Baskin swallowed this information like it was a dry old walnut. Still in its shell. 'My new neighbour, you say?'

Waters nodded benignly. 'Looks that way.'

'I thought he was just visiting?'

'Why would he just visit?' asked Frost. 'It's Denton, not Disneyland.'

'Once you're out of town . . . Some of the best scenery in the country,' insisted Waters.

'Really?' Baskin looked bemused.

'It is if you're from Bermondsey, which he is.'

'How do you know this, because that's not—' Baskin pulled out of what he was going to say sharply, but not sharply enough.

'Not what?' asked Frost.

'Not . . . not what I imagined he'd do.'

'Well, how do you know? You said you haven't seen him.'

'I haven't. I'm from Stepney, we were from different sides of the river, we didn't fraternize.'

Frost said, 'Anyway, mate, just thought we'd warn you.'

'Warn me?'

'I think what Jack means, Harry, is that if McVale does decide to settle here, and it looks that way, we don't want any trouble.'

'Why would there be?'

'You've been good to us in the past, Harry,' said Frost, 'we just thought we'd tip you the wink. Jimmy McVale could be serious competition for you, right?'

'He's retired. Writes books.'

Frost let out a bit of laughter. 'Do they ever really retire, Harry? Men like Jimmy McVale? Nah, it's in the blood.'

Frost and Waters finished their drinks with lavish 'ahhs' of satisfaction; not only because of the smoothness of the superior blend, but because of the smoothness of the execution of their strategy. It was working a treat.

Harry Baskin grabbed the bottle of Johnnie Walker Blue and quickly refilled their glasses. 'Hold up, lads, hold up. You've just told me you've heard it from the top that he committed the 1967 Bond Street job – you'll be nicking him for that, won't you?'

'No evidence,' said Waters. 'The only witness, the only person who saw him, was Conrad Wilde. And he's dead.'

'How did Jimmy McVale find out where Conrad had buried the box?'

Frost and Waters, now feeling the effects of the booze, slumped in their chairs, barely managed some who-gives-a-monkey's shrugs.

'I have to say, I'm disappointed in you, Mr Frost, Mr Waters. Especially you, son, you've just won copper of the year. This isn't what I pay my taxes for: murderers and robbers left alone to walk the streets of our fair town.'

'You're showing a lot of civic pride all of a sudden,' said Waters.

'Denton's been very good to me.'

'And you want it to remain so, right?'

'I have nothing to fear, Inspector Frost, I pay my taxes and I'm a legitimate businessman.'

Waters said, 'But with Jimmy McVale around, that could put a serious dent in your margins, no?'

Baskin countered, 'Make a tasty titbit for the *Echo*. Imagine the headline: "Hidden bank robbery haul in Denton funds convicted murderer's property portfolio." '

'Very good, Harry, you'll give Sandy Lane a run for his money with headlines like that one,' said Frost.

'I'll run it by him next time I see him. Denton's top crime reporter is very easy to find. If he spent any more time in this place he'd be a bar stool.'

'What do you care?' asked Waters with a face full of mock confusion.

'Like you said, I'm very civic-minded these days.'

Frost said, 'It's an old case, Harry, and we've got bigger fish to fry, like getting that little girl back.'

This stymied Baskin's faux outrage; he couldn't argue that point. He took a thick slug of his drink.

John Waters offered, 'And anyway, we can't move on the case unless we hear anything worth moving on. We need hard evidence. All trails have gone cold on that job. It was almost twenty years ago.'

Frost agreed wholeheartedly with his colleague, couldn't have put it better himself. Though when they were rehearsing the routine in the back of the cab, he was pretty sure he'd phrased it a little more emphatically, so he added, 'That is, of course, unless you hear anything about McVale and the robbery that might liven things up. Or anything about McVale at all that we could use.'

'Grass? What do you take me for?'

'The number two in town?' said Frost.

Harry Baskin's bottom jaw lurched forward, his brows knitted and his eyes darkened, and he looked like the intimidating presence that must have first set him up in business all those years ago, and had made him the number-one gangster in Denton.

Frost said, 'Relax, Harry, keep your toupee on.'

'Another vicious rumour. Anyway, that's rich coming from a man in a PVC keyboard tie.'

Frost glanced down at the offending item, whilst Baskin contemplated the contents of his crystal tumbler. Knowing they'd given Baskin quite enough to think about, the two Denton detectives got to their feet. They told Harry they'd talk later, they wanted to get back to the darts. There were some big names making an appearance, more for the appearance money than the sporting prestige. Jocky Wilson was on next, and there were bound to be more 180s flying around – a small man, but a big player. It was worth it, just to see one of Baskin's Bunnies hold up the score card.

They stepped out of the office and closed the door behind them, leaving Harry nursing his whisky and mulling over his fragile-looking future as the self-appointed *capo di tutti i capi* of Denton.

'Look at you, the sexy inspector, all dressed up and looking like the cat that got the cream.'

Frost, who was patting himself down in search of his keys, and whistling a jaunty little tune, shot his head around to see Shirley walking behind him in the hallway of Paradise Lodge. She was wearing a little black number with high-heeled red pumps. She'd obviously been out for a big night herself.

'Shirley, I didn't see you . . .' Frost sniffed the air, and an imperceptible smile slipped into place.

'Chanel N°5. Looks like it brings back memories?'

'Recognize it anywhere. Dead give-away.'

'Don't worry, sweetie, I'm not following you. I just caught sight of you hobbling into the lift. I was going to get you to hold it, but I wasn't fast enough and you got away from me. Been doing the town, all dressed up? Nice tie, does it play a tune? Bet I could get one out of it.'

'I bet you could.' Frost pulled out his key.

'You seem pleased with yourself? Have you just brought down Mr Big?'

Frost gave it some thought. 'Well, in my line of work, sometimes we're the last people in the world who can catch the crooks. Sometimes it takes a crook to catch a crook. But to do it, you have to set it up carefully. And I think that's what I've achieved tonight.'

'Do you think you'll catch him?'

'I don't even know if he's done anything yet, not for sure. But sometimes you have to shake the tree as hard as you can to bear fruit.'

'A man after my own heart, that could be my motto.'

Shirley leaned seductively against the wall.

Maybe it was the booze throwing his world into soft focus; expensive whisky had a delightful tendency to dapple the light, give everything a glow. But she looked good. The fur jacket she was holding fell to the ground like a bored cat jumping from its owner's clasp. It was clear to Frost that she was shaking the tree. He considered the fruits. Then he dutifully bent down to pick the jacket up. Maybe it was all the talk of spooks, '60s capers, and all the tuxedos on display that night, but Frost was aware of the moist-lipped smirk he was wearing, Sean Connery-style. But the veneer of 007 sophistication quickly fell away as his hand grabbed the fur and his face contorted in pain like one of Blofeld's hastily dispatched henchmen.

'Oh . . . Jesus Christ!'

'Oh, Jack, let's not bring him into the equation, and spoil the mood.' She looked concerned as he ratcheted himself up and handed her the fur. 'You all right, pet?'

'Just a twinge,' he said, his voice wavering with pain and hitting all the high notes. 'All . . . all in the line of duty . . .'

'Where does it hurt?'

Frost made a vague gesture with his hand to indicate the area of pain.

Shirley puckered her lips and considered him with the demeanour of a well-practised doctor. 'Lower back pain. Common enough. There's a tight pack of nerves around there.'

She jolted herself away from the wall and put her hands around his waist, her right hand reaching under his jacket. She could feel the involuntary spasm of him sucking in his gut. She smiled. Touch a man just about anywhere and he'll try and flex something. Her right hand dug into the zone of pain. She could tell by the flutter of his eyelashes that it felt good. Painful, but good. She disengaged from the detective, then fished out her own key from the little red clutch that matched her red pumps and opened her front door.

'Those muscles need a good going-over, your nerves are in need of some relief. I've got the hands and the know-how.'

'No need, Shirley. I'll get Dr Maltby at work to give me the once-over.'

'Most doctors know bugger-all about back pain. My old man was in the profession.'

'I thought he was a chiropodist?'

'He was.'

'That's feet, isn't it?'

'Same field.'

'I'd say not even the same country.'

'Oh, Jack, haven't you heard the song?'

He shook his head. She, in a low, breathless and impossibly sexy voice crooned it for him: 'The foot bone's connected to the ankle bone, the ankle bone's connected to the leg bone, the leg bone's connected to the thigh bone . . .'

She grabbed his keyboard tie and pulled him in. Frost knew what the thigh bone was connected to, and Shirley was reminding him of that anatomical fact with each tug of his keyboard tie. She was playing him beautifully.

Monday (1)

It must have been during the second volley of thunderous banging on the side of the van that Clive Banes opened his eyes. His clothes were stuck to his skin, soaked in cold sweat. He'd woken up in the middle of the night shaking, nauseous, dry-heaving. It felt like the flu. He cursed at the idea of this, the bloody flu. A common cold was bad enough, but it was a mere niggle compared to the flu, which could wipe you out for weeks. He didn't have weeks. He had days, maybe even just a day, and the clock was ticking. He knew that the net would close in soon. It always does. And he knew that the ones who get caught are the ones who lose sight of that and can't walk away.

'Is anyone in there?'

'Who is it?'

'Police.'

Of course it is, he thought, who else would bang on the side of your van like that? The sheer persistence of it was authoritative, demanding, and somehow spelt out the fact they had plenty of back-up if things turned nasty and they didn't get the response they were after.

'Hold up, mate, just getting dressed.'

His eyes did a quick sweep of the back of the van: everything that might have looked suspicious, or raised questions, was covered. He lifted the lid off the tool box. There was a hacksaw with a selection of varying blades, a red-handled Stanley knife, three chisels and two hammers. He then removed the top section of the three-layered box to retrieve the right tool for the job. It was a blue nylon fold-out wallet with a Velcro fastener. Wallet number five he called it, five out of a possible seventeen. But he'd taken only six with him for this trip. He took a deep breath, closed his eyes, concentrated, and ran the legend through his head until it was locked in there. There could be some creative improvising along the way, but his history was solid. He climbed into the cab of the Bedford and rolled down the window. The first thing he saw was their badges.

'What you doing parked here?'

There were two coppers: a WPC and a plain clothes one. Spotty young fella, certainly looks too young to be out of uniform, thought Banes. But it's comments like that that age you. The copper was wearing what looked like a dinner jacket and bow-tie under his navy-blue mac.

Which seems a bit over the top for this time of the morning, thought Banes. Then he said, 'I had a couple of pints in the pub up the road, then I started to feel ill, so I pulled over, ended up staying the night. Better safe than sorry.'

The plain clothes, or rather very flash clothes, copper considered Banes with some suspicious little nods. This didn't unduly bother him, that's what coppers did. It was their job to unsettle you, catch you off guard.

'Can I see your driving licence, please?'

Banes smiled his acquiescence, reached into his jeans pocket and pulled out the grubby blue nylon wallet. He took out his driving licence, in its own little clear plastic wallet, and handed it to the policeman.

'Reading? What you doing around here, Mr Phelps?'

The spotty young copper handed the driving licence to the WPC, who detached herself from the conversation and went back to the patrol car. She retrieved from the dashboard what looked like a scroll of fax paper, and began checking through it.

'I said, what you doing around here?'

Annoyed with himself that he'd been caught out being distracted by the actions of the WPC, Banes tried to smooth it over with some run-of-the-mill paranoia. 'I've got the MOT in the back of the van if you want to see?'

'It's OK, we're just running a check on some names.'

'My name won't come up, never does. I've played the Pools and Spot the Ball for yonks, not so much as a tickle.' This elicited a whiff of amusement from the copper. 'I was going to go to the protest, Denton Woods.'

The copper gave a weary look of disapproval. 'I think they've got enough protestors down there now, Mr Phelps. But it's a free country.'

Banes fished out a card from his wallet, a union card. 'I'm not a protestor, I'm a chippy, a carpenter by trade. Mate of mine said they needed blokes who can handle a chainsaw. I'm between jobs, so I thought I'd give it a go. Like Norman Tebbit said, get on your bike and go look for work.'

The plain clothes guy's face seemed to lighten at this. There were now some nods of approval. The WPC came back and handed Thomas Phelps his driving licence. 'Thank you, Mr Phelps.'

Banes put it back in the nylon wallet. 'Pleasure. I take it I haven't won the Pools, then?'

The WPC threw her colleague a questioning look.

'Mr Phelps says his name never comes up for the Pools prize.'

'To be honest, sir,' said the WPC, 'you wouldn't want your name coming up on this list.'

'I'm intrigued. If I see anything . . . suspicious, as you say, I could give you a call.'

The tuxedo copper looked appreciative. 'We're looking for someone from Longthorn mental hospital.'

'Blimey, an escaped patient? Do you have a name?'

'Someone who worked there, actually, and we've got a whole list of names.'

'Blimey, I heard about something in the pub last night. There was a murder, some bloke in a caravan in the woods. Gruesome, I heard. Is it this bloke from the nuthouse – must be, right?'

The WPC, more circumspect than her colleague, said, 'We don't know yet, it's an ongoing enquiry.'

'What's his name, the bloke you're after?'

'Like I say, sir, we're working from a list. I'm not at liberty to say.'

'Nutters on the loose, people getting smashed over the head in the woods, and there's a kid missing too, right?' Banes didn't wait for an answer, he was too busy looking mildly terrified. 'I think I'll turn back. It's a lot safer in Reading.'

'You OK to drive?' asked the WPC.

'Look that rough, do I?'

'My dad's got the flu, lot of it about.'

'Yeah, I'll be OK. Safer than hanging on around here.'

'Someone's got a spring in their step.'

Frost turned his head, faster than he'd turned it in a while, certainly since being pushed down the stairs, and saw John Waters getting out of a red Ford Fiesta. His wife, Kim, was driving. She gave Frost a beaming smile and a fluttery little wave. It was certainly the biggest smile he'd seen her give since her husband came out of hospital. Frost returned both the smile and the wave, just not so fluttery. She drove off and Waters jogged over; he too had a spring in his step as they headed towards the station.

'Good morning, Detective *Inspector* Waters.'

'Easy, easy, not yet, I'm not.'

'Area copper of the year, looks like you could win the nationals too – you're a shoo-in.'

'That's not why I'm smiling.'

Frost grinned and winked. 'And I assume that's not why Kim is smiling too.'

John Waters stopped and grabbed Frost firmly by the shoulders, forcing the DI to stop too. Once the animated and about-to-be-DI had loosened his grip on the actual DI, Frost dipped into his bomber jacket and pulled out a fag from the pack of ten he'd nicked off the three girls and lit it up.

'Go on, you've got until the end of this,' he said, gripping the B&H betwixt thumb and forefinger and sucking down a huge tube of smoke that made the paper and noxious weed crackle and fizz. 'Then I'll just lose interest.'

'I think I've sorted it out with Kim.'

'Good to hear. I knew me giving absolutely no advice whatsoever was the right thing to do.'

'When I got in last night, I was getting ready to kip on the sofa. And then I hear her call my name. I go into the bedroom—'

'I might have to light up another smoke.'

'It was great, the best ever, but that's not the point!'

'When you're in my shoes, that's the *only* point.'

'She was smiling . . . she was smiling! It was like all the pain and hurt had left her. The ghost was gone, and Kim was back. That's what really did it for me. She was happy to see me. The first time I'd seen that in a long time. And I was happy to see her, the old Kim, the girl I married . . .'

It had been a while for him, but Frost got what his friend and colleague was talking about. That smile; sometimes that's all that mattered. Frost looked down at his cigarette. There was probably another minute left on the clock, but Waters was right, Frost did have a spring in his step, so he gestured for his colleague to follow him.

'You look . . . different, sort of taller,' said Waters.

'Yeah, my back's cleared up.'

'Sleeping on the floor must have done the trick.'

Frost winked, beamed a smile and bounded off like a cheetah to take the steps to Eagle Lane two at a time.

Five minutes later, Frost was standing in the incident room before the blackboard and the flip chart, which were now completely covered in names, dates, locations, arrows, hot tips, wrong turns and dead ends and positive sightings. It was the morning briefing, and the room was packed. Everyone in CID was in attendance. And there was a fair scattering of uniforms, too.

'Ladies and gentlemen – and Arthur – so far we have two prime suspects for Ruby Hanson's abduction. One of whom, Gordon Alistair Dellinpile, known as "Degsy" to everyone who doesn't really know him, is currently in custody, but will be released later today, without charge, due to lack of evidence. And then there's Louisa Hamilton, who is in custody in Bristol.' Frost checked his watch. 'And will be joining us shortly, and will certainly be charged with perverting the course of justice and wasting police time. Kidnapping? No. So where does that leave us? A random snatch off the streets of Denton? Every parent's nightmare, every policeman's too.'

Superintendent Stanley Mullett, who may well have been lurking at the back as was sometimes his wont during the morning briefing, now made his presence felt. He advanced towards the front, with reassuring utterances of 'Morning' and 'As you were, as you were.' He was now standing between DC Susan Clarke and Arthur Hanlon. Hanlon pocketed the oily sausage roll he'd been feasting on behind the broad-shouldered cover of John Waters' back.

Frost continued: 'Can we link Ruby's abduction to the murder of Kevin Wheaton in Denton Woods, and indeed of Wheaton's mother in West Norwood? I believe we can.'

Groans and gasps went up from those gathered in the incident room, as they considered the brutal nature of the murders. The idea that this killer was in the orbit of the little girl was unfathomable.

But amongst all the collective anxiety, Stanley Mullett didn't move, flinch, utter a sound or even seem to modulate his breathing. He just stared ahead of him, and ahead of him stood Jack Frost. Catching Mullett's glacial gaze didn't freeze the detective. Frost quietened everyone down and continued.

'OK, listen up. First of all, and thanks to the stellar work performed by the team in questioning the protestors in Denton Woods, I believe we can eliminate those actually involved in the demo. As far as we've been able to establish, Kevin Wheaton had no interest, and was not involved in the protest. No one knew him, interacted with him, or was even really aware of him. Wheaton was just camped up there. The Wheaton murders, with our assistance, are, as you all know, being investigated by the south-east London murder squad. Working with DI David Garside, who's heading the investigation, we've established that Kevin Wheaton spent time at Longthorn Secure Hospital – not as a patient, I stress, but as a visitor. Visiting one Conrad Wilde.'

Now Frost heard a sound out of Mullett, not speech, but he could actually hear him bristle. He pushed on regardless.

'This brings us back to the case of Ivan Fielding, who I believe died in suspicious circumstances—'

'Jack, can I have a word, please,' said Mullett, already on the half-turn towards the exit.

'Sorry, sir, but I need to make this point to my team, now. It's a matter of life and death.'

'And I need to talk to you in private, *now*.'

'I'll repeat that, Superintendent Mullett, a matter of life and death. Time is of the essence, and above and beyond anything, my career included, my officers will be made aware of all the facts that we have uncovered to help bring Ruby Hanson home.'

There wasn't a pin to hand to test the theory, but you could certainly hear the rustle of the greaseproof paper that contained Arthur Hanlon's jumbo sausage roll. Frost didn't budge, stayed stock-still with a determination that emboldened his team. The mutterings of agreement and solidarity with Frost from the assembled officers made it damned clear to Mullett that if he wanted to stifle the information Frost had, he'd be writing out

D11 reprimand notices to the whole incident room. Even the new civilian part-timer Rita, with the colourful hair, was craning her neck over the desk partition to see what was happening.

Mullett was shrewd enough to know that if he didn't want a mutiny on his hands, he'd have to let Frost speak. And Frost was astute enough to throw Mullett a bone so he wouldn't be publicly humiliated, so he pretended to ask for permission.

'May I carry on, sir?'

'Very good, Jack, we can talk after.'

'Indeed we can, sir, indeed we can.'

Mullett exited the incident room nodding his approval, but obviously bruised by the episode. Once he was gone, Frost breathed easy, unravelled his red scarf from around his neck and unzipped his bomber jacket, to reveal he was wearing the same duds as last night. They smelt of whisky, cigarette smoke, and Hai Karate. But most of all they smelt of Chanel N°5.

From the floor came groans and titters and, 'I was hoping I'd never see that tie ever again, guv.'

'Don't talk with your mouth full, Arthur!'

Frost then straightened the offending keyboard tie, and reached into his inside jacket pocket to pull out a photograph. He pinned it up on the incident board.

'Here's something else we need to consider very, very seriously. Ruby's abduction might well be a case of mistaken identity.'

Monday (2)

She was going to go last night. But as brave as she was, she was still scared of the dark. And on a practical level, she knew that it was colder at night, and in the countryside it was even colder still. For she was sure she wasn't in a town or a city. All she heard was the occasional caw of crows, and what she thought was the hoot of an owl. There was no *whoosh* of passing traffic, no chatter of human voices. I could be anywhere, she thought, miles from other houses, and certainly miles from home.

At night, out there, in the woods, the forest, wherever they had taken her, she would stumble and fall and get eaten by wolves, her blood would be sucked by vampire bats, and her bones picked over by zombies. That was bound to happen. It's *bleedin' well* bound to, she thought. She then laughed to herself, she'd picked up some swear words from listening to the two Ronnie Reagans. Worse ones than *bleedin'*, but she wasn't sure what they meant, so she wouldn't use them. She'd ask Darren Blake, the boy whose dad ran the garage (Mum said they weren't their sort), he was bound to know. Then she'd use them, she was sure.

So morning was the best time for her to make her escape. After they'd given her some breakfast. It was usually Rice Krispies; or toast with lots of jam, more than Mummy gave her. She always said it was bad for her teeth. It was toast this time. Elevenses was in two hours' time. She had a 'gap in the diary', as her daddy always said when he had some spare time. Then he'd write it down in his expensive Filofax. She hid the Filofax once when she heard him shout at Mummy. He almost cried, said he was lost without his Filofax. Ruby 'found it' for him, and he hugged her, said she'd saved his life. Shame he's not here to save *my* life now, she thought. But she'd given up on that happening, it was up to her now. She knew you couldn't rely on the grown-ups.

She carefully pulled back the little chest of drawers and saw the light showing through the loose floorboards. They came away easily, because she had removed them once already. But this time it was for real. She lowered her head into the hole and saw the grate where the light flooded in. It looked like a bright day. Cold, but bright. She pulled her head out of the hole, glanced around the room and located her *Cockleshell Bay* rucksack, with her Little Miss Lucy doll inside. She realized that she hadn't even taken it out of her bag the whole time she'd been here. And she knew that she wouldn't be taking it with her now.

Then down the hole in the floor she went, head first. She'd dithered about this, but decided this way she would see where she was going and so wouldn't get stuck. The gap under the floorboards looked big enough to crawl along, but she suspected there was only a small amount of space between the top and the bottom. And if she got stuck, she couldn't exactly call out for help. Wiggling herself through the oblong hole, she was soon down the floor, which seemed to be made up of hard earth. She then saw that the space was much bigger than she expected. It looked like it stretched under half the house. But height-wise, it was fairly restricted, so she gave herself a gold star for going down head first, it had been the right thing to do.

Even with the light from outside, it was still spooky down there. There were cobwebs like flavourless candy floss spread between the joists above her head, and lots of dead daddy-long-legs. It smelt earthy and damp, of rotting wood, with the curled-up corpses of dead woodlice like little cannonballs dotted around the dirt. The ground was cold and hard. Her knees were soon raw and bleeding as she crawled along, and she knew she'd end up with some big scabs. But she quite liked scabs on her knees, they tingled, and when you peeled them off, you could eat them, they tasted like salt and were chewy. She thought about the scabs because it stopped her thinking about the cobwebs that were brushing against her face and the dead insects caught in her hair. And she really didn't want to see any live spiders.

She had reached the grate. It was almost big enough to crawl through as most of the terracotta slats were broken and crumbling. With the heel of her hand, and pure determination, she punched away at the remaining ones until spots of blood bubbled up on her hand and trickled down her wrist. But she couldn't feel the pain because the adrenalin that was pumping through her little frame was numbing everything. She was powered on by fear, determination and a newly found rage which she couldn't quite account for. The hole was widening as the terracotta slats crumbled under her blows.

She'd done it! She crawled through the vent, pulling herself along the ground with blunt little fingers digging in the grassy earth – until her feet shook free of the ventilation hole, and the house, and her captives. She stood up and looked around her. The house was a mixture of grey stone and timber – a cottage, she supposed, but without a picturesque thatched roof, just dark slates. Actually, she thought, it's more of a chalet than a cottage. But whatever it was, it was in a state of disrepair, with most of the windows boarded up. What looked like a lot of builder's materials was stacked up against one wall, planks of wood and sheets of plasterboard in plastic covers. They reminded her of Daddy. He drew houses and buildings and sometimes at the weekends she'd go with him when he had to visit a building site.

The house was in a large clearing, though you couldn't call it a garden, because the grass was patchy and long. There was a blue Land Rover, looked like an army vehicle. She'd seen one outside school, Lindsey Klebb's dad's car, but he wasn't in the army, he was a farmer. Did Lindsey Klebb's dad steal her? No, now she remembered, Lindsey's dad's one was green, and it was always muddy.

She turned suddenly back towards the house as, in her peripheral vision, a light went on in one of the downstairs windows. She quickly realized that it wasn't actually a window, but a thick sheet of clear plastic replacing the glass. But it was too murky and smeared with dirt to see who was inside. But she did detect some movement. The Ronald Reagans . . . who else? There were only two of them involved in stealing her, she was sure. And the other man, the angry man on the end of the line who shouted at them and told them off. It was when the two Ronald Reagans put the phone down, after these heated conversations with the angry man, that Ruby learned most of her new swear words. The Ronald Reagans sounded funny. But they were also dangerous.

She ran.

'Lovely morning for it.'

Stephen Parker lifted his gaze from the cracks in the pavement he was walking along and turned sharply to his left, towards the road, to see the white Bedford van creeping alongside him. It stopped and Banes opened the passenger door, letting it swing ominously open. Parker glanced nervously around him. He had just stepped out of his home, and had gone about a hundred yards down the road to where he'd parked his 2CV.

'I hadn't heard from you . . . I thought it was over.'

'Far from it, Doctor. It's just begun. Our friend, Mr Wilkes, has had a change of heart. He's happy for us to have the painting. It's all been sorted out.'

'I have to be at work.'

'It won't take long. Get in.'

Parker edged towards the van and held the open door, but didn't commit himself to climbing in.

'My . . . my third of the painting is at work, in my office. Vanessa thinks I've thrown it out.'

'Very duplicitous of you. You don't plan on sharing your new-found wealth with her?'

Parker barked an inappropriate little laugh, like it was all a bit of a joke. 'I haven't really thought about it. I just want to find out what it is that's worth so much money and has cost people their lives. Like a good research problem, it's about solving the mystery.'

'Then get in.'

'I can't, I have rather a full day today.'

'Doing what?'

'Lots of papers to mark, a seminar, then I have to pick up Vanessa's grandchild from school, her mother's working today up in London, and Vanessa's seeing her sister, so I said I would. Then I'm cooking dinner tonight. Sorry, another day. How are you fixed for tomorrow? Mm?'

Banes stared at him. At first he was incredulous. Then he glared at Parker as anger took over. This – this was proving to be his life's work and this idiot was boring him to death with his tiresome little domestic plans. Treating the whole thing as an appointment in a diary, something to get to, like a haircut or a trip to the cinema.

'Marking papers? Picking kids up from school? *Are you mad?* Do you know what we're involved in here? Because if you don't, why don't you just give me your painting, and we'll call it quits. Pretend we never met.'

'No.'

'No what? No, you don't know what we're involved in, or no, you don't want to give me the painting?'

'I don't want to give you the painting.'

'Maybe I should ask your delightful girlfriend, Vanessa, the glamorous granny, because I believe the painting belongs to her, right?'

'I don't want you anywhere near her!'

Banes' thin mouth rippled into a smile. That was exactly what he wanted to hear from Parker. You mendacious little prick, thought Banes.

'Ah, so you do know what you're involved in. You see, Doctor, I'm no dilettante. This is a serious business. Not a "research" project. It's a once-in-a-lifetime opportunity, if you will. You've got a nice little girlfriend, your nice little family, your nice little job . . . But me? This is it for me. This is all I have. And I'm not going to blow a once-in-a-lifetime opportunity because you've got to . . .' He paused to get some equanimity back in his voice. 'I'm a serious man. And you, you're in this, you're in this too. Up to your neck.' And more than he knows, thought Banes. 'So. Get. In. The. Van.'

Parker got in the van. 'Where are we going?'

'To see our friend Mr Wilkes.'

'How did you get him to sell you the painting?'

Banes changed the subject. 'She's very lovely, your girlfriend. And her daughter, and granddaughter. And you, not a lot older than the daughter. But really, Vanessa is quite the beauty.'

'How did you see . . . You followed us?'

Banes had been waiting outside Parker's house when he and Vanessa had emerged earlier. The two of them had walked to Sally's block of flats on Howland Street. And then they all walked Ella to school. It was busy at the school gates this morning. It was the first day Mountview Juniors had opened since the disappearance of Ruby Hanson. There were parents and grandparents in force, and even the mayor had shown up to show support for the returning children. There were yellow ribbons threaded through the cast-iron railings. Two WPCs were on hand, and a patrol car was parked outside. The press and TV cameras kept a respectful distance. The school reopening was news, but not big enough news for them to get excited about.

Once the little girl had kissed her mummy and grandmother goodbye, Vanessa and Stephen Parker headed back home, and Sally to the train station.

'I followed you only because I didn't think you'd want me knocking on your door. It would be difficult for you. And I didn't think it was right for us to be seen together.'

Parker looked content with this answer, maybe relieved that Banes had got the parameters of their relationship right.

'Here's the plan, Stephen. We go to Wilkes', pick up the painting, then go to the university and pick up your painting.'

'And yours?'

Banes gestured with a flick of his head that his painting was in the back. Parker turned and saw what he assumed was the painting, leaning against the side. It had a floral sheet over it. Parker looked concerned – there appeared to be deep-red blotches on it, and they weren't roses . . .

'Stephen? *Stephen?*'

Parker turned away from the painting, and the red blotches on the floral sheet. 'Yes?'

'Then, *then*, when we have all three paintings together, we'll work out where it is, and finally get our hands on it.'

'You sound so confident?'

'You have to be, or why bother? You have to think like the man who stole the treasure in the first place. No disrespect, but unlike you, they weren't scholars; if they had thought about it too much, they'd never have undertaken such a daring robbery in the first place. Of course, for any high-risk undertaking, you need the right amount of planning, the right timing, a little bit of luck. But more than anything, you need guile. When I first heard about the possibility of the treasure being in Denton, I knew it was in my grasp. I'm not a religious man, God knows, I know how cruel He can be. But I do believe in fate. Some guiding force leading us through this life, this "vale of tears". And when I heard what I heard from Conrad Wilde, well, I knew it was put in my path for a reason. All the ... all the pain, hardship, it had been for a reason.'

Parker blinked twice in quick succession. It could have been nerves, or he could have been re-evaluating Banes. Refocusing his view of him. *The pain ... the hardship*. He realized how little he knew about this man, this man who he had let into his life on the most tenuous of notions. And, also, the most dangerous. His mind scrolled back, to something the detective had said when he visited his office ... Frost, that was his name. He'd come to see him about the ad he'd put in the *Denton Echo* offering a reward for the painting. Frost had warned him – *maybe you should be careful* – but then Banes turned up. He said he hadn't stolen the painting from Ivan's ... but he had it. Parker was overtaken by two guiding thoughts: great pity, and great fear. With another feeling maybe overriding both: great excitement. Banes was right, this wasn't an academic exercise; Parker was mixing and dealing with criminals, with real consequences to his actions. Then there was the floral sheet to consider, with the big red blotches ...

'Are you OK?'

'Yes,' said Parker, refocusing on the driver. 'I could ask the same of you. You're not looking too good.'

Banes adjusted the rear-view mirror to be met with a sallow visage, sweat beading his brow, murky rings under his eyes, and the eyes themselves a filigree of red veins. He didn't want to feel weak, and he didn't want to be perceived as such, not now.

'You're a doctor of philosophy, you said, so I'll ask you to keep your opinions to yourself. Bit of a cold, nothing some paracetamol won't cure.'

A fifteen-minute silent drive and they were soon in the picturesque village of Gisborough. It was only when they were at the door of the ancient little shop, with its peeling green fascia and faded gold lettering spelling out 'Wilkes' Village Arts', and

Banes pulled out a large bunch of keys, that Parker asked where Wilkes was. 'Are those his keys? Why have you got them?'

Banes ignored him, busy as he was with trying each of the dozen-odd keys in succession. It was around number nine that he hit the jackpot, and the big old lock gave and they gained entry.

The shop was, ostensibly, a little gallery, with also a small offering of artist's materials for sale: tubes of paint, brushes, pallet knives. Not that it appeared to derive much of a profit from the dusty-looking stock in the cabinet. The whole place was a vanity project for its owner. Every inch of wall space was taken up with Wilkes' own paintings. They were mostly oils of the surrounding countryside. Every building in the village looked like it had been immortalized by Wilkes at one time or another.

At least he was better at buildings and the broad strokes of landscapes than the up-close-and-personal of portraiture. The skill of capturing the human form had eluded his heavy-handed approach. The people in the paintings just didn't look like people, and you'd be horrified to find any of them actually walking about. Hands, always a problem for even the most gifted of artists, were reduced to mitten-clad flippers. But compared to Conrad Wilde's efforts, Wilkes' pictures were masterpieces worthy of a wall, even a wing, of the Louvre. No comparison. And that, at first glance for Banes and Parker, was precisely the problem. There was no comparison. For Conrad Wilde's painting was nowhere to be seen.

But after the feverish initial search for the painting, which lasted a good ten minutes, Parker resumed his questioning.

'Where is Wilkes? Why isn't he here to show us . . . and why do you have his keys . . . this is breaking and entering, is it not?'

Banes, who had locked the door after them, now reinforced this by standing in front of it to block anyone's attempt at an escape.

'Don't worry about Wilkes.'

'What . . . what does that mean . . . ?'

'No one will find him.'

'What have you done to him?'

'No one will ever know what, because no one will find him.'

Stephen Parker took a backward step, then another, and another until he was as far away from Banes as he could put himself. What alerted him to this fact was the clatter of paintings being knocked from the wall as he pressed himself against it.

He balled his fists in panic, and looked like he wanted to fight his way out of there. But Banes was guarding the door, his hands thrust deep in the pockets of his duffel coat, and Parker dreaded to think what he was concealing in there – a knife, a gun? He was taller than Banes, but he knew he couldn't hit him, not with any great impact anyway. The idea of violence appalled him, and his ineffectuality at it just embarrassed him. He even had trouble making a fist properly, his long wispy fingers somehow buckling under the strain. But I can certainly stand up straight and try not to look like a submissive victim, he told himself.

'You've killed him?' Parker struggled to keep his voice even.

'Prove it.'

'I . . . I can stop this. This has to stop.'

'OK.' Banes leaned back against the door; it was a casual pose and full of confidence, like he was totally at ease with the situation. 'Why don't you go to the police? Tell them everything. Tell them who I am. Tell them what *we've* been up to. Because they'll want to know. They'll want to know everything. You can't pick and choose what you tell them. It's like pulling on the thread of your favourite old jumper, it just unravels until you're left with nothing and you wish you hadn't started. You set out on a journey, Dr Parker, and you're not even halfway through it.'

'This isn't what I want . . . I've had enough, I want out.'

'Tough. I won't let you. Not until we're done. Then – then you're free to do as you please. But until then, you belong to me.'

'Don't threaten me.'

'I'm not. In fact, if anyone's been doing any threatening around here, it's you.'

Banes took his hands out of his duffel coat to reveal not a knife or a gun, but some photos. He moved away from the door and placed the five snaps on the counter for Parker to look at.

'I took these when you were first trying to convince Mr Wilkes to part with his painting. I've had a few psychological assessments in my time, and whilst I'm no *doctor* . . . I definitely detect interpersonal issues with you. Easily frustrated, quick to anger, the overactive id of the completely unempathetic narcissist demanding that its needs are met, and totally prepared to use violence to get those needs met . . .' He drew a deep breath. '. . . But enough about me, how about you? Because that's what they'll see, because a picture says more than words ever can. Just ask Wilkes . . . he looks positively terrified in some of these . . . Being hounded on his own front doorstep. By you.'

Parker's eyes flitted from photo to photo, each one more incriminating and damning than the last. He wasn't aware he could be so animated. Yet there he was, on Wilkes' doorstep – eyes bulging, mouth contorted into a vicious snarl, hands gesticulating wildly in pure rage and frustration. It looked like a different man, a man very much, as Banes had pointed out, capable of violence, capable of killing someone. And yet very visibly still Parker. And Wilkes, his 'victim', on one photo meeting the challenge, but on all the others looking cowed and intimidated. He remembered Wilkes being a completely intractable old prick, ignoring his pleas, and his overly generous offers, but he didn't . . .

'Probably not as you remember it at all, right? But the camera doesn't lie, Stephen. You were proper pissed off. Angry. I remember sitting in your tin can of a car taking the snaps on my little Olympus Trip, thinking they would tell a tale. And they do. You look like you could *kill* him. And seeing as you're the one in the photo, and not me, you probably *fucking well* did.'

Parker went to gather up the photos and tear them up – but stopped. Pointless, Banes would have the negatives.

'Think about it, the police have already spoken to you, and you've already expressed an interest in the Bond Street job. Your field of academic interest. You're Vanessa's boyfriend, the estranged wife of Ivan Fielding. You're a suspect for his murder.'

'It's not murder – he had a heart attack.'

'Oh, don't worry, Inspector Frost will soon reopen the case once these photos come to light. Maybe your relationship with Vanessa is a sham, you're just with her to get your hands on the money.'

'You . . . you did it!'

'Me? Who am I? No one knows who I am. No one has seen me. Not even Charles Wilkes. He just felt a sharp pain to the back of his head. They all do. But they never see me. No one sees me or knows who I am.'

'You're Banes . . . You're Clive Banes.'

He smiled. 'Am I?'

When Parker lifted his hands away from his weeping eyes, he found himself crouched on the floor. On realizing just how compromised he was, he felt his bones imperceptibly slip from his body, and he slumped forward. What broke him out of his torpor was a cry of fury. '*Shit!*'

Banes was no longer by the door, he too was crouched down, but by the opposite wall, looking at a canvas that had been painted over with a base colour wash to cover the garish green that lay beneath, but not enough to obliterate it. Parker recognized it immediately: it was the exact same size as the others. Banes had found the final third of the triptych.

'Shit!' Banes repeated.

'It's OK,' assured Stephen Parker, not bothering to get up, but crawling along on his hands and knees to the painting propped up against the wall.

'How the hell is it OK, he's painted over it!' said Banes, also still crouched on the floor examining the canvas.

'Yes, he told me he was going to. But like I told you before, there's a technician in the art department at work, Ralph Collins, he can remove the new paint and restore it back to the original. Remember? And anyway, it's freshly done, and looks like he only gave it one layer.'

It was true, Conrad's garish composition was visible in patches under the light-grey coating.

'Trust me, Banes, Ralph can get this painting back to its original form.' Stephen Parker stood up, seemingly excited by a thought. 'And, of course, if there are any secret messages under the painting, Ralph has the latest ultraviolet equipment that can expose everything. That might be where the secret is hidden, *under* the painting! A map, directions. It's not unheard of for prisoners to do that, to get messages to the outside world, to their criminal cohorts. When they send letters to their loved ones, they also write other messages on the paper that aren't visible to the naked eye, so the warders can't detect them. They use their urine, it works as invisible ink. You just put a light behind the paper, and it becomes visible.'

Banes managed to arch an impressed-looking eyebrow. 'How do you know about all this?'

'One of my degrees is in criminology. I did my thesis on the coded language of criminality. The amount of time that Conrad Wilde spent in prison, I'm sure he must have picked up the trick.'

'And your mate Ralph can detect it?'

Parker gave some enthusiastic nods at this.

'Right, let's go and see Ralph,' said a grinning Banes, also rising to his feet.

Parker aped Banes' grin, as once again his moral compass swung wildly, and all the horror was gone, and he was once again caught up in the excitement and the fantasy.

Monday (3)

She ran and ran and ran until she had stitches in her tummy and her thumping little heart felt like it wanted to burst through her chest; like that space monster that Ranjit Patel showed her in the film magazine he hid in his desk. But most importantly, she ran until she was sure she was far away from the house. She didn't know where she was, she didn't recognize the woods. Mummy and Daddy, when Daddy wasn't working, often took her for drives in the countryside, but none of this looked familiar to her. She could have been on the other side of the world for all she knew.

The trees were tall and clustered closely together, the tops were waving, a moving canopy that made everything dark. The ground was thick with ferns and tangled skeins of dead roots. The undergrowth was deep enough to hide things, the things she was scared of. So she pressed forward, letting the woods lead her. The trees stretched on far beyond her field of vision, yet seemed to open up to her, maybe leading her to a path. She listened, above the sounds of nature, the birds, the *whoosh* of the wind in the tall trees. Then she heard it, a familiar sound: the steady thrum of a car engine drawing closer.

She ran towards it. Faster and faster. The stitches returned, but she ran through them. But however fast she ran towards the sound of the car, it didn't seem fast enough. A pain shot through her left heel, like she'd trodden barefoot on a piece of Lego at home. She saw that she'd lost one of her shoes. She didn't even think of retrieving it, didn't care that Mummy might be angry, she just pressed on.

There was a bank of mud, mulch, bracken and shrubs that led to the lip of what she was sure was a road. Ruby scrambled up it, grabbing at the vegetation to climb up to what she now thought of as civilization. She ran into the centre of the gravelly track but saw nothing. Then she heard the harsh screech of tyres, the engine cutting out, a long skidding sound getting louder and louder. Ruby turned around to see the maroon car with its chrome bumper looming towards her, almost on top of her.

She lay there, the cold gravel pressing into her back, her eyes closed, wondering if this was what getting run over and dying felt like. She was pretty sure it was.

'Are you OK? . . . Are you . . . ?'

She heard the voice, it was soft, comforting. She felt hands gently cupping her cheeks.

'Can you hear me . . . can you hear me?'

The man's voice was panicked this time, it had an urgency about it that made everything real. Ruby now knew she wasn't dead. She opened her eyes and said, 'I think so.'

The man was crouched at her side. He was big, with a broad kind-looking face, and brown eyes that seemed close to tears. He muttered something like 'Thank God for that.' He carefully moved her head from side to side, as if inspecting it for cuts and blood, she thought.

'You're all right, sweetheart, nothing is broken. You weren't hit, I stopped just in time. You must have fainted. Can you get up?'

'Yes, I think so.'

Holding the man's hand, Ruby got to her feet.

'What are you doing out here?'

'I've escaped.'

'Escaped?' The big man's eyes narrowed and he looked confused. 'Where are your parents?'

'I was kidnapped, by some men. They put a pillowcase over my head and drove me to a house. I don't know who they are . . . they wear Ronald Reagan masks.'

'Jesus . . . You're . . . you're Ruby?'

'How do you know?'

'I recognize you, you've been in all the papers, on the TV.'

He held her hand and guided her to the passenger seat of his car, and secured her with the seatbelt.

'Can you take me home, please?'

'Yes, of course, your poor parents must be worried sick. But before we do that, the first thing I have to do is call the police, let them know you're safe, and they can tell your parents. OK?'

Ruby nodded at the man, and whispered thank you. He smiled, his kind face letting her know she was safe. He started the engine.

'Let's get you home, Ruby.'

'I think we're wasting precious time discussing this, sir.'

Mullett stood at his desk, with his hands clasped behind him. Seemingly solid and unmoving, yet Frost suspected he was sticking pins in an effigy he'd made of his recalcitrant DI. Frost almost felt sorry for him, but not quite. As soon as Mullett realized he was outgunned and outmanoeuvred during the briefing in the incident room, feeling the whole of CID turn against him, he decided to take the fight away from the nitty-gritty of investigative police work. And into his home ground, the realm of unquestioned authority, his oak-panelled office.

'You lied to me, Frost, you lied to a superior officer when asked about your actions in an ongoing investigation.'

'The clock is ticking, sir.'

'You will tell me, Frost, or I will issue you with a disciplinary notice and remove you from duty.'

'I didn't *lie* to you, sir.'

'You're lying now.'

'Bit strong. Do I need to call my union rep?'

'Call bloody Arthur Scargill, for all I care – I have it on very good authority that you were seen with Captain Lionel Cavanagh at the Prince Albert Hotel yesterday afternoon.'

'I won't lie. Bang to rights. I was. But I wasn't lying earlier. I wasn't *actively* pursuing the case. When first investigating the death of Ivan Fielding and the signs of forced entry, you will recall, *sir*, we uncovered a hidden stash of stolen antiques. I took pictures of said hidden stash and showed them to DI Anthony Dorking, and—'

'Frost, we've been over this before!' Mullett interrupted angrily.

'Yes, and you wouldn't listen then either, sir. Just hear me out. Dorking told me Conrad Wilde's and Ivan Fielding's files have a D-Notice on them. Restricted access to only the most—'

'I know what a D-Notice is, Frost. Get on with it.'

'DI Dorking said he'd pass on my details to Captain Cavanagh, who headed up the Stolen Art and Antiques Squad in the '60s, when Fielding and Wilde were criminally active. And because the captain was Ivan Fielding's handler. I mentioned it to you before: Ivan was an informant. For Scotland Yard.'

On hearing this, Mullett's chest rose up like he was on parade. The mention of Scotland Yard always seemed to have that effect on him, like a man who had missed his true calling or position in life, and was destined for the provinces. Frost could see it had piqued his interest.

'What did Cavanagh tell you yesterday?'

'I thought you weren't interested in 1967, and all that?'

'Don't be snide, Frost, I just have a penchant for solving cases in the correct manner.'

Frost gave an internal groan at this, which must have escaped and made it out into the office.

'You don't understand my position, never have,' said Mullett.

Frost shrugged. 'What do they say, you have to walk a mile in a man's shoes to understand him? And your size elevens are far too big for me.'

'I'm squeezed from the top and the bottom.'

'Lucky you.'

'ACC Winslow informed me there's special interest in this case. The security services, Special Branch, who knows.'

'I thought as much. Has he had me followed? Is that how you know I met with Cavanagh?'

Mullett's hornrimmed eyes, magnified as they were, gave nothing away, remaining impenetrable and steadfast. He ignored Frost and carried on with his own agenda.

'And then I have to contend with you. You're smug, Frost. You carry the smugness of a man who avoids responsibility. With your grossly inappropriate attire, and your sneering contempt for propriety and the ethics of your role, you just think the world revolves around you and only you can solve cases.'

'My heart bleeds, and that clock is still ticking.'

'If this really does relate to Ruby Hanson in some way – and I can't imagine how – tell me what Captain Cavanagh said.'

'In a nutshell: Jimmy McVale pulled off the '67 Bond Street caper. Then had his haul stolen off him by Conrad Wilde. Who then buried it in Denton. Now Jimmy McVale is out of prison and wants to get his hands on the treasure. He's gone the direct route: kidnap Ivan Fielding's granddaughter, in the hope that Vanessa and Sally Fielding will give up whatever secrets they have. It's McVale's MO, he used to rob banks that way. Kidnapped the family of the manager to put pressure on him. Johnny Johnson, who read his book, told me all about it.'

Stanley Mullett moved for the first time, and began to pace the dark parquet floor with a stiff and thoughtful gait. 'And, as your photo showed, Sally Fielding looks remarkably like Gail Hanson, similar attractive features, same dark colouring. And this also applies to their two children, Ruby and . . . ?'

'Ella Fielding.'

'Yes, they are also very similar, very similar.'

'Right down to them having the same haircuts, both mothers and both daughters. Purdey cuts?'

'What?' Incomprehension blazed on Mullett's face.

'That's the name of the haircut.'

'I thought it was a Lady Di?'

Frost shrugged.

Mullett did the same, then said, 'And you believe the killer of the Wheatons has a connection to Longthorn Secure Hospital, where Conrad Wilde was kept . . . and this business with the missing painting?'

Frost gave a solid nod to this.

Mullett shook his head and puffed out some breaths of exasperated air. He eventually stopped pacing and stood exactly where he'd set out from, a monolith encased in its inky-blue uniform with its shiny brass buttons. Unmovable and authoritative. Apart from sometimes, and this was one of those times.

'OK, Inspector, you've convinced me. Do what you need to do, bring McVale in.'

'Yes, sir, good call.'

Of course, before joining Mullett in his office, the defiant detective had already given DS Waters the nod to bring Jimmy McVale in for questioning. He suspected that Mullett would see reason, and with all the facts laid out before him, the obdurate super indeed had little choice.

And if he didn't agree, well, Frost couldn't give the proverbial monkey's. Mullett was right, he wasn't squeezed like him: the ambition, the politics, the raging upward mobility. Frost suffered none of this. Unburdened as he was, when he opened the door to leave he felt emboldened to ask, 'With ACC Winslow content to suppress the case, have me followed, and no doubt come down on me like a ton of bricks, I would like to know where you stand. Not for my sake, you understand. I'll be happily directing traffic in the next few months if all goes to plan. It's just so that *our* terrific and hardworking team here at Eagle Lane aren't wasting their bloody time.'

'Bring in McVale and Ruby Hanson and I'll handle the ACC.'

'Very good, sir.'

He hammered on the old front door, the coil of his clenched fist making the rustic old wooden planks dance and jostle and almost collapse. Inside he heard desperate sounds, like the stage whispers of some overcooked cockney *Play for Today*, about a pair of criminals holed up in an abandoned house in the woods.

'Avon calling!' Jimmy McVale laughed and quelled their fears. 'Relax, it's me.'

'Jimmy?'

'Course it is. I said I'd be down here today, didn't I?'

The door opened a crack, and a sliver of Tony Minton appeared. Seeing that it wasn't a baritone Avon lady, he opened the door fully and let McVale in.

The room looked like it was midway through some extensive building work. The walls had just been plastered. There was a pine kitchen table and some chairs gathered around it. A Calor gas heater in the hearth was waiting to be installed, and the floor was made up of some ancient-looking flagstones with some cheap old rugs thrown over them to warm the place up.

On the pine table were the rubber Ronald Reagan masks. Eddie Tobin and Tony Minton sat down.

'Not even so much as an offer of a cup of tea?' said Jimmy McVale, peering into the adjacent kitchen that looked like it had just been fitted, or half of it anyway. There was a brushed-steel sink and a new fridge, a Baby Belling and a kettle. The cottage was obviously liveable in, with all essentials present.

'You took your time,' said Eddie.

'I had some speaking engagements, some book signings. What would it look like if I dropped everything and rushed back down here? But seeing as you snatched the wrong bloody kid in the first place, it's a bit of a moot point. How the hell did you manage it?' he asked with a plangent sigh.

'We've been through all this!' barked Tony. 'I knew it was a bad idea.'

McVale didn't raise his voice. It would seem that all the shouting that needed to be done had been done, down the phone. 'Take it easy, Tone. I just want to point out that it's worked before.'

'We used to have more time before, we had better planning before,' said Minton.

McVale gave a humourless laugh. 'We had a run-through, we followed the kid, Ella, Ella Fielding. You saw what she looked like. You said you'd got it.'

Eddie was firm on the point: 'It was rushed, we needed to find out her routine!'

'Bullshit, you two just panicked, you saw a kid that might have looked like her, and you got sloppy and stupid and scared and just grabbed her like a couple of amateurs. If you had any doubts, you should have just driven past them, double-checked, or waited for the next day. You had a whole week to do it, and you fucked up royally.'

Eddie Tobin balled his fist like he wanted to hit someone, but made do with thumping the table. Tony Minton, the more volatile of the two, shot up from his spindle-backed pine chair so fast he sent it crashing to the floor.

Jimmy McVale stood his ground with the two men, his eyes full of challenge flitting from one to the other. But neither took him up on it, and McVale could see they were each as ineffectual as the other. Full of sound and fury, piss and vinegar, and pointless posturing. They were middle-aged, soft, had lost their edge, their ruthlessness. But McVale hadn't. In prison he wasn't afforded that luxury. You had to stay sharp, stay fit, stay strong, always on the alert because there was always someone ready to take you on. They might come at you with just their fists, but nine times out of ten they'd come tooled up with a shiv. Ready to cut your throat with a razor blade stuck to a toothbrush.

Once McVale felt sure the two men had absorbed the clear fact that he, at least, was unchanged, he spoke, softly: 'Remember, lads, it was *you* who came to *me*. I didn't force you to do this. I just laid out a plan that you agreed to execute. Because it was a good plan.'

Tony Minton picked up his chair and sat back down, hunched and beaten. Eddie Tobin took the half-smoked cigar that had been mouldering in the ashtray, stuck it in his mouth and breathed some life back into it. It had the same effect as a baby's pacifier and calmed him down. Then both men eventually muttered, in unison, that it was a good plan and proceeded to offer explanations as to why it had gone wrong.

Eddie said, 'You're right, we've been out of the game too long, not as sharp as we used to be. When you're right, you're right.'

Tony said, 'We saw the kid, what looked like the kid, and we wanted to get the job done. We was running on adrenalin, not brains. We'll hold our hands up to that.'

'So what do we do now?' asked Eddie.

'Get her back home,' said Tony, like it was the only viable option.

McVale crossed his arms and paced around the room, mulling over their predicament. 'Tell me, when exactly did she tell you her name was Ruby?'

'We grabbed her,' said Minton, 'put some gaffer tape over her mouth to stop her screaming, a pillowcase over her head so she wouldn't know where she was, then drove straight here. Then we calmed her down, said we wouldn't hurt her.'

'Promised we wouldn't.'

'Then . . . then she calmed down and said . . .' Tony Minton turned to Eddie Tobin to finish off his thought, as he so often did.

' "My name's not Ella, it's Ruby." Thought she was being a smart-arse at first, they can be at that age . . . then we realized.'

'We thought about trying to go after the real one,' said Tony. 'But it was too late by then. Police everywhere. The school was closed the next day. A patrol car parked outside the school gates, coppers going door to door.'

Jimmy McVale's face lightened out of its deep contemplative state. He then moseyed over to the table and picked up one of the Ronald Reagan masks. 'And little Ruby, she's not seen either of your faces?'

'No, absolutely not,' insisted Eddie Tobin. 'We was very careful about that, very careful. When we snatched her we had stockings over our heads and baseball caps.' He pointed at the masks on the table. 'And we've been wearing these when we've been in her room.'

Jimmy McVale nodded his approval. 'So, that's good, then. She's not seen your faces, so we can just put the pillowcase back over her head, drive her into town and drop her back home. Right?'

Tobin and Minton glanced at each other, heads bobbing up and down in agreement. It was clear they liked the idea, that it really did sound like a fine plan.

'Where is she now?'

'In her room, of course,' said Minton.

McVale moved slowly into the hallway, as if not to disturb anyone, especially a scared little girl. He then pointed to a door, and mouthed the words, *In here?*

Tobin and Minton gave the thumbs-up, to which McVale responded with the rounded thumb to forefinger sign of OK.

McVale came back into the living room, all smiles. 'Right, lads, follow me.'

Tony and Eddie got up from the table and did as Jimmy McVale asked. They followed him out of the cottage into the thin silvery light of the cold January day, and watched as he sprang his car keys from the pocket of his artificially distressed, designer brown leather jacket. McVale went around to the rear of his BMW, twirled the key in the lock, and the boot opened without so much as a squeak. With a come-hither gesture he invited Tony and Eddie to take a look. They peered in.

'Christ!'

'What's she doing . . . !'

Both men reeled back in shock. Jimmy McVale wasn't smiling now. His prominent brow was ridged in a vicious V, and everything about him that had been light and charming was now transformed into dark and menacing. He stopped Eddie and Tony scuttling away by grabbing the collars of their matching blue quilted ski jackets. He then forced their faces almost into the boot of the car, inches away from its terrified cargo.

'Look! Take a *good, hard look* . . . Ruby.'

Monday (4)

'You really, really don't look very well. It looks like you've got some kind of virus. I don't want Ella catching anything.'

Banes glanced in the rear-view mirror. Parker was right. The pallid had turned to white and waxy. He'd swallowed some paracetamol, but still his head throbbed. He could feel a permanent sheen of sweat over his body. Whilst driving he tried to rest his right hand off the steering wheel as much as possible because it throbbed with pain now, and when it didn't, it was weirdly numb. The scratch he'd received from that vicious cat in Norwood was now livid and clearly septic, sticking to his shirt; his whole arm had turned a greenish-yellow colour. And his leg ached too. The leg that had been bitten by that brutal little bastard of a dog that belonged to Charles Wilkes. He'd always thought he liked animals, or certainly didn't hate them like he hated most humans, but he was reconsidering that position now.

'She won't catch anything, we're only picking her up and dropping her off, aren't we?'

'Yes, of course.'

'Then don't complain. Not my idea. If I had my way we wouldn't be bloody wasting time doing this. She should bloody well walk . . .'

Banes carried on muttering his complaints – the aches and pains in his arm and leg, and the overall feeling of illness, darkened his mood. They were in the white van heading towards Ella Fielding's school, and Banes wasn't happy about it, not one little bit. But Parker had insisted, as he'd promised to pick Ella up. And as Parker had pointed out, they would only be waiting about anyway for Ralph Collins to do his work. So by the time they'd picked her up and dropped her off at home, the technician would have some conclusive news for them.

On leaving Wilkes' gallery, they had taken the painting to the university's art department. Collins, a bluntly spoken and blunt-looking Yorkshireman, was initially curious as to why Parker wanted the new paint removed, and what they hoped to find. Parker spun him a tale, not too far from the truth, so as to make it believable. It was a piece of art created by a con with a hidden message. Parker said that he wanted it for an ongoing research project and then proceeded to waffle on about the project, until Collins, a technician and not an academic, cut him short by telling him he'd get straight on with it. Which was the desired effect.

Collins had already cleaned off enough of the paint to start to reveal the image that lay beneath whilst they were still in the lab with him. It was another hill, or a mountain. But this one was bigger than the other two. And it had something on it: it was, by the looks of it, some kind of bird. A swan? A duck? A chicken? It was hard to determine. But Ralph Collins assured them that he would be able to clean the picture back to its original state.

In the hour or so it would take, Parker and Banes could pick up Ella and drop her at home. Vanessa was due back from seeing her sister shortly, and would wait with Ella for Sally to return from London. Parker wanted to go on his own, and it was clear to Banes that he didn't want him anywhere near his new family.

But Banes insisted – at this stage of the game, this close to the prize, he didn't want Parker out of his sight.

And Parker could see the logic of this. He'd seen how these things could go badly wrong, men undone by greed. Of course, he'd seen this mainly in films, like *The Treasure of the Sierra Madre*. But he understood the logic.

The white van pulled up at the school gates.

Frost dropped the receiver into the cradle from enough of a height to make an exclamatory clatter, and then mouthed one of his lesser-used swear words.

'No go?' asked John Waters, sat opposite him at Frost's desk.

'The station at Peckham Rye where McVale was supposed to sign in today haven't seen him. The address he's registered at in Dulwich, he's not at. He had a book reading at Goldsmiths College in New Cross last night, but he didn't turn up for it.'

'Which tells you?'

'Well, he's either on the run and out of the country because he knows we're on to him . . . or he's in Denton.'

Frost and Waters both craned their necks to look out of the office door to discover the source of some frenzied yapping. Desk Sergeant Johnny Johnson had just escorted a man and his dog through to the incident room, and sat the man down at DC Arthur Hanlon's desk.

Frost then spotted something more interesting. DC Clarke was coming through with a young woman with long, shiny henna-red hair. Her entire face looked red and moist with tears.

Frost leapt up from his chair. Waters again looked surprised at the new-found agility.

'Good to see your back has completely cleared up. We were going to have a whip-round for a walking stick. When I saw you first thing, I couldn't believe it.'

'Never felt better, John. I might have to move house, but it was worth it.'

Waters was about to question him further but the sprightly

detective was out through his office door and bounding over to Clarke, who was taking the still-weeping girl to the interview room.

As Frost made his way over, the dog, a wiry-haired Jack Russell, sprang out from under the chair his owner was sitting on and fired off a barrage of barks at him. The detective tried to stare him down. 'Ssssit! Ssssit!' he hissed out, just like that dog-training woman on the telly. To no avail – the terrier kept straining at its lead and yapping away.

Arthur Hanlon said to the owner, 'He recognizes a dog's dinner when he sees one.'

The owner laughed. Frost didn't have time to muster a retort and carried on over to Clarke.

'I take it this is Louisa Hamilton?'

Clarke turned towards Frost, still keeping a firm guiding hand on the uncuffed Louisa Hamilton. 'That's right. She eventually contacted Richard Hanson at his work number, just like we thought. She wanted the £70,000 in used notes, or she was going to tell Gail Hanson the whole story.'

'Shame Gail had already heard the story.'

'I'm . . . I'm . . . sorry . . .'

She burst into tears – again. Her face looked waterlogged. Any more and she'd drown.

'I'm sure you are,' said an impatient Frost. 'But just for the record, tell me, Louisa, tell me you don't have Ruby.'

Louisa Hamilton shook her head so vigorously that she resembled a garden sprinkler. Frost and Clarke had to take a step back from her.

'He made me . . . he made me do it.'

'Who did?'

'Ryan Grayson, her new boyfriend,' said Clarke when Louisa was unable to. 'Apparently it was all his idea.'

'Take a statement and nick her for blackmail, obstructing police business, going out with idiots, and anything else you see fit to throw at her.'

DC Clarke took the busted drain away.

Frost skirted the snappy Jack Russell whilst announcing to everyone in the incident room, 'Right, listen up, we need to find Jimmy McVale. Let's assume he's in sunny Denton or its environs.'

Everyone who wasn't on the phone making enquiries, and even some that were, shouted back, 'Yes, guv!' or words to that effect.

'So, I want coppers posted at—'

'Hold on, Frost!' called out Superintendent Mullett as he stalked into the incident room. 'Just got confirmation through from the courts that the council planning department and Jarrett & Sons have won the appeal, and have permission to start stage one of clearing Denton Woods for the new development.'

Groans went up from the entire room, even the dog barked. No one could deny there was a heavy bias amongst them in favour of keeping the woods and not building some Legoland housing estate. Most of the Eagle Lane coppers were local, and most knew the woods intimately and loved the trees almost as much as the dog did, which now aimed its barks at Mullett.

'We've also received intelligence that there will be more protestors coming into the area, and the present ones at the site are actively blocking the way to the bulldozers. I need every available officer at the site immediately! I predict a riot.'

Now Frost groaned, and swore. Loudly.

'What have you got there, Ella?'

'It's for Granddad,' said Ella Fielding, showing Stephen Parker what she had on her lap: a scroll of thick and fibrous grey paper.

Ella was sat between Parker and Banes in the front of the white Bedford van, on their way to drop her off at home. Banes kept on nudging the scroll of paper out of the way with his hand every time he had to change gear. Not that it particularly impeded his driving, but it was just a way of registering his continued annoyance at having to do the school run. He was vexed. I just don't have time for this bollocks, he told himself.

'I'm sure he would have appreciated it, Ella, you know how much he loved art.'

'Fucking hell,' muttered Banes, under his breath but loud enough for the 'naughty' swear word to register with the little girl. She screwed up her face and gave him a challenging look.

Parker shot a look at Banes too, obviously wanting to prevent him from making any insensitive remarks. He turned his attention back to mollifying the little girl, who now looked upset.

'Your grandmother told me you were taking the loss of your grandfather quite hard, Ella. I know that he was . . . at times like a father to you. Right?'

She nodded. 'My teacher said that I should celebrate Granddad, and try not to feel sad. Just remember all the happy times.'

'That's a wonderful idea, Ella.'

'I never knew either of my granddads,' said Banes.

'That's sad,' said Ella, with genuine emotion in her voice.

'Or my dad, for that matter.'

Parker gave a loud warning cough and pulled a *shut-up* face, or certainly that's how Clive interpreted it. Banes smiled slyly; he enjoyed winding the dopey academic up, it was so easy.

'I don't know my dad either,' said the little girl.

She then put her hand on Clive Banes' hand as it idled on the gearstick. He flinched and moved it away, as if the sensation of being touched kindly was completely new to him.

'Are you not well?' asked Ella Fielding, suddenly looking concerned.

Parker cleared his throat again and tapped Ella's shoulder to draw her attention away from Banes, who clearly wasn't enjoying it.

'I'd love to have a look at your painting,' encouraged Parker. 'I know that you've been getting top marks at school for your art. That's your granddad's influence, that is, the same one that sent your mother to art school. Do you think you'll go to art school when you're older, study painting?'

Ella nodded, and happily unrolled her work. 'It's not a painting, I used pastels and some crayons for this one. What do you think?'

Parker's eyes widened on the picture, he looked impressed. It showed a blue sky and fluffy white clouds, and the pastels were carefully smeared to make the clouds distended and wispy; there were also some well-proportioned little ticks to represent birds in flight. Parker's gaze was soon drawn down to the main subject of the piece, a pirate in his tricorne hat, an eyepatch, pantaloons, a long brocaded jacket, and with a broad cutlass gripped in his hand. The pirate stood with his Jim Hawkins, as Parker scrolled back to his childhood reading of *Treasure Island*. But this Jim was also dressed as a pirate, and was obviously a girl, and obviously Ella. And even though the pirate, with his eyepatch and beard, was not a faithful representation of Ivan Fielding, it was safe to assume it was him.

'Jesus bloody Christ!'

'That's rude, *again*, Mr Banes,' chided Ella.

Banes slowed the van, then, rather recklessly, swerved against the traffic and pulled over at a bus stop. They were just a street away from Ella's home. Parker didn't complain about the dangerous driving as he, like Banes, was fixated on the colourful drawing.

'Is that . . . is that Conrad's painting?' asked Banes.

'It's not a painting, it's pastels and crayons, and it's mine. It's Granddad and me,' explained Ella.

Parker nodded in agreement, with both parties.

The two pirates stood on a mound with a smaller hill at either side. It was instantly clear to Parker and Banes that the mound in the middle was the centre panel of the triptych, the one Wilkes had painted over – it had to be. The composition was more realistic (and just better) than Conrad's. There were fallen leaves and bracken on the ground, and the hills were more earthy and grassy, with a mossy tree stump at the base of the larger one, covered in foliage and roots. The scene was set in a clearing in the woods.

'Where is that, Ella?' asked Parker.

'Granddad used to take me there. He said he used to take Mummy there when she was young, but she didn't like the woods, so she doesn't remember it. But I do.'

'The woods – Denton Woods?' prompted Banes.

Ella shrugged. 'Yes. But I don't think it's the part where they're going to take all the trees, it's nearer Granddad's house.'

Parker said to Banes, 'The very north end of Denton Woods backs on to Ivan's property.'

Banes attempted some congeniality. 'Please, Ella, we'd love to see it too, so can you show us where these hills are?'

'They're not hills. They're islands. And that one in the middle is Treasure Island.'

'*Treasure* Island!' exclaimed Banes, looking at Parker meaningfully. Now they were certain they didn't need to retrieve the painting from the university lab – the little girl had the golden ticket right in her hand.

'That's what Granddaddy called it. You see there?' She pointed to the mossy tree stump at the base of the middle hill, which had red-capped toadstools sprouting out of it and was draped in rope-like roots. 'That's the ship, the ship that got wrecked on the island, and Granddad and his friend used to play there when they were my age.'

'Who was Granddad's friend?' asked Parker.

'He said when he grew up he became a real pirate and went off and sailed the seven seas and had lots of adventures.'

'And then ended up in an insane asylum.'

'You're very mean, Mr Banes.'

Parker hissed at him, 'You're not helping.' He tapped Ella gently on the shoulder, as she now had her arms firmly crossed, with her mouth in a petulant pout and her eyes shooting arrows at Banes. 'Ella, can you show us where Treasure Island is?'

'You. Not *him*.'

'Him' put the van into gear, and released the handbrake.

Monday (5) _____

'There's only one thing for it. She's left us no choice.'

Eddie Tobin and Tony Minton knew what this meant. They knew *exactly* what this meant. And there was no disguising it, it made them sick to hear it. But still they asked in turn:

'What are you talking about, Jimmy?'

'What only thing?'

'Why has she left us no choice, Jimmy?'

But McVale remained impassive in the face of their questions. The three men were back at the pine kitchen table. There was a bottle of brandy being drunk from chipped teacups. Ruby was back in her room. Her hands and feet had been tied, and she wasn't going anywhere. McVale was all for keeping her locked in the boot of the car, but Eddie and Tony, who both had daughters a little older than Ruby, vetoed the idea. Around the table, the mood was sombre, measured, maybe because they all knew it could easily tip over into excitable and uncontrollable violence at any moment.

'You know what I mean. She's seen us. She's not stupid, she'll recognize us all when the Old Bill show her the old mugshots.'

'Well, whose fault's that?' said Tony Minton. 'She didn't have to see our faces. You made sure she did.'

McVale shook his head. 'No, *you* made sure she did. I told you to secure her, make sure she didn't leave the room. Keep her blindfolded, tie her to the bed—'

'Jesus, Jimmy, she's a little kid,' said Eddie Tobin. 'She's done nothing wrong.'

'That's right, I've got two girls, you can't do that—'

'What the fuck are you two talking about? You used to do that, you used to do whatever was necessary to get your hands on the money. Now look at you, you're soft and fat and fucking useless! Bit of luck it was me who found her, picked her up. But then again, you make your own luck. And I plan on keeping on being lucky. She can't leave these woods. It's simple. I put one in the back of her head. She'll never know. Do it when she's asleep. Slip her a Mickey. Pillow over her head, then pull the trigger.'

Both Tobin and Minton straightened up from their miserable slouches over their mugs of supermarket brandy, and exchanged troubled looks.

'That's cold.'

'Ice-cold.'

'I've just got out of prison, I've got no intention of going back. And you two, you couldn't do the time,' hissed McVale.

'I'd rather do the time than kill a kid.'

Eddie Tobin agreed wholeheartedly and said, 'I'll take my chances. She's only seen us briefly, and she was crying her eyes out, terrified. A good brief could turn that around: she was scared, crying, confused, she didn't know what she saw. Forget it, Jimmy, I'll take my chances in a courtroom.'

'Me too. Kill a kid? There's a special place in hell for that kind of shit.'

Their telepathy still intact, Eddie Tobin and Tony Minton rose up simultaneously from their chairs without needing to say a word to each other.

Then Jimmy McVale did likewise.

'So now what, Jimmy?'

'Yeah. You carrying the shooter now?'

'No. It's in the car, under the seat. The car's rented. That way if I get pulled over by the Old Bill, I can just deny the shooter's mine, and tell them that's the last time I rent a car from Avis.'

They laughed. It was an old one, but a good one. But what hung over them was too heavy to bear, and they stopped laughing as swiftly as they had started.

McVale said, 'Gun or no gun, this is still a Mexican stand-off.'

'Dunno, never been to Mexico,' said Tony Minton.

'Trust me,' said McVale. 'Me and you two, both wanting different things. Only one of us can prevail. Equally matched.'

'But there's two of us, only one of you,' clarified Eddie Tobin.

Tony nodded. 'Yeah. It's more like *The Alamo*. And you're John Wayne.'

'*Zulu*. And you're Michael Caine,' suggested Eddie.

All three men's brows crinkled at that analogy, unsure of that film's final outcome.

Then Tony Minton shrugged and said to McVale, 'Either way, you're fucked.'

'And you're fat. The pair of you. I could take you ponces at twenty-five, and I can take you at forty-five.'

'We'll see about that.'

'Will you shut up and stop moving about?'

'I can't help it, Harry, I'm itching like crazy.'

Harry Baskin was in the bushes with Bad Manners Bob. Bad Manners Bob, the giant bald bouncer, was in a bad way. Before they'd got in the bushes to hide where they could get a good view of the cottage, he'd slipped on the wet leaves and mud and fallen down what he'd described as a ravine. Though the minute he'd climbed out, Harry had redesignated it a ditch.

Whatever it was, it was full of poison ivy. Which was bad news for Bad Manners Bob, who had the complexion of a baby, very pale, yet surprisingly, and pleasingly for Mrs Bad Manners Bob, very soft; but, also like a baby's, it was red and blotchy at the best of times. And now it was inflamed and itchy. Given his bulk, that was an awful lot of skin to be itching. His hands were working overtime, going like the clappers, reaching into his nylon tracksuit to scratch and pick and soothe his burning and bubbling rind.

'Stop moving, Bob! You're rustling, you're rustling!'

'I can't help it . . . I need some calamine lotion, sharpish!'

Baskin peered intently through his binoculars, zooming in on the door, his front door, an original feature of the cottage he'd bought at a snip, together with a good plot of land. Harry and Bob were perched on a rise, deep in a thicket of bushes and ferns and, as it turned out, nettles.

'I can't help it, Aitch, I'm on fire!'

'Shut up, Bob . . . I see something.' Baskin again adjusted the zoom on his binoculars and spotted three men leaving the cottage. One of them was McVale. The other two he recognized, not by name, but by type.

'Are we sweet, then?'

'That's not the word I'd use.'

'That's the deal. You walk away from here, and never look back. Don't think about it or ever contact me again. You were never here and we never spoke. That's the deal.'

McVale, Tobin and Minton had just stepped out of the house and were making their way over to the dark-blue Land Rover. It was just the three of them, there was no Ruby.

'I don't care about the money, Jimmy. It makes me sick to think—'

'To think about how you two messed up? Have no doubt about it, this is *your* mess and I'm clearing it up. Your choice.'

Eddie Tobin and Tony Minton, unable to look at each other, to see the same guilt and horror reflected in each other's eyes, turned their backs on McVale. They had the look of men that had been hung, drawn and quartered, yet were still, just about, alive. They'd made a deal with the devil. But they knew they couldn't stomach the alternative. They had kids themselves, and the idea of being away from them, banged up in a prison cell, missing them grow up, unable to provide for them, it was too much to bear. Put like that, and the countless other justifications they knew they'd be using for the rest of their lives, it was a sacrifice they were prepared to make. They climbed into the Land Rover and made off down the muddy track that would eventually lead them to a road, the same road McVale had driven up with Ruby earlier.

It was getting dark, or more intensely so. It would be pitch-black soon. The tall trees did a pretty good job of forming a canopy, veiling the sun, feeble as it was for this time of year anyway. It was a darkness that McVale contemplated. It was a darkness McVale wanted to hold back. Would the little girl be asleep, would it be that easy, as easy as he said it would be? A painless death in the dark as she slept, barely a movement as he ensured she would never wake up again. He somehow doubted it, nothing was ever that easy. His eyes flitted away from the trail that the Land Rover had wobbled its way down, and he turned to go back into the cottage. To the little girl that would soon be—

A howl. A howl like a wounded animal seized McVale's attention. He spun around to see a large figure rolling down the slope in the distance. McVale's eyes widened, not to adjust to the encroaching darkness, but to the descending figure. It looked like a . . . a giant baby . . . bald, pink, bulbous and naked. And it sounded like it was crying. McVale went to his car to retrieve his gun.

The big fat naked baby didn't run, even when he saw the gun McVale was holding. He just carried on rolling around, scratching himself, looking like he was in tears. McVale realized that the fat man wasn't actually naked, and when he rolled over Jimmy was able to read the legend embroidered on the back of his flesh-coloured shell suit: 'The Coconut Gr—'.

'Don't shoot!'

McVale turned sharply to his right to see Harry Baskin edging his way down the hill, trying not to slip and fall like his cohort. He too was kitted up in the same flesh-pink tracksuit.

'Don't shoot him, Jimmy, he's with me!'

McVale aimed the gun at Harry Baskin instead. 'What the hell are you doing here?'

'You forget, it's mine, I own the property,' said Baskin, with his hands half raised in the air in a gesture of surrender. He wondered if he should raise them further, because even though Jimmy McVale had clocked who the two men were, he still had the gun directed straight at Harry's head. Bad Manners Bob was slumped where he had come to rest, and was too busy scratching himself to even notice the gun pointed at his boss's head.

'You spying on me, Harry?'

'No, we was out running.'

'*Running?*'

'Yeah. Look at me, where else would we be going in this get-up?'

Jimmy McVale ran his narrow suspicious eyes over Baskin, as if seeing him for the first time. He probably would have laughed at the sight of the club-owner and his bouncer if his own situation hadn't been so grave.

'What the hell are you wearing?'

'A tracksuit. Like I said, I'm getting back into sports promotion—'

'You look like a pair of fat streakers coming down that hill. I thought you were having it off in the bushes up there.'

Baskin, stood in his muddy Dunlop Green Flash plimsolls, and figure-hugging nylon tracksuit, could understand McVale's antipathy towards his outfit. 'It's flesh-coloured . . . sort of pink. It's supposed to be the Coconut Grove team colours. To repre- sent the naked girls at the club, you know, flashing all that skin—'

'Yeah, I get it. You quite literally look like you're in your birthday suit. Your birthday tracksuit. You look like a prick. I mean it, you actually look like a prick. It's disgusting. I should shoot you on principle.' McVale turned his disgust to Bad Man- ners Bob. 'What's wrong with him?'

'He fell in some poison ivy.'

'Yeah? When did this happen, out on your run?'

'Bob's going in the ring next week. Needs to lose a few pounds, build up his stamina. You know how these unlicensed fights go. Can be over in the gouge of an eye, the bite of a nose, or they drag on for hours. Like I said, I'm getting back into sports promotion. It's the final of the darts tournament tonight. Big success. Local boy and Coconut Grove-sponsored athlete, Denton's very own Mr Talent, Keith "Keefy" Keathson, faces the great Jocky "At the Oche" Wilson.' Harry Baskin pulled up the cloying nylon sleeve of his tracksuit to reveal his gold Rolex, then read its diamond-encrusted face. 'I need to get back, Jimmy, make sure all's OK back at the ranch. I'll put your name on the door, front-row seats, complimentary bottle of Moët, and I'm sure a couple of the girls would be happy to give you a complimentary blo—'

'What are those?'

Harry followed the barrel of the gun, which was pointing to the binoculars around his neck. Baskin stuttered and spluttered for an excuse; but McVale beat him to the punch with a pretty on-the-nose explanation.

'Here's what I think. I think you've sussed, or been told, what I've been up to. I knew it wouldn't take you long. You're a fat man, Harry, but you move fast, don't you? Smart as a whip.'

'No, not me, Jimmy, I know nothing. We'll be on our way, mate. Bob's in desperate need of the calamine.'

McVale gestured towards the cottage with the barrel of the gun. 'I'll make you a nice cup of tea.'

Never had the invite for a cuppa sounded less inviting. 'No, we don't want to put you to any trouble.'

'Warm up by the fire. It's cold.'

'Is it? Hadn't noticed. All that running's kept me warm.'

'Then why are you shaking?'

Baskin looked down at his hands. His armpits were on fire and he could feel the sweat gullying down his arse crack.

Jimmy McVale raised the gun to Baskin's head and cocked the hammer.

'So, the dog walked into the pub.'

'That's right.'

'He was a regular, you say?'

'Plato was a good customer.'

'*Plato?*' asked Frost.

The dog barked.

'The name of the dog.'

'Not Pluto?'

'Why would you call a dog Pluto?'

Frost shook his head. 'Fair enough. Carry on.'

'With Charlie Wilkes, his owner, he was in four or five times a week.'

Frost was perched on the corner of the desk, where PC Simms, supervised by DC Hanlon, was taking the details of Mr Malky Balon, landlord of the Coach and Horses. Balon was a bulky, short man in his late fifties with thick, smoky-golden hair, the hue of nicotine.

Simms said, 'I thought you'd be interested, Inspector, as Mr Charles Wilkes, the owner of Plato, lives in Gisborough, a village just north of Denton—'

'I've lived here all my life, I know where it bloody is.'

'Sorry, guv. Anyway, Mr Wilkes runs an art gallery—'

'Art gallery, my arse!' said the bellicose publican. 'It's just a little shop full of his stuff. Charlie Wilkes is a keen amateur painter at best, with pretensions to being a bit of an undiscovered genius.'

At this, the wiry Jack Russell barked again, either in defence of its master's reputation, or to speed things up. Frost looked down at the beast, which was on its haunches, right by his feet. Frost's ankle felt exposed.

'The Coach and Horses is on Mantle Street, near the Denton Repertory Theatre, isn't it? From Gisborough, that's quite a distance. On foot, forty, forty-five minutes to an hour?'

'He sometimes got the bus,' said Malky Balon, 'or a taxi. Money was never a problem for Charlie Wilkes. I think he was left a fair bit when his mother died. That's why he's able to run his "gallery". He hated the local village pub, and we've got some colourful regulars at our place. Lots of theatricals from the Denton Rep use it: stage hands, actors. We had that fella from *Bergerac* in the other night; and that sexy-looking lass from *Triangle*, Kate something, with the big—'

'And the dog was always with him?' asked Frost.

The publican nodded. 'Always had his bowl of water and dog chocolates ready for him.' The dog made a sad whining sound, like the chocolate treats were now a distant memory. 'Charlie and Plato, they were always together, he'd never leave him. Something must have happened.'

Frost glanced down at the dog. The dog met his gaze, its head tilted slightly, heartbreak in its guileless little eyes. But Frost glimpsed something else, too.

An hour later and Frost and Simms, armed with torches, and with Plato in the PC's arms, were outside Charles Wilkes' cottage home cum gallery.

'He may not be a bloodhound, but the way he was looking at me, he knows more than we do. But when your name's Plato, you're bound to,' said Frost as Simms put the dog down on the pavement and let it lead the way.

Plato turned away from the cottage's front door and trotted off down the road like Frost had just thrown a stick for it. When it saw the men weren't at its side, it stopped, turned around and barked at them. Frost and Simms followed its lead like it was Sir Kenneth Newham, the Met Commissioner, himself.

Another thirty or so minutes later and they were in a forest clearing. Plato had raced ahead and was sniffing the ground, making a pained, whinnying sound, and circling an area of grass. Frost and Simms ran over to it. They aimed their torches and saw there was a reddish-black viscous substance on the long grass, glistening under the torchlight. There were some marks, probably from the heel of a man's shoe. Some of the grass was flattened and torn up, like there had been some kind of violent activity.

'What do you see, Simms?'

'Here, just here. He was attacked here?'

'I'd say that's about right.' Frost looked around him. 'Killed here, but I don't think he was buried here. It's open ground, no cover.' He then looked down at the dog, sat alert at his feet. It looked like it wanted to go.

Plato led Frost and Simms back into the village and to Wilkes' house, then around to the back where the clever pooch clawed at a loose paving stone where Wilkes kept a spare key. Once inside, they checked every room. Every door that Frost opened, he steeled himself for what he might find. Of course, he'd seen more than his fair share of dead bodies, but being bludgeoned with a hammer held its own special horrors away from the gun, the knife, the rope. He didn't think he'd ever shake the images of the Wheatons, mother and son, so ferociously dispatched. But then again, if he thought back through the annals of his crimes – because that's how he thought about them, they were as much his to solve as they were the perpetrator's to try to get away with – he was sure he could remember in detail every murder victim he'd seen. Maybe they never leave you, he thought, and maybe they never should.

But in the upstairs apartment where Charles Wilkes had made his home, separate from the gallery below, there was no sign of him, or indeed of any crime having taken place. Down in the gallery, Plato the wonder dog had beaten them to it again as far as detective work went; it'd sniffed out traces of blood on the floor and on the doormat where the killer had obviously trodden.

'Simmo, go to the car and radio this one in. We need scene of crime officers and Forensics, both here and in the woods.'

Simms gave an efficient nod and went out. Frost quickly scoped the walls of the gallery and the paintings on offer. For some reason he found himself muttering, 'Not bad, not bad,' then realized he was doing this for the benefit of Plato the dog, who was sat looking at him attentively. His eye soon wandered over to the wastepaper basket behind the glass display counter; inside it, Frost saw amongst the usual debris of screwed-up paper, pencil shavings, and a brown apple core, a business card. He fished it out. It had been torn, but not quite in half, and was perfectly legible. It was the business card of Dr Stephen M. Parker, of the social sciences department at the university.

Frost smiled. Plato the dog barked. And Simms ran in and told him the bad news.

Monday (6)

It was 9.35 p.m. when Frost and PC Simms arrived at the home of Sally and Ella Fielding. They were met by DC Arthur Hanlon, who made to move towards the yellow Metro, but when it mounted the pavement, quickly jumped out of the way. Frost and Simms – who looked as pale as any passenger of Frost's would when he was in a hurry – climbed out of the car.

'You move fast for a big man.'

'You keep me on my toes, guv. WPC Begbie is upstairs with Ms Fielding.'

'Which one?' asked Frost.

'The grandmother, Vanessa.'

They entered the lobby of Summerhill Court, the small modern block of flats where Sally Fielding and her daughter Ella lived. Frost gestured for Hanlon to get him up to speed, and he complied by pulling out his notebook.

'It was Vanessa Fielding who called us. Ella and Stephen Parker, who was supposed to be picking Ella up from school, should have been here when she arrived. First she thought there'd been a mix-up and they'd gone to Parker's house. So she called him at his home, and then at the university, but just got his answerphone. Then she called the school and one of the teachers was still there and told her that Ella was seen getting into a white transit van. Then Vanessa called us.'

'Did the teacher get a look at the driver?'

'Afraid not. No number plates, not even sure of the make of the van.'

'That's the beauty of white vans, no one takes any notice of them. No sign of Parker?'

Hanlon shook his head.

'Where is the mother, Sally Fielding?'

Hanlon flicked through his notebook. 'She was in London today, she had a day's work with an advertising agency, and was staying on to meet up for a drink with some friends. We managed to contact her at the agency and she's on her way, should be home any time soon.'

'Guv?'

Frost shot a questioning look at Simms.

'First thing this morning we checked a white transit van, found it pulled over on the Rimmington road. The driver said he was looking for work with Jarrett's, clearing the woods. Said he was a carpenter. Said he stayed the night in the van, he felt ill. The story sounded like it stacked up. Driver's licence checked out. Seemed genuine, and he did look ill, I remember – flu.'

'There's a lot of it about,' offered Arthur Hanlon.

'Thank you, Dr Kildare. Did you get a name?'

Now it was Simms's turn to check his notebook. As he flicked through it they stepped deeper into the lobby until they were at the lift. Frost pressed the button, even though the Fieldings' apartment was only on the second floor.

'Thomas Phelps. Got the registration, too.'

'Good, go run a check on it and find the driver. See if it was the same white van the teacher saw. Show her a photo of the model, see if it jogs her memory.'

Simms trotted back out to the Metro to radio through, and Frost and Hanlon rode the lift up to Sally's flat where Vanessa Fielding was anxiously waiting. WPC Hannah Begbie was with her.

It was a cosy purpose-built flat. There was a red corduroy three-piece suite, the floor was covered in modern Habitat rugs, and there were lush rubber and spider plants in cheerful pots. And lots of art on the walls, bright splashes of primary colours, by the looks of them mainly the work of young Ella Fielding.

Vanessa Fielding was dressed in a black roll-neck sweater, black slacks and black patent-leather shoes with a silver buckle. She looked elegant and sophisticated as ever, in what Frost took to be her usual tasteful attire, and not sombre widow's weeds. She was on the couch, her back straight, her hands clasped together, looking stoic and ready to answer any question with a clear head. But before she had the chance, and within minutes of the detectives being there, Sally Fielding arrived.

She had been met at Denton train station by two officers who had blue-lighted her home. The siren hastened their journey through the clogged-up one-way traffic system. But as fast as they went, it was still probably the longest journey Sally Fielding had ever made.

Frost stood back as WPC Begbie and Vanessa attempted to calm Sally down. Once that had been achieved, Frost filled her in on the details of what they knew so far. He then stood by the hearth, arms clasped behind his back like he was taking advantage of the electric fire. He wasn't, it wasn't even on. The central heating was doing a good enough job of warming the neat little flat. He just wanted to get some distance from the mother and daughter sat on the couch. To observe them, catch minor details, read any body language that flowed between them, to see if they were lying.

Frost reached into his bomber jacket, pulled out the photo he had taken off the Hansons' fridge and handed it to Sally Fielding. She wasn't crying now. In fact, dressed in her smart navy-blue trouser suit, she looked efficient and capable of answering any questions he put to her.

'Yes, it's the netball team.'

'Ruby Hanson and her mother. You and Ella. What struck me is how similar you all look.'

Sally Fielding stared at the picture; it was clear from her expression just how uncanny she found the likeness too, once it had been pointed out. 'Ruby is still missing . . . and now Ella.' She no longer looked composed.

Vanessa, who had her arm around Sally on the three-seater couch, intensified her grip and tried to prevent any more tears with her words: 'I know, darling, I know, but we must hear what the inspector has to say.'

Sally took a deep breath and gestured for the detective to continue.

Frost counted to three to himself, knowing that what he was about to say would make things sound a hell of a lot worse for Ella. 'I believe that the abduction of Ruby Hanson was a case of mistaken identity, and who they were really after was Ella.'

Sally took another deep breath, absorbing the information. 'Is this anything to do with . . . to do with my father and his past?'

Frost nodded. 'I don't think this is a random abduction, I don't think the motive is . . . is sexual or to cause her physical harm.'

Sally Fielding squeezed her eyes shut at this, like it was the worst thing in the world she'd ever heard. But also, for now, maybe the best.

'I don't think they have any interest in Ella other than financial gain. It's you they're interested in.' Frost's eyes moved from Vanessa to Sally and back. 'They want information, information from you.'

'What the hell do we have . . . ? We have no money, Daddy spent it all, lost it all, drank it all away . . . They can have what they want in the house, they can have the bloody house and everything in it, if it brings Ella back.'

Frost now focused his gaze on Vanessa and didn't let go. Sally followed it.

'Mum, what's happening?'

Frost said, 'You're right, it's all about your father's past. In 1967 your father was involved in a robbery—'

'That's not true!' protested Vanessa.

The detective's tone changed, he went in hard this time. 'Are you still trying to protect Ivan's reputation? I'd worry about getting your granddaughter back if I was you.'

Sally broke free of her mother's grip, then grabbed Vanessa by the shoulders and shook her violently. 'Come on, tell me!'

Frost made a calming gesture, and WPC Hannah Begbie, standing in the doorway, looked ready to move in and separate them. Sally quickly realized what she was doing, wrung her hands, apologized; her gaze swivelled between Frost and her mother repeatedly, her expression confused, angry, demanding.

Frost knew that time had caught up with Vanessa Fielding. She now had two inquisitors against her, two accusers staring at her, and she wasn't going to get off the hook with a protracted tale of innocence. The swinging '60s dolly bird, the arm candy, the trophy wife, the dumb blonde. She was none of those things. The soirées, the salons, the parties, the happenings, the Chelsea set: she was integral to them, she was the one with the connections. Ivan may have been the brains, but she was the glamour, the honeypot that drew them in. And maybe that's why she had stayed as long as she did. But the past and its secrets were no longer trapped in old photographs. It was written all over her daughter's face, and even more uncannily all over her granddaughter's face, too.

'Mother, *please*, what's going on?'

Vanessa ignored her daughter and looked straight at Frost, again stoic and businesslike. 'Once Conrad sent those awful paintings to Ivan – one for me, one for him, and one for Sally – I knew it was a curse. Conrad probably thought he was giving us the golden ticket to some fabulous prize. Split three ways, so we could all share in it. But I knew all about it, I wasn't stupid. I just turned a blind eye to Ivan ... and Conrad's activities because it suited me. And yes, I played my part, too. But they didn't want me to know about this, they wanted to protect me. But I knew what went on, I made it my business to know so I could protect my family, and of course it was in all the papers, and the rumours swirled around about what had been taken. Then when I read that Jimmy McVale was in Denton . . .'

'I read about him,' said Sally, eager to join the fray. 'Do you think he has the girls?'

'At this stage, I think there's a strong possibility. We've been trying to find McVale, but we can't. He's disappeared,' Frost answered.

'He's a killer, isn't he?' Frost gave a bleak nod to this. 'And what is he after?'

Frost told her.

'You can't kill her . . . you just can't.'

'She's left me no choice.'

Harry Baskin was on his feet and moving, moving fast. The fastest anyone would have seen him move in quite some time. Because now Harry Baskin was up to speed on what had happened with Ruby Hanson. Granted, Baskin was only pacing around the kitchen table in his cottage, wringing his meaty and by now sweaty hands, but his mind was racing, at light speed, because he knew he didn't have long to talk Jimmy McVale out of doing what he fully intended doing.

The sound of a sneeze broke Baskin's morose thoughts. It was so loud that he could still hear it all the way from the Roller that was now parked outside. Bad Manners Bob could be seen through the plastic-sheet windows stuffing his face between bouts of sneezing and scratching. He'd been sent to fetch the Corniche. Baskin had earlier parked it in the lay-by beside the little hut that sold piping-hot tea the colour, consistency and taste of stewed rust. With what was about to happen – unless Harry could talk him out of it – Baskin wanted his distinctive wheels off the road and out of sight. There was only one other person in Denton, as far as he was aware, who had a Roller, and that was the mayor. And it seemed unlikely he would be complicit in murder.

'Poison-ivy rash, hay fever in January? Not too good out in nature, is he?' said Jimmy McVale with an amused but sour expression.

'Bob? No. Not too good in the boxing ring, either.'

'Don't worry, I didn't believe you in the first place, Harry. It was obvious you were spying on me. I must say, though, you've got some nerve running around in that get-up. You look like you're bollock-naked.'

Harry Baskin stopped pacing nervously around the room, maybe feeling the ridiculousness of his outfit. He sat down at the pine table, as if to cover his manhood.

'The two chaps who left earlier – they didn't look well.'

'They don't have the stomach for the work.'

'No one does, Jimmy. Not this kind of work.'

'Funny thing was, *they* came to *me*. Obviously, they knew I was out. But they'd monitored the situation, shall we say.'

'They were on the old firm, right? They were two of the famed "Bond Street Burrowers"?'

Keep him talking, thought Baskin, until I've had time to work something out. Play for time. He was playing not only for the little girl's life, but for his and Bad Manners Bob's lives, too. There was an old saying and rule to live by in the underworld: three can keep a secret – if two are dead.

'They were good in their day, Eddie and Tony,' said Jimmy McVale, 'but I was the one who got nicked for the lawyer's murder.'

'A murder you committed?'

'Course I fuckin' well did.'

Baskin gave a nod of acceptance at this. Not at the fact of the murder, that was always a given. But at the sheer menace in

McVale's voice. All pretence of a changed, educated and enlightened man was gone now. Normal service has been resumed, thought Harry.

'And you didn't grass, Jimmy. You could have got a reduced sentence, but you stayed staunch. Lot of people were impressed with that. I know Nice One was.'

'How about you, Harry, is your nose in the trough? Just how friendly are you with Detective Inspector Jack Frost?'

Baskin considered the DI for a moment. The information Frost had given him was obviously wrong. It was unlike Frost to get something so badly wrong. 'I throw him a bone every now and again. You know how it is, never a bad thing to cultivate a copper. I tried to get him on the firm, a thick brown envelope every week to turn a blind eye, maybe feed me information. No go. He may look like the type who would, scruffy so-and-so who doesn't give a shit, but he wouldn't take the money. Said if I tried it again he'd be all over me like one of the cheap suits he occasionally wears.'

'He doesn't know about me being here, does he?'

'I said I throw him a bone every now and again, not the sirloin steak with all the trimmings. And if he did, he'd be here by now, wouldn't he?'

Jimmy McVale raised his elbow and plucked back the sleeve of his navy cashmere jumper to commune with his wristwatch. The steel and gold square-faced Cartier Santos told him time was moving on, and things needed to get done *now*.

'So it's just us, Harry.'

'And Ruby.'

'No. She's gone. Whatever was going to happen to her, as far as I'm concerned, it's already happened. My mind's made up, it's done. It's you and Mr Sneezy and Scratchy out there that bother me now.'

Baskin cocked an ear: he could indeed hear Bad Manners Bob sneezing, and even thought he could hear him *scratching*. But it was a momentary distraction, as Baskin focused back on the man opposite. The luxurious cashmere couldn't soften him. He was granite.

'Listen, Jimmy, you've got options. For the safe return of their daughter, I'm sure I could get you a deal.'

'And your pal Jack Frost?'

'He's a reasonable man, we could work something out.'

'Forget it. There's powers that be who want me put away. Because I know the secrets. I know what was in the bank vault.'

Baskin's eyes widened, his mouth opened, he could feel drool pooling in the gully of his bottom lip. He'd forgotten about the 'treasure', caught up as he was in the fate of little Ruby Hanson. A thought struck him: maybe this was a moral and ethical breakthrough for him. It wasn't all about money. It wasn't even all about criminal intrigue.

'Fuck that, Jimmy! I don't care about that. It's the kid. You can't kill her, and you're not thinking straight.'

'Don't talk to me like that.'

'Bit of luck I did turn up. You need to think, think fast. Your old firm . . . ? Eddie and Tony? They didn't have the stomach for it, and weren't going to argue with you, right? How do you know they're not at a service station right now, putting in an anonymous phone call to the Old Bill?'

McVale shook his head. 'They wouldn't grass.'

'This goes beyond grassing, Jimmy. You've been away too long. Prison time's different from the real world. They got kids, those two?'

McVale gave a slow thoughtful nod. He then got up from the chair, and did what Harry had done earlier, taking the exact same route as he paced the cottage.

Baskin chipped away at the granite. 'Maybe . . . maybe I could reach out to Ruby's father. He's an architect, so I read. Has his own business. One thing I know about having your own business is that it costs money. Everyone has a price. We let it be known it was a mistake, how sorry we are, pay him off, whatever it takes . . .'

Jimmy McVale continued his figure of eights around the cottage, picking up pace.

'. . . I find out what his price is and get it to him. He gets the kid back and a good few quid on top. And anyway, if it comes to the kid picking you out in a line-up, maybe she'll get it wrong. It was dark, she was scared. Maybe she'd seen you in the paper, recognized your face, got confused – you're a known figure. A good brief could take her story apart . . .'

McVale speeded up, punching his big left fist into the heel of his right hand. 'That's what Tony and Eddie said, but *I'm* the one in the dock, I'm the one they want to put away!'

'But of course, you won't be around, you won't be in the dock. The kid gets delivered, you disappear. You must have your exit plan? You stashed some cash away just in case it all goes tits up . . . all good criminals do, right?'

McVale let out a plangent sigh. 'The plan was to head down to Rio and see an old mate and colleague, then to Colombia, meet some new contacts. But I needed the money from the Bond Street job to make it happen.'

Harry Baskin chose his words carefully, knowing what would come next. 'I'd like to help you out, Jimmy, honest I would.'

Jimmy McVale sat down opposite Harry, hands clasped in front of him on the table. His demeanour had changed. No longer the intransigent and unyielding block of cold granite, he was hunched forward, engaging, his broad smile beaming out at Baskin.

'I like the sound of your plan. And it looks like the kid in there will be going home. But me going away is going to take money. *Lots* of money. I need what's in your safe.'

'*My* safe?'

'*Your* safe.'

'There's nothing in my safe. Just the prize money for the darts . . . and Jocky Wilson's gonna get most of it if he beats Keith.'

'Don't lie to me, Harry. You must have it too, your escape

plan. You must have some readies stashed away, just in case things go pear-shaped for you, right?'

'Nothing.'

'Think again. Because right now I've got a gun aimed right at your orchestra stalls.'

Harry Baskin was so rapt at McVale's malevolence – the pitiless slits for eyes; the whiter-than-white teeth that looked like they could bite your throat out; the malign words slipping between them – that he hadn't noticed him unclasp his hands and move them off the table. He glanced down, trying to see over his belly, trying to see if the gun was in fact aimed at his 'orchestra stalls'. He couldn't see past his gut, but he didn't need to. He heard the click of the hammer being cocked, for the second time that day, and for some reason this seemed far more painful than when the gun had been aimed at his head.

There was a creak, a *whoosh*, a blast of cold air.

'I really need to get home, Harry, I'm not feeling too good—'

McVale raised the gun and shot Bad Manners Bob.

Monday (7)

'Just thought you should know, guv.'

'Go on, Simms,' said Frost, trying to keep a lid on the mounting impatience in his voice. He was in the hallway of Sally Fielding's flat, using her phone. The address book on the side table was one of those that replicated the dial of a phone. Fiddling about whilst waiting to get put through to Simms back at Eagle Lane, he'd managed to get his forefinger stuck in the DEFG hole.

'The bloke we pulled over in the white transit van, Thomas Phelps. Well, his ID checked out, but on further inspection, two names came up with exactly the same name and date of birth.'

Frost weighed this up with a little wobble of his head. 'Sounds like a fairly common name.'

'Yeah. But one is now registered as living in Germany, he's in the army. The other one died twelve years ago. Murdered in a pub car park. Had his throat cut. Suspected weapon, a Stanley knife. He was a carpenter. The culprit was never found.'

Frost stopped trying to free his finger from the hole of the address book as he leaned heavily against the wall. He could feel a sudden rush of cold sweat eddying down his back, like someone had just turned on the tap.

'Guv? You there?'

'I'm still here.'

'Also, the lab boys came back with the blood samples found where Wilkes walks Plato, and from the shop. O-Negative. Same blood group as Wilkes.'

Frost wanted to say, 'It's a fairly common blood group,' just like he had with the name Thomas Phelps, but knew he couldn't. He knew Charles Wilkes was dead.

'The bloke in the white van, do you remember the face? Could you pull it out of some photos?'

'Don't know, maybe, I think so.'

Frost was getting annoyed. 'What do you mean, maybe, you think so? Was he ginger with a big hooked nose and one eye in the middle of his forehead?'

'That's the problem, guv, now I think of it, he had no real distinguishing features. He was sort of mousy . . . brown eyes . . . not blue . . . hard to describe . . . very . . . forgettable?'

'You've just remembered that he's forgettable, I guess that counts as something. Check him against the photo IDs we have of employees or patients of Longthorn. Anything comes up, call me here or on the radio.'

Frost dropped the phone down in its cradle, pulled the now-broken address book off his finger, and went back into the living room. Relations between mother and daughter had settled after the emotional Geiger-counter reading had gone off the scale. They were holding hands, more of an effort on Vanessa's part than Sally's.

'What do you know about Charles Wilkes?' asked Frost, to no one in particular, waiting to see who picked it up first.

'He's an artist. He bought the painting Dad gave me, my third of it, anyway.'

The detective frowned. 'Why did he buy the painting if he's an artist? I think we're all agreed it was rubbish.'

'He bought it at our school jumble sale for ten pence or something. He wanted it because it was a stretched canvas. He was going to paint over it. Lots of artists do that.' Sally turned to her mother. 'Stephen asked me about it the other day. He said that you wanted the painting, or something.'

Vanessa shook her head. 'No, that's not true, I didn't want it at all. In fact, I threw the one I had out.'

Sally turned back to Frost. 'I remember he got quite tetchy about it.'

'Parker?'

'Yes. I didn't think anything of it, what with what's been happening lately.'

'Charles Wilkes was reported missing today. I think he may be in danger because he had Sally's third of the painting. And I think Stephen Parker and Ella are in danger because Parker has your third of the painting, Vanessa. I found Stephen's business card in Wilkes' wastepaper basket.'

Frost watched intently as Vanessa Fielding's eyes flicked up from the carpet she'd been staring at. 'You think . . . you think Stephen is involved in this?' she asked.

He ignored her question. 'Did *you* actually throw it out, or did Stephen do it?'

She thought for a moment. 'Stephen did.'

'You saw him do it, or you just assumed he had?'

She shrugged. 'Assumed. Only because he always takes the rubbish out . . . You think Stephen is after the—'

'The treasure!' Sally cut her mother off and went over to the dining table which looked like it served as her workspace. Frost had never seen a graphic designer's desk before, but imagined it would look something like the table that Sally was searching now. There were lots of loose leaves of artist's paper with perfectly executed drawings and logo designs on them, artist's sketchpads, stacks of magazines for inspiration, and scissors and scalpels for cutting out patterns. Frost felt a camaraderie with Sally and her cluttered desk, it was just like his. He also felt the same sense of triumph when she eventually found what she was looking for under the pile of papers and clippings.

'I didn't think it was important. It's Treasure Island. Ella drew pictures of it. She's like me, not very verbal, couldn't express how she felt about losing her granddad, so her teacher told her to draw her memories of Dad.'

Sally handed Frost and her mother Ella's drawings. Frost had three of them, Vanessa had two. But they were almost identical. It was Ivan and Ella, dressed as pirates, on the mounds in the woods, which through the magical mind of a child were easily transformed into Treasure Island.

'Ella said she and Dad played there. I remember when she told me, I felt a twinge of jealousy, because he never had with me. But then I remembered – Dad did take me there once. It was where he used to play as a kid . . .' Her voice quaked, a tear escaped. '. . . I didn't show any interest then. I was already a teenager when I moved to the area, or certainly felt like one. I was eleven or twelve. And I hated Denton, resented being taken away from London and my friends. Hated the house. But Dad used to play with Ella there. They used to dress up like pirates. This was before he got really ill with the drinking, about two, three years ago. Dad swore her to secrecy. Said it was a special place for him and his best friend. She did these a couple of days ago. I usually pin her work up in the kitchen or somewhere, but I'd forgotten all about them, what with everything—'

Vanessa stood up sharply and said, 'Ella's drawings are the same as Conrad's. It's a place in the woods.'

'Do you know where this is?'

'I'll show you,' she said, going to put on her coat.

'He's hurting me.'

Parker attempted a stern look at Banes. It didn't work. Banes, whose hand was firmly clasped around Ella Fielding's shoulder, just stared back blankly at Parker and issued the first of what would be his many instructions.

'She's fine, don't want her running off and getting lost, do we?' With his free hand Banes tossed Parker the van keys. 'Get the shovel out of the back. There are two torches in there as well.'

'You're well prepared, aren't you?'

Banes smirked. 'That's not the half of it. Rolled up in the grey blanket by the wheel mount is a C Scope CS2M.'

'What the hell's that?'

'It's a metal detector. Don't drop it, it's brand new.'

They were on the other side of Denton Woods, the part that abutted Ivan Fielding's property, well away from where the tree-clearing work was to take place. They had parked the white Bedford van on a dirt track as far into the woods as possible. It was dark now, the moon was a slim crescent providing little light. The twinkle, twinkle of little stars was muted by misty clouds that hung over the woods. The ground felt damp, slippery, the air smelt of mulch and pine.

It had been little Ella who had led the way, taking them up this track, away from the road and the houses. She insisted that she knew where she was going. She would never forget her and Granddad's Treasure Island, because to do so would be to forget him. And she would never do that.

As she led the way, she obviously grew dissatisfied with the two grown-ups' explanation of why they wanted to see the place where she'd played pirates with her grandfather.

'Why do you want to see it now, why not in the morning?'

'That's a good question,' said Parker. 'Why not wait until the morning?'

Banes, his voice raspy now, said, 'Because I don't have the time. It's now or never.'

Ella said, 'But why? Why do you have to go *now*? What's so important—'

Banes groaned. 'Because, kid, there really is bloody treasure buried on that island of yours, and when we find it, Uncle Stephen over there will buy you Barbie dolls—'

'I don't like Barbie dolls,' she said, suddenly stopping in her tracks.

'Cabbage Patch dolls? I hear that's what all the kids like today.'

'Ruby Hanson had a Cabbage Patch doll. Did you take her away in your van?'

Exasperated, Banes turned to Parker. 'What the hell is she talking about?'

Ella, full of anger for her missing classmate, shouted and punched Banes in the stomach. 'You did! I know you did! I know you did . . .'.

Banes, doubled up, hunched over, his breathing laboured, uttered curses, caught out by the strength of the little girl's anger and her powerful little punch.

Parker grabbed Ella's hand. 'OK, that's enough . . . this is over with. I'm taking Ella home.'

Banes straightened up suddenly and as he did so, he grabbed Ella by the hair and snatched her out of Parker's weak grip. She screamed, then stopped, as she felt the blade of the Stanley knife press into her throat.

'Maybe you should wait here?'

'No way,' said Sally to her mother.

They were just about to leave Sally Fielding's flat. Frost stepped in. 'That might not be such a bad idea, Sally, just in case Ella does comes home. She'll need someone here.'

Sally gestured to the WPC standing behind her. 'I thought she was staying here?'

'But Ella doesn't know WPC Begbie.'

Sally Fielding obviously saw the logic of this, but still looked set to protest, when she was cut short by an urgent knock on the door. It was Simms. The PC was brandishing an A4 Manila envelope like a sixteen-year-old with some good O-Level results. Frost was expecting him. But he wasn't expecting what was stood by his side looking up at him.

'Plato?'

Plato the dog dutifully barked back at Frost. It was an offi-
cious bark, almost like a salute, like it was reporting for duty.

'He was in the incident room, we were waiting for the RSPCA
to pick him up, then I thought . . .'

'He's clever, he can sniff things out, like a bloodhound . . .
Good thinking, Simmo!' He gestured to the envelope. 'What
else you got?'

'I've got a name and a picture. Clive Banes. He worked at
Longthorn as an orderly and then he quit. Nothing unusual
there, you're right, guv, they quit all the time. But this one . . .'
Simms handed over the envelope and Frost reached in to look at
the picture. Brownish thinning hair, glasses and a goatee beard,
mid-thirties. '. . . He left a couple of days after Conrad Wilde
died, and he worked in the infirmary, had full access to—'

Frost raised his nicotine-stained finger for Simms to shut up.
'Excuse us for just a second,' he said to Sally and Vanessa as he
hustled Simms and Plato out of the flat into the hallway by the
lifts for some privacy. But he still spoke in a hushed voice.
'Sally Fielding doesn't know about the Wheaton murders and
the potential connection.'

'You think their killer has Ella?'

Frost didn't want to say it, but gave a strained look that suggested he did. Simms pointed at the picture in Frost's hand.
'That's a close enough likeness to the man we spoke to, Thomas
Phelps. Phelps didn't have the beard and wasn't wearing
glasses, but he had the same hair. Sort of combed forward
because it looked like it was thinning.'

'Tell me about it,' mumbled Frost, examining the photo and
running a hand over his receding hairline.

'I've got Rita going through the database, seeing if we can
get an address.'

'I bet pound notes for peanuts she won't turn up anything.
Because there's a really good chance that this Clive Banes
doesn't exist. Just like Thomas Phelps.' Frost again considered

the photo in his hands of Clive Banes . . . Thomas Phelps . . . or whoever the hell he was, and even though Simms had recognized the man in it, the image still seemed out of focus, indistinct, and anonymous.

'Where to now, guv?'

'Take Plato for a walk in the woods.'

Ten minutes later, Simms was at the steering wheel of the Metro with Frost in the front telling him to put his foot down, and Vanessa Fielding sat in the back gently petting Plato. Reason had prevailed and Sally was waiting at home for Ella's return, which Frost had promised her.

They drove in silence to Ivan Fielding's house. Vanessa knew the spot they were headed to, of course she did. She didn't need Conrad's terrible depictions of the three little mounds that had been 'treasure islands' in the childhood imaginations of three generations, and, now, were possibly so in reality.

As they reached the village, the car radio crackled into life. It was John Waters for Frost.

'. . . *Me and Clarke have just arrived at an RTA . . . Harry Baskin's Rolls-Royce has been driven into a ditch. Over.*'

'How is he – alive? Over.'

'*Harry's not in the car. A really big bald bloke is. One of his men. Over.*'

'Bad Manners Bob, probably. So where's Harry? Over.'

'*No sign of him. But Bob's in a bad way, paramedics are tending him now. Unconscious, and looks like he's been shot. Over.*'

'Gordon bleedin' Bennett. Over.'

'*I thought you'd say that. He's still breathing, got an oxygen mask on. But they can't get him to the hospital yet, they're going to have to cut him out of the car. Over.*'

Frost winced. 'So how bad was the accident? Over.'

'*Not bad at all. The car wasn't going at speed, it just sort of rolled into a tree, by the looks of it. Barely dented the bumper. Over.*'

'So why are they cutting him out of the car? Over.'

'*Because he's so fat. Over.*'

Frost couldn't argue with that. 'Get looking for Harry Baskin. The Coconut Grove, his home, his car lot, that pub he's got in town. Let me know the minute you hear anything. Over and out.'

'Drive slowly, Harry, we don't want to attract any attention, do we?'

McVale said this as his BMW, which Baskin was driving, passed a string of coppers surrounding the floodlit site of Jarrett & Sons. The number of protestors had trebled. A busload of uniforms had been pulled in from all over the county to counter them. Truncheons weren't drawn yet, but with the anger and chanting from the angry mob raising the temperature, this part of Denton Woods was dry tinder about to ignite at any minute.

Harry Baskin dropped his speed. He knew that even though he was at the wheel, it was Jimmy McVale who had control of the car. His gun was concealed in his leather jacket, but again, Harry knew that if he made one wrong move it would be quickly out of McVale's pocket and aimed at his head.

'You still mad at me, Harry?'

'You shouldn't have shot him.'

'He shouldn't have sneaked up on me like that. We kept him outside for his own good. Doesn't he know how to knock?'

'Bad Manners Bob is a good man, I wouldn't have him with me if I couldn't trust him.'

'I didn't mean to, it was just a reflex reaction.'

Baskin gave a mounful shake of his head. 'Shouldn't have left him there. Could have taken him to the hospital, seen what they could do.'

'When someone comes in with a bullet wound, the doctors are duty-bound to call the law. Who knows what he'd have said, if he was alive? And anyway, I can't have him bleeding all over the motor. And let's face it, he's not exactly inconspicuous. Scratching and sneezing all over the place. He was getting on my fuckin' nerves, better off where he is.'

Harry Baskin considered this. That was more like the truth.

Jimmy McVale didn't like Bob, so he shot him. But Harry knew there was also another motive behind his actions, and wondered when it would be his turn to start 'getting on Jimmy's fuckin' nerves'. When McVale had the bearer bonds in his hands, he suspected.

'Oh, well. One of them things. Bob knew what he was getting into when he came to work for me. Don't know what I'm gonna say when they find him, though.'

Jimmy McVale smiled – a smile of recognition, perhaps. Harry was just like him, a fully paid-up member of the self-preservation society. 'Say you heard there was activity down at your cottage. Burglars. You sent Bob down to take a look. They must have shot him. You know what the countryside is like, more dangerous than the city, everyone's got a gun and is out shooting things.'

Harry Baskin made some satisfied humming noises as he weighed this up. He liked it. And he made sure that Jimmy McVale saw that he liked it, and that they were squared off and on good terms again.

'One thing about all this I don't understand is . . . the books. I mean, you wrote one, you're writing another, I thought you were set to earn a lot of money with the books. I heard they were going to make a film. You could go to Hollywood, might get the opportunity to rump Raquel Welch!'

McVale laughed. 'No money in writing, it's a mug's game.'

'The missus loves Harold Robbins, I'm sure he earns a few quid.'

'You want the truth? I've never written a book in my life.'

Harry Baskin scrunched up his face in confusion.

'It was all a ruse to get parole.'

Harry Baskin banged his fist on the steering wheel. 'I knew it! I fucking knew it! But you were so convincing . . . even I thought . . .'

'I convinced a parole board too.'

'How did you . . . ?'

343

'I used a ghost writer. I've never even read the book I was supposed to have written. Well, bits, at book signings. Writing books, fuck that, it's boring, sat on your arse all day. No, mate, mug's game.'

'But didn't you get some degrees?'

'I cheated. I got College Charlie to write all my papers. He was at Cambridge before he got into the forgery game. He was doing a five stretch, so I had to work fast. Or rather he did. Or I'd break his fuckin' hands.'

Harry Baskin shook his head, finding it hard to fathom the depths of McVale's dishonesty, or of his own gullibility. The momentary self-loathing was cut short when he heard a thump, like he'd hit something, or maybe just a bump in the road.

'What was that?'

It happened again, but it was clear it was no bump, it was coming from the rear of the car. The two gangsters looked around them, then at each other, mouths agape.

'You're joking? No?'

'No . . . It's not . . . It can't be.'

There came two more bumps in quick succession.

'What the . . . ? You've got to pull over.'

'Pull over . . . ?'

'What else . . . ? Pull over.'

Harry Baskin slowed the car and stopped at the side of the road. They were still deep in the Denton countryside, and had been studiously taking the B-roads wherever possible since skirting the Jarrett site so as to avoid the law. The car rested at an angle on the verge of the narrow road. Jimmy McVale was armed with a torch, as they got out and made their way to the back of the car. There it was again, a thumping emanating from the boot.

'You've got to be joking . . .'

'She's still . . . ?'

'She *can't* be . . . ?'

Baskin sent his dense brows skywards a couple of times like

that in itself would open the boot. When it didn't, Jimmy McVale took the hint and went to pop it open.

'I can't believe she's still . . .'

'I know, I thought for sure she'd be dead . . .'

The boot opened and there was Ruby, a blindfold on, greeting them with a big yawn.

'. . . dead, dead to the world! How many sleeping pills did you put in her Nesquik?'

Jimmy McVale said, 'I put two pills in. I have two and I'm out like a light, all night, and I'm a big bloke. She should be fast asleep.'

Harry Baskin looked surprised at this; with what McVale had on his conscience, he'd have thought he'd need the whole bottle just to get a wink of sleep.

'Where am I?' asked Ruby in a drowsy voice.

Harry said, 'You're safe, sweetheart. You're going home, darling, back to Mummy and Daddy, I promise you. You just have to be brave for a little longer, okey-dokey?'

She yawned and nodded and let out a wispy little sigh. Jimmy McVale closed the boot.

Tuesday (1) _____

The black and yellow police tape was still up across the door
and the ground-floor windows, barring entry to Grey Gables.
Vanessa Fielding, in a long black woollen coat with a fur-
trimmed hood, stood on the path looking at the house. At just
gone midnight, Grey Gables seemed to suit the night better
than the day. Gothic, crumbling, overgrown, its life snuffed out.
It would take new blood to restore it to its former glory, fix the
brickwork, strip the peeling and mouldering Regency-stripe
wallpaper and replace it with something new, light and vibrant.

'Are you ready?' asked Frost.

Vanessa took a deep breath, and gave a resigned smile. Frost
interpreted this to mean she was ready to face her past, too,
lurking there hidden in the woods all these years.

So, armed with torches, Frost, Simms, Vanessa and Plato the
dog made their way up the path. Frost couldn't help but smile –
the decrepit old house, the dark woods, the buried treasure,
and the faithful dog. His report to Mullett would read like a
script for an episode of *Scooby-Doo*. Still, with a killer like Banes
on the loose, as long as it didn't turn into *Friday the 13th* . . .

They made their way around to the back of the house, wading through the long damp grass, then up some scattered paving stones that led to the broken garden fence, which gave them access to the woods.

The luminous dial of Simms's Swatch told them they'd walked a good ten minutes into the wilds of Denton. With Vanessa guiding them, they knew they were on track. And with a low and sustained growl as it sniffed the air around it, Plato must have sensed they were drawing closer.

'Good boy . . . good boy,' encouraged Frost. He could have been saying it to Simms, too, for Frost had instructed the enthusiastic young PC to keep his mouth shut and let the DI do all the talking. He had a feeling that the closer they got, the deeper into the woods they ventured, the more likely it was that Vanessa, who had been virtually silent, would begin to open up. She did.

'I hope it won't disappoint you, Inspector, this "treasure island" we're after. It's where Ivan and Conrad used to play as children, just as Ella said. They played pirates. They were always more than just business partners. They were like brothers. Conrad was a local boy, but very much from the wrong side of the tracks, as it were. His mother cleaned for the Fieldings, but she was also more or less Ivan's nanny. Ivan's mother was rather an aloof, hands-off sort of woman. I found her rather cold.

'When Conrad's mother died suddenly, the father, who wasn't around much anyway, left him with Ivan's family whilst he went to look for work. But, of course, he never returned. Apparently, he'd gone abroad, joined a merchant ship to the South Seas or somewhere. Conrad was only about six or seven, so he and Ivan grew up together. Just how happy his life with the Fieldings was, is hard to say. Taking Conrad in was very much Ivan's father's idea, who was, according to Ivan and Conrad, a wonderful man. But when he died, I think the mother became resentful of having to look after Conrad as well as her own son. So

Conrad ran away when he was fourteen and, like his father, joined a ship to somewhere exotic, looking for adventure. Maybe hoping to become a real pirate.

'Ivan and Conrad met up again in London years later. By that time they'd both learned their "trades": Ivan with an uncanny knowledge of fine art and antiques, Conrad with an uncanny ability to steal them. Together again, inseparable. Brothers, again.'

Frost said, 'Their childhood fantasies came true: they both became pirates, after a fashion. And when you saw the paintings, you knew that's where Conrad had buried the haul from the 1967 job?'

'Yes. And I knew it could only mean trouble. Some things are better off left buried. Like the dead.'

Frost didn't know if that statement was supposed to send a chill up his spine, but it did. It also cued up his next line of questioning perfectly. 'You say they were like brothers – and yet Ivan betrayed him. Got him sent to prison.'

'Ivan believed that Conrad betrayed *him*. Believed he'd kept for himself the Vermeer he was at Eaton Square to steal for Ivan.'

'Yes, that's what I heard. But that's not the betrayal I'm talking about, Vanessa.'

She stopped dead in her tracks and stared ahead of her, into the blackness of the woods. 'When did you find out?'

'A friend of Ivan and Conrad, Captain Cavanagh, he saw a picture of Sally and Ella. He said it was unmistakable. It was like seeing a ghost. And once I dug out an old photo of Conrad Wilde, I saw it too. It's written all over their faces. Conrad Wilde is Sally's father.'

'It's not what it seems.'

'Nothing ever is, and I'm not making any judgements, just stating some facts.'

Vanessa wrapped her coat around her more tightly, as something seemed to move in on her, a cold blast. 'It's over here,' she said, still refusing to face him, and stalking off. The detective couldn't see if she was crying, but he suspected she was.

'I imagine that for both men, you were always the real object of desire for them, not the paintings, the treasures.'

She managed a laugh. 'What a romantic you are, Inspector.'

'And yet you chose Ivan over Conrad?'

'When I first met them, of course I was attracted to Conrad initally. But I knew Conrad couldn't give me what I wanted. Security. He was too much the lothario, the adventurer, risk-taker, and liable to take off at any minute. Much like his own father.'

'And yet, you had Conrad's child?'

She stopped again, and turned to him, her face full of rage. 'No! No, it wasn't like that! Don't make me out to be some stupid scarlet woman, because it fits your simple-minded profile—'

'Nanna!'

They all turned towards the direction of the little girl's voice. It was distant, but desperate. Plato barked, slipped its leash and ran ahead. They followed the smart little terrier. They were in the thick of the woods on a mulchy ribbon of track that snaked its way through the cluster of trees, to what would hopefully soon be a clearing.

Vanessa called out to her granddaughter, just as desperate, but nothing came back.

A light glowed in the sky, a spotlight bearing down. And Vanessa's desperate cries for Ella were now drowned out by the sound of a helicopter whirling overhead. With its arrival, in the distance, came also the roar of a crowd, the protestors, their battle cry rising up, '. . . WE'LL BRING JARRETT'S TO THEIR KNEES IF THEY CUT DOWN OUR PRECIOUS TREES!'

Frost realized they'd been walking at a good clip for about twenty minutes, and were heading south, closer and closer to the Jarrett site.

The three of them raced ahead after Plato, its barking lead-ing the way, and soon their torch beams showed they were in a clearing covered in long grass and thick with ferns. But there they were – unmistakable – the three little hillocks. The largest one, the 'treasure island' in the centre, the remains of a fallen tree in front of it, its gnarled and bulbous stump still in the ground, its thick curlicue roots resembling coiled rope on the deck of a galleon.

'Nanna!' called out Ella Fielding once more.

'Ella!' Vanessa ran towards her granddaughter who stood by the tree stump at the foot of her Treasure Island.

Frost's torchlight fell on the little girl, but she started scream-ing, then stopped, just as the blade of a Stanley knife was pressed against her throat again.

'You touch her and I'll kill you!' hissed Vanessa.

Frost grabbed Vanessa by her arm to stop her.

Banes backed away, taking Ella with him, the blade steady at her throat.

They were about twenty feet away from them. Frost was holding Vanessa back, who between sobs was hissing curses and threats at Banes. Simms was now holding Plato, who was growling with the same threatening intensity as Vanessa.

But louder than all this came a groan, a groan of pain. Frost aimed his torch in its direction, and saw that at the base of the central mound, almost hidden, lay Stephen Parker, face down in a hole about three foot deep. It looked like it had the makings of his grave. And he had a shovel in his hand with which he'd been digging it.

'You, copper!'

Frost didn't know if Banes was addressing him or Simms, but he took it up. 'What do you want, Banes?'

'You know who I am, eh?'

'Yes, Clive, I do. If that really is your name.'

'It was Thomas Phelps, last time we spoke,' said Simms.

Banes flashed the torch in Simms's face. 'It's you again. The spotty young plod in the bow-tie. Don't feel too bad. I've slipped past sharper coppers than you. People have been underestimating me all my life.' He focused back on Frost. 'Underneath Parker, you'll find it.'

'The treasure?'

Banes added, 'Lift him up, and put it at my feet, and the little girl lives. Then I'm out of here. Like I never existed.'

'That's your speciality, isn't it?' Frost aimed his torch squarely at Banes' face and was shocked at what he saw. His eyes looked like they were sunken into his skull, his skin was bloodless, yet there were livid red blotches on it, like welts, or septic scabs. He glistened with a sheen of sweat. 'You don't look like you're going anywhere, apart from hospital.'

Banes, his voice sounding both raspy and restricted, like he was choking, insisted, 'Like I said, it's a big mistake to underestimate me . . . I'll kill you all before anything happens to me.'

Plato barked, seemingly pleased at the state of its erstwhile aggressor.

'Keep that bloody thing away from me!'

Simms reined Plato in, whispering to it to be patient.

Frost calmed the agitated killer. 'My name's Frost, Inspector Frost—'

'I know who you are . . . seen you in the paper . . . looking for the kid. Well now you've found her . . . just the wrong one.'

'Or the right one, depends on how you look at it.'

'That's right . . . I got the *right* one . . . so like I said, Frost, don't underestimate me.'

Frost saw that Ella had her eyes squeezed shut now, her lips were trembling, through fear and the cold, or maybe she was mouthing a prayer. Either way, he had to act fast. Banes was desperation personified, there wasn't anyone he wouldn't kill to get what he wanted. Frost knew he had to keep him talking, keep him engaged, stop him sinking into that psychotic head of his.

'Let's take it nice and easy, Clive. There's no need for anything rash to happen. We can all get what we want without anyone getting hurt.'

'I don't need you to tell me that. I'm getting exactly what I want, it's right here. There's no way I'm walking away without it. Come and take a look.'

Frost edged closer to the hole and shined his torch in. The first thing that grabbed his attention was the open wound at the back of Parker's head. It had all the hallmarks of a Banes killing. Parker had been hit over the head with a hammer, and most certainly would have been completely dispatched if they hadn't arrived when they had. The lecturer was face down in the earth with his bloody wound glistening, and his legs twitching in spasms as the blows to his head still worked through his system, destroying the thing that Parker held most precious and believed to be superior to others: his grey matter, his brain cells. There was a metal detector on the ground too.

But that wasn't what Banes was so keen for Frost to see. Underneath the academic, protruding from his side, was a metal box. *The* box.

'You see it, Frost? You see it?'

He glanced up to see Banes grinning maniacally like the psychotic killer Frost knew him to be. Or maybe that was too easy, too obvious. And he was right, Frost didn't want to under-estimate him. 'I see it. But others have been just as close, and look what good it did them.'

'I'm different. I've got nothing to lose. I never have. Now, do as I say . . . Get the box, and place it at my feet. Slowly. Try any-thing, and I will cut the girl's jugular and she will die in her granny's arms.'

It was said with such intent and authority that no one doubted it. A deep silence fell over the clearing. Simms breathed heav-ily. Vanessa closed her eyes, like Ella, and she too looked like she was praying. And Frost eased himself down into the hole. He crouched down, and whispered in Parker's ear, 'Can you hear me, Stephen?'

Parker's breathing was torturously laboured, sounding like every breath would be his last. But he seemed to be semi-conscious and responded with a grunting sound that Frost suspected he would be using for a while. But at least he was alive. The poor fool, thought the detective. Banes obviously had no intention of sharing the spoils with Parker and went to kill him as soon as he hit, literally, pay dirt.

'Hurry up, Frost!'

The detective carefully moved Parker's head to the side so he was no longer breathing in and eating mud. He then took off his jacket and made a pillow for him, hoping that it would also help to staunch the blood. Banes, impatient, angry, told him to pull his finger out. Frost complied and lifted the box free from under Parker and climbed out of the shallow hole, looking back at Parker as he did so, hoping it wouldn't become what Banes had intended it to be, his shallow grave.

The metal box was about the size and dimensions of a shoe-box. Given its heft and dull colour, Frost suspected it was made of lead. And even though it had oxidized through the years, and was now a greenish colour, it was still very solid and secure and more than capable of protecting its precious cargo with its heavy padlock.

He took the four or five paces necessary to deliver it at Banes' feet. If he was going to make a move, he was close enough. But Banes' Stanley knife was even closer to Ella's jugular. He could see the blade pressing in, her delicate skin looking ready to part at the slightest increase in pressure.

Frost placed the box before the killer, and saw his dead eyes spark into life once again. Banes' tongue slipped out of his mouth and he looked like he was going to lick his cracked lips.

But instead he told Frost, 'Now stand back, back with the others.'

Frost did as he was told, but not before saying, 'I've done my part, and as far as I'm concerned you can have it. Just let the girl go.'

'Throw your torches over there . . .' instructed Banes '. . . way over there, by the trees.'

Simms, Vanessa and Frost looked at each other, knowing they would be plunged into darkness. Frost gave them the nod, and led the way by throwing his torch to the ground. They all did the same. Plato barked its disapproval. But it was immediately drowned out by a thunderous sound and a whirlwind churning up the leaves and loose dirt in the clearing. A spotlight beamed down on them as the low-flying helicopter lit up 'Treasure Island'.

By the time they'd lowered their eyes from the sky, Frost saw that Ella lay face down on the ground. Banes and the box were gone.

'One . . . hundred . . . and . . . eighty!'

The audience roared. Stamped their feet. And Keith 'Keefy' Keathson raised his arms and pumped his fists as he faced his adoring home crowd. He pulled his darts out of the board, and the lager-fuelled chorus from the punters grew even louder as Jocky stepped up to the oche. It was poetry in motion as the arrow left his hand.

Jimmy McVale pulled the gun out of his jacket, spooked by the sudden and incredibly loud roar from inside the Coconut Grove. Harry Baskin and McVale had just hauled themselves out of McVale's BMW that Harry (the designated driver – at gunpoint) had parked in his own private spot at the rear of the club. It was Harry's idea to go around the back so they wouldn't be seen. It suited both men.

'Put that bleedin' thing away! Jeez, relax, Jimmy.'

McVale slipped the gun in his waistband. 'Sounds like you've got quite a crowd in there.'

Harry Baskin smiled at the thought. At ten quid a ticket, he knew he'd be in the money. The coffers would be full. He just hoped he would get through tonight and get a chance to spend it. 'Follow me.'

They made their way into the club, through the back door, through the kitchen, through the caged area where the booze was locked up, and into Harry's inner sanctum: his office.

Once inside, Harry went straight for the bottle of Johnnie Walker Blue, and filled two glasses to the brim. Jimmy McVale, even though time was of the essence, didn't argue. They raised their glasses to each other and took some sizeable glugs. It was much needed. The supermarket brandy they'd been swigging in the cabin in the woods couldn't do what Johnnie Blue did: settle the nerves, sack the tension and give you that warm glow.

The two men sat in silence as they sipped their drinks. Partly because in Harry Baskin's inner sanctum it was eerily silent. He'd had the windowless room soundproofed. When they were done, Jimmy McVale placed his glass on the desk with an emphatic thud.

'The money, Harry.'

Harry Baskin got up from his swivel chair and padded over to the concealed safe. He took down the portrait of Margaret Thatcher, which was squeezed in between one of the Queen and a Spitfire majestically making its way over the white cliffs of Dover, and revealed the perfectly flush wall safe. He spun the dial and opened her up with a banker's ease. He reached in with both hands and pulled out a thick yellow Jiffy envelope that looked stuffed with money. He then spun around and shot Jimmy McVale in the head with the Beretta pistol that was concealed inside the padded envelope.

McVale slumped forward on the desk. Perfectly dead.

Tuesday (3)

'Simmo? Where are you? Plato?'

Nothing. Not a sound. Not even a bark. Frost cursed Simms. Hadn't he told him, the last bloody time they were out here, to wait up for his colleagues? But no, the enthusiastic young copper had raced off again.

He knew that every time he called out for Simms, he was potentially alerting the killer that he was alone, and in need of help. The one thing he knew was that he was heading south, towards the ever-closer voices of the protestors, who sounded like they were kicking off royally now. Frost was glad to hear it, happy that the forces from County were unable to quell them. Because right now they were leading him back to civilization.

Frost stopped – he thought he heard a crackling behind him, not heavy enough for a man, surely, but maybe an animal. In his peripheral vision – though all of it seemed that way now, in the dark, uncertain – he thought he saw a low black figure darting between the trees, indistinct, flickering in what little light there was from the sickle of the moon. It seemed to be encircling him. Frost spun around, trying to keep up with it.

He yelled out in pain as the dull cold thud of metal glanced against the side of his head. Frost spun around again and managed to push his fist into his attacker's face, before he fell to the ground as the force of the blow from the hammer took effect.

On his back, he saw the hammer zooming down on him again – but managed to roll away from it. They were both on the ground now. Frost's punch had connected with Banes' nose. Frost had felt it give way under his knuckles. Still he couldn't see the murderous bastard, still he was in the dark, but he shouted out anyway, hoping Simms would hear him.

'There's nowhere to go, Banes! You're finished! Whatever is wrong with you, you need to get to the hospital! You listening to me?'

Frost couldn't understand the reply. Banes' voice was reduced to a raspy and pained low growl – whatever was eating its way through his body was gathering pace and shutting him down.

As the DI's eyes adjusted to the seemingly ever-changing scene, he could just make out Banes scuttling off, back into the trees. Frost stood up, fists at the ready, sure that Banes' body was failing him, he'd had his last hurrah. But, again, he'd underestimated his quarry, as he was charged to the ground. He could feel the hammer in the small of his back. He was now face down, with Banes on top of him, straddling him.

There was something unyielding and strong about Banes, even in his depleted state, and Frost knew that if he stayed in this position he was a dead man. He needed a miracle – he got a helicopter. The searchlight beamed down on them and lit up the scene. It flew in low enough to churn up the forest floor, and dirt and leaves and bracken spun around them.

He felt the gloved hand that was pressing down on the back of his neck, as if to hold a piece of wood in place before hammering in a nail, release its grip. And Frost managed to twist himself around to face his attacker. He sniffed the air. It was rancid, like putrefying flesh and . . . death. Banes was holding his hands to his eyes, eyes that were obviously full of the swirling grit and dirt. The hammer was in one hand, the lead box was stuffed in a deep pocket of his duffel coat.

Then there was a bark, followed by Simms's voice encouraging Plato, 'Where, boy? Where are they?'

Banes took his gloved hands from his face – a face that looked like a death mask – just long enough for Frost to grab Banes' ears, pull his head towards him, and deliver a textbook head-butt to his nose. He could feel the bone crack where it had connected with the sweet spot at the top of his forehead, just below the hairline. Banes' nose, already weakened from the earlier punch, now exploded in a blast of blood.

The killer reeled back, emitting a high-pitched yelp as he did so, like a dog. (Though Frost thought the comparison an insult to the venerable Plato, whose stately barking was getting closer and closer.)

The helicopter must have veered away, because it went dark again. Frost got to his feet, searching around for Banes, clenched fists at the ready.

'Guv! You all right?' asked Simms, shining a torch in his face.

Frost grabbed the torch, and raked its light over the ground and trees – Banes was gone. Simms, breathless, excited by the chase, talked away, but Frost ignored him. He was concentrating on his surroudings; for once, he seemed to be getting his bearings. This neck of the woods looked familiar to him.

Plato barked up ahead of them, its powerful little nose naturally on to something. Frost shone the torch at a tree. 'Recognize that one, Simms?'

'Oh yeah. It's the one that—'

'Come on, son!'

Frost and Simms steamed ahead, following Plato who was again on Banes' trail. And they were heading in just the direction that the DI wanted them to. Two police helicopters flew over, low and loud. The roar of the protestors intensified. But above the melee, the sudden cry was unmistakable to Frost. He recognized it, because he'd lived it himself. He raced ahead of

Simms and Plato, his torch aimed at the ground, then he slowed and held up his arms, and managed to raise one leg, too, to stop Plato and Simms from falling in.

'Degsy, you bloody wonderful stupid little toffee-nosed twat!'

Lying in the deep hole, the hole that Frost had fallen in only days before, was Clive Banes. The hammer in one hand, the lead box containing the 'treasure' beside him. Banes, unmoving, looked up at them, his red-rimmed eyes in his bloodied face were wide open and unblinking. He remained that way until he was lifted out of there by the ambulance crew that arrived thirty minutes later.

Frost wondered whether they shouldn't have left him there, with his hammer, with his 'treasure', and just shovelled the dirt over him. He wasn't being cruel, far from it. He suspected it would be what the lone, unknown, unknowable and anonymous killer would have wanted.

'Cheers, Jimmy, God bless, bottoms up and your good health.'

Harry Baskin raised his tumbler of whisky, then took a slug and expelled a lavish 'Ahhh' as it burnished the back of his throat and slipped down like satin. He inspected the glass in his hand. Not so much as a tremor. Nerves of steel, brass balls, and a game boy to the last. Harry still had it. And Jimmy McVale got it. Right between the eyes.

'I don't want to speak ill of the dead, Jimmy, but you had it coming, son. You was always heading this way, just a matter of time. You always was a horrible bastard. Not well liked amongst the "chaps".' Harry's face curdled in disgust. 'Kill a kid? You piece of shit. No, you had it coming. Not only for her, but for Bob. He's got a wife, a kid. I'm gonna have to tell them. And another thing, you half-baked, two-bob, piece of shi—'

'Harry?'

Baskin turned towards the locked door. There was a faint knock. Followed by a series of them and another call of his name, but with added urgency this time. Harry recognized the voice: it was his barman, Dino, hammering on the padded door to be heard.

'What is it?'

'You've got visitors.'

Harry Baskin knew what that meant. 'How many of them, and who?'

'Two. There's a bird, pretty. And that black fella, always wears great clobber. They've just walked in.'

'OK. If they ask, say you haven't seen me. The usual, you know nothing, right?'

'Right, Aitch.'

Harry Baskin downed the Johnnie Walker and put plan B into action. Or was it plan A? He hadn't quite decided what the plan was to be. All he knew was that he was going to kill Jimmy McVale. He'd decided that long ago. But with Denton's finest, Waters and Clarke, in his club – his mind needed to focus.

Harry moved with lethal efficiency now, the same lethal efficiency that had put him in this predicament. He took a pair of leather driving gloves from his desk drawer and pulled them over his meaty hands. He then lifted McVale out of his chair and laid him on the floor. He removed the revolver from the dead man's waistband and went over to the bottle of Johnnie Walker. He picked it up by the neck and took some mighty swigs. He needed the Dutch, and hopefully it would blunt some of the pain. The plan he was enacting now was definitely plan B.

Plan A was to roll McVale up in the rug on the floor, stick him in the boot of the car, and drive him out to Felixstowe where an associate of his had a commercial fishing boat and could be relied on to take care of such things. Burials at sea where they don't get washed up, or end up bobbing about on the surface. It was Davy Jones' locker for Jimmy McVale.

Plan B was a different kettle of fish altogether. Harry gripped

McVale's gun, and fired a shot into his own left arm. Not right in it, not the muscle, the bone, but enough to blow away a big flap of flesh and get it bleeding good and proper; and enough to make him bite down on his bottom lip and draw blood from there too. But he knew he'd survived far worse gunshot wounds. He then put four shots into the wall around the safe. And, regrettably, the Queen caught one in the bonce too.

There was now a banging on the door that grew into a thorough pounding, like they were putting their foot to it.

'Harry! Open up!'

'Mr Baskin, it's the police! Are you OK?'

It was DS Waters and DC Susan Clarke, in that order.

He went over to Jimmy McVale and put the revolver in his hand, pressing his dead fingers around the butt and on the trigger. He took off his gloves and put them back in the drawer, went over to the safe, and slumped down on the floor and called out, 'Help! *Help!* He shot me . . . robbery . . . he shot me!'

The room was soundproofed, but not to the extent that they hadn't heard the gunfire, because now the door was flexing and bulging and just about to burst free of its lock, which it duly did, letting in the roar of the crowd and the bellowing voice of the MC: '*Keith, you know what you need, three in a row, top of the board . . .*'

Waters and Clarke stood in the doorway, taking in the scene.

'The kid . . . Ruby . . . she's in the boot of McVale's car . . . a Beamer, round the back . . . the keys are on the desk . . . She's OK . . . she's . . .' Harry tried to say something else but his pained voice was drowned out by the ecstatic cheering of the crowd.

'*ONE . . . HUNDRED . . . AND . . . EIGH-TY!*'

Keith 'Keefy' Keathson had just beaten Jocky Wilson with a maximum finish in the final of the very first Coconut Grove Darts Classic.

Harry Baskin smiled as he thought to himself, life doesn't get much sweeter than this.

Wednesday (1)

Frost, Simms and Hanlon considered the box on the desk. They were in Frost's office. The door was closed. It could have been seen as an unnecessary precaution given the incident room was empty. It was 1.30 a.m. Most were in bed, fast asleep after their gruelling forty-eight-hour shifts in the search for Ruby Hanson. The poor sods that weren't were on duty at Denton Woods.

Frost's usual paper-strewn and file-heaped desk had been cleared – almost in just one sweeping move – by the DI to accommodate the box.

'Shall we?' asked Arthur Hanlon.

Simms said, 'We're this close, be madness not to, wouldn't it?'

Frost considered this statement. It was apt. Because madness was at the very heart of this case. The 'treasure' had joined a long and unhappy lineage of inanimate objects that man had put greater store in than life itself.

There was a chisel and a hammer on the table. They were both from the store room, and not part of Clive Banes' arsenal. Frost picked them up. He gave Arthur Hanlon the nod, and

Hanlon's big hands gripped the box, securing it to the desk so Frost could hammer down on the chisel and break off the padlock . . . and get to the prize.

'Don't miss, Jack.'

'Don't worry, Arthur, I was a dab hand at woodwork at school.'

Frost put the business end of the chisel on to the weakest and thinnest part of the padlock. He was pretty sure one swift blow would break it open. He took a deep breath. He raised the hammer and—

'Don't you dare, Frost!'

Crammed in the doorway were Superintendent Stanley Mullett, Captain Lionel Cavanagh and some plain-clothes bods who had 'spook' written all over them.

Mullett and Cavanagh parted to let the dark-suited men enter the office. The four of them moved to take the hammer and chisel from Frost's hand and the box off the desk with such a close-drilled precision that by the time Frost managed to ask what the hell was going on . . . they were gone.

Simms and Hanlon were just as quickly dispatched by Mullett.

'How are you, Jack?' asked a concerned Captain Cavanagh as he tilted his head to inspect the lump on the detective's temple. 'Looks like you caught one for the cause.'

'It's nothing.'

On hearing this, Captain Cavanagh beamed a big smile. 'Good man, good man. My utmost congratulations. Absolutely marvellous work. Bravo. Shall be making the highest commendations about your impeccable conduct throughout this case. You really are an outstanding detective, a credit to Denton and the force.'

Frost knew when he was having smoke blown up his arse, and didn't greet the praise with the requisite obsequiousness. 'You're not retired at all, are you, Captain Cavanagh?'

'One never really retires in this game, Jack. When duty calls, when England expects.'

'And you're not really with the Stolen Art and Antiques Squad, are you?'

'Frost, you've been told by the captain—'

Cavanagh turned to Mullett and with barely a gesture cut him off.

'Jack has every right to ask. Let's just say, I'm a serving officer without portfolio. My remit is wide and rewarding, I like to think.'

'A spook?'

'I'm in the service of Her Majesty. Just like you.'

Mullett muttered a 'Hear, hear' to this.

'And I take it you're not going to tell me what's in the box?'

'But I did tell you. A fabulous jewelled Fabergé egg.'

'Yes, you did tell me. But why don't I believe you?'

The smile vanished from the captain's face. He took a breath and released it on the back of a sigh that was tinged with genuine sadness. Sad that he'd underestimated Frost and been caught out? Or maybe sad because it was the age-old question, and one that he could never answer. 'My dear Inspector Jack Frost, may I ask *you* a question?'

'You may.'

'What do you *want* there to be in the box?'

Frost considered this. Then smiled, then shrugged. Cavanagh returned both gestures with the slightest of winks. They understood each other. Cavanagh touched the brim of his green Harris tweed cap and turned to leave.

Mullett opened the door for him. 'I have a rather good sherry in my office, if you have time for a . . .'

Cavanagh didn't answer Mullett, just repositioned that beaming, slightly buffoonish smile on his face, which Frost now realized was as much play-acting as anything else in a well-rounded spook's repertory. The good captain stalked out of the incident room with the gait of a man half his age.

Mullett, maybe to cover his embarrassment, adopted Cavanagh's demeanour, and beamed broadly at the DI. 'Yes,

Jack. Good work. Both the little girls are back home safely with their parents. This box, or whatever it is, has been found. The Wheatons' murders solved. As for Jimmy McVale, Harry Baskin is claiming McVale tried to rob him.'

'That sounds about right to me.'

'Said when he opened the safe McVale shot him. So he shot him back. Of course, I will suggest further investigation into Baskin. What's he doing with a gun in his safe in the first place? This is Denton, not Dodge City.'

'Stopping people from killing him? Sounds like self-defence to me.'

Mullett looked unconvinced. But happy enough. 'Anyway, despite Baskin, the one blemish on the case, that's all of them closed.'

'Almost, sir. Almost.'

Wednesday (2)

'How is it?'

'No brain damage,' said Frost, making his way across Denton General's car park to where Susan Clarke was leaning against the yellow Metro. There was a decent-sized plaster spread across his forehead.

'Could have told you that. It would take the Burundi drummers two days beating out a tune on your bonce before they located your brain.'

'You've been rehearsing that one.'

She winked and nodded towards the report he was holding. 'What's that?'

He held it up to stress its importance. 'This? This is serious trouble for someone. It's Dr Death's path report on Clive Banes. He died of massive organ failure brought on by encephalitis.'

'What's that and who's in trouble?'

'Encephalitis is potentially deadly brain inflammation. Often caused by animal bites, like dog bites.'

Frost and Clarke gazed down at the 'felon' at their feet. Plato, the tenacious little terrier, barked, proud of its handiwork.

'Of course we can't just blame him, he did have an accomplice. Banes, it seems, had an allergy to cats. And the cat scratches he had on his arm, presumably the work of Flossy Wheaton's cat, went septic and caused a blood infection. And when mixed with the untreated encephalitis, it was lethal.'

'You're kidding?'

'Nope.'

Susan couldn't help but look impressed. 'Cat and dog working together. Rather like you and me, Jack.'

'What's the old saying? "Revenge is a dish best served with a saucer of milk and a bone."'

'What are we going to do with him?'

'Keep him in custody. Until we find him a good home, I suppose?'

Plato and the two detectives got in the car. Twenty minutes later and they were pulling up at Grey Gables. Frost went inside, Clarke stayed in the car and tickled the tummy of the 'prisoner'.

Frost found Vanessa in the living room. There were cardboard boxes, some tea chests and piles of newspapers and bubble wrap, as Vanessa prepared to pack the house up.

'Emptying a house can be quite emotional, Inspector. I didn't think it would be, quite so much. All these things have memories attached to them. You wonder if they'll return, or just stay in the boxes.'

'I had to go through it when my wife passed away.'

'I'm sorry.'

'My in-laws took care of most of it. The house was officially theirs, and most of the furniture, too. I just came away with a couple of boxes.'

'Have you unpacked them?'

'No.' Frost swiftly changed the subject. 'I've just come from the hospital. It seems Mr Parker will make a full recovery.'

'Yes, I was there this morning. They induced a coma while

the swelling goes down. He should be out of it by tomorrow. Is he in trouble for what he did?'

'Let's just say, we will need to talk to him in some detail.'

'But that's not why you're here, is it?'

'No.'

Vanessa, who had been stood at a side table, wrapping her old photos in newspaper, stopped what she was doing and sat down on the sofa. Frost didn't join her.

'I believe that you were the last person to see Ivan alive.'

'How do you know?'

'Because when you went around to see him, or maybe confront him, he was still in his pyjamas and dressing gown, which he had been in for the last few months. He was unshaven, unwashed, dishevelled. Pretty typical condition for a bottoming-out alcoholic. And you shaved him, and dressed him. Gave him back some of his dignity. But he was dead by then. He died an alcoholic's death, no doubt about that. It's written in black and white in the post-mortem report: heart attack, organ failure. But the bruising and marks around his neck and shoulders suggest that—'

'Yes, you're right, of course,' said Vanessa, cutting him short. 'Once he gave me and Sally those paintings from Conrad, I knew it was too much for him. It always had been.'

'Your affair with Conrad Wilde, and Sally being his daughter – Ivan knew about this?'

'As I tried to tell you, it was complicated. Sally in many ways was Conrad's gift to Ivan. Conrad didn't want children. And as we discovered, Ivan couldn't have children. So, they worked it out between themselves. And of course, I knew, but didn't say anything to either of them. I wanted a baby. So it all remained unsaid. It just happened.' She smiled. 'And nine months later the stork flew over and delivered me a baby. My beautiful Sally. And Ivan was the proud father, and Conrad was happy for us. But soon after, the dynamic changed. As, in hindsight, it was always going to. Conrad slowly began to distance himself from us. He was always at our house before Sally arrived, but then he just stopped coming. I never said anything. Again, it was between Ivan and Conrad. Closer than brothers. They kept up their . . . their business arrangement, though.'

'Did you have any contact with Conrad, without Ivan knowing?'

'No. But I did keep track of him. I knew what happened to him. Prison, insane asylums. The tragedy of it.'

'And you blamed Ivan?'

'Not entirely – how could I? We were all complicit. But what seemed like an amicable arrangement for everyone quickly soured.'

'Ivan couldn't accept that Sally wasn't his biological child. Looking the image of Conrad as she did, how could he? And he also couldn't accept that you had always secretly loved Conrad? And maybe Conrad couldn't accept that he had given up a daughter?'

'Exactly. It turned Ivan into a drunk. But also his guilt at putting Conrad away to save his own skin. He knew Conrad better than anyone. He knew that he couldn't bear being caged. They were that close, and being close, like brothers, brings its own familial rivalries. It had all remained unsaid all these years, buried in the past. Then Ivan gave us the paintings. A gift from Conrad, who had just died. Ivan said we should talk. So I came here. He'd been drinking . . . and all the bile, the resentment came out . . . On both sides, Inspector. I must admit to that. He said he was going to tell Sally the truth. There was some pushing and shoving and . . . yes . . . yes, I grabbed him . . . and he died in my arms . . .'

There was a silence. Frost let her mind scroll back to the moment.

'. . . I held him . . . I told him I loved him, that I always had . . . He smiled, said he knew that. Said he was sorry . . . and . . . and we hugged each other. We didn't want to let go.

Then it happened. I could feel it. It wasn't what they said in the medical report . . . in black and white, as you say. It wasn't a heart attack. It was just broken . . . just broken . . .'

Frost took out the pack of tissues from his jacket pocket and handed her one.

'Of course, I'll . . . I'll make a statement.'

'I think I've heard all I need to.'

'I'm guilty, Inspector.'

Frost considered this, then let his mind seek out a memory. The time when he was in uniform and was called to a house. The milk bottles lined up on the doorstep. The man in the chair, surrounded by empty bottles and little else.

'It could have been a lot different. I, or one of my colleagues, could have been called to Grey Gables to break open the door. And find Ivan, as you found him. As far as I'm concerned, the only difference from what's written in the doc's report is that he died in your arms, Mrs Fielding. And not alone.'

The detective made his way down the path, leaving Vanessa to her packing. The art, the antiques, the objects of desire and the memories. He'd leave the medical report and the theory of Ivan's demise as they were. If it was good enough for Superintendent Mullett and the powers that be, then it was good enough for him. Now that he had all the facts. But as she had agreed, nothing was ever black and white, it was usually a heady swirl of foggy grey. Jack Frost enjoyed solving cases and finding out who did what, and when. And sometimes why. But he reckoned working out where true justice lay, having that moral certainty, without question or doubt, was at times tantamount to trying to figure out the meaning of life. It was way beyond his comprehension. You needed to be a philosopher. Or a dog.

Read the previous books in the series . . .

FIRST FROST
by James Henry

A *Sunday Times* Top 10 Bestseller

Denton, 1981. Britain is in recession, the
IRA is becoming increasingly active and the
country's on alert for an outbreak of rabies.

Detective Jack Frost is working under his mentor and
inspiration DI Bert Williams, and coping badly
with his increasingly strained marriage.

But DI Williams is nowhere to be seen.
So when a 12-year-old girl goes missing from a
department store changing room, DS Frost is
put in charge of the investigation . . .

'*Not only a gripping mystery, but an exclusive look
at Jack Frost's early years*'
David Jason

'*The success of* First Frost *is incontestable. This is a
palpable hit . . . [a] dark, but glittering pearl*'
Barry Forshaw, *Independent*

FATAL FROST

by James Henry

May, 1982. Britain celebrates the sinking of the
Belgrano, Princess Diana welcomes the birth of her
first child and Denton Police Division welcomes
its first black policeman, DC Waters – recently
relocated from Bethnal Green.

While the force is busy dealing with a spate of local
burglaries, the body of fifteen-year-old Samantha Evans
is discovered in woodland next to the nearby railway
track. Then a fifteen-year-old boy is found dead on
Denton's golf course, his organs removed.

Detective Sergeant Jack Frost is sent to investigate – a
welcome distraction from troubles at home. And when
the murdered boy's sister goes missing, Frost and Waters
must work together to find her . . . before it's too late.

'I can't recommend it highly enough'
Martina Cole

'A palpable hit'
Independent

MORNING FROST
by James Henry

November 1982. It's been one of the worst days of **DS Jack Frost**'s life. He has buried his wife Mary, and must now endure the wake, attended by all of Denton's finest.

All, that is, apart from DC Sue Clarke, who has been summoned to the discovery of a human foot in a farmer's field. And things get worse with the shooting of local entrepreneur Harry Baskin inside his club.

As the week goes on, a cyclist is found dead in suspicious circumstances. Frost is on the case, but another disaster – one he is entirely unprepared for – is about to strike . . .

'Funny, shocking, unpredictable'
Daily Mirror

FROST AT MIDNIGHT

by James Henry

August, 1983. Denton is preparing for a wedding, with less than a week to go until Detective Sergeant Waters marries Kim Myles. But the Sunday before the big day, the body of a young woman is found in the churchyard. Their idyllic wedding venue has become a crime scene.

As best man to Waters, **Detective Inspector Jack Frost** has a responsibility to solve the mystery before the wedding. But with nowhere to live since his wife's family sold the matrimonial home, Frost's got other things on his mind.

Can he put his own troubles aside and step up to be the detective they need him to be?

'One of the most successful ventriloquial acts in crime writing'
Financial Times